DINNER WITH ANNA KARENINA

Also by GLORIA GOLDREICH

WALKING HOME

Gloria Goldreich

DINNER WITH ANNA KARENINA

MIRA®

ISBN 0-7783-2227-0

DINNER WITH ANNA KARENINA

For my favorite readers:

Ruthy Gal, Saul Eitan and Ilan Yehuda Amkraut,
Gila Rose, Samuel Nathan and Lily Esther Sheldon

Chapter One

Trish Bartlett glanced at her watch as she hurried up East Eighty-Third Street. A quarter to six. She was not late but she didn't want to be either exactly on time or the first to arrive. She slowed her pace and lingered at the Korean market on Cynthia's corner, where she appraised the cut flowers, the irises wilting and fading, the last roses of the season already shedding their petals. She settled at last on a pot of amber-colored zinnias that would, she decided, make a festive centerpiece for the dinner that marked their first book club meeting of the year. But even as she paid for it, she regretted the purchase. Knowing Cynthia, there would be an expensive flower arrangement, color-coded to match the table linens and china. That was Cynthia's style—a casual elegance, easily achieved with a flash of plastic and the knowledge that Mae, her housekeeper, would be on hand to clip the stems and position the vase in exactly the right place on the tastefully set table.

Trish balanced the flowers and shifted her briefcase, grimacing at its weight. It bulged with the files of patients, which she was determined to update that night. There would be little enough time after the book club, after Jason's swift bout of passion (a given on nights when she returned late from a meeting, an assertion of his power over her, compensation for his moody solitude), after comforting Mandy, who inevitably, perhaps instinctively, wakened when her parents' lovemaking had reached its weary climax. Still, the patient records had to be completed. A state inspection of the hospital loomed and her regular hours were overscheduled, hardly allowing time for the inevitable emergencies. She had dealt with two that very afternoon—a thirteen-year-old girl whose self-mutilation had escalated to what appeared to be an actual suicide attempt, and an anorexic Sarah Lawrence student who had collapsed in her dorm, unable to speak, unable to stop weeping.

"I chose the wrong profession," Trish told herself bitterly as she waited for the light to change. "Cynthia made the right choice, damn her." She spoke the last two words aloud and the harshness of her own voice startled her. Cynthia, after all, was her friend, her very good friend.

"Just whom are you damning?"

Jen, who must have been walking just a few paces behind, sidled up to her and grinned mischievously. Although she carried her own oversize leather portfolio, she relieved Trish of the briefcase so that she could hold the zinnias more easily.

"Jen. Don't sneak up on your friends like that! I was just thinking about some idiot at the hospital who screwed up a diagnosis," Trish lied. "No biggie."

She stooped slightly and dropped a kiss on her diminutive friend's head, pleased to have these few moments alone with her before the frenetic rush of hugs and breathless greetings as the members of the book club reconvened after the summer hiatus, each of the women clutching a much underlined, dog-eared paperback of *Anna Karenina*. Of all the members of the group, Trish felt closest to Jen, who was never demanding, never confrontational, as calmly acquiescent in interchanges as she was with Ian, her longtime partner.

"You look terrific, Jen. How was the summer?"

Elfin, smiling Jen did look wonderful. The sun had brushed her skin to a rose-gold hue and her short dark hair curled about her head in a helmet of ringlets; a coral knit dress hugged her small compact body.

"Not bad. A couple of good weekends and a really boring stretch at the Rhode Island shore. Ian had a sudden urge to paint seascapes and someone lent him a shack near Westerly. So he painted and I read *Anna Karenina* and tried to keep the sand out of my bathing suit. Do you think the lovely Anna ever worried about getting sand up her crotch?"

"If she did, she wouldn't have talked about it," Trish replied, laughing. "Count Leo wasn't too strong on intimacy between women."

"Let's talk about that tonight. After the cassoulet. That's the menu. Cynthia said it was to celebrate the first meeting of the year. Although she didn't look all that celebratory when I saw her at the office today. Something was bugging her. Maybe her new assistant is too smart or too pretty or both."

"I can't recall ever seeing our Princess Cynthia bugged by anything," Trish reflected. "My professional opinion is that she's free of that *All About Eve* syndrome."

"Maybe."

Jen frowned and looked up at the tall elm that stood sentinel in front of Cynthia's town house. The narrow leaves were gold-edged and trembled in the early evening breeze. Several, newly fallen, skittered across the pavement, brittle reminders of encroaching autumn. Although the air was warm, she shivered involuntarily.

"Then you're doing another project with her?" Trish asked.

"There's always another project for Cynthia. No rest for the weary or for the marketing director of Nightingale's. This time she's rushing through a Thanksgiving catalog—turkey-shaped pot holders, pumpkin-colored satin aprons—upscale kitchen stuff for upscale customers who will never go near a kitchen. It's a close deadline and I'll probably be up all night working on it, but I'm not complaining. We can use the money. Ian hasn't sold anything for a couple of months now and things are sort of tight. I'm glad to have the work. A lot of freelance graphic designers are hurting now, so I'm pretty lucky that Cynthia knows my phone number by heart."

"And Cynthia's pretty lucky to have you," Trish insisted loyally.

She had seen the brochures and catalogs Jen produced so effortlessly and she admired her friend's skill. Like many scientists, she was awed by artistic talent, by the intuitive creativity that was totally independent of data, research or experiment but mysteriously flew onto canvas and paper.

"Cynthia's a pretty lucky lady in general," Jen said without bitterness, and Trish nodded and marveled at Jen's generosity. Her own appraisal of Cynthia's life was tinged with an envy that she supposed was understandable but hardly admirable.

The truth was that Cynthia did have it all—the great job as marketing director of Nightingale's, the high-end boutique department store, with the great salary and even greater perks. There was Eric, the perfect handsome husband whose documentary films garnered award after award. Liza and Julie, the golden-haired twin girls who were the same age as Mandy but who were as self-assured as Mandy was shy (the twins, Trish was certain, never wakened in the darkness, fearful and trembling.) And, of course, there was Mae, the live-in housekeeper assisted by a procession of European au pairs who spoke charmingly accented English and took exquisite care of the children and of the wide-windowed, many-roomed house, with the gleaming hardwood floors and the terrace that led out to an elegantly landscaped garden. And there were, of course, trips to exotic locations for the premieres of Eric's films or the launching of new Nightingale's lines. A fairy-tale life replete with the fairy-tale echo—Cynthia was as good and generous as she was fortunate.

Trish's own envy mystified her. She had, she knew, no real reason to envy Cynthia. She herself was living the life she had envisaged during her dreamy undergraduate days when medical school and marriage lay in the distant future and she was uncertain that either could be attained. Even in the nineties, women med students had an uphill climb, and for scholarship students like herself the ascent had been that much steeper. It amazed her still that against all odds she had her career, Jason's ring snug upon her finger, and Mandy's smiling kindergarten portrait, discreetly placed on her desk. Jason's work was not as glamorous as Eric's, but he was successfully chairing his own venture capital group, his name appeared occasionally in the *Wall Street Journal,* and recently he had been urging her to look at larger co-ops and to think of buying a summer place in the Berkshires. They were on their way, he confided after each financial triumph, his cheeks ruddy with success as though he were a mountain climber approaching a long, elusive peak. Always Trish offered him an affectionate hug, a warm smile of approval, willing her enthusiasm to match his own. *He's terrific,* she told herself severely. *I have a terrific husband.*

And Mandy was a precocious and affectionate child (Cynthia's twins, Trish secretly thought, were a bit cold, or what her colleagues in child psychology would call emotionally stingy.) Trish knew herself to be admired by the young women interns on her staff. One attractive psychiatric resident had even styled her hair in imitation of Trish's shaggy layered cut. She overheard them speaking softly, admiringly, of her ability to juggle family and career. Her success offered them hope. "She has such a terrific life," she had overheard one intern say wistfully to another. "She was smart to put off having a kid until she was through with her residency and on staff." And it was true. *I have a terrific life,* she told herself. It was a mantra that, if repeated often enough, she might come to believe.

Why then did she find herself comparing her life to Cynthia's? Why did she struggle each morning to free herself from the cocoon of sadness that ensnared her in the night? She shrugged. Exhaustion, perhaps. Too frenetic a pace. She should think about getting more help at home. They could afford it. This very evening she would ask Cynthia for the name of the agency that provided her with all those attractive, helpful au pairs.

Her mood lifted, as though the fleeting thought was a decision taken, and she smiled at Jen as they climbed the broad stone steps to the polished oak door. It was Jen who lifted the heavy brass knocker, burnished to a subtle glow. The windows were open and they heard the strains of a simplified "Für Elise" plucked from the strings of small Suzuki violins. The twins were practicing and their music wafted through the soft evening air.

The aroma of roasting meat mingled with mysterious spices teased their nostrils and Trish realized that she was hungry. She tried to remember whether she had eaten lunch and could recall only nibbling an apple between a conference with a distraught parent and a consultation with a gastroenterologist concerned about the dietary needs of a bulimic patient. She had referred him to Donna, who would, no doubt, express her annoyance at the intrusion at some point during the book club gathering, probably between the dessert and the analysis of *Anna Karenina*.

It was, in fact, Donna who opened the door to them and beamed a welcome, hugging Jen and placing a collegial (and perhaps forgiving) arm on Trish's shoulder. It occurred to Trish, not for the first time, that Donna took on a different persona when she left the hospital. At work in her nutritionist's office, its institutional green walls devoid of anything except charts of food pyramids and stark drawings of the digestive system, Donna confined her ash-blond hair to a severe bun. Her pale skin was washed free of makeup, a long white lab coat concealed her soft and appealing plumpness, and high white oxford shoes reached her slender ankles. But here in Cynthia's entryway, her loosened hair caped her shoulders in silken sheaths, pale blue eye shadow that exactly matched her large eyes dusted her eyelids, and blush, subtly applied, rouged her high cheekbones. She wore a pale violet breast-hugging sweater and matching pants; flat-heeled shoes of the same color caressed her feet like the softest of gloves. She had the look of a woman who had dressed for a man, and surely one of the two men in her life would be waiting for her after tonight's meeting, a patient lover, summoned by cell phone to the corner of East Eighty-Third Street—either Tim, the jazz musician, or Ray, the scholarly neurologist. She expertly juggled the hours of her evenings, the evenings of her week; dinner with Ray, a concert with Tim, alternate weekends spent with one or the other of the two men, to the wonder and admiration of the other women. They would not want Donna's life, they assured one another, but they marveled at the skill with which she managed it. Of course, they told themselves, Donna was younger than they were, which might account for her resilience. She and Rina were the babies of the group, tiptoeing their way through the treacherous terrain of their early thirties.

"You're late," she gently chided Trish and Jen. "Everyone else is here. Some of us are on our second glass of Chablis. And you missed Liza and Julie's duet."

"Probably they planned it that way," Elizabeth, Jen's sister, called caustically from the living room where she sat beside Rina on the leather couch.

Trish flashed Jen a commiserative glance. Elizabeth seldom missed an opportunity for a negative barb, a cynical thrust.

Trish marveled, not for the first time, at the complete dissimilarity between the sisters—tall Elizabeth with her mousy hair and tense, narrow face, and elfin Jen, relaxed and almost submissive, swift to laugh at herself and offer affection to others. They gave a new dimension to the nature-and-nurture argument so dear to the hearts of Trish's colleagues. It was difficult to believe that they had grown up in the same household, had the same parents, but then, of course, life had treated them very differently. She reminded herself to feel sorry for Elizabeth. It was not easy to be the mother of an autistic son and the wife of an uncompromising chauvinist like that son of a bitch, Bert.

And Elizabeth was a valuable member of the group, perceptive and insightful. She shared their addiction to literary analysis and in-depth reading. Jen had been right to ask her sister to join them when Carla, a former member, moved to Los Angeles after her divorce. The original book group had lost members over the years, and the women who took their places were carefully evaluated before being invited to join. They were, they told themselves, no ordinary group, gathering together to kill an evening, to fill time, to seek refuge from critical husbands and demanding children while idly discussing a new bestseller. They met because literature was their shared passion. Books were as important to them as breath itself. They shared the ability to immerse themselves in the lives of fictional characters, to argue passionately about the development of plots, about decisions taken, dilemmas resolved. Each of them brought unique insights, both personal and professional, to the titles they discussed, and Elizabeth, for all her sarcasm and rigidity, had an incisive intellect. Her own problems might overwhelm her, but she could deal easily with those of Anna Karenina. Trish wondered suddenly how Elizabeth, who had sacrificed her own life on the altar of her son's disability, perceived Anna's contemplated abandonment of her only child.

She smiled at Rina, who was, as always, too pale and too thin, her slender body lost in an oversize white sweater and baggy black pants, the nails of her ringless fingers bitten down to the quick. Rina, in turn, acknowledged her with a weak wave of her hand, as though any exertion at all was too wearying.

Cynthia herself, smiling and radiant, her amber-colored hair pulled loosely back, a smoky topaz on a long gold chain adding understated elegance to her simple jade-green silk dress, sat comfortably on a deep leather chair. Liza and Julie, each in Winnie the Pooh pajamas and holding a small violin, perched on her lap, their smiling faces turned toward her as though posing for an unseen artist. The last light of the slowly dying sun briefly crowned mother and daughters with fiery aureoles.

"Jen, Trish. What lovely flowers. Thanks." Cynthia smiled and waved them toward the glasses of wine.

As though on cue, Mae padded up to them and took the zinnias.

Mae, Cynthia's stout Irish housekeeper, her hazel eyes faded, her pale hair thin enough to reveal the pinkness of her scalp, wore a peach-colored sweatsuit, part of a rotating wardrobe of similar outfits, with sneakers to match.

"Where does she get those sneakers?" Elizabeth had once asked when Mae appeared in olive green and Jen had calmly told her sister that the marketing director of Nightingale's could locate any product anywhere with minimal difficulty.

"If a manufacturer doesn't have it they'll make it for her," Jen had explained.

"Lucky Mae. It must beat having a life." Elizabeth's reply had been predictably sour.

"Thanks, Mae," Jen said pleasantly. "Have a good summer?"

"Good enough."

The housekeeper, they all knew, disapproved of them, disapproved of their impassioned discussions, begrudged them the time Cynthia surrendered to them and the extra work their meetings created for her. It was Mae, after all, who cooked their meals (following the gourmet recipes that Cynthia selected), set the table (according to Cynthia's instructions) and cleaned up while they sat in the living room arguing over plot and character development. They knew, too, that Cynthia was indifferent to Mae's attitude, concerned only with her efficiency and her reliability. In return, she paid Mae a hefty salary and special-ordered her pastel-colored sneakers. Like many women whose lives are built on a sense of entitlement, Cynthia was prepared to pay more than the going rate for the assurance that her home was expertly managed, her family's needs effortlessly satisfied.

"Dinner almost ready?" she asked Mae's retreating back.

"Just tell me when," Mae said, and slammed the door that led to the kitchen behind her.

"Ingrid," Cynthia called, and turned to her daughters, one perfectly manicured hand on each golden head. "Time for you two to get to bed. Give me a kiss and go along with Ingrid."

Obedient cherubs, the little girls pressed the soft red petals of their lips to their mother's cheeks and then, playing for time, insisted on circling the room and giving each of the women a bubble-gum-scented kiss, gig-

gling as they did so. Slender, flaxen-haired Ingrid, a new
au pair who wore tight sequin-studded jeans and a T-shirt
that revealed her pierced navel, waited patiently and un-
smilingly until Liza and Julie ran up to her and took her
hands. They led her away, their minder made captive,
submissive to their whims.

Cynthia sat very still until she heard the door of their
bedroom close, and then she turned to her friends. Her
voice was very soft and they leaned forward to listen.
Trish was reminded of Dr. Tremont, her training analyst
whose barely audible speech pattern was a technique.
"When a patient strains to listen, that patient actually
hears," he had told her. Did Cynthia perhaps use such a
technique in the high-level meetings convened in Nightingale's boardroom? Trish wondered but dismissed the
thought at once. Cynthia's eyes were dangerously bright,
her cheeks were flushed and her words, for all the faint-
ness of their utterance, were verbal knots of pain.

"I want to tell you all something very important. I am
divorcing Eric. He left the house this morning and he'll
come by tomorrow when I'm at the office and the twins
are in school to collect his things. It was all very sudden.
Neither of us was prepared. But last night I discovered
something that makes it impossible for me to spend another day of my life with him. I couldn't allow him to
sleep here even for one more night. Please don't ask me
any questions because I won't answer them. I wanted you
all to know because we've all shared so much. I know I
have your support, but really, I'm fine. I don't need anything. Everything is under control. Even I'm under control. I don't want to talk about it."

A thin smile played at her lips, but her friends, frozen
into a shocked silence, remained very still, as though

their slightest movement might upset a treacherously uneasy balance. Their eyes were downcast, their faces veiled in sadness.

The tinkling sound of shattered crystal startled them and they stared down at the shards that glittered like teardrops on the hardwood floor where Rina had dropped her wineglass. As though released from their trance, they all turned to Cynthia at once, their voices a chorus of concern and bewilderment.

"Cynthia!"

The questions she had forbidden them to ask tumbled from their lips in shrill confusion.

"But what on earth could have happened?"

"You can't work out, whatever it is. Think about the children. It will be so terrible for them."

"Cynthia, what are you saying? You can't mean it."

They struggled for words of consolation, suggestions. Trish wondered softly, almost inaudibly, if they had thought of seeing a marriage counselor. Jen, ever the conciliator, as close to Eric as she was to Cynthia, murmured something about time putting things into perspective.

Shock morphed into disbelief. This was Cynthia, capable, privileged Cynthia, her life a dream to be marveled at and gently envied. They had no advice to offer a woman who had never needed any. Lucky Cynthia made so suddenly unlucky.

It was Jen who stood and put her arms around Cynthia, placed her dark pixielike head on her shoulder. Cynthia ran her fingers through Jen's hair, absently comforting the comforter. Cynthia was very pale now and they saw that beneath her expertly applied cream, her eyes were rimmed with red.

"Hey," she said, rising from her chair, clapping her hands sharply, changing mood as she changed position. "This is a book club meeting, not a bereavement support session. Let's have dinner and get on with discussing the lovely Anna. I take it no one had the guts to come tonight without finishing the book. After all, we had the whole summer."

She spoke with determined lightness, and linking arms with Jen, she led the way into the dining room, where the set table covered with an ochre-colored linen cloth awaited them. Gleaming glassware and polished cutlery flanked each terra-cotta plate. Order and beauty challenged emotional chaos.

Trish noted wryly that she had been right. A beautiful spray of asters in an earth-colored ceramic vase stood in the center of the table. Her own zinnias had been placed on the coffee wagon and were dwarfed by the huge copper urn Mae had already filled with aromatic coffee. But at that moment she did not envy Cynthia. Her earlier thoughts shamed her; envy had morphed into pity. She watched her friend, who was busily ladling out the cassoulet, her lovely angular face flushed but her movements steady, her smile fixed. Trish wondered if Cynthia had selected the recipe and the color scheme before or after she had made the discovery that led her to unequivocally banish Eric from their shared home, their shared life. That unbidden malice shamed her anew and she turned her attention to the delicious lamb-and-white-bean mixture and added her compliments to those already floating toward Cynthia.

"Delicious."

"Everything looks so lovely."

"Are these dishes new?"

They did not discuss *Anna Karenina* during dinner but instead chatted about their summer vacations. Trish, Jason and Mandy had spent a week in the Berkshires and another week in the Hamptons. They were looking for a summer place, Trish confided, but she did not know if she wanted the seashore or the mountains. She did not tell her friends that in the quiet of the night, as Jason breathed lightly beside her, she did not know if she wanted either.

Although Cynthia did not discuss her own summer, they all knew that she and Eric and the twins had flown to the Riviera for a film festival and had spent a week on a Greek island at a cinema verité conference. Pictures of the glamorous couple with their beautiful twin daughters, arriving and departing, had appeared in *New York* magazine and in the Styles section of the *Times*. It was incongruous to think of them now.

What could handsome Eric have done to nullify his family's beautiful, perfect life? Trish knew that they all shared the same thought, that they all pondered the possibilities as they chewed their lamb, sipped their wine and listened to the ongoing exchange of summer experiences. As they spoke, struggling for normalcy, they shot covert glances at Cynthia, who ate very little but replenished her wineglass more than once.

Donna had spent one week with Tim at the Newport jazz festival and the second week with Ray at a Connecticut spa. Cheerfully, she told them that she recommended neither experience.

"A little-known fact about jazz musicians—they don't bathe often enough. Not Tim, of course, but his friends. Seven days of listening to combos in rooms that stank of BO and really bad weed."

They smiled sympathetically and did not ask her about the spa.

Rina and Jeremy, her six-year-old son, had traveled to London so that Rina might retrace Sylvia Plath's steps during the last tortured months of her life. The tragic American poet's death wish and its impact on her work was the subject of Rina's long-delayed doctoral dissertation, begun during her pregnancy and repeatedly set aside because of Jeremy's needs.

"My adviser is very sympathetic," she told them with wry bitterness. "He said that a single mother shouldn't think about getting a doctorate."

"You could get him on sexism charges for that," Elizabeth said.

"Not politic when I'm that close to finishing," Rina replied. "All I need is built-in hostility at my defense. Jeremy was a terrific traveler. Genetic, I guess." She took another helping of the cassoulet and ate it too swiftly, as though fearful that the food might disappear, leaving her hunger unsatisfied. It was understood that she would leave with a plastic dish of leftovers and the remaining heel of the baguette.

They were silent. Rina, they all knew, was a terrible traveler and they dared not ask who Jeremy's father, the man with the good travel DNA was. Even Donna, who had been her college roommate, acknowledged that she had suspicions but no real information about the liaison that had led to Jeremy's birth. Rina had not confided in her and (this Donna did not tell the others) if she had, her confidences might be fabrication. Donna had always recognized Rina's ability to reinvent herself, to redesign the truth to fit the odd demands of her imagined life. Rina had called her one day to announce her pregnancy and ask for a healthy prenatal diet, then called Donna back to tell her that the calcium-rich foods she had recommended were too expensive. Donna had suggested that the father of the child be asked to share the expense and Rina had replied tersely that she would manage and, apparently, she had. Donna had seen her grazing at the Food Emporium salad bar, filling a container with raw broccoli and spinach, which she nibbled on while filling her shopping cart with dented cans and day-old bread. She tucked samples of cheese into her bulging purse, filled paper cups with milk at the coffee bar, which she sipped without embarrassment as she ambled over to the cash register.

Donna, ever the nurturer, invited her friend for dinner, sent her home with leftovers and, after Jeremy's birth, carried containers of puréed fruits and vegetables across town.

"Remember, he has to be properly nourished," she had advised Rina, professional severity commingled with caring friendship.

Rina had accepted the food and accepted the advice, because in this, as in all things, she was a taker, a girl who had smiled at her dorm mates' dates as they waited in the common room, an expert applicant for grants, an excellent interviewee before committees. The trip to London had been underwritten by a foundation; the Hampstead apartment where she and Jeremy had stayed belonged to a friend of a friend.

"London sounds wonderful," Elizabeth said grudgingly. "Of course we've never been to Europe, Bert and I. We planned to go just after we were married but that never happened, of course. And now with all the expenses for Adam's school we're lucky if we even take a trip out of state. I taught summer school, which helped us get ahead of the bills and we did spend a week at a motel not far from Adam. Bert thinks it's wrong to leave him for any length of time and the doctors and social workers agree with him."

Nine-year-old Adam was autistic, a beautiful dark-eyed boy in the photos Elizabeth occasionally shared with them, who had spent much of his childhood spinning around on the floor, arranging and rearranging a wooden set of farm animals, their painted surfaces faded from years of being licked and sucked. As he grew older, he bit his fingers until blood spurted from the punctured capillaries. It had been the spilled blood and the refusal of aides to continue to work with him that had, at last, compelled Bert and Elizabeth to place him in the rural residential facility that they could ill afford.

"And you, do you agree with him?" Trish asked quietly.

"Of course I do." Elizabeth flushed angrily. "This isn't a therapy session, Trish, and I am not your patient. Some of us are here to discuss *Anna Karenina.*"

"Then why don't we do just that?" Cynthia said. "Bring your coffee into the living room and let's get started."

Again Mae padded in, as though on cue, placed a platter of miniature Danish pastries on the polished oak table in front of the sofa and sullenly began to clear the table.

Balancing their coffee cups, fumbling for their books, they arranged themselves in a semicircle and turned to Trish, who would launch the discussion. Their pattern never varied. One member, her role assigned in advance, served as leader and summarized the book's general background, both social and historical, offered relevant information about the author and suggested themes for discussion. Trish, as always, took her responsibility seriously, and rummaged through her briefcase for the notes she had made while sitting beside Jason on the East Hampton beach weeks earlier. She found the file folder, and as she opened it, granules of pure white sand fell to the polished hardwood floor. They all laughed and leaned back, a new and familiar ease established.

Briskly, Trish discussed Tolstoy's life, the impact of the new science of the nineteenth century on his work, his disgust with materialism and his complicated relationships with women, including his own wife.

"Here's an important thing to remember about a man who is supposed to be sensitive to a woman's feelings," Trish said. "His poor wife, the mother of his nine children, give or take a couple of miscarriages probably, handwrote seven copies of *War and Peace*. Seven copies of that monster of a book, written out in pen and ink, while she managed an estate and wiped the noses of all those kids."

"Which means what, that we should all be grateful that we don't live in the nineteenth century?" Elizabeth asked. "Or that she gets the red-star award for masochism?"

"Which means that we have to be a little wary of how much the great count actually knew about the logistics of a woman's life, of his own wife's life. If he couldn't understand that, how could he understand Anna Karenina?" Trish retorted, and returned to her notes.

"I want to read a quote from him that I think is really important. He wrote, 'History is an accumulation of accidental events relying on an element of chance.' I think that, by extension, that's how he felt about his characters' lives, that their individual destinies rely on accident, on chance. Anna's whole story depends on chance. Her brother bumps into Count Vronsky at the train station and introduces him to Anna, his married sister—married and bored. Vronsky and Anna fall in love. Mad meetings, passionate nights. Divorce wasn't exactly a choice in imperial Russia. Vronsky wavers. Anna despairs and finally she throws herself onto the railroad tracks. Which brings us back to the idea of chance. If her brother had never met Vronsky—a chance meeting, remember—Anna would have stayed married to boring old Alexey and died in a nursing home instead of beneath the wheels of a train."

"Meaning that we don't have control of our own lives, that we can't opt for change or make calculated decisions. Twelve-step programs are out, the winds of chance are in," Rina said. "Which might put you out of business, Trish."

"Even therapy is affected by chance," Trish admitted.

They discussed that single point for a while, each of them relating a chance encounter that had changed their own lives. Elizabeth spoke of meeting Bert at a party she had almost decided not to attend. Donna had decided to move to New York because her acceptance to a program in Boston had been wrongly addressed and had arrived a week after she had already committed to accepting the job offer at the metropolitan hospital. A friend of Rina's had developed mononucleosis and she had stepped into the community college lectureship in her place. Ian and Jen had met at a painting workshop. He had critiqued her work and taken her home to bed. The "what ifs" compounded—*what if* Elizabeth had not gone to the party, *what if* Donna's letter of acceptance had arrived on time, *what if* Jen had not attended that particular workshop—

they fantasized and speculated, intimacy escalating, unexpected laughter erupting. Like Tolstoy's Anna, they were all pawns in a wild game of chance.

Only Cynthia remained silent, rising suddenly to draw the drapes, to turn the wedding portrait of herself and Eric that stood on the piano facedown. She had made an accidental discovery the previous evening, they knew, that had changed her life, and they wondered when she would speak of it. Not now. It was too soon. She was, of all of them, the most private, her secrets always closely held, but any intimacy that she shared was completely honest. Truth, she had told them once, was her obsession. Employees were fired for telling even the smallest lie. Friendships were severed over casual untruths. She abhorred deception. It occurred to all of them that in some way Eric had deceived her, and she, in turn, had discovered his deception.

But the question lingered. *What if* she had not made that discovery, *what if* that mysterious secret had remained unrevealed? Would she have banished Eric, spoken of divorce, or would her life have continued on its own enchanted way? They looked at one another, recognizing the commonality of the thought and, swiftly, changed the topic, took up another of Trish's talking points.

"Here's a quote from the count—I can't remember who it refers to, maybe Levin," Trish said. "But it resonates. 'If there are as many minds as there are heads, then there are as many kinds of love as there are hearts.'"

They were silent, digesting the words, lassoing them to thoughts and feelings.

"Maternal love. Erotic love," Elizabeth suggested. "Different for each mother and child, different for each pair of lovers." She poured herself another cup of coffee and did not elaborate.

They admired her courage and asked no questions. How did maternal love translate for Elizabeth, the mother of a damaged child who held her life hostage to his infirmity? That Adam had scratched and bitten Elizabeth, drawing blood, they knew. They had seen the scars, heard the truth from Jen. When could maternal love be forfeit?

They argued, referred to the novel. Hadn't Anna's love for Vronsky caused her to abandon her eight-year-old son Seryozha—erotic love canceling the maternal mandate? The discussion expanded, contracted, their voices rose and fell, their faces flushed with the exhilaration of the exchange. They were Anna, they were Vronsky, they were Kitty and Levin, the confusion of the Oblonsky household dizzied them. The summer's reading erupted into life.

"But when Dolly, Anna's sister-in-law, speaks about her own marriage, her own situation, here's what she says," Trish said excitedly, thumbing through her dog-eared book in search of the exact quote, "Oh, here it is. 'The worst of it all is, you see, that I can't cast him off: there are the children, I am tied. And I can't live with him. It's a torture to see him.' You see, it's a woman's dilemma—a terrible choice."

Cynthia's spoon clattered against her cup. She stood abruptly and left the room. Trish's hand flew to her mouth.

"So stupid of me. I didn't think, I was so caught up in what were saying…I forgot. Should I go to her?"

They looked at one another, upset, undecided, but before anyone could say anything Cynthia returned. Her makeup was refreshed and she carried a basket of beautifully wrapped small boxes.

"Sorry. I went to get an aspirin. I feel a headache coming on. And I forgot to give you these. I found them in a small shop in Florence and thought of you guys."

She was again the benevolent friend, sharing her good fortune, inviting their vicarious participation in the excitement and luxury of her life. Always on her return from one glamorous odyssey or another she brought them small but very expensive mementos—pendants from Athens, key chains of rose quartz from Turkey, silk handkerchiefs from Paris.

Pleased, relieved, they tore off the wrapping, opened the boxes and found soft leather bookmarks, each dyed to a different pastel shade. Exuberantly, they thanked her, thrust the bookmarks into place.

"*Madame Bovary* next?" Jen asked.

They all nodded.

"Trish, as long as you're into European infidelities, why don't you lead that one, too, and then we'll pass the baton," Elizabeth said, her voice flat. It often fell to her to structure their meetings. She was used to making decisions without offering alternatives. They imagined her meeting with parents in the guidance office of the inner-city school where she worked, issuing ultimatums, accepting no excuses. And they admitted that her decisions were usually wise. They nodded their agreement, recorded the scheduled date in their pocket calendars. They would meet at Rina's apartment and call her in advance to see what they could bring. Rina would not prepare a cassoulet. She would be responsible only for the soft drinks and they would all be store brand.

They hugged Cynthia goodbye, murmured their support, their availability.

"Call any time, Cyn."

"If there's anything we can do for you…if you just want to talk…"

"Really, we're here for you."

Their voices trilled with concern, throbbed with compassion.

She smiled pleasantly at each of them, nodded, shrugged.

"A great meeting," she said, ignoring their solicitude. "A great discussion, Trish."

Trish's cheeks blazed but she nodded her thanks.

The heavy oak door slammed behind them and they walked to the corner, then turned to stare at the house. But because the drapes were drawn they could not tell whether or not lights still burned in the room they had just left. They did not want to think of Cynthia alone, weeping in the dark.

By tacit agreement they did not separate when they crossed Third Avenue. Donna did not summon either of her lovers and the others called their homes on their cell phones to lie away their lateness.

"I have to stop back at the hospital to pick up some files," Trish told Jason.

"My friend isn't feeling well so I'm staying with her for a while," Rina told her babysitter.

"Cynthia wants to discuss the Thanksgiving catalog with me, so I'll be home when I'm home," Jen informed her answering machine. She did not speculate about where Ian might be. She had once told her friends that she made no demands on him.

"Trish wants to talk to me about some new drugs that might be helpful to Adam," Elizabeth told Bert. "No, I don't know how long it will take." She clicked off when he was still in midsentence of protest.

Grinning guiltily at one another, they filed into a coffee shop and sat around a newly wiped table sipping bitter, tepid cups of decaf.

"What could Eric have done? What could have made her act so drastically?" Jen gave voice to their thoughts. "I mean it can't be just an affair. Not even a couple of affairs. That wouldn't make it impossible for her to have him in the house for another night. She's not Tolstoy's Dolly and this isn't the nineteenth century. If it was an affair they'd throw things at each other, go to a marriage counselor like Trish suggested and then do in-depth therapy at the Ackerman Institute and take a two-month cruise."

"Child molestation," Elizabeth suggested. "I'm seeing a lot of that in my office and it's not limited to low-end inner-city families. Maybe she accidentally found something on his e-mail, some juvey porn site."

"Eric doesn't seem to fit the profile," Donna protested. "He's too with it, too concerned with self-image, too confident, successful."

"There's no real profile for sex offenders," Trish added. "But I'm inclined to agree with Donna."

"Besides, he was great with kids. I mean, you can tell something about a guy when you see him with kids," Rina said. "He once took Jeremy to the set of a documentary he was shooting, Jeremy *and* a friend—they were doing some sort of a project—and he just gave them a terrific time."

"There you go," Elizabeth asserted, and, in spite of themselves, they laughed.

They floated other ideas, as their cups were refilled by a waitress who glanced pointedly at her watch. Drugs.

Homosexuality. It was Rina, her eyes always on the finances of others, who suggested embezzlement, which in the end caused them all to laugh.

"Look, we just have to be there for Cynthia," Jen said at last.

"As though she's going to need us," Elizabeth retorted bitterly.

"Some people *do* need other people," Jen said. She blushed hotly and looked at her sister, who turned away from her. The others busied themselves with reapplying lipstick, draining their cups. There was a silent agreement among them that they ignore the sororial bitterness that occasionally erupted between Elizabeth and Jen. Trish had once discussed the odd dynamic between them with Donna.

"It's not an atypical sister relationship," she had said. "They're locked in a fatal embrace. Shared history, shared responsibility for their mother. They love each other but they don't like each other."

She had thought briefly of doing a psychoanalytic study of relationships between sisters but had not followed up. As she listened to Jen and Elizabeth, the idea recurred and she thought she might actually develop it.

She glanced at the check and put a ten dollar bill on the table. It was time to go. Enough had been said. Too much had been revealed.

They parted at the corner and she raced to catch the crosstown bus. She fumbled for her Metrocard, setting down her briefcase, which suddenly seemed unbearably heavy.

Chapter Two

Rina Samuelson prepared for the book club meeting with a meticulous care that would have surprised her friends. They thought of Rina as the eternal graduate student, always living on the edge but happily casual about her surroundings, content with her rent-stabilized West Side apartment, which she herself described with wry indifference as being furnished in "early hand-me-down" and "late divorce." The beige pullout sofa in the living room on which she slept had belonged to Trish and Jason when they were first married. Rina scattered brightly patterned Indian pillows across its faded cushions. A batik spread was tossed across the wicker armchair she had rescued from a curb on West End Avenue. The blue woven rug had been in the apartment when she rented it, its faded surface covered with geometric stains and a rust-colored spot that might have been blood. The previous tenants had divorced shortly after breaking their

lease and Rina imagined desperate arguments grown violent, plates of food and half-full cups of coffee hurled
across the room and landing on the rug that had perhaps
been carried back from a honeymoon on a Greek island.
Hadn't Ted Hughes once aimed a dish of food at Sylvia
Plath? Rina vaguely remembered reading about it. She
would have to check its accuracy and perhaps relate it
to one of the poems in *Ariel*.

The low coffee table had traveled with her from the
apartment she and Donna had shared in their undergraduate days.

"You don't need it and I can't afford a new one," she
had told Donna, and Donna, who did need it and who
also could not afford a new one then, had not protested.
Rina had a talent for generating pity.

For the book club meeting, Rina cleared the table of
the small mountain of literary journals that dominated
one corner, carrying them into Jeremy's bedroom and
concealing them beneath the youth bed Cynthia had
given her when she redecorated the twins' room. She
gathered up the past week's newspapers from the middle of the table and brought them to the incinerator
room, where she paused long enough to pluck two
month-old copies of the *New Yorker* out of the commu-
nal bin. She lingered briefly over the most recent copy
of *Vanity Fair,* but the grease stain on the cover deterred
her. Shrugging, she returned to her apartment, cleared
the floor of Jeremy's Lego construction, and vacuumed
before calling Ellen, the mother of Jeremy's best friend,
to make sure the sleepover she had scheduled so carefully was going well.

"Thanks so much for having him," she told Ellen. "He
hates it when my book club meets here."

That, in fact, was not true. Jeremy loved it when the book club members gathered in the living room, reveling in their attention and the small gifts they brought him. But Rina felt constrained by the thought that he lay awake listening to their talk, now and again wandering into the room to ask for a drink of water or to complain of a stomachache. She did not have the luxury of Cynthia's large home with the children's room at a remove nor the assistance of an unsmiling but capable au pair to deal with nocturnal requests. *Lucky Cynthia,* she thought, and then swiftly amended the thought. *Newly unlucky Cynthia.* Besides, it was good for Jeremy to adjust to another family's rhythms, and she did need his room for the coats and briefcases her friends would pile on his narrow bed.

"We'd love to have Seth stay over sometime soon," she said, and Ellen's evasive reply did not surprise her. Ellen, an attorney, married to an investment banker, had proudly abandoned the law to be a stay-at-home mother. She was uneasy about Rina's single status (described to her friends as a "lifestyle"), Jeremy's conspicuously absent and unexplained father and the Samuelsons' cluttered and possibly unsanitary apartment. Once, as she waited for Seth, Rina had caught her sliding a finger across the kitchen table and wiping away the grease stain with a delicate linen handkerchief. When Rina told her that her book group would be meeting that evening, Ellen eagerly told her that she belonged to a book club that met in the afternoons. They were reading Isabel Allende, she reported brightly.

"Bitch," Rina thought, and did not tell Ellen that her group had read Allende three years ago and thought her work pretentious and boring.

"Well, thanks for everything," she told Ellen after being reassured that the boys were playing well together and that Ellen had lent Jeremy a pair of pajamas because the ones Rina had sent appeared too small. She hung up, plucked a soiled napkin from the phone table (an incinerator find) and thrust it into her pocket.

She shut her computer down and carefully filed the newly printed hard copy into a folder, which she shoved into a drawer. She did not want to leave the opening chapter of the novel she might never continue writing in plain sight. She left only the pile of ungraded essays from her composition class on the table. The very sight of them wearied her. She would get to them. She had to get to them. This was the year she was up for tenure and she didn't need the strikes against her to be compounded by students' complaints.

In the kitchen, she checked the progress of her avocado plant, which seemed to have stopped growing, wistfully and bitterly remembering the colorful potted flowers and wide-leafed plants that had flourished in her parents' Florida sunroom. She rummaged in her cabinets for paper plates and cups and plastic cutlery which she arranged in neat piles on the table, and then scraped away a clot of Play-Doh, abandoning it to answer the triple ring of the doorbell.

Donna and Trish burst in, talking and laughing. The grease-stained brown bags they carried filled the small apartment with the garlic-tinged fragrance of lobster and beef Szechuan-style and the mingled odors of stir-fried vegetables and shrimp fried rice.

"I had the order delivered to the office and it arrived just as I was discussing diet with one of my morbidly obese patients. Great timing," Donna said, laughing, as they handed the bags to Rina.

"Oh, well, even nutritionists are entitled to a meal outside of the food pyramid now and again," Trish assured her. "But it might not be a good idea to have it happen again."

"I don't make a habit of it," Donna retorted irritably. "And you're off duty now, Trish."

"Sorry. You're right. Sometimes it seems that I'm never off duty." Sadness edged her voice and Donna's expression softened.

Rina set the white cardboard containers on the table and opened the door for Jen and Cynthia, who added their own upscale plastic containers from Shun Lee East—scallion toast, hot and sour soup and delicate spring rolls. The requisite kisses were exchanged, each of them hugging Cynthia just a moment too long and searching her carefully made-up face for any new clue of distress or fragility.

"How are you, Cynthia? Really, how are you?" Trish asked daringly, and they busied themselves with setting out the food as they waited impatiently for her reply. But Cynthia was, as always, controlled and calm, her tone steady.

"Fine. Really, I'm fine," she replied, and asked Rina to heat the soup, adding that she had asked for disposable soup bowls because she wasn't sure Rina would have any on hand.

"You're right, I don't," Rina said. "I never thought about soup bowls."

She marveled that Cynthia, engulfed as she surely had to be in emotional trauma, managed to think about disposable soup bowls. At such an emotional crossroad she herself would be paralyzed with despair. She remembered the early days of her pregnancy with Jeremy. Three weeks curled up on the couch in a fetal position, rising only to eat saltines, drink tea and lie to friends and her adviser, who phoned regularly.

"Fine," she assured them. "I'm managing. This is exactly what I want to do."

She wondered if they really believed that what she "exactly wanted to do" was have a child alone whom she would raise alone but then it did not matter what they thought. All that mattered was that she needed this child to be born, to reconnect her with the world, to be someone with whom she would have a biological tie.

She had spent hours struggling to devise a plan that would make it possible for her to have the baby and survive. There were finances to be arranged, a larger graduate stipend to be negotiated, the small inheritance from her parents to be invested prudently enough so that there would be money for food and rent and medical expenses. She lay awake and created budgets, mentally transferred dollars from one column to another. Once she had played at poverty, milked it for its drama, for the sympathy it brought her. Now that imagined poverty had morphed into reality.

She did not even think of asking the man who had impregnated her (never did she think of him as her baby's father) for money. She wanted him gone from her life as swiftly as he had entered it. She had met him only weeks after her parents had been killed in an automobile accident on a Florida highway, only six months after their move from New York to begin their new life, a modest retirement in the Garden of Eden, a gated senior community. Their condo was newly constructed, their furnishings, wicker couches and chairs, wheat-colored sisal rugs, a pale wood bedroom suite. Even the dishes in the kitchen were new, bright orange-and-yellow ceramic replacing the chipped china of her childhood. The only child of only children, Rina sat *shiva* alone in the apartment that still smelled of fresh paint. Only her framed college graduation picture gave proof that she had a connection to the sun-drenched rooms to which elderly neighbors came with offerings of casseroles and store-bought pies, uneasy as to what one might bring to a solitary mourner. She had felt herself doubly bereft. Her parents were gone and all the furnishings of her past had vanished. Neither family nor history anchored her. Donna flew down, helped her to sell the condo and everything in it. Together, they returned to New York.

She resumed her graduate work, but she moved slowly, shrouded in loss and loneliness. Always thin, she grew even thinner, her cheekbones rising high in her angular face. She wore her long dark hair in a single braid. She dressed in black, but she was wearing a bright red sweater over her standard black turtleneck the night she met Jeremy's father. He was older, a visiting lecturer persuaded to teach a single seminar on British poetry in her department. He was a renowned academic, always en route from one university to another, jetting across the Atlantic to a conference at Oxford, a fellowship in Italy.

As he spoke of Wilfred Owen, he twisted his broad gold wedding band, but his bright blue eyes never left Rina's face. She was not surprised when he approached her after the class and invited her for coffee.

"You look like a Modigliani portrait," he told her as they sat in a booth drinking the bitter brew neither of them wanted. "But why are you sad? Are Jews always so sad?"

She recoiled from the question, studied his pale patrician face for an expression of malice but found none. His sympathy melted her. She longed to be comforted, to be touched, to belong however briefly to someone else. They walked very slowly to her apartment, but they made love with a swiftness that astonished them both. He stayed the night, and when he left in the morning she realized that he had not even asked her name. Two months later she had known for certain that she was pregnant and the news exhilarated her. She would have a child, a blood tie to someone else in the world. The child would be hers alone. The father would never know of the birth, would never know he had a Jewish child, whether sad or happy. She would be independent yet connected. *Connected.* The word intrigued her.

"It's what I want," she told Donna, who spoke gently of other choices. *Roe v. Wade* had changed the world.

"I don't want an abortion," she said. "I want this baby."

"But how will you support yourself?"

Donna had been her roommate throughout college. She knew that Rina had always worried about money, sometimes irrationally. Checks arrived from her parents, but Rina hoarded them, uncashed, and borrowed small amounts from their dorm mates. Donna had been silent when one girl's necklace disappeared and she saw Rina fingering a necklace she had not seen before. Someone else worriedly reported that a ten dollar bill was gone from her wallet. Rina, always so careful of money, had insisted on paying for dinner that night. The bill had come to just under ten dollars. She had asked no questions. Rina was her friend, her sharer of confidences and, like Donna, a compulsive reader. Their passion for literature, their closely hugged privacy, bonded them. Donna would say nothing that would hurt her.

I'll manage," Rina had replied, and Donna had not argued.

Rina saw that she could manage, that she would manage. She haunted thrift shops and day-old bakeries and made do. There was, after all, no alternative. And then came the melancholy, as heavy upon her heart as the new weight within her womb, the fetus that slowed her steps and strangled her breath. It abided with her still, that strange and lingering sadness, ambushing her just as she thought she had overcome it, reducing her to sudden tears, to inexplicable outbursts of bitterness. It had frightened Jeremy during their visit to London, as they stood on the steps of the house where Sylvia Plath, who could not subdue her own demons, had put her head in the oven as her small children slept.

"Are you all right?" friends and colleagues asked her, frightened by her pallor and the dark circles beneath her eyes, her listlessness. They offered advice and support, small gifts, large loans, baby-sitting hours. Donna invited her for dinner, brought platters of food to her apartment, called often, late at night, early in the morning. They watched television together wearing the oversize bright pink bunny slippers, ratty with age, that they had given each other during their sophomore year. They mocked the commercials, muted the volume and invented their own dialogue, collapsing with laughter at their own cleverness. They recreated the dormitory world they had left behind a decade earlier. Donna invited her to join the book club and then there was a new group of friends who worried over her, called her during lonely evening hours, always prefacing the conversation with the inevitable query—"Are you all right?"

It was a question that only Trish had dared ask Cynthia now, who in fact looked very all right, radiating, as she always had, confidence and control. Her color was high, her skin smooth, and she moved through Rina's small kitchen with graceful energy, ferreting out a pot large enough for the soup, a ladle, a pot holder. Her hands did not tremble as Rina's had, as they still did. But then, of course, Cynthia's situation was radically different from Rina's. She had a support system—family, friends, professional colleagues, a comfortable home and a staff to ensure its smooth operation. And she had no financial worries. She was a high earner, a savvy investor. Money cushioned her life, guaranteed her comfort, her security. No matter what Eric had done (*and really what could it be?*), no matter that she was newly alone, Cynthia would never search through supermarket bins for dented cans or wear the so-called "gently used" clothing that smelled of a stranger's perfume.

Rina watched her as she carried the soup to the table and began to fill the plastic bowls. Did money and financial security really guarantee such ease of gesture? She did not know. Probably she would never know. Still, it was among the questions that the friends had asked one another during the flurry of phone conversations about Cynthia's situation. Rina and Donna, during their late night exchanges, had discussed it.

"At least she doesn't have to worry about money," Rina had said wryly.

"How do you know?"

"I sort of hinted at it and she said flatly that she was fine about that, more than fine."

Jen and Trish, meeting for a hurried cup of coffee, had spoken worriedly about Cynthia being lonely. All of them were concerned. All of them were curious. They imagined Cynthia's long nights in that large house. They imagined themselves in her situation. They had no truths to offer each other and their conversations ended abruptly. They were annoyed with themselves and, yes, annoyed with Cynthia, and sorry for her, so sorry.

"Shouldn't we wait for Elizabeth?" Rina asked, brandishing the ladle over the steaming soup. "You're sure she's coming?"

"Oh, she'll be here. She's bringing the video," Trish said.

"The video?" Jen asked in surprise.

"Yes. She didn't tell you? I thought it would be fun to watch the video of *Madame Bovary*. It's a golden oldie, Van Heflin, Jennifer Jones, Louis Jourdan, and I mentioned it to Elizabeth, who said that her school had a copy. It's a bit of a change, but I thought we could indulge. We'll watch it while we eat."

Trish smiled, pleased with her idea, pleased that the group was surprised. It would be a relief to sit back and watch the film in silence. Her day had been too full of words—the outpourings of her patients, earnest conferences with her colleagues, a too-short exchange with Jason, a too-long phone discussion with Mandy over a theme for a birthday party that would not take place for months. She longed for the companionable silence that would come as the film drifted across Rina's small television screen and the actors' voices rose and fell accompanied by the click of chopsticks and idle comments about Jennifer Jones's absurd costumes.

"She never told me," Jen said, "but then, of course, we really haven't talked that much. She's had a rough week—Adam's been going through a difficult phase again and Bert hasn't exactly been understanding. To say nothing of our mother's usual litany of complaints."

The women said nothing. They had heard about Adam's difficult stages before, his total withdrawals, his wild attacks on the caregivers who tried to penetrate his inexplicable emotional world. And they knew, too, what Bert's lack of understanding meant. He was at odds with Elizabeth over Adam's treatment, angry at the cost of the residential facility that depleted their income, that prevented him from taking a job in the private sector that would be less secure than his civil service position as a statistician with a state agency. He went online and printed out theoretical articles on autism, showing Elizabeth those that insinuated it was rooted in maternal rejection, toxic amniotic fluids during gestation, a genetic predisposition linked to the female line. Obscure, unproven theories guaranteed to cause Elizabeth stress. He was a tall man whose bulk ran to muscle rather than to fat, whose fingers were clenched into fists even during casual conversations. His pale hair was thinning and his wife's friends were maliciously amused to note that freckles dotted his scalp. And all of them knew about Jen and Elizabeth's mother, the disgruntled old woman who had complained about them throughout their childhoods and now, during her infirm old age, complained to them.

Trish looked at her watch.

"She did say she had to stop at home before she came here, but she was sure she wouldn't be late." She spoke hesitantly, worry darkening her words. Bert was a clinical example of latent violence, she thought, although she would never articulate such an idea. Trish had thought of discussing it with Jen. Still, the relationship between the sisters was strained enough as it was.

"I could call," Jen suggested, but even as she spoke the door opened and Elizabeth came in, nodding in apology because it was not in Elizabeth's nature to smile.

"Sorry. I had to discuss something with Bert. But I have the video."

She gave it to Rina, who also took her coat, noting the fresh bruise on Elizabeth's arm before she could pull the sleeve of her blouse down.

Elizabeth followed her gaze.

"Oh, that," she said. "I bumped into a filing cabinet. Clumsy of me."

Rina said nothing. There was, after all, nothing to say. She saw Cynthia stare hard at Elizabeth and turn away. She watched as Cynthia twisted her handkerchief, pursed her lips and left the room abruptly, her eyes dangerously bright. That might have been it. Perhaps Eric had been abusive, physically abusive, to Cynthia or even to the twins. That could be the solution to the mystery, to the raging "why" that absorbed them. It was certainly a possibility that had not yet occurred to any of them. They had always thought Eric so gentle, actually a Manhattan anachronism—a highly successful man who was also mild mannered and soft of tone. She might ask Trish about it. No. Not Trish, who was so damn analytical. She imagined Trish's reaction. *And why should you think that, Rina? Are you perhaps projecting?* Donna. She would suggest it to Donna.

The toilet flushed. Cynthia returned, her lipstick refreshed, her bright yellow scarf newly knotted. Elizabeth inserted the video and they filled their plates as Trish dimmed the lamp. They slipped off their shoes, settled themselves on the couch and the floor, smiling in guilty anticipation. Spearing bits of beef and lobster, munching on spring rolls, slurping soup and tea, they leaned back and watched Dr. Charles Bovary enter a small farmhouse in rural France and share that first fatal breakfast with the beautiful Emma. They chewed slowly as the story unfolded with Charles and Emma marrying, and Emma, inevitably bored with marriage and mother-hood, slipping into ill-fated affairs, and the extravagant ending that would drive her poor husband into bank-ruptcy and Emma to surrender to suicide. But only Donna wept during the final tragic scene. Her tears mys-tified and embarrassed them. The acting was appalling, the writing worse and Donna was usually a discerning critic.

"Oh, come off it, Donna. It was so damn corny," Jen said as Rina replenished Donna's teacup but did not meet her friend's eyes.

"Well, I think we can safely say that in this case the book was way better than the movie," Elizabeth said dryly as the final credits rolled.

"Oh, I don't know. It had its moments." Cynthia poured herself another cup of tea. "It would have been better if Jennifer Jones could act, but even so she man-aged to get a grip on Emma's character."

"Or lack thereof," Trish interjected. "Although I think Flaubert was basically sympathetic to Emma. Remember when they asked him on whom he had based the char-acter, he said…"

"'*Madame Bovary, c'est moi,*'" they called out in unison, and laughed, pleased with themselves and their shared memory.

"Certainly, that's the way James Mason played Flau-bert," Trish said. "Although the rest of the film was pretty harsh on Emma and very soft on poor Charles Bovary. I guess Hollywood in those days wasn't too soft on unfaith-ful wives. A happy marriage was the American dream, and the prevailing philosophy was that marriage, any marriage, had to be preserved at all costs. So Emma, who betrayed her own wedding vows, had to become their villain."

"Oh, I imagine that even those Hollywood bigwigs might agree that there are times when the acts of one partner or the other would make divorce inevitable," Cynthia said.

She wandered over to the window and stared down at the deserted street.

The others looked at her, a single thought mutely telegraphed from one to the other. *What acts would make her divorce inevitable? What had Eric done?* Sitting in the coffee shop, trading ideas during their late-night calls to one another, they had discounted the idea of Eric having an affair. He would have to be mad, they had agreed. Cynthia was gorgeous, their life together a dream. But now, given Cynthia's reaction to Emma Bovary's infidelity, it loomed again as a possibility. But almost as swiftly as Cynthia had invited the supposition, she dispelled it.

"Of course, just routine unfaithfulness wouldn't provide enough of a plot for the Hollywood moguls. It wouldn't be enough to wreck any marriage, not then, not now," she said dispassionately. "It would take a great deal more than that." She sat down on the couch and briefly closed her eyes.

It occurred to Trish that Cynthia might be teasing them, toying with them, tossing out flickering clues and extinguishing them before they could properly ignite. The unkindness of the thought shocked her and hurriedly, she changed the subject.

"Flaubert was more interested in character than in marriage," she said. "He himself never married and he looked down on those who did. He hated his sister's husband, his brother's wife. I think he saw marriage as a kind of prison, as an end to freedom."

"Not such an absurd idea," Donna murmured. "I sort of share it. If I married I'd be giving up my freedom. Right now I'm my own person. I have my own career, my own apartment. I can have dinner with Tim one night, take off with Ray for a weekend. No excuses, no apologies, no lies."

"Emma Bovary would have envied your freedom. I can see her juggling lovers, holding herself accountable to no one, a woman in charge of her own finances, her own life. But in the novel she thought herself a prisoner," Trish observed.

Donna blushed hotly.

"I don't *juggle* lovers," she murmured. "I just happen to have two men in my life."

"And that's your right, and your terrific good luck," Rina assured her. In any such exchange she would always spring to Donna's defense.

"What sort of prisoner?" Jen asked, looking at Trish, who was carelessly turning pages, in search of a passage that would back her up.

"A prisoner of boredom. Chained to her own yearnings," Rina interjected, and grinned at the facility of her answer. Academic language had entrapped her. She was quoting from her own thesis in which she described Sylvia Plath as chained to her own yearnings, an idea which she had yet to prove. "But what the film emphasized— very different from what Flaubert wrote—was that there was something terribly wrong with that boredom, with those yearnings. Sure, she wanted beautiful things, fashionable clothing, hats, handbags. Is that a crime?"

"It is when you'll do anything for those beautiful things. Buying what you can't afford. Driving your husband into bankruptcy. Which is what Emma did," Elizabeth said. "I'd like a lot of things but I know I'll never have them. So I do without. Probably I'll always do without." She sat very straight, her lips pursed, her fingers lightly stroking the slowly darkening bruise on her arm.

"But there are certain women who can't do without, who will do anything to get the things they think they need, the things they deserve," Rina persisted. "I'm thinking of a woman I saw at Saks the other day."

"You were at Saks?" Donna asked mockingly. "Rina the Frugal was at Saks Fifth Avenue?"

Rina laughed.

"It has been known to happen that lowly academics are allowed to pass into the halls of opulence. There was a terrific one-day sale in the children's department and Jeremy needed new shirts. So I bought them and then I wandered about. And that's when I saw her, plowing her way through a sale table of women's handbags."

Rina fell silent and they all leaned forward expectantly. Rina's anecdotes, her observations of life in the city, always amused them. She had a keen eye and a sharp delivery. Donna had told them that during their college days Rina had written short pieces for the campus newspapers and held court in the common room.

"But that was the old Rina," she had added, and they had understood. The pre-Jeremy, pre-disappointment Rina who was going to finish her dissertation in record time, write novels in a book-lined, thickly carpeted study and marry someone as handsome as Sylvia Plath's Ted Hughes. Still, vestiges of the old Rina surfaced when she had a good story to tell.

"And who was she and what was she doing?" Jen asked, eager for the story to be told, glad to avoid discussing Emma Bovary for the moment. Although Jen had

liked Flaubert's heroine, had even condoned her duplic-
ity, Emma's silence was not mysterious to her. Jen understood that sometimes it was necessary to withhold the
truth to maintain the peace. And it had always been Jen's
priority to avoid confrontations and maintain the peace.
Growing up in the same house as Elizabeth had taught
her that much. She glanced at her sister, but Elizabeth's
attention was focused on Rina.

"She was an attractive woman, shoulder-length silvery
hair, with that fresh-from-the-beauty-salon look, an angular face very well made up and very sad, long fingers,
her nails newly manicured and polished with a subtle
shade of coral, tall, slender, a sleek black suit and a red
silk scarf, red shoes, Moroccan leather, probably." Rina's
voice was pensive as though she were struggling to recall
every detail because every detail was of utmost im-
portance.

"Jewelry?" Cynthia prodded, fingering her own
chunky bracelet, touching her own heavy gold earrings.
She loved jewelry and Eric had given her exquisite pieces
on her birthdays, their anniversaries, on holidays. They
wondered if she would miss those gifts, if she would
continue to wear the pins and necklaces that were the
milestones of their marriage. *Why, if you could not bear
to have your husband in your house for one more night,
could you bear to keep his gifts?* Trish touched her own
silver-and-turquoise bracelet—Jason's gift when Mandy
was born, combining gratitude and apology. She closed
her eyes. She did not want to think of what had occa-
sioned the need for apology, of his betrayal, of her cow-
ardice.

"A wedding band. Diamond. And the scarf held in
place with a silver pin shaped like an arrow. But here's the

funny thing. She wasn't carrying a purse. Using both hands, she was digging through that table piled high with evening bags, handbags, leather totes—you know how they lump everything together during those monster sales—as though she was Moses parting the Red Sea. Somehow she fascinated me, so I kept watching her and I saw her dive deep and pull out an oversize bag, a pouch, sort of, black leather with a tortoiseshell handle, and, without even looking around to see if anyone was watching…"

"Which you were, of course," Elizabeth said harshly.

Rina ignored her and continued.

"Without looking around, with one swift jerk of her hand, she yanked off the sales tags, reached into her jacket pocket and filled that bag with her wallet, her makeup case and two sets of keys, and holding it oh-so-casually, she strolled away to another department. And here's the funny thing. The sadness had drained from her face. She was smiling."

"And you thought this was relevant to a discussion of *Madame Bovary* because…" Elizabeth's tone was impatient.

"Because as Rina saw it, and as I see it, this woman shares an addiction with Emma Bovary—an addiction to beautiful things. She may hope that owning such things, making them part of her life, will relieve the terrible boredom that she feels, the sameness of her daily existence. You remember how Emma was always looking out of the window waiting for something to happen and nothing ever did. In a way she's typical of all women who have no control over their own lives and so they try to take control, sometimes in perverse ways."

Trish spoke rapidly, her own words surprising her, but she had understood suddenly why Rina had told the story. The small incident provided her with a clarity of insight that had been elusive during her own reading of the novel.

She paused. Her words were coming too swiftly, her thoughts flying in unfamiliar directions. Was she projecting her own discontents onto Emma Bovary? It was irrelevant that her dynamic twenty-first century Manhattan life bore not the slightest similarity to the boring existence of the wife of a rural doctor in nineteenth-century Normandy. As she read she had strongly identified with the incipient boredom that had overcome Emma in provincial Yonville. Often, late at night, as she turned the pages, with Jason asleep and snoring lightly beside her, she had suddenly closed the book, overcome by the sense that despite its external order, her own life and her own commitments were beyond her control. Like Emma, she was powerless, her own choices preempted by the demands of her patients, of Jason, of Mandy. She knew that was what her young anorexic patients were doing when they stopped eating, when they forced themselves to vomit. They were trying to exercise some sort of dominance over their own lives, their own bodies. It was no accident that she, who had waged a struggle from childhood on to exercise control over her own life, had chosen to specialize in eating disorders. Her own emotional needs had become her professional compass. She had a new understanding of Emma Bovary and, perhaps, a new understanding of herself. An obvious insight but one that strangely enough had eluded her.

"You're assuming that having an affair is perverse," Jen said mildly. "I suppose you could consider my relationship with Ian an affair, at least by conventional standards. We're not married. We've made no formal

commitment to each other. But I don't think of it as perverse."

"No. Of course not," Trish said swiftly.

"But there are affairs and affairs." Cynthia's tone was
flat and they met her words with an awkward silence, sti-
fling their question, that persistent, unarticulated why.
*Was Eric having an affair that breached acceptable bound-
aries? A liaison with a pubescent girl, an aged woman, one
of the handsome young men always to be found in the pre-
cincts of filmmaking?* The possibilities were endless. *There
were, as Cynthia herself had said, affairs and affairs.*

Trish touched her bracelet again, thought of how Jason
had wept when he gave it to her, when he had told her that
during her pregnancy, her difficult pregnancy, he had had
a brief liaison with a colleague in a distant city. A stupid,
run-of-the-mill affair, he had said. He loved Trish, only
Trish. He had to be honest. It would never happen again.
He had promised and she had believed him, allowed him
to slip the bracelet on her wrist, to take her hand and kiss
it, forgiving him because it seemed impossible to do anything else. She had tried not to blame him, had found excuses for him. She had been bedridden, sexually distant. He
had been far away and lonely. They had a new baby. It was
no big deal, a one-time fling. *There were affairs and affairs.*

It was Donna who changed the subject.

"I think we're thinking only of Emma as a wife, as a
frustrated bourgeois woman. But what about Emma as a
mother? When a woman has a child doesn't the equation
change?"

"Irrevocably." Elizabeth's reply was swift and firm.

They had no doubt that she would have left Bert if not
for Adam. It had never been a happy marriage. That
much Jen had intimated, although she was too loyal to

her sister to elaborate. They knew that Elizabeth and Bert had separated during her pregnancy and even lived apart until Adam was diagnosed as autistic. It was his condition, his need, that had brought them together and kept them together, ensnared in a marital net of bitterness and blame. Divorce was expensive and caring for a child like Adam was expensive. They had made their choice and trapped themselves in their secure but unrewarding jobs, in their unrewarding marriage, their lives governed by Adam's suffering and their own.

"But Emma Bovary, just like Anna Karenina, never thought of her child. She thought only of herself, of her own happiness," Elizabeth added, her words brushed by a veneer of righteousness, of self-approval. She herself was not happy, she would never be happy, but she was doing her duty. She looked at Jen, who would not look at her, who, just as she had when they were children, stifled her own response, refused to be drawn into an argument that might begin as an abstract discussion of *Madame Bovary* but would surely end in accusations and recriminations. Elizabeth turned away as Jen poured herself more tea.

"There are times when you have to think beyond yourself," Cynthia said. "It's not only forgivable, it's necessary. A mother who protects herself protects her children."

She fell silent, but they imagined her thoughts, her words unspoken (*"Which is what I did, which is why I forced Eric to leave"*), and tossed them into the hopper of their speculations. They would talk about that comment in the weeks to come during hurried phone conversations, and over quick meals in neighborhood restaurants. Their coffee would grow cold as they spoke of Cynthia, analyzed her words, probed her secret. *How had Eric threatened the twins? Had he threatened them at all? Why had Cynthia seen herself as their protector?*

The enigma of her drastic decision obsessed them. They seized upon each hint she dropped as though they had been presented with a magic thread that, if carefully followed, would lead them through an emotional maze to an exit where all would be made clear, the cloudy "why" of their imaginings answered with a defining clarity.

"Neither Emma Bovary nor Anna Karenina thought about protecting their children. It's only on her deathbed that Emma even remembers she has a child," Donna observed. "Which is understandable. It's not as though children are the center of every woman's universe. Her daughter was certainly not the center of Emma's life. Believe it or not, there are some women who don't even want children."

"Haven't you ever wanted children, Donna?" Trish asked.

How strange it was that she worked so closely with Donna, felt so close to her, and yet knew so little about her. So much lay hidden beneath that mask of calm and serenity, so briefly shaken by her question. She supposed that Rina knew a lot more about Donna, but of course she could not be sure.

"We're discussing Emma Bovary, not Donna Saunders," Donna replied tersely. "But since you ask, I'm not sure that I do want children, no more than I'm sure I want to be married. And maybe it would have been better for Emma Bovary if she hadn't married. Maybe she wouldn't have died with the taste of arsenic on her tongue and the song of the blind man in her ears."

The discussion veered then as to what Emma's life might have been if she had not married Charles Bovary.

Excitedly they introduced a range of possibilities, giggled over their own literary alternatives. Emma might have moved to Paris, become a George Sand, spurned Rodolfe, her lover, instead of waiting for him to spurn her. Then again, she might have stayed on in Yonville, her daughter Berthe might have become a beautiful young woman who fell in love with Rodolfe and lived the life of her mother's yearnings.

Charles Bovary might have perfected his surgical skills, become a member of the Legion of Honor. Emma might have danced at gala balls in Paris, curtseyed to royalty, lived out the girlish fantasies of her convent school days.

Cynthia imagined her as an old woman, a dowager denizen of a five-star hotel, beautifully gowned, layered with makeup, hair lacquered into place, a young man trailing behind her, holding her bag, her cloak.

"I've seen women like that in hotels on the Riviera. Bored prima donnas of yesteryear. Each one of them an Emma Bovary with money," she said. "Eric actually thought of doing a documentary about them." She flinched at her own mention of her husband's name.

Jen saw Emma living peaceably with Charles Bovary, reconciled to wifehood, content to act as mistress to rich older men who would pay for her ball gowns and music lessons.

"Someone might even commission an artist to paint her. Or she herself might discover a talent for art and become a painter."

She clapped her hands, delighted with the destiny she had invented and they nodded in approval. They no more wanted Emma to poison herself than they had wanted Anna Karenina to die beneath the wheels of a train.

"Why should women always be the victims?" Elizabeth asked plaintively.

"We're talking nineteenth century," Rina replied. "What would a twenty-first-century Emma be like?"

They were briefly silent, thinking and then allowing their thoughts to spill over into spirited conversation, trading theories, juggling options—Emma on Prozac, Emma as a day trader, Emma as Martha Stewart.

Their ideas energized them. They soared on the wings of their creative imaginings, vested the men and women of Yonville with new and dramatic choices, argued over the historic and social details that fleshed out the novel. Immersed in Flaubert's fictional world, they left their own lives behind, forgot the small irritations and perplexing, ongoing dilemmas that encroached upon them daily. Briefly, Cynthia's situation receded from their consciousness, Trish forgot her emotional lethargy, Elizabeth her nagging worry about Adam. Rina's phone rang, but she allowed the answering machine to pick up. Jen doodled on a paper napkin, a line drawing of a woman and a child, Emma and Berthe, perhaps. Donna's face was bright with excitement as she listened and spoke and listened again.

They were readers for whom literature was a drug, each complex plot line delivering a new high, suspending them above reality, allowing them a magical crossover— now onto the snowbound avenues of St. Petersburg, now into the pretentious opera house of provincial Rouen. They had spoken often, with rueful honesty, of how the books they read represented escape, offered pathways to literary landscapes that intrigued and engrossed.

From childhood on, books had been the hot air balloons that carried them above the angry mutterings of

quarreling parents, schoolyard rejections, academic boredom. The sisters, Elizabeth and Jen, divided on so many
things, were united in their addiction to reading, concealing volumes of fairy tales in odd corners of their subur-
ban home, claiming introductory and valedictory
sentences as their magical mantras—*Once upon a time…*
And they lived happily ever after. Rina and Trish had each
confessed to reading by flashlights hidden beneath their
blankets. Donna had never gone to sleep without a book
beneath her pillow, had listened to recordings of books
as she worked beside her mother in their kitchen. Cynthia had read walking to school, walking home, stumbling and scraping her knee only to get up and continue
on her way still reading.

Such revelations had evoked their laughter and instant recognition. They were of a kind, readers from
birth, as genetically marked as those born with blue eyes
or a predisposition to alcoholism.

Theirs was no ordinary book group, because they
themselves were not ordinary readers. Each of them had
visited other book groups, heard superficial comments,
pseudoanalysis, words offered in games of intellectual
one-upmanship. *What I think the author really meant*
was… Let's talk about the symbolism, which I think
means… I hated the ending…. Maybe we should try a bi-
ography next month.

They themselves were different. Literature was their
passion, each book they discussed a challenge to heart
and mind, each of their meetings a celebration of ideas.
Their friendship, their intimacy, was rooted in that
shared passion, unarticulated but silently acknowledged.
In discussing books, they revealed themselves to one another, exposed their dreams, their deepest fears, their

brightest hopes. As they did now, immersed as they were in the life of Emma Bovary, whom they neither pitied nor admired.

Exhausted at last, they sank back and allowed their copies of the book to fall to the floor.

"So," Trish said, "who really is Madame Bovary?"

"Nous sommes Madame Bovary," they replied in chorus, and laughed, amused by their own presumption and the kernel of truth they knew it to contain.

It was Cynthia who found the bag of fortune cookies and passed it around as Rina refilled their cups and Elizabeth, who abhorred disorder of any kind (*How had she managed,* they wondered, *when Adam, in the throes of inexplicable tantrums, had trashed the living room?*), tossed the paper plates and plastic cutlery into a black garbage bag.

It did not escape their notice that Rina scraped the remnants of the Chinese food into a single plastic container, indifferently mingling shrimp in lobster sauce with Szechuan beef. She would eat them together without flinching, Donna knew. The minifridge in their college dorm room had been crowded with slices of pizza rescued from the take-out orders of their neighbors, wilting greens purloined from the cafeteria salad bar and half-eaten bars of chocolate slowly turning white. Rina's compulsive scavenging had amused her then. Now it was a worry and an irritation.

"What the hell are you trying to prove?" she had asked her friend more than once, never waiting for an answer, never expecting one. A mute acceptance informed their intimacy. She turned away from Rina and passed the dish of fortune cookies.

One by one they broke open the small cookies and read the fading predictions on the flimsy bits of tissue paper aloud.

"'A mystery man in your future,'" Donna read, and grimaced. "Just what I need, another man to complicate my life."

"Do you want to trade?" Elizabeth asked. "Oh, never mind. I like mine. 'A financial bonanza awaits you.' I suppose I'd rather have a financial bonanza than a mystery man."

Jen and Trish each drew the same warning. "'Make no plans until the next full moon,'" Jen read aloud.

"They really have to exercise quality control at that great fortune cookie factory in the sky," Trish said. "Suppose an entire group got the same fortune. They might stop believing it. But hey, I'm not going to make any plans until the next full moon. That's the best advice I've gotten all day."

"Me, neither," Jen agreed. "I'll leave all the planning up to Ian."

"Nothing new about that." Elizabeth's tone was cutting. Jen flinched but said nothing.

"Mine is fairly apt," Rina said. "'Complete the task at hand.'" She glanced over to her pile of ungraded papers. "I'm trying," she told the slip of paper, and ripped it in half.

"Cynthia?" Trish probed.

"Not worth reading," Cynthia said, and tossed it into the garbage bag. "Anyway, I have to rush. The new au pair and Mae are having issues and I promised to get home early enough to discuss things with Mae."

"Who works for whom?" Elizabeth asked dryly.

Cynthia did not reply but thrust her book into her soft leather briefcase and tossed the camel-hair cape that matched her A-line dress over her shoulders. She stooped to lace up her boots and her auburn hair shimmered in the lamplight. She looked, for the moment, like an advertisement in her own catalog, the logo appropriate to her casual composure—"the Nightingale's woman, her life and her closets in order." She smiled at them, as though posing for the unseen photographer.

"Someone call me when you decide on the next book," she said, and blowing a perfunctory kiss, she darted out, closing the door softly behind her.

It was Rina who pulled Cynthia's discarded fortune out of the garbage bag and read it aloud.

"'Decisions made in haste will be regretted at leisure.'"

"Apt. Truly apt," Elizabeth murmured.

"It must have affected her," Trish said. "She wouldn't read it aloud."

"Maybe she thought it was true. It's crazy how you believe these throwaway predictions. I always read my horoscope in those ridiculous magazine and newspaper columns, and the weird thing is I always find myself half trusting them," Donna confessed.

"She might have seen some truth in that stupid fortune. She did decide in haste and maybe she's beginning to have regrets. Life without Eric can't be easy," Rina said. "But at least she doesn't have any financial worries. If I can manage so will she. But that's not the issue. The issue is why. What the hell did he do? And why won't she talk about it?"

They were in familiar territory now, all their speculations of the past weeks renewed and reviewed. Each of them, over the weeks, had reached out to Cynthia, tried to arrange lunch dates, dinner dates, asked tentative questions, extended emotional lifelines.

"It must be so hard to go through this alone."

"How are the twins doing?"

"How are you doing?"

Cynthia had remained politely unreceptive. She was fine. Yes, it was a difficult time. The twins were coping.

"What do you think?" they asked one another yet again, but the question was rhetorical. All suggestions were exhausted, all options seemed stale. They turned again to a discussion of the next book.

"Donna's choice," Trish said, consulting her notebook. "You facilitate, it's at your apartment, you choose."

"Away from the nineteenth century. No more European heroines who commit suicide," Donna said placidly. "I started *The Letters of Edith Wharton*. I think it gives us a lot to work with. And if there's time we could read one of the novels. Maybe *The Reef*."

"*The Reef* or the letters. Or both. But it'll be a Wharton evening." Trish, as always, set the course.

They all nodded in agreement, almost in relief. A good choice. It would be meaty. It would be fun.

"I want to try some new recipes," Donna said, and again they laughed. Donna was a professional foodie; she cooked with a gourmet's flair. At her apartment they would not have to depend on Chinese food. The date was set and copied into their Filofaxes and PDAs.

"I'll tell Cynthia," Jen said. "I'm meeting with her tomorrow to talk about the graphics for a new promotion."

"Great." They spoke in unison.

Each of them would invent an excuse to call Jen the next evening, to find out what Cynthia's mood had been, if she had said anything new, if Eric's name had been mentioned. Shamed by their curiosity, they did not meet one another's eyes as they exchanged the light, indifferent kisses that always punctuated their leave-taking.

* * *

Because the evening was unseasonably warm, Trish decided to walk home. The frenetic discussion, her own memories tumbling to mind unbidden, the inevitable discussion of Cynthia's situation, had left her feeling strangely depleted, as fatigued as she often felt after a particularly challenging therapy session. Late night walkers brushed past her. A white-haired woman, bent with age, weighed down by a dark wool coat too heavy for the season, walked a small poodle and talked to it in a high, gentle voice. A bike messenger, balancing a pizza, sped by. A couple wearing matching gray sweatsuits jogged in companionable silence, broke their pace at the corner and kissed, the girl's face turned upward, her lover's hand gentle upon her head. Trish briefly slowed her steps to watch them. A cab stopped in front of a brownstone and a young woman in a business suit, holding a briefcase, jumped out, waved toward an upstairs window and hurried inside.

Why wasn't she herself hurrying home to Jason and Mandy? Trish wondered, envying the other woman's eager haste, as, she realized now, she had envied the sweet spontaneity of that street-corner kiss. She tried to remember the last time she and Jason had moved toward each other, eager for touch and tenderness, and, impatient with herself, abandoned the effort.

Theirs, after all, had never been a relationship forged in inexplicable passion and attraction. They had come together sensibly, introduced by mutual friends who rightly thought that they would have much in common. She had been in her first year of residency, the hard-fought battle to complete medical school, against all odds, newly won. The years of competing for scholarships, of filling out forms for loans, of holding down menial part time jobs while frantically studying, were finally over. There would be no more furnished rooms and meals cooked on a hot plate, one package of macaroni and cheese stretched over dinner and lunch. She was a doctor. She had a studio apartment. She saw her loneliness as another obstacle that would soon be cleared. She was on her way.

Jason had just been made junior partner in a venture-capital firm, bought his first car, his first subscription to the Met, tickets for two as though intuiting that he would soon meet someone with whom to share his Family Circle seats. He took perverse pleasure in writing a check to his parents when his father had suffered a stroke. That check made a statement to the family, who had cynically mocked his aspirations, to the brother who had hidden his textbooks, imitated his use of words he considered pretentious.

Trish and Jason, meeting when they did, as they did, two young professionals, appreciative of each other's intelligence, of each other's achievements, veterans of the requisite failed love affairs, were poised for permanence. It overwhelmed them that they shared so much. They both loved the opera, held hands as they sat in his hard-earned seats, wept together as Madame Butterfly died (she wiped his tears and, yes, she remembered, kissed one away, loving the saline taste of his sorrow on her tongue), joined standing ovations, hugged each other at the conclusion of a wonderful *Pagliacci*. The theater engaged them, and for a short while they cooked together, amassing a collection of spices that now gathered dust in the rear of their pantry.

"We have so much in common," they told their friends, fulfilling the prophecy of the couple who had brought them together. "We have so much in common," they told each other, and took that commonality for love. It did not matter that he did not share her passion for literature. They shared so much else, and she had already found the book group, which satisfied without threatening.

They exchanged family stories, spoke sadly of their working-class parents—his in rural Pennsylvania, hers in a blue-collar Delaware town—who had offered little encouragement, little support, bewildered as they were by the son and daughter whose ambitions and dreams were so far beyond their scope. That parental bewilderment had morphed into bitterness, a muted estrangement and, finally, a cool indifference. Phone calls on birthdays, excuses on Thanksgiving, Christmas cards carelessly chosen.

Both Trish and Jason felt themselves very alone in their chosen worlds. It had seemed natural then, that finding each other, they would banish that loneliness and marry. Their wedding was small and sensible. A gathering of friends and colleagues. Only Trish's mother attended. Jason's family sent a large glass fruit bowl, which they donated to a thrift shop.

They worked hard. Trish was engrossed in her residency. Psychiatry had seemed an obvious choice born, she sometimes thought, of her enchantment with literature, her need to understand the motivation of the fictional personalities who had peopled her lonely childhood. Slowly, her focus had shifted to patients with eating disorders, young people struggling to understand those voids so familiar to her, the emptiness she had felt in that world where no one seemed to speak the language of her mind and heart. She understood their need to seize control, however perverted, of the bodies that be-

trayed them. Her patients became her other selves. Her
involvement with them was intense.

She worked late into the night and often arrived home
to find Jason slumped in front of the television set, half
asleep. His hours, too, were long, the climb up the partnership ladder exhausting. There were business trips to
distant cities, late-night meetings with research and development teams. They saw each other less and less.
There were no more afternoons of shared cooking. More
often than not they offered their opera tickets to other
couples. She was on call. He would be out of town.

And then she became pregnant with Mandy. An un-
planned but sensibly timed pregnancy. Her residency
was completed and she was on staff. He had closed the
first of what would be a succession of excellent deals. At
last they could afford a convenient and comfortable
apartment in the city.

But her pregnancy was difficult, requiring long weeks
of bed rest, and his travel had accelerated. She felt the
first stirrings of uneasiness. Was this really the life she
wanted? She confessed to a boredom that she blamed on
his absence, the strain and loneliness of her pregnancy.
She thought of returning to her analyst, but therapy was
not supposed to be a cure for boredom. She learned of
the divorce of Carl and Rita, the couple who had introduced them, and felt a cold chill of terror. Divorce was
not an option and why should it be? She and Jason were
so right for each other. They had such a good life. She
dismissed even the thought, cut her long dark hair, now
lightly streaked with gray, into the layered shaggy cut that
softly framed her angular face, and bought silky pastel-
colored negligees that she would wear after the birth. She
was determined to renavigate her marriage, to avoid the

shoals that had ambushed Carl and Rita. She felt a new sexual energy, an anticipatory excitement that swelled when she first held Mandy in her arms.

She was wearing such a negligee, the color of buttercups, when Jason gave her the bracelet, when he told her of his affair. Again, he had wept, but this time she had not tasted his tears.

There had been forgiveness but something had withered. She felt a small death, a rotting in a corner of her heart. She struggled against it, buried it in increasing busyness. She could not imagine destroying the life she—they—had built with such effort. Secretly, as she read, she had envied Emma's daring at engaging in the affair with Rodolphe, planning her escape from Charles Bovary and the dullness of a life that no longer interested her. She herself would not have such courage. Immediately, she regretted the thought. *Her life was not dull.* Still, she admired Emma as she reluctantly admired Cynthia.

"It took courage for her to ask Eric to leave," she had told Donna over coffee in the hospital cafeteria.

"It doesn't require courage if you feel you have no choice," Donna said. "What Eric did must have been pretty horrific." Pensively, she stirred her coffee. "What would make you end your marriage? What would Jason have to do?"

The question, so idly asked, caused Trish to seize up with fear. Her stomach knotted, as it had when Cynthia had so calmly (too calmly?) told them of her decision. The vulnerability of one marriage, deemed safe and enviable, like a game of dominoes, threatened other marriages. Couple after couple might topple into disunion. Her answer to Donna, who was staring at her intently, whose question might not be so idle after all, was disarmingly vague.

"I don't know. I suppose it would have to be something extreme." *And Jason, her cautious, gentle Jason, was not given to extremes. He did not live in Eric's world of frenetic glamour, first-class journeys to Greek islands and Tuscan villages, beautiful women and, yes, beautiful men. His was the quiet, tense world of late-night meetings and faxes, business trips to cities defined by shopping malls and high-rise office buildings. Occasionally, very occasionally, a weary traveler might seek a brief escape, a tentative venture into uneasy sex, but that could not be called extreme. His affair had been a one-time thing, out of character, never repeated.*

"An affair?" Donna had suggested, and Trish had shrugged, unwilling to venture further into the now-familiar wilderness of speculation.

"Hardly extreme. Not in the post-Clinton world. Hillary set new standards for all of us."

They had laughed then, hurriedly finished their coffee and rushed to their respective offices to confront that afternoon's calendar of misery.

She had not told Donna that she had not left Jason, had not even thought of leaving him, when he confessed his affair, piercing her joy at Mandy's birth, tumbling her hopes for a new and better beginning. Other women might have reacted with fury, with tears and threats. She herself had merely turned away and allowed his tears to fall on the bracelet, which, as it turned out, was too large for her wrist.

Why was that? Why didn't I even float the idea of a trial separation? she asked herself as she stood in front of her own apartment building, a vagrant wind ruffling her hair. The answer came to her with startling simplicity. *Be-*

cause I did not want to. Because I wanted to stay married to Jason. And I still want to be married to him.

They were alone in the world, she and Jason, severed from their first families, the parents and siblings who did not even send Mandy cards for her birthday. She admitted that it might be fear that bound them together, but, if so, it was a fear founded on reality, interwoven with the affection and the mutual determination that had led them to this place in their lives. She was a doctor, a psychiatrist. She understood symptoms and syndromes. She knew that when there was no cure, palliatives could apply. And always, like small invasive tumors, emotional rot could be cut away. Neither Emma nor Charles, doctor though he was, had had such knowledge. She was suddenly impatient with the Bovarys and with the Kareninas. They had not tried hard enough. *And Cynthia— had she tried hard enough?* The question teased and faded away. Cynthia held her secret too close.

Trish looked up at their window, golden in the darkness, only a small table lamp aglow. Jason stood in that patch of light, looking down at the street. Always, when she was out late, he waited for her, leaning forward, his face etched with anxiety, a tall, graying man who had known little love as a child and feared to lose the tenderness that had been theirs from the beginning. Those tears shed all those years ago, never mentioned since, had sprung from that fear.

He moved into the shadow and her heart stirred with a new compassion. Swiftly, then, she entered the building, eager suddenly to see him, to walk with him into Mandy's room, to stand beside him as they looked down at their sleeping child.

Perhaps, afterward, they could speak of the summer home he wanted to buy. Perhaps tomorrow she would phone Cynthia for the name of the agency that recruited au pairs.

Unlike Emma Bovary, perhaps, unlike Cynthia, she had choices, and she would make good use of them. A new lightness of heart spurred her on. She did not wait for the elevator but hurried up the stairwell, unsurprised to find him in the doorway waiting for her.

Chapter Three

"Jen! Jen Reardon!"

Standing on the corner of Madison and Fifty-Fifth, buffeted by the first fierce wind of late autumn, her huge black leather portfolio tugging at her arm, as she tried vainly to hail a taxi, Jen turned in annoyance. She was already late for her weekly visit to the nursing home where her mother waited, impatience souring her deeply lined face, her pale eyes dulled by a lifetime's accumulation of disappointments. Jen had thought she might manage a stop at the loft to exchange her long dark coat and too closely fitting black wool beret for her hooded denim jacket, and to offer Ian the smoked-salmon sandwich she had scrounged at the Nightingale's brunch buffet. That hadn't happened. The meeting with Cynthia had continued well past the time she had allotted and there was no way she could leave. Cynthia's schedule took priority. Her voice was gentle but controlling, her criticisms of Jen's graphics apologetic but uncompromising. She wanted more prominence for the products on one storyboard, a subtler use of color on another.

"Those new spice racks from Sweden have to grab the consumer's eye. Everyone owns a spice rack. We're selling something no one really needs except maybe a bride, so we have to go for the aesthetic approach, Jen. We want the page flipper to pause and study your graphic."

Jen might disagree, but she acknowledged that Cynthia was a marketing genius and she was also the boss, the dispenser of projects, the woman who wrote the checks. Their meeting had extended into an early lunch. It was only over coffee, when all of Cynthia's corrections had been carefully notated that they relaxed and spoke as friends. Cynthia remarked on Jen's outfit, a zany rainbow-colored sweater with huge pockets for Jen's ever-present drawing pens.

"It suits you, Jen," she said approvingly.

"Ian bought it, actually," Jen said, and immediately regretted her words. She had not wanted to remind Cynthia she had a lover who bought her gifts, not when Cynthia was so newly alone.

She looked at her friend, noted that she was pale beneath her carefully applied makeup and so thin that her crimson wool dress (daring Cynthia, to choose a color that clashed with her bright hair) hung too loosely.

"You look a little tired, Cyn." Her voice was edged with concern.

"Well, it is a rough time," Cynthia admitted, and added cream to her coffee.

"Do you want to talk about it?" Jen asked carefully. She was trespassing into treacherous emotional terrain, she knew, but she wanted Cynthia to know that she cared, that she was available.

Cynthia had hesitated and then shook her head.

"Not now. Not yet."

And Jen, of course, had not persisted, had in fact glanced at her watch and made a hurried, unapologetic departure. Her mother. She had to get to her mother.

"Jen!" Her name was called again, more urgently now, just as a taxi pulled up. She turned, and the driver, spotting another fare, careened away.

It was Eric. He hurried toward her, his open coat flapping, his face wind-reddened, the thick fair hair that photographed so well falling across his similarly photogenic high forehead. She forced herself to smile, to veil her irritation, to keep her voice even. She was well schooled in such control, which was mocked, in turn, by Elizabeth, her sister, by Ian, her lover.

"Anything to avoid a confrontation." Elizabeth's frequently repeated taunt was designed to trigger confrontations, but Jen was seldom sucked in. Years of experience had taught her when to leave a room, when to hang up the phone, when to vanish into a kitchen and busy herself with chores.

"People spit in your face, Jen, and you act as though it's raining." Ian's contempt was careless, tossed out at her if he thought she had accepted a project at too low a fee, if she had agreed to do a favor (usually for Elizabeth) at great inconvenience, if the supermarket cashier shortchanged her or their landlord ignored her complaints of burned-out bulbs in the stairwell and a lack of hot water in the shower. She did not tell him that more often than not, he was among those who launched small verbal attacks because they were out of toilet paper, a bill had not been paid, he had mislaid his sketch pad. She seldom answered him. It was easier to buy the toilet paper, pay the bill, find the sketch pad, call the landlord yet again. The lessons of her childhood in Elizabeth's shadow, avoiding her parents' fierce and irrational anger, had been well learned.

"Eric, hi." She kept her tone even, concealing her surprise that he should be outside Nightingale's, almost too obviously waiting for Cynthia. *Waiting or stalking?* Looking at him, she dismissed her own mental accusation. She pitied the desperation in his expression and the new gauntness of his face; the dark circles beneath his eyes saddened her. His elegant camel-hair coat seemed too large for him, his thin wrists dangled from sleeves suddenly oversize, and when he bent to kiss her she thought she smelled liquor on his breath.

"Coming from a meeting with Cynthia?" he asked.

"Just plans for the post-holiday sale." Thanksgiving was still weeks away and Cynthia was already thinking January. But that was Cynthia, in control, organized, always thinking ahead, which was why she was now seated comfortably behind her huge uncluttered mahogany desk while Jen was frantically trying to grab a cab.

"How is Cynthia?" His voice was light, but pain flashed across his face; her compassion intensified. She had always liked Eric. He had always been kind to her. He had even bought a painting from Ian, although she sensed that he did not like Ian's huge abstract splashes of color.

"Well, you know," she said vaguely. "She's coping." She never knew what people meant by that. It was borrowed from Elizabeth's lexicon. Her sister's standard answer to questions about Adam, her job, her marriage, was always "I'm coping."

It seemed an appropriate reply to Eric. And in fact it was almost true. Cynthia was coping. Despite her obvious fatigue, throughout their meeting she had been focused on her work, her critique of Jen's graphics right on target. Twice during the morning she had taken personal calls. She had spoken to Mae, reminded her that she should serve an early supper to the twins, and to Ingrid, because there was an evening dinner meeting at Nightingale's. "Wild salmon, not farmed," she had told Mae. She would not be home to eat with her children but she would control the menu. The second call was from the headmistress of the twins' school to confirm a parents' conference. All the while her eyes had been fixed on Jen's storyboards. Even Jen's sympathy, her offer to listen, to share, had been gently rejected and relegated to Cynthia's own emotional timetable. She was hardly the portrait of a woman whose dream life had unexpectedly turned into a nightmare. She was clearly a woman who coped, who knew how to compartmentalize.

"I want to talk to her," he said. "I have to talk to her."

"Eric, I can't help you. You must know that."

"Then let me talk to you." Not a demand, a plea.

Pleas were harder for Jen to resist, but this afternoon she had no choice. She had promised Elizabeth that she would make the weekly visit and meet with the nursing home bookkeeper about the usual overcharges. Elizabeth could not be expected to manage their mother's affairs, to submit to her moods, not with her full-time job, her responsibility to Adam and Bert's constant demands. Jen ignored Ian's too-frequent reminders that Jen might not keep regular office hours but her work consumed as much time as Elizabeth's, that Elizabeth did not have the right to dictate what Jen's obligations should be.

Another cab approached and she waved frantically to the driver.

"I'm sorry, Eric. But I'm in a terrible hurry. My mother…I'm late already."

The cab drew up and he opened the door for her. Always he had been gentle, bred to courtesy. "But another time," he insisted.

"Call me." The invitation, she knew, was acquiescence. Speaking to him, meeting him for coffee, was harmless. In no way could it be seen as a betrayal of Cynthia. How, after all, could she betray Cynthia? She had no information to offer him, no secrets to share.

Impulsively, as he bent forward, she kissed him on the cheek. Looking back, as the cab sped away, she saw him stare up at the Nightingale's building and then swiftly walk away.

She reached into her bag for the Library of America Edith Wharton collection, relishing the smooth feel of the black cover, the newness of the thin paper on which it was printed. She did not read but turned the pages slowly as the cab raced northward. Donna had suggested that they read *The Reef* in addition to Wharton's letters, and Cynthia had told her that she had completed the novel in the early hours of the morning.

"I stayed up until about three to get to the end," she had said, and Jen had imagined her propped up in the huge bed she and Eric had shared, her rose-colored bed lamp casting its glow across the book, her fingers threaded with rhomboids of light while Eric's side of the bed, barriered by a pillow, remained shrouded in darkness. No wonder Cynthia had been tired. Loneliness had banished sleep.

Jen wondered if the twins wakened in the night calling for their father. It had occurred only to Rina to wonder how Cynthia had explained Eric's sudden disappearance to Liza and Julie, but it had become a question that teased all of them.

Jen sighed and read the first two words of *The Reef*, "Unexpected obstacle…" Those were words that Cynthia could relate to, she knew. After all, an unexpected obstacle, an unexpected catastrophe, had derailed her marriage. Jen knew that the other members of the book group, aware that she was working with Cynthia, would call during the week, as they always did, hungry for nuggets of information. *How did she seem? What did she say?* Their questions would be insistent, their need to know intense. Even her sister, Elizabeth, angry and self-absorbed as she was, freed herself from the mire of her own misery to ask about Cynthia. *Was she managing her department as efficiently as always? Did she seem in control?* Elizabeth, Jen knew, prided herself on managing her own job efficiently despite Adam's difficulties and Bert's barely contained anger—she never missed a day of work, wrote careful reports on problem students and their even more problematic parents, organized faculty meetings and individual conferences. She was definitely in control. Would Cynthia be capable of as much?

Always Jen gave her friends accurate reports. Cynthia, she told them, perhaps too brusquely, remained the capable, organized marketing executive she always had been. Jen did not speak to Elizabeth or the others of the sadness that clouded her green eyes, once so gimlet bright, of her loss of weight or how, as they bent over page proofs, her astute critical assessment drifted into a whisper and then into a sudden silence. As she had that very morning, Jen waited patiently then until Cynthia shook her head and, as suddenly as she had fallen silent, resumed her clear and reasoned critique. Cynthia had offered her no confidences to be hugged close or to be shared. *Not yet,* she had said. She could report that exchange to her friends and they would have to be content with that.

The cab braked for a light and she thought she might tell the other women about her brief encounter with Eric. She was to meet Donna for coffee that evening. Should she mention it in casual conversation?

She closed the book and remembered to eat the smoked-salmon sandwich only blocks before the cab pulled up in front of the nursing home where her mother waited, frozen into an aphasic anger.

"Jen, that you?"

Ian's strong voice, echoing across the cavernous loft, surprised her when she returned home that evening.

"Who else would it be?" She struggled to keep her tone light, to mask the annoyance she felt at finding him there. He taught a class at the Art Students' League on Wednesday nights and was usually gone when she arrived home. She had looked forward to an hour of solitude, of lamp-lit quiet, a respite from the long hours at Nightingale's working on the catalog layout and then what had seemed like the even longer hours at the nursing home, struggling to make conversation with her mother, arguing with the bookkeeper about mysterious charges.

"Aren't you teaching tonight?" she asked, setting her portfolio down and tossing her beret onto the butcher-block counter, which was littered with the remains of Ian's lunch. Dried scabs of tomato soup bloodied her yellow soup bowl and stale crusts of brown bread had been tossed into his empty coffee mug. Automatically she carried bowl and mug to the sink and, still wearing her heavy coat, took up a sponge and wiped the table clean.

"I was too tired. I got Patrick to cover for me."

He was lying on the day bed, a tall lanky man, slightly heavier now than when she had first met him in a life-drawing class three years earlier. The red hair that he usually wore in a ponytail was loosely spread across the pillow and she noted for the first time, with a stab of sadness, that it was streaked with silver. Ian, who still wore the plaid shirts and jeans of his undergraduate days, who still kept a few joints in the Gauloise tin he had brought back from his junior year in Paris, who had yet to open a checking account, was not supposed to grow old. Only weeks ago they had celebrated their thirty-fifth birthdays together and thirty-five was not old. Impulsively, she bent over him and kissed his cheek, just above a streak of blue paint that was slowly hardening.

He lifted his hand to her hair and stroked it gently, then moved his fingers down her back, kneading the tensed muscles of her spine until they loosened and relaxed beneath his touch, humming as he worked. "Let It Be," the Beatles song, Jen's favorite. It was this swift sweetness of his, a quality she had not known before, that had bonded him to her from the beginning.

"Sorry about missing the class. I know we need the money, but I finished the canvas today, didn't stop painting for maybe seven hours. I couldn't have done a stint at a classroom easel."

"I know. It's all right," she said, calculating the balance in her checkbook against the month's rent for the loft and the credit card bill that lay unopened on her desk.

They did need the money. She had had to write a check at the nursing home for her mother's supplementary medication, an expense she could not ask Elizabeth to share. A new one-on-one program that had been recommended for Adam meant paying an exorbitant amount for extra therapy hours. But she would manage. A millinery shop had asked her to design their promotional package, and Cynthia had given her name to a mail order company that had admired the Nightingale's catalog and wanted her to do some work for them. All right. So she'd work a couple of extra hours, maybe up her rates. Cynthia herself had told her that she wasn't charging enough.

She turned to look at the canvas.

It was oversize, stretched across two easels, a bold and arresting abstract of an evening sky, great splashes of cobalt threaded with shafts of silver and the delicate pastel wash of the slowly sinking sun.

"It's wonderful, Ian."

She walked over to it and studied it more closely, marveling at both the daring and subtlety of his brushwork.

"With the work you did at the shore in the summer and three more major canvases you'll have enough for that one-man show the Maestrato Gallery wants to put on," she said.

"Three more major canvases? You say that as though I can just knock them off as easily as you turn out graphics for the Nightingale's catalogs." His voice rang with sarcasm and she winced. Immediately, sensing her hurt, he placed his arms around her.

"I'm sorry," he said.

"It's all right," she sighed.

His words had wounded but she recognized their truth.

She had long since recognized the limitations of her own talent, acknowledged, with disappointment, that she was not good enough to be a serious painter, and concentrated her efforts on developing her commercial art business. It was a practical choice and it worked, providing them with a reasonably steady income so that Ian could concentrate full-time on his painting and Jen could arrange her hours as she pleased. It was an arrangement that Elizabeth viewed with contempt. But then, Jen knew, Elizabeth would view any decision she made with the harsh criticism that had endured beyond their tempestuous childhood when their parents' incessant quarrels had sent the two sisters scurrying for refuge in opposite corners of the large overheated house that was more battlefield than home.

Their mother and father argued about money, and Elizabeth and Jen shut the doors of their rooms and read. They argued about vacation plans, her mother's cooking, her father's indifferent sloppiness, and their daughters turned the pages of their books and lost themselves in the lives of fictional families who said cheerful good mornings to one another and sat together beside glowing fires. The sisters did not play together, did not even read in the same room, but they exchanged books, their tastes in literature, from earliest childhood, as similar as their reactions to the turbulent ambience of their home was different.

Elizabeth had thrust herself into the role of the arbiter, now criticizing her mother, now her father, arguing for a reasonableness of which they were incapable, sternly pointing out their faults to the weak, angry man, the complaining, emotionally starved woman they called Mother and Father. Elizabeth confronted while Jen withdrew. The raised voices frightened her, the irrational invective caused her to tremble. She sued for peace with her silence, her acquiescence. Elizabeth's early marriage was an escape of a kind, a strike for control. Unable to control her parents' lives, she would control her own. Bert was a steady, quiet suitor. There had been no hint of the emotional whirlpool concealed beneath the still water of his silence. But that, too, Elizabeth might have been able to control if Adam had been a normal child, if he had not stared through people with that vacant gaze, if his small graceful hands had ever ceased their incessant drumming and his few words had not been endless repetitions. It was a condition that defied Elizabeth's control, and Jen, who understood her sister, pitied her and said nothing. It did not surprise her that Elizabeth had opted for a career in which she exercised control over her students' lives. "This is the college you must apply to," she told them. "These are the courses you must take." "This is what must be done," she informed troubled parents. Unable to guide her own life, she was guidance counselor to others. Similarly, she would impose her unwanted guidance on Jen. Where was Jen's life going? What did she get out of her arrangement with Ian? What did he contribute to their shared life? Why wasn't Jen taking studio classes instead of making it possible for Ian to paint?

Jen avoided answering her sister. It did not matter to her that Elizabeth disliked Ian, that she thought he exploited their relationship.

"Do you ever speak of marriage?" Elizabeth had asked her sister more than once.

Always Jen shrugged off the question. She would not tell Elizabeth that she treasured the very impermanence of her life with Ian, an impermanence that offered her freedom and power of a kind. Unlike her sister, unlike her mother, whose ragged marriage had ended in lonely and infirm widowhood, she was not trapped. She would not counter those prying words, that tangle of malice and concern, with accusing questions about Elizabeth's own life with Bert, a bitter alliance, cemented by their shared obligation to Adam and fired by a volcanic anger that erupted with increasing frequency. She would not tell her sister that while she recognized Ian's irresponsibility, the narcissism that she forgave because of his talent, she reveled in the safe harbor he had offered her with his ability to comfort and to surprise.

"Oh, by the way, Elizabeth called while you were out," Ian said, moving away from her, standing back to appraise the canvas from another angle.

"Did she say what she wanted?" Jen asked.

"She wanted to know how your mother was. She said to call her."

It occurred to Jen that Ian had not asked about her mother, but then he never did. It was only their life together that was of concern to him.

"Oh, well, she'll have to wait until tomorrow. I'm meeting Donna for dinner and I'm already late."

"Hey, I thought we'd order in pizza, have some time together." Petulance punctuated his words.

"I'm sorry. You were scheduled to teach when I made this date with Donna."

"Right."

Their mutual disappointment dissolved into a contained civility. He heated leftovers while she changed into jeans and a loose shirt. He walked her to the door and kissed her on the cheek. She smiled, remorsefully, forgivingly. Tenderness, as always, was his hold over her.

* * *

Donna was waiting for her at Gino's, the small Italian restaurant on Ninth Avenue where the tables were just far enough apart so that conversations could not be overheard. The clean but not quite white tablecloths were streaked with stubborn tomato sauce stains that would not wash out, and candles that were never lit stood clumsily in dusty wax-encrusted Chianti bottles. Donna had already moved a pot of plastic flowers from the center of the table to the side and was grimly wiping her water glass with a napkin. The food, however, was excellent, the service swift, and it was possible to linger over coffee without feeling any pressure to leave. It also pleased them that Gino's was not a "couples" restaurant but a meeting place for same-sex friends. Groups of women sat together, talking softly, laughing softly. Men leaned toward each other, speaking with great seriousness and bursting into laughter with muscular spontaneity.

Gino's was Donna's discovery, one she had shared only with Jen. Rina, after all, would have complained even about the modestly priced menu, guilting them always with the poverty she flaunted as other women might show off a new dress. It was too downscale for Trish and Cynthia, who in any case were always frantic to get home to their families in time to share a meal whenever possible, which was seldom enough. Elizabeth almost never went out for dinner. It was the only time she and Bert got to talk, she had explained self-righteously the few times they had thought to invite her. Although her excuse was dubious, they never challenged her. Jen had known from childhood on that it was a mistake to ever question her sister's decisions, and Donna admitted that although she respected Elizabeth for her dedication to her son and appreciated her perceptive insights during book club discussions, she did not really like her.

It was natural then that Jen and Donna, both of them single and childless, their respective lovers undemanding, had drifted into sharing an occasional casual dinner and exchanging confidences that were more than casual.

Jen sat opposite Donna and she, too, took her napkin and vigorously wiped away a vagrant clump of pasta that had adhered to the oversize soup spoon at her place setting.

"Can you imagine what Cynthia would say if she saw this?" she asked Donna.

"Probably look at it in disgust and ask politely for a clean spoon. And then she'd never come here again. You know Cynthia."

"Do we?" Jen asked.

It was a question that had teased her for weeks, as she had taken meetings with Cynthia, the graphics spread on the table in front of them, as she had listened to her discuss Madame Bovary, as she observed her on the phone at Nightingale's, discussing her weekly menus with Mae, her children's schedules with the au pair, threatening a supplier, cajoling a printer, taking off one hat and donning another. How well, after all, did she know her friend, her client, who, with such calm, had tossed a grenade into their midst and retreated while they tossed it about, speculating, guessing, fumbling for the pin that would release the answer to the ever constant "why"?

Jen studied the menu. Linguini with clam sauce, she decided at once, and asked the hovering waiter to bring a glass of red wine with it.

"Comfort food," she told Donna. "I'm definitely in need of comfort."

"The same," Donna told the waiter, and buttered a piece of bread as he disappeared with their order. "A long day?"

"No longer than usual," Jen replied. "Except for a visit to my mother. A fairly long conference with Cynthia at Nightingale's stretching into the afternoon. It went past lunch, although she knew I was desperate to get to the nursing home and see my mother. Not like Cynthia."

"But then what is like Cynthia? Or rather, what is Cynthia really like, beneath all the razzle-dazzle?" Donna asked. Jen's question rephrased, her doubts articulated.

Jen hesitated, reflected.

"I suppose we've got the basic bio straight," she said at last. "Cynthia Anders, born Cynthia Simmons. Comfortable parents, comfortable home, although she never mentions her father. She did say once that he was a man who disappointed, whatever that means. A bachelors from Bryn Mawr, an MBA from Penn, a dream job. A romantic courtship in Italy, a dream marriage to Eric Anders, genius documentary maker, angelic children and then…"

"A nightmare separation and probably a nightmare divorce on the horizon," Donna finished. "Which may or may not give lie to everything else we know, or thought we knew, about her. I'm kind of ashamed to admit it now, but I always envied her—the stable family. The drop-dead house, the jet-set stories in *People*, the job, Eric. Nice, talented gentle Eric. I always liked him. We all did, I think."

"I saw him today," Jen said, sipping her red wine.

"You did? Where?"

"I was just leaving Nightingale's, struggling to get a taxi—you know that midday, Midtown madness—and suddenly there he was, calling my name, running up to me."

"Outside *Nightingale's?* What was he doing there?"

"I don't know. I didn't really have time to ask."

"Stalking Cynthia, probably." Donna swirled the wine in her glass, tasted it and grimaced.

"I don't see Eric as a stalker," Jen protested mildly.

"Me, neither." Donna smiled sadly.

She was right. They had all liked Eric and he had been kind to all of them, quietly dispensing the odd favor, buying the painting from Ian, arranging for Jeremy's class to visit the set of a documentary he was filming, somehow finding a rent-controlled apartment for Donna.

"How did he seem?" she asked.

"Sad. Very thin. His clothes seemed to hang on him." *As Cynthia's scarlet dress had hung on her.* She was newly saddened by the odd parallel that had just occurred to her.

"Not unusual for people in a depression. One of the first symptoms is a lack of appetite and weight loss. I deal with a lot of patients like that, and no matter what terrific eating plans I create for them I know that my best bet is Ensure or some other liquid diet supplement." Donna slipped easily, too easily, into professionalism. She loved her work, loved being able to make assessments and design solutions. Low carbs, reinforced proteins, vitamin supplements. She and Trish had co-authored an article for a psychiatric journal, "Diets and Depression."

"Do they serve much Ensure at the Brasserie?" Jen asked wryly, and Donna laughed. Eric had invited each of them to lunch there at different times.

"Maybe they pour it into an oversize crystal goblet," she said. "What did you talk about with him?"

"Not much. I told him I was in a hurry to get to my mother's, which was the truth, but I said that maybe we could talk another time." She hesitated.

"And?" Donna prodded.

The waiter set down their bowls of linguini, the garlic sauce steaming fragrantly between them. Jen twirled several strands about on her fork and then set it down.

"And I thought I smelled liquor on his breath," she admitted. "He wasn't drunk, I'm sure of that. But I did smell the liquor."

She blushed guiltily. She had not meant to tell Donna that, and in telling she felt that she had betrayed Eric, but she did want Donna's reaction. She wanted Donna to ask the questions that had occurred to her, to partner her curiosity.

"Do you think he's an alcoholic?" Donna asked. "Do you think that's what made Cynthia kick him out?"

That was a supposition that had not arisen during all those weeks of speculation, but it had occurred to Jen during her ride home from the nursing home just as it occurred to Donna as she peered at Jen over her glass of wine.

"He always seemed just a social drinker. I mean, we've seen him sip wine at openings, maybe a martini at a cocktail party. Never more and sometimes not even that much. We would have noticed. And even if he did drink a little too much, or a lot too much, would that have caused Cynthia to say she couldn't even allow him to stay in their home with the children for one more night? I think that would be a pretty extreme reaction," Jen reasoned.

"Unless of course there was some other kind of substance abuse and the liquor was the least of it. We see that sometimes at the hospital," Donna persisted.

"You mean drugs?"

"Sometimes drugs are an alcoholic's next step. It happens. Pot, then cocaine. Heroin. Maybe Ecstasy. Cynthia wouldn't have him in the house if he was doing drugs there, not with the children. And given his profession, it's not so difficult to think that he could get them. Film people. You know. It's a big drug scene. That could be why she acted so quickly."

Donna spoke more slowly, the scenario she was creating gathering momentum, her words gaining validity. A teenage actress had been admitted to the hospital that very afternoon, high on crack, spinning through intake half naked, her esophagus so damaged by constant vomiting that Donna had to create recipes for protein shakes to sustain her. She had scanned the girl's case history. Her highs had begun with wine, drifted to liquor and weed and then the hard drugs that had landed her chart on Donna's desk.

"Eric's not Hollywood. He's not television. He makes documentaries. Serious stuff. He works with serious people. We've met a lot of them at his previews and their parties. Not exactly cokeheads," Jen protested. "Look, let's forget it. He had a couple of drinks at lunch, maybe because he was depressed as he damn well has every right to be. That doesn't mean he's an alkie or a druggie. I never should have said anything about it. Let's talk about something else."

Jen turned her attention back to the pasta, but it was suddenly tasteless. She was relieved when Donna's cell phone rang and she listened as Donna made after-dinner plans to meet Tim at the jazz club where he had a gig.

"You don't mind, do you?" Donna asked.

She shook her head. She did not mind. She was anxious suddenly to rush home to Ian, to be gathered up in his arms, to be reassured by his warm breath against her cheek, his tender touch upon her arm.

But Ian was not home when she returned to the loft. The only message on the answering machine was from Elizabeth, her voice annoyed, accusatory. Jen ignored it. She turned to study the new painting again and discerned a gathering storm in that restless sky splashed across the oversize canvas. A sadness gripped her and she fought it in the same way she had fought sadness all her life. Reading, as always was her refuge.

She reached for her book, crept into the protective cave of fiction and lost herself in the world Edith Wharton had created in *The Reef*. She absorbed herself in the story of Anna Leath, a widow waiting for her lover's arrival, unaware that he had a brief romantic involvement with Sophy Viner, now engaged to her stepson. She read on. The mysterious outcropping that gave the novel its title became her own precipice; the garden of the Leath home in Normandy was transformed into her own landscape, engrossing but unthreatening. She submitted to the magic of Wharton's narrative. Anna Leath's uncertainty dislodged her own. Sophy Viner's dilemma obscured Cynthia's sadness, the real pain in Eric's eyes. The story absorbed her, dulled her anxiety. Jen fell asleep reading and wakened only as Ian's lips gently brushed one eyelid and then the other. The heavy book fell soundlessly to the floor.

Donna prepared carefully for the book-group meeting. She planned the menu as meticulously as she designed meal plans for the hospital, conscious, as always, of taste, nutrition and aesthetics. There was a new spice blend she had bought in the Italian market on Eighth Avenue that she was particularly anxious to try. Perhaps she would use it in a Tuscan eggplant appetizer she had found on the Internet. That recipe called for canned tomatoes, but she would use the vine-ripened ones she had bought at Whole Foods. She closed her eyes and smiled at the thought of the multicolored dish simmering on her stove, filling her bright kitchen with its garlic-tinged steam. Tim, who occasionally perched on a high stool and watched her cook, had once wryly observed that she seemed happier in the kitchen than in the bedroom, and she had laughed but she had not contradicted him. She was, in fact, happiest when she was cooking, especially when she cooked alone.

Her choice of profession, after all, had not been accidental. Nutrition had been an obvious choice, and she had gravitated toward it without the endless conflict that obsessed her classmates who agonized over their choice of majors. She remembered how Rina, her accidental roommate and now her closest friend, had switched from a concentration in creative writing, then flirted with history, before finally settling on literature. Donna Saunders had never wavered. She had known what she would study the day she registered as a freshman.

The preparation of food had always filled her with an excited contentment. Her mother's kitchen had been her own private fairyland, a magical island suffused with the fragrance of herbs and spices, of slowly simmering soups and golden loaves of bread rising in the huge oven that wafted its heat throughout the house. It was from that kitchen that her mother, Anne, ran the small catering enterprise that supported the family. It was a way of making a living, an occupation that had been thrust upon her.

Ed Saunders, the strong dynamic man Anne had married after a courtship so swift that she remembered it only in fragments—sitting beside him in a theater, wearing the gardenia he had bought her from a street vendor, dancing with him in a small, dimly lit club, the metal buttons of his uniform cool upon her cheek—had returned from Korea a shadow of a man, veteran of a forgotten war, whose hands trembled uncontrollably and whose eyes filled with tears inexplicably and unexpectedly. He wept when small Donna showed him a book, a toy. He wept when the doorbell rang, when a familiar song played on the radio, always tuned to the same station, in the living room where he spent his days huddled beneath a blanket in the sagging easy chair. A burn had seared away the flesh on his left thigh, making it difficult for him to move easily. He left the house only to go to the Veterans Hospital where his prescriptions were filled, his wasting body examined, and where harried doctors shrugged in answer to Anne's questions. There was nothing to be done, they told her, but she did what she could. She was wife and nurse, laying out his clothes, helping him in and out of the bath, feeding him, doling out the tranquilizers that controlled neither the tears nor the trembling nor the aimless wandering from one room of the house to another. The pills did not keep him from touching one object and then another, from turning on faucets and leaving the water running, from searching through the linen closet for something he was sure he had lost amid the sheets and towels, which he scattered across the hallway floor. Posttraumatic stress syndrome, the doctors told her knowingly. Get used to it. Live with it.

But she was a mother and there was a daughter to care for and a life to be lived. The disability checks that arrived each month would not pay for Donna's education, would not even cover the new shoes and the pretty pastel clothing that Anne bought for the child. Dressing her beautiful blond daughter was her only luxury and her only delight. And so she cooked, turning what had been a pleasant hobby into a business that rewarded her with enough income to start a college fund, to take out credit cards on which she never never made a late payment.

The soups and breads, the wine-based stews and the roasts decorated with sprigs of rosemary were meant for the tables of strangers. Anne arranged for a van service to deliver them to elegant homes, churches and synagogues, American Legion halls and high school gymnasiums. She was proud of the food she packed in the cartons of her own design, and Donna, from childhood on, felt herself complicit in their creation. She stood on a stool to stir a broth, to mix a roux, to add a dash of fennel to a sauce.

It did not occur to her to wonder why her mother had affixed a latch to the kitchen door so that it remained locked as they cooked together, her mother's small tape player whirring. They listened to books on tape as they diced and chopped, plunged parboiled vegetables into water and thrust salad greens into a spinner. It was in her mother's kitchen that Donna listened to *Charlotte's Web, Stuart Little, Hans Brinker, Little Women*, then slowly graduating into the novels of Jane Austen, the short stories of Dorothy Parker, the adventures of J.D. Salinger's Glass family. George Eliot spirited them off to England; Balzac was their guide to France.

Donna had been a teenager when she confided to her mother that she would be content to spend her life reading. Anne had turned to her, her eyes bright with fear and anger.

"Live your life, Donna. Don't imagine it. Don't waste it. That's not what I've worked for all these years. I'm giving you choices that I never had. College, travel, a career. Promise me that you'll use them." She had gripped Donna's hands and held them tight.

Frightened, Donna had whispered, "I promise. I promise."

Still, literature and cooking remained intertwined, joint refuges, joint escapes, the shared joy of mother and daughter, not even interrupted by the occasional rattling of the latch as Ed Saunders tried to open the door and then padded to another part of the house.

It was only years later, during a medical training session on the habits of Alzheimer's patients and untreatable depressives, that Donna learned that the restless roaming typical of their behavior described her own father. It was fear that had caused her mother to latch the kitchen door and fear that sent her dashing from the kitchen to the living room at regular intervals, calling in a high-pitched, anxious voice, "Ed, are you all right?" knowing, of course, that he was not all right and that he would never be all right.

But for Donna, in her mother's kitchen, everything was all right. There was the beauty of fruits and vegetables, of meat and chicken fresh from the butcher, of gleaming fish wrapped in thick white paper, the fragrance of sauce and spice, light and warmth, stories unfolding as the tape recorder gently played, and her mother beside her. And in all the kitchens she would work in afterward, the laboratory kitchens in which she studied, the institutional kitchens she supervised when she began to work, the cheerful kitchen in her own apartment, everything was always all right, always clean, always organized, and always the cultivated voices of readers narrating novels and stories to soothe her as she sliced, chopped and basted.

But the maternal mandate was not forgotten. She lived her life as fully as her mother would have wished. There was her job, friends and lovers and trips to Eliot's England and Balzac's France, books in her bags, books on her bedside table, books in her kitchen, an open volume always propped up against the file box that contained her mother's recipes written in violet ink on fraying index cards.

The day before the book club was to meet at her apartment she arranged to leave the hospital early, stopping in at Trish's office to drop off a menu she had created for a newly admitted patient.

"All liquid. Vegetable and fruit smoothies. The gastroenterologist's report showed esophageal damage, possible throat ulcers."

"Typical of bulimics," Trish said. "Serial vomiting does terrible things to the esophagus. Can you add some ice cream? She's a recovering druggie with a sweetness craving." She sighed and slammed the file shut. "What makes people self-destruct like that? Here's a kid who has everything—rich parents who seem really to care, brains, looks and she gets hooked on crap. I could practice for a hundred years, read every paper written, take a thousand case histories and I'll never really fathom addiction—maybe I can see how it would grab the inner-city population, but our patients aren't from that world. They're people who have virtually everything. Why do they go for the bottle or the needle? Why do they have to snort snow up their nostrils and stick their fingers down their throats? Oh, I know the textbook answers… addictive personality, stress, predisposition, emotional vacuums. That's all we have to work with and it's not enough."

Donna studied the chart, penciled in the ice cream addition.

"Would you say offhand that Eric has an addictive personality?" she asked too casually.

Trish looked at her sharply.

"Why do you ask?"

"Jen met him. By chance. Or maybe not really by chance. He was waiting outside Nightingale's. She smelled liquor on his breath. And she said that he looked sort of gaunt. She wondered, actually, we both wondered, if maybe that was why Cynthia wanted him out of the house."

"A drink in the middle of the afternoon doesn't make him an alcoholic," Trish said dryly. "Drugs, real substance abuse—that would be another story. Then I could understand Cynthia making that sort of preemptive strike."

"We did think of drugs," Donna admitted.

A wave of shame washed over her. It was somehow wrong for her, for all of them, to be so absorbed in the small sad drama of Cynthia's life. What had happened between her and Eric was their own concern. The book group had no business being so caught up in a web of speculation, meeting in coffee shops to juggle ideas, phoning one another with new and improbable conjectures. It was not right. They had invaded Cynthia's emotional territory, flying the flag of friendship. Of course, they cared about Cynthia, of course they wanted to help her, but they should have respected her rules, her penchant for privacy. And yet, even acknowledging all that, Donna knew that she could not and would not surrender her own curiosity, a curiosity that seemed to gather intensity as the weeks went by. She had, after all, wondered from childhood on, what it was that made a marriage intolerable, what it was that might trigger a grim finality, an irrevocable ending. Would it have to be something even worse than her father's overwhelming and hopeless disability? When did the latch on a door become permanent, never to be released? It was a question she had never dared ask her mother, not during her father's life and not after his death. And then there had been no time to ask.

She knew, of course she knew, that every marriage and every family, whether happy or unhappy, was different. Tolstoy had not gotten that right, she had thought to herself the first time she had read the opening line of *Anna Karenina*: *"Happy families are all alike; every unhappy family is unhappy in its own way."* Still, she was in pursuit of a common denominator, a rationale, and Cynthia's secret might offer her an answer of a kind and if not an answer, at least a clue.

"No. I wouldn't think that Eric fit the profile of an addictive personality," Trish said at last. "He's goal-oriented, disciplined. You don't achieve his kind of success without organization and hard work. He never seemed to have any problems relating to other people. He and Cynthia had loads of friends—remember the parties they gave for his premieres—and he seemed to have friends of his own, college pals, professional colleagues. Jason and I went to dinner with them a couple of times. He never ordered more than a glass of wine. Drugs? Definitely not. I'd have spotted it."

"You're sure?" Donna was insistent.

"Donna, you know damn well that no psychiatrist is ever sure of anything. I'm not even sure that ice cream will be good for our bulimic. But I'd be willing to bet on it. Now, get the hell out of here. You're supposed to be food shopping and I'm scheduled to see the angry father of one patient and the grateful mother of another. I think I'm going to find the angry father easier to deal with."

They both laughed then and Donna left, loosening her hair from the bun as she stepped out of the hospital and onto the windswept street.

She shopped quickly, sweeping the produce into her large net bag and carefully cradling the trout, wrapped in the familiar heavy white paper, in her arms. She had briefly thought of doing a shrimp dish, but she was uncertain as to whether this was a year when Rina was observing Jewish dietary laws. Like everything else about Rina, her religious observance was erratic.

She cooked that night, having fielded phone calls from both Tim and Ray, each of whom wanted to take her to dinner.

"I'm cooking," she said. "You know, for my book group."

Neither of them offered an argument. They understood her priorities and understood, too, her need for independence. It suited their own needs for a relationship with no commitment, no questions asked. Ray had been married, briefly and unhappily, Tim wanted a life free of constraints, allowing him to play gigs in distant cities, jam into the early hours of the morning. Each had a vague knowledge of the existence of the other, but early on Donna's terms of "don't ask, don't tell" had been accepted. It was an arrangement that was comfortable enough for all of them. For now, for the present. They were not people who worried about the future. No demands would be made, no ultimatums issued. Donna did not think about them as she studied the ingredients ranged on the counter and slipped the CD of The *House of Mirth* into her player.

"Selden paused in surprise," the male reader said in a mellifluous tone, and Donna smiled and reached for her dicing knife as the story of Lily Bart unfolded.

It stormed the next day, a wild downpour after weeks of autumnal mildness, reminding them that winter edged closer and closer. The members of the book group burst into Donna's apartment with dripping umbrellas, their faces wet and glistening, rain-drops sparkling in their hair. Laughing at their adventures—the jostling competition for cabs, the daring sprints over puddles, Rina's detour to guide a blind woman home, Cynthia's rush back to Nightingale's to collect a proposal forgotten on her desk—they deposited their umbrellas in Donna's bathtub, draped their coats over her shower bar and collapsed onto the piles of cushions scattered across her living room floor, peeling off their soaked stockings like small girls. Even Elizabeth chatted gaily, her damp pale hair helmeting her head, the hem of her long denim skirt soaked. Proudly, she described how she had managed to flag down a cab and how she had poked at a man who tried to push his way into it with her umbrella.

"But I got it. I got it," she said gleefully, and they applauded her.

The rain had excited them. Released from their overheated workplaces, they had dashed through wind and water in their bright coats and capes, hurrying toward friends and warmth, toward the long evening of good food and good talk.

And Donna, her face flushed from the heat of the oven, her long blond hair tied back with a pale blue scarf that matched her pantsuit, circulated gaily, offering them the Tuscan eggplant spread on crisp pieces of toast, filling their glasses from the ceramic jug of sparkling cider that Cynthia had brought.

"A Nightingale's Thanksgiving special," she said proudly. "You can refill the jug or use it for flowers. I found it in Ireland last spring."

They sipped the cider slowly. They remembered her trip to Ireland. Eric's documentary on Irish-American families had won a prize at the Dublin Film Festival and Cynthia had returned raving about the landscape, the warmth of the people, the brilliant speech Eric had delivered before the showing. She had given each of them a lavender sachet wrapped in Irish linen. They wondered if she was even thinking of Eric as she drank her cider. Had it occurred to her that separation from Eric meant separation from his world of prizes and premieres, brightly lit marquees and hushed and darkened theaters, cocktail parties filled with admiring fans? Donna suddenly remembered words her mother had uttered one winter evening as she stared out at a slowly falling snow, her shoulders stooped with fatigue, her face pale.

"You don't marry the man," Anne Saunders had said bitterly. "You marry the life."

Donna had wondered then, and wondered now, if the marriage ended, did the life end? If her mother had left her father, as so many of her friends and relatives had urged her to do (*"He doesn't even know you're there, Anne. He'd be better off in a nursing home"*—the unsolicited advice had riddled her childhood, frightened her, caused her mother's face to freeze into a mask of bewildered anger), would her life, their life as they knew it, have ended as well? Looking back, she knew that those relatives and friends had been right. Her mother might have met another man, might have entered into a new life. There might have been leisure, travel, companionship. Her sadness might have lifted, morphed into a vaporous regret.

She brushed the memory away and hurried into the kitchen. The trout in its sauce of white wine and shallots was cooked to perfection, the rice pilaf was a golden brown, the tossed green salad, pearled with pine nuts, shimmered.

"Dinner's ready," she called, and her friends, all barefoot, their bright faces rain washed, gathered around the table covered with a green linen cloth and set with the wedding china and wedding silver her mother had never used.

"A table fit for Edith Wharton," Cynthia observed approvingly.

Donna smiled. Praise from Cynthia, ever the perfectionist, was hard to come by.

"Well, maybe for her Newport summerhouse before she hit her stride. Definitely not elegant enough for the Mount, her Berkshire home, or the Paris apartments," Elizabeth countered sourly, and Jen cringed.

Why did her sister have to shoot down the mildest of compliments? Not for the first time, she regretted having invited Elizabeth into the group, but that regret typified her relationship with her sister. Always she had felt herself uneasily balanced on an emotional seesaw of affection and resentment, guilt and sadness. Elizabeth's unhappy marriage and Adam's autism had compounded those feelings. Jen was free while Elizabeth was encumbered. When Carla, who had been a longtime member of the group left and they discussed who would replace her, Jen, with some hesitation, suggested her sister. Elizabeth had a passion for literature, she had told her friends who had raised no objections. They wanted to please clever, elfin Jen who was always gentle, always agreeable. And in the end Elizabeth's insights and contributions to the discussions had proved valuable. On that they all agreed. And Jen knew that although Elizabeth had never thanked her for the invitation, her sister welcomed the escape and the companionship. The occasional irritation was a small price to pay for the assuaging of the latent guilt that was the legacy of her childhood.

"But this meal would certainly be worthy of the dinner table either at the Mount or one of the Paris or English homes," Trish said, lifting a forkful of the trout. "Delicious, Donna."

"Thanks." Donna circled the table, refilling wineglasses. "But, of course, Wharton herself would never have had anything to do with the cooking of a meal. What she excelled at was planning dinner parties, guest lists, menus, specifying china, cutlery, table linens, that sort of thing."

"Sort of like Cynthia," Rina said slyly. "She proposes and Mae disposes."

"Not quite." Cynthia's protest was languid. "I don't mind being compared to Edith Wharton, Rina, but let's at least be accurate. I have a housekeeper and au pairs who come and go, mostly go. Edith, I think we ought to call her Edith…."

"Edith!" they all called in happy unison and lifted their glasses. "To Edith."

"Okay," Cynthia continued, "at least we agree on that. Anyway, Edith had a staff, a full crew of maids and cooks and manservants. And I have two children to care for while our Edith had only those disgusting little dogs."

"Whom she thought of as her children," Trish said. "Do you remember the letter she wrote to some friend when her dog died, brimming over with pathos and sorrow. You would have thought she was devastated with grief over the death of a child. Clinically, I'd call it an emotional displacement."

"Nothing clinical tonight, Trish," Rina said. "Remember, this is a night when we leave our work behind."

They nodded in agreement. Book club meetings were time out, an oasis of escape. Their only obligation was to the book under discussion, to the honesty of their exchange.

"I've got a ton of papers to grade, but I'm not going to think about them."

Elizabeth leaned forward to take another helping of salad. "Still, Trish has raised a pretty interesting point," she said in the mediating tone she probably used when speaking to the parents of a problem student. "Was I the only one here who read the letters and thought that Wharton really did feel a kind of disconnect? And why not? She was betrayed by her husband and then by her lover."

Jen avoided looking at her sister. Elizabeth, she knew, was probably thinking of the betrayals she herself had endured—Bert's harshness, Adam's illness.

"At least her cook never betrayed her. And her accountant was probably pretty faithful," Cynthia observed, and they all laughed.

"I could use a cook. I could use an accountant," Rina said plaintively. "In any future life I would like to come back as Edith Wharton."

"A Jewish Edith Wharton?" Trish asked, and they all laughed again. "Somehow I can't see that happening. You'd have to organize a kosher kitchen at the Mount."

"And Henry James would abandon you. Unless he was reincarnated as a Jew," Jen suggested, and giggled.

"A straight Jew. There's a literary concept for you—a newly imagined Henry James—straight and Jewish," Cynthia said as she reached for another roll.

They smiled. It pleased them to see her eat with some appetite. All of them had noticed her weight loss. Elizabeth surreptitiously slid a piece of fish onto Cynthia's plate. That was how she had fed Adam, how she sometimes fed her mother, who often rejected the meals served at the nursing home. Cynthia, too, disabled by misery, had need of her care.

"Ah, but if he was straight, and thus available, and Jewish and thus unacceptable, Dame Wharton would have dropped him," Trish said. "It would be her pattern."

"Oh, let's not psychoanalyze poor Edith." Donna rose to remove the serving dishes. "Let me just get everything into the kitchen and we'll have coffee in the living room. Do you all have your books?"

They all nodded. It was their habit to bring the books to their meetings so that if a textual reference was made they could all find the exact page and paragraph. This, too, they considered a mark of their seriousness, of their deep involvement in the books they chose. They rose from the table and clustered in the living room, each holding a mug, the books on their laps.

Donna joined them with a plate of pistachio cookies, which she set on the low coffee table, her own notes in hand. Briefly she described the author's life, her lonely childhood, her early ability to make up stories and her love affair with literature from the time her doting father taught her to read.

"Listen to this excerpt from a letter she wrote to her sister-in-law. She wrote that she thinks of reading as 'a secret ecstasy of communion.' What a great phrase. That's how I felt about books and stories, when I first began listening to them while my mother cooked, when I first began reading by myself. I remember how my mother used to come up and make sure my bedroom light was out, and I'd open the door and read by the sliver of light that came in from the hallway. I didn't want to give up that communion Wharton talks about. I didn't want to be alone again." Donna's voice was weighted with sadness. Almost involuntarily, she glanced at the picture of her parents on their wedding day that stood on her bookcase— Anne, like Donna herself, fair haired and full figured, her father robust and healthy, a man she had only known when he was weakened and hollowed out by wounds and memories. Her friends followed her eyes and turned away.

They were silent, reflective. The writer's words had touched each of them to the core. They too understood that "secret ecstasy" that offered escape from loneliness, a startling recognition of shared thoughts and feelings.

"I wonder if she felt the same way about writing," Rina mused. "When she describes writing, there always seems to be so much emphasis on the effort it took, how it exhausted her—"

"And how her publishers were cheating her," Elizabeth interjected. "She was clearly a woman with money on her mind always. And she didn't really need the money. First her father and then her mother left her substantial trust funds, and then she had a windfall inheritance from some distant cousin."

Donna consulted her notes.

"That inheritance was $120,000. A huge amount in 1885, probably the equivalent of a couple of million today. So yes, her obsession with money is curious."

"Not really. Money bought her freedom," Cynthia's tone was flat, her words matter-of-fact. "It meant she could function independently, make decisions, travel. Eventually it meant she could divorce Teddy Wharton. No matter what his indiscretions, she couldn't have done it if she hadn't had money of her own and a way of making even more money. I had a—" she paused as though searching for a word and then continued "—a relation, a woman, whose husband had a mistress, a secret family. He deceived her, deceived their children, turned their whole life into a living lie. But she was stuck. She couldn't divorce him because she had no money, no profession. Her life made me decide that I would always have a way to support myself—not that I thought it would ever be necessary—but now…"

Her voice faded, her cheeks were flushed, and when she lifted her coffee cup it clattered against the saucer until she controlled her trembling fingers.

Donna glanced at Jen, Rina at Trish, the same thought flashing between them. *Could Cynthia have separated from Eric if she did not have money of her own, if she was not a consistently high earner? Without money, without her power to generate significant income, would she, like that "relation" of hers, have been stuck in a marriage that had morphed into a living lie?*

Elizabeth twisted her wedding ring, removed it and re-placed it.

"Still, she could have made a good case against Teddy Wharton even if she had no money of her own. She could have worked out some sort of alimony. She had every reason to leave him. He was an adulterer, he had embezzled money from her accounts and spent it on prostitutes, he was a playboy who lived off her, who had never worked a day in his life," Donna pointed out. "The real mystery isn't that she divorced him but that she stayed with him all those years. She wasn't exactly a fan of the marriage vow. She wrote a letter about how the marriage tie had the power to strangle. So you'd think she wouldn't have any problem with the untying of such a knot. She wasn't particularly religious, so that wouldn't have kept her back. So my question is, how could she have continued to live with Teddy Wharton, who of-fered her absolutely nothing—not love, not children, not financial support?"

"Maybe because nothing that he did surprised her," Trish suggested. "She had put up with his behavior, re-ally his craziness, from the day they married. She prob-ably intuited everything about him at their first meeting, but she still thought she could make it work. Still, like Donna, I have to wonder. When she saw that it didn't work, that there was absolutely nothing holding them to-gether, why did it take her twenty-eight years to divorce him? Even the most frightened, neurotic woman would have given him his walking papers. I can think of a pa-tient I saw during my training who did exactly that."

Cynthia leaned forward, impatiently thumbing through the biography of Wharton she had brought with her. "Because after twenty-eight years things came to a head. Because his patterns changed and suddenly his be-havior intensified and she found that she could no longer accept things she once thought she could accept. It hap-pens. People change. Levels of tolerance change. The man you married may not be the husband you're living with. Essentially, you've made a contract with a partner who no longer exists."

She spoke too rapidly, her words clipped and unhesitating. They wondered if she was speaking of Edith and Edward Wharton or of her own marriage. Embarrassed for her, for themselves, they looked away, and as though sensing their discomfort, she rose abruptly and disappeared into the bathroom.

Hurriedly then, they resumed the discussion, Donna reading aloud from the correspondence that had engaged her.

"The letters she wrote to her lover, Morton Fullerton, really grabbed me," she said. "She kind of knew from the beginning that their affair was doomed, but she wasn't afraid to plunge in, to go traveling with him, even to invite him to the Mount."

"Even to offer him advice on how to deal with a former mistress," Elizabeth said. "Which means she knew exactly the kind of man he was, unreliable, untrustworthy, inconsistent. It's one thing to enter into a relationship with someone without recognizing his faults, but it's another to have the knowledge and ignore it."

Her tone was harsh, condemning, and Jen, watching her sister, thought that as always, Elizabeth was self-forgiving, her own mistakes condoned. She had married Bert too quickly. There had been no time to see the darkness of his recurring moods, the resentments that triggered his irrational bursts of fury, all compounded by the shame and anguish of Adam's autism. She had not had the luxury of that early recognition. As always, she saw herself as the victim, ostentatiously and bitterly accepting the joint miseries of her marriage and her motherhood.

She noticed suddenly that Elizabeth was staring at her, her lips curled in the hurtful, knowing sneer Jen remembered from their shared childhood. She realized with a shudder that the man whom Elizabeth was describing was not her own husband but Ian, and the woman she was describing was Jen. It followed. Elizabeth consistently accused Jen of weakness, of ignoring Ian's faults, his unreliability. She turned away, gripped by the familiar anger she had suppressed throughout her girlhood. *Damn Elizabeth*, she thought. *Damn her. Why on earth did I ever invite her to join the group?* And Elizabeth, smirking now, turned away.

"But she understood exactly what she was doing," Trish insisted. "It was her choice. She was honest both with herself and with Fullerton." She turned the pages of her book rapidly. "Here, she writes to him in 1909, 'My only dread is lest my love blind me and my heart whisper *tomorrow* when my reason says *today*.' That's a pretty daring thing to write to a lover. But she was a woman who was used to taking risks."

"Because she was strong and because she knew her own strength," Rina added. "And she had the money and the talent to back that strength. Still, I love it that when she breaks with him she writes, 'I think I am worth more than that.' Pretty advanced thinking for a woman of that era."

"Or even for a woman of today." Cynthia had rejoined them, her face washed clean of makeup, her auburn hair pulled back, her self-defining composure restored. "Too many women have no idea of their worth. It's something we recognize when we do a promotion at Nightingale's.

Buy it. You're worth it. You deserve it. Our advertising gurus tell me that there are too many women out there who don't believe that they deserve anything."

"It's okay for an ad campaign," Trish said. "But I can't see myself counseling a woman who comes to me for marital advice like that. What would I say—*divorce him. You're worth more. You deserve more.* It's not Oil of Olay we're talking about here, it's her life. I couldn't tell her that."

"Why not?" Cynthia asked calmly as she refilled her coffee cup. "If it was the truth."

Donna stood, her eyes flashing, her color high.

"Because not all solutions are that simplistic. If they were, my mother should have divorced my father the day he got back from Korea because she knew damn well then what her life would be like. She'd be a nurse, a care-giver, but never a wife. Still, she stayed married to him and took care of him until the day he died even though, like Wharton, she had to know she was worth more. And she was, she was! But she thought about more than her own worth. She thought about him and about me and— although no one uses these words anymore—she thought about doing her *duty.* And she paid a price for it. There was a whole life she never got to live. And then when he died, she didn't want to live it. She was ex-hausted. He was dead, I was on my own. The night be-fore she died she spoke to my aunt on the phone. 'I'm tired,' she said. 'I'm too tired to get up in the morning and there's really no reason anymore. I just want to rest.'"

She fought back tears and turned again to the wedding portrait she had found on the bedside table the morning of her mother's death, neatly placed beside the five small, empty vials of sleeping pills and the note written in the violet ink reserved for menus and recipes, the note that asked for love and forgiveness and told Donna where her will, her bank books and her small cache of savings bonds were hidden. Only Rina knew about that note, only Rina knew about those tiny empty vials.

Donna picked the framed photo up, set it down again, and her friends saw that she was weeping. Disconcerted, they looked away. They considered that they knew one another well, that they were close enough to own one another's histories. They were of an age when the death of a parent was wrenching but not unusual. Aging mothers and fathers developed infirmities, died of cancer, were killed in accidents. Donna's mother had already passed away when she joined the group and now, for the first time, they wondered how Anne Saunders had died. They realized that there were boundaries to their intimacy. Donna's inexplicable grief startled them just as Cynthia's words, so decisive, so unexplained, mystified them. They watched as Rina went up to Donna and hugged her, as Jen brought her a glass of water, offered her a tissue. She emptied the glass, wiped her eyes and smiled shyly, apologetically, but the gaiety of the evening was shattered. They felt themselves bewildered and helpless.

It was Trish who, with professional deftness, steered them back onto the safer ground of the novel. They resumed a dispassionate discussion, and after some minutes, Donna disappeared into the kitchen and emerged, minutes later, newly composed, carrying a plate of russet-and-gold miniature pears, which she set down on the low coffee table, an offering to normalcy restored.

Swiftly, Trish, following the prescribed pattern of their meetings, summarized the novel. Although they had each read *The Reef,* they listened attentively as she spoke of Darrow, the eligible young diplomat and his chance encounter with the impoverished Sophy Viner in Paris. She described the brief interlude of their affair when his journey to see his true love, Anna Leath, is inexplicably postponed, and then Sophy's reappearance as the governess of Anna's young daughter and the fiancée of her stepson.

Now and again, other members of the group interrupted her. Cynthia thought the detailed descriptions of Sophy Viner's clothing were important. Rina speculated about her family, her economic circumstances. Elizabeth wondered about the mysterious unnamed sister.

Their discussion, as always, was intense. They were not casual readers, intellectual voyeurs. The books that engrossed them throbbed with reality, immersed them in the lives of the characters, in the nuances of the narrative. They juggled ideas, tossed out insights.

"I see what you mean."

"I never thought of that."

They agreed and disagreed. They laughed and sighed.

"I loved the book," Elizabeth said, "but even loving it I thought that so much of it was contrived. Too many coincidences. Out of all the estates in all of France Sophy Viner turns up at Givre, Anna Leath's home."

"But how else could the story have evolved?" Donna asked reasonably. "There would have been no plot for *Casablanca* if Ilse hadn't turned up in Rick's Bar. What was Bogey's great line—'of all the bars in all the cities, in all the world, you had to pick this one'? Something like that. That's how fiction works. And sometimes real life, too. I met Ray at a medical conference in San Francisco and two weeks later he turns up at a party in New York.

No contrivance. Just coincidence. So Darrow meets Sophy in Paris and months later she turns up at Givre. Same thing. I don't think Wharton herself knew how she was going to develop the plot. None of her letters to her publishers give story outlines for the books she was writing. She didn't submit proposals."

"How much of Wharton's personal life do you think spilled into *The Reef?*" Trish asked.

It was the sort of question Rina loved, a question she frequently tossed out to her lit students. Motivation obsessed her, the *whys* of other people's lives, the *whys* of her own decisions. *Why* should a well-dressed woman steal an expensive purse that she could obviously afford? *Why* had Sylvia Plath opted for suicide on that particular night? *Why* had she herself opted for single motherhood when other options were open to her? *Why* had childless Edith Wharton immersed herself in a novel about a widow who prioritized the duties of motherhood over romantic love?

She leaned forward, flipping through the collection of letters, pausing at last at the one she wanted to quote.

"Here's a letter she wrote to Bernard Berenson, while she was working on *The Reef*. I suppose he had written to ask if it was at all autobiographical and she answered, 'Anyway, remember it's not me though I thought it was when I was writing it,'" Rina read from the text. "So I guess the answer to your question, Trish, is, yes and no and even maybe. A writer gets lost in the work, slides in and out of the personality of the characters he or she is creating until the boundaries between author and subject are blurred. Remember Flaubert's *'Madame Bovary, c'est moi.'* Wharton could have said *'Anna Leath, c'est moi.'* It wasn't her real life that spilled into her work. It was her imaginative life."

She sat back, plucked a pear from the dish and bit into it, satisfied with her answer.

"I suppose it's similar to Flannery O'Connor saying, 'I write so I'll know what I'm thinking,'" Elizabeth said thoughtfully.

Jen glanced at her sister in admiring surprise as the others nodded. That was Elizabeth's strength, the eclectic bits of literary knowledge she tossed into the stew of their discussions, as a talented chef might add a secret spice. That was why they valued her participation and tolerated her cynicism and the shadow of depression that trailed her wherever she went. They did not like her but they respected her.

"Perhaps I should become a writer—so that I'll know what I'm thinking," Cynthia said. "And then maybe I'll know what I'm doing and why I'm doing it." She smiled sadly.

"You don't know?" Trish asked her sharply.

"Sometimes yes, sometimes no," Cynthia admitted. "There are days when I feel like Anna Leath. One day she was going to marry Darrow. The next day she was going to break with him. Back and forth, back and forth. As though she were playing against herself in an emotional ping-pong match. And what Darrow had done was not really awful. He hadn't hurt anyone. At least he hadn't meant to hurt anyone. He became involved with Sophy Viner because he wanted to be kind. He presented no danger."

"Are you saying that you yourself waver from day to day about your decision?" Jen asked, her voice very soft, as though any change of tone might shatter Cynthia's fragile confidence.

But Cynthia only nodded unhappily and pressed her finger to her lips, like a child who fears that she has spoken out of turn, revealing a secret she had sworn to keep.

Her friends looked uneasily at one another. Cynthia's words, however cryptic, triggered new speculation, stirred up suppositions they had cast aside. She had emphasized that Darrow had not hurt anyone, that he presented no danger. *Did Eric present a danger, had he hurt anyone?* They contemplated the varied forms such a danger might take—physical, emotional, sexual, each discrete or all in concert. But they were silent, obedient to the boundaries she had imposed. And Cynthia, as though to protect herself from that curiosity, that concern held so carefully in check, glanced at her watch and sprang to her feet.

"I didn't realize how late it was. I promised Mae I'd be home early. She doesn't like to go to sleep if I'm not home because her room is so far from the twins' that she's not sure she'll hear them, and Ingrid, that new au pair, is a real zero. I'm sorry. I've got to rush now. Someone call me about what we're reading next and where we'll be meeting."

She dashed into the bedroom to retrieve her briefcase and her cape and after a moment Jen followed her, closing the door behind her. She watched as Cynthia slipped on her shoes and fumbled for her briefcase.

"Cynthia," Jen said quietly, "I saw Eric."

Cynthia froze. She stared at Jen.

"And?" she asked, her lips barely moving.

"He came up to me on the street. He said he wants to meet with me, talk to me. I wouldn't do it without speaking to you about it first." She did not tell Cynthia that it was outside of Nightingale's that Eric had approached her, that his eyes had been heavy with sadness and that his voice had trembled, that she could not bear the idea of refusing him.

"I appreciate that," Cynthia said. "But I have no right to ask you not to meet him. You'll have to decide that for yourself."

She tossed her gold-colored rain cape over her shoulders and adjusted the hood so that it fell in graceful folds, barely concealing her flame-colored hair. With her hand on the doorknob, she turned to Jen.

"I can't tell you I'd be happy about your seeing him, but maybe, just maybe, it could be helpful."

And before Jen could respond, she left. Jen, wondering how it could be helpful, watched as Cynthia sailed through the living room, waved her goodbyes and disappeared through the front door. She imagined Cynthia entering her home, the carpet soft beneath her feet, the fragrance of yellow roses filling the air, new books in brilliant jackets neatly arranged on the mahogany coffee table. She would tiptoe upstairs to the bedroom where her daughters slept, their coppery hair streaming across the mint-colored pillowcases decorated with drawings of Kermit the Frog, and then she would go to her own room, to the vast queen bed in which she would sleep alone, the bedside radio softly playing because, she had told Jen, she could not bear the silence of the solitary night.

The women had regrouped around the dining room table, where Donna filled their mugs with freshly brewed decaf.

"I think Cynthia's having second thoughts," Rina said. "She sure didn't sound as certain as she did when she first told us about it."

"It can't be easy for her. To be alone again after all those years with Eric. I haven't been with Ian for that long, but I can't imagine coming home to an empty apartment, an empty life," Jen murmured.

"Hardly a good-enough reason to stay in a marriage or a relationship," Elizabeth countered. "You can be more alone in a lousy partnership than if you're on your own. Independence means freedom."

Again, she twisted her wedding band. The independence she had thought to claim when she married had vaporized. She was not free. She would never be free. She was hostage to her son's needs, to her husband's demands. Jen, at least, had not locked herself in. Ian was a leech, sapping her resources, contributing nothing, but Jen could kick him out anytime. Jen's seemingly unresistant acceptance of difficult situations did not fool Elizabeth, had never fooled her. Her sister was an emotional survivor, her weapon of choice a superficial acquiescence.

"But Cynthia and Eric seemed so perfect together," Trish said. "Really in synch. I wonder what she meant about Darrow presenting no danger. She must have been thinking of Eric, but what sort of danger could Eric present?"

Rina's bitter laughter was drowned out by the talk that suddenly flooded the room. The ideas that had teased them when Cynthia spoke were released in verbal balloons that sailed across the table, now and again colliding with one another in the sudden rush of conjectures that could no longer be contained. Their voices rose in an odd excitement, an urgent need to know, to understand. Without facts they would guess. *Why and again why?*

"She specified actual danger," Elizabeth said. "It could be that Eric was abusive to the twins or even to Cynthia. We've talked about that. Or maybe she suddenly found out that he'd been abusive in the past, maybe in another relationship. An old girlfriend surfaces. Accusations are made. And she begins to worry that it's a pattern that could be repeated."

"A pretty extreme scenario," Trish said wryly. "And not one I find credible. I always thought Eric was incredibly gentle, almost too gentle. But he did seem to drift in and out of depressions, especially between film projects. He told me once, when he had finished that documentary about the mill workers in South Carolina, the one that got him a Film Critics Award, that he couldn't enjoy its success because he was already frightened about not having another idea. Maybe Cynthia saw those depressions as a danger to her kids, an emotional danger. I have one chronically depressed patient whose wife filed for divorce as soon as I shared my diagnosis with her. 'I don't want my kids growing up in a home dominated by depression,' she said, and I can't say I blamed her."

"Kids survive depressed parents," Donna said moodily. Again her eyes drifted to the photograph of her parents, again Rina touched her hand, a gesture of comfort, of protection. "I don't think Cynthia would see depression as a clear and present danger—something that would make her say that she couldn't bear having him in the house another night. There had to be something else."

"There's a case in my school now," Elizabeth said. "I've been working on it with child services. A kid whose father was tapping into kiddie porn sites on the Internet. The social worker thinks that's behavior that is dangerous enough for the mother to ask the guy to leave and to request an order of restraint."

Jen felt a sudden surge of anger. She clanged her spoon angrily against her cup, and when she spoke her voice trembled.

"Listen to us. We're like a bunch of vultures, pecking away at a couple of rotting words. So Cynthia said 'danger.' So she said 'harm.' But that's all she said and we're wallowing in innuendoes, in suspicions based on nothing at all, talking about physical brutality, pervert net surfing. We've known Eric for years. Has he ever been anything but kind to us? Generous, gentle? Where are we going with all of this and why?"

They were silent. They recognized the truth of her accusations, but they had no answer to offer. They could not apologize because they knew that their curiosity would not abate, that they would continue to juggle questions and answers, that their quest for Cynthia's truth had, somehow, become a quest for the truth of their own lives, their own decisions, a testing ground of their own perceptions. They had been deceived. Cynthia and Eric had spun through their orbit for years, the brightest stars in their small constellation of friends, boarding jet planes, inviting them to glamorous parties and openings, smiling at them across beautifully set tables, heavy with silver and crystal and flowers so fresh that dew shimmered on their petals—Cynthia and Eric, the golden couple, envied and enviable. How could they all have been so wrong? And if they had all been so wrong about Cynthia and Eric, how sound were their other judgments, how safe were their other relationships? Jen's question unnerved them. The answers they might offer her would reveal their own weaknesses and fears.

"Oh, enough of this," Elizabeth said at last. "Don't be so damn holier-than-thou, Jen. You're as caught up in the great Cynthia-and-Eric mystery as the rest of us. Maybe more because you see Cynthia more than we do. You work for her. Maybe you think you owe her special loyalty because she signs your paychecks, and unless Ian gets featured in *Art News* you need the money. You wouldn't want to make waves, anyway. It's not your style. It never has been."

Jen flushed and rose from the table. She ignored her sister and busily stacked saucers and cake plates, sparking a spurt of activity. Donna circled the table refilling coffee cups. The others, embarrassed by Elizabeth's bitterness, made a great show of passing the sugar and cream. Rina complimented Donna on the meal. Trish asked her for the pistachio cookie recipe.

"Mandy loves pistachio. And so does Jason," she added after a brief pause. She introduced her husband's name into the conversation as though to remind herself, to remind her friends, that her own marriage was intact. "We're looking for a summer home with a really big kitchen," she added. "I want to get into cooking and baking. I suppose it's the impact of dealing with bulimics and anorexics." She laughed, mocking herself, inviting them to share her amusement.

"And I'm looking for an apartment with another bedroom," Rina said. "Forget about a summer home. I just want to go to sleep at night without having to pull open a sofa bed. Do you think Wharton even knew what a sofa bed was?"

They all laughed, the tension broken.

"Listen," Elizabeth said. "I have to go. Bert's probably waiting up for me because Adam's therapist was supposed to call. What are we reading next and where and when are we meeting?"

They whipped out pocket calendars and PDAs.

"After Thanksgiving. Before Christmas," Trish decided briskly, and they settled on an evening in mid-December. "I think it's your turn to host, Jen."

"Great," Jen agreed.

"If it's no good for you, we can have it at my place, Jen," Elizabeth said, and they understood that she was trying to make amends, to restore equilibrium.

"Thanks, but it's fine," Jen responded pleasantly. Jen, who avoided confrontations, also did not hold grudges.

"Your choice of book and author, Jen," Donna called from the kitchen.

"Shirley Jackson's short story, *The Lottery* and *Life Among the Savages*. I picked them up with a whole pile of books in a paperback exchange when I was trapped with Ian in that shack on Rhode Island last summer. He got to paint his seascapes and I got to read paperbacks, all of them smelling of the ocean and a lot of them with missing pages. But the Shirley Jacksons were intact."

"Okay. Shirley Jackson it is and we meet at Jen's." As always Trish was the organizer.

"I'll tell Cynthia," Jen said.

"Fine. And I think that it's important we all keep in close touch with her. Maybe ask her if she wants to have dinner, catch a flick. She needs our support at a time like this."

Trish was in her clinician's mode but they did not mind. They nodded in agreement. They had each decided to call Cynthia, to offer their time, their understanding, to ask only the most guarded question during the most casual of conversations. Kindness and curiosity would meld in those cautious phone calls carefully planned for an hour when the twins would be asleep and there would be time for talk.

They snapped shut their calendars and PDAs, finished helping Donna clear the table and gathered up their bags and coats. Donna walked them to the door. The rain had stopped and a sweet freshness trembled on the night air. They hurried on their way, each of them waving to

Donna as they descended the steps of the brownstone. She waved back and went inside.

Alone in her kitchen, she turned on her CD player and wrapped leftovers and scraped plates, lost again in the unfolding story of Lily Bart. She listened to the single line that formed Wharton's damning assessment of her ill-fated heroine: "It was a relief to Lily when her father died." The phone rang but she did not answer it. She had become one with Lily Bart; she did not question Lily's reaction to her father's death. Donna, too, had been relieved when her father died, guiltily and honestly relieved. It was her mother's death that had devastated her.

The phone rang yet again but she made no move to answer it. The caller was either Tim, who often called just to say good night, or Raymond, who called when he had difficulty falling asleep. Her undemanding lovers, like Morton Fullerton, Edith Wharton's own lover, wanted their presence felt even in their absence. She muted the phone's ring and wondered if *House of Mirth* had been among the novels her mother had listened to on tape in that warm kitchen, its air fragrant with spices, its door latched against her father's irrational wanderings. Tears, unbidden, rolled down her cheeks, as she plunged her hands into a dishpan overflowing with suds.

Chapter Four

Jen did not like "The Lottery." She had read it in college and recalled that it had left her feeling oddly bewildered. Rereading it on the Rhode Island beach during the summer, as Ian painted and the sun moved in and out of the windswept clouds that shadowed the pages of the tattered second-hand anthology, she had felt a vague anger. Shirley Jackson's world was so damn dark; ignorance and evil danced hand in hand through a narrative that inevitably ended in sadness and solitude. Still, the writing had intrigued her, and finishing it, she had known that she wanted to discuss it with her book group, to hear their interpretations and impressions of Jackson's work.

She read it yet again, in preparation for the book club meeting, as she lay on their disordered futon. She wore the paint-stained shirt Ian had discarded moments before, and as she read, she threaded her fingers through her dark hair, still damp from the shower. Now and again she glanced across at Ian who stood before his easel bare chested, lifting his brush in lazy strokes. The "Spring" movement from Vivaldi's *The Four Seasons* drifted into its sweet conclusion as she read the last terrifying paragraph of "The Lottery." Yet again the ending unnerved her and she tossed the book across the room. It landed softly at Ian's feet.

He turned to her in surprise.

"Hey," he said. "What's happening?"

"Nothing. I'm the so-called facilitator for the book group's next meeting and I can't get a handle on one lousy story."

She picked the book up and went to her desk. Idly she took a stick of charcoal and began to doodle in her sketchbook. Frowning, she saw that the doodle had turned into a drawing, a single stick figure surrounded by others, large and small, each with an arm outstretched.

"So what are you doing now?" Ian asked.

"It would appear that I'm drawing that lousy story," she replied. "Which, in fact, is a magnificent story."

She drew a circle onto each extended arm. Stones. She was drawing stones. "I can't talk about it but I can draw it," she said as she added a small pile of stones at the feet of each figure.

"Well, you are an artist," he said, and stepped back to observe his own work.

"Am I?" she asked.

"Oh, come on. Let's not have a self-pity session." He put his brush down and strode toward her, bending down to encircle her in his arms. "Pixie," he said, nibbling her ear, causing her to laugh as he knew she would. "My pixie." The other ear. She laughed again but continued drawing. She took her ruler and drew panels.

"A comic strip?" he asked.

"It seems to be turning into one."

Oblivious to his touch, to his quickened breathing, she worked on the first panel. A smiling sun. A flower-spangled field. New shoots of grass darting up between blossoms. A village square, the clock in the tower reading ten o'clock. The charcoal moved swiftly. She was, she knew, drawing the first paragraph of "The Lottery," re-creating Jackson's description of an ordinary town on a bucolic summer day. Jen worked quickly, effortlessly. She loved it when a drawing grew with such ease, springing to life as though from a hidden source, independent of her conscious will. That was how Ian worked, his brush moving from palette to canvas in a charge of creative energy, but for her, it was a rare experience.

The phone rang. She continued drawing. Ian's hand slipped into the pocket of his shirt and cupped her breast. His cheek rested on her bent head.

"Don't answer it," he said. "Let the machine pick it up."

She nodded, and after three rings, the answering machine clicked on and Eric's voice, muted and tentative, echoed through the loft, mingling oddly with Vivaldi's string quartet.

"Jen, I'm sorry I startled you the other day but I do want to talk to you. Please call me so we can arrange something…coffee, lunch, dinner, whatever." He paused, as though there were words that he wanted to add that now eluded him. "Okay then. Let's talk soon." He hung up.

She put the charcoal stick down, the mood broken. She had heard the urgency in Eric's tone and it triggered both pity and uncertainty. Ian stepped back.

"What was that about?" he asked.

"Eric. He wants to meet me. Talk to me. About Cynthia, I guess."

"You're Cynthia's friend, aren't you?"

"Yes. I told her about it. She thought it would be okay. She thought it might even be helpful."

"I don't want you to meet him," he said flatly.

The disk ended and he slipped it carefully back into its case. Careless in most things, allowing dirty dishes to accumulate in the sink, wet towels to litter the bathroom, never bothering to sweep up the shards of a dropped mug, Ian was scrupulously careful of his compact disk collection and his painting equipment. Just as his palette was always wiped clean, his brushes plunged into turpentine, each paint tube screwed closed when he finished work, each CD was replaced in its case and neatly restored to the holder. Jen had once mentioned this to Elizabeth, who had shrugged.

"Of course he's careful of his own things. It's consistent with his pattern."

Jen had not asked her what pattern that might be. She had, almost immediately, regretted her comment. She knew that her sister disliked Ian and thought him a parasitic user. Any judgment she made would be negative. But watching Ian as he rearranged his CDs, resentful of his proprietary reaction to Eric's call, she recalled Elizabeth's words.

He is careful only of his own property, she thought. *But I am not his property. I don't want him to take that kind of care of me.* She wondered suddenly if his possessiveness, his need to control, would ever grow invasive enough to cause a break between them. What, in fact, could cause her to make a decision that matched Cynthia's, to ask him to leave, to tell him that it was over between them? Of course, her situation was different from Cynthia's on every level. She and Ian were not married. They had both studiously avoided commitment. She had never met his family and he had never visited her mother. There were no children, no bright-haired twins who would be devastated by their split. *And yet, and yet.* Involuntarily, possibilities occurred to her. They were, after all, a couple, as Cynthia and Eric had been.

She glanced at the pile of bills on her desk, at the storyboard on her worktable. Because he had not taught his last two studio classes at the League, she had had to take a boring assignment, designing a fund-raising brochure for an obscure foundation.

"It's all right," she had assured Ian when he had murmured a laconic apology. But it was not all right. The truth of Elizabeth's insinuations about Ian nagged at her, weighted the scales of her gathering discontent. She thought of Shirley Jackson's helpless heroines, the yearning women at the mercy of careless, uncaring men. She was not like them; she would not be like them.

"Why not? Why shouldn't I meet Eric?" she asked with a calm she did not feel. She was trained to mask irritation.

"You don't know why Cynthia kicked him out," he replied sullenly. "You could get yourself in trouble. There are things we don't know about him, things that she knows. I'm only trying to protect you."

"We're talking about *Eric* here," she said evenly. "Eric, who bought your black-and-white abstract and hung it in his office so that your work would get some exposure. Eric, who came to your show and brought friends with him, two of whom bought paintings. Eric, who never raised his voice, who was never anything but nice to us. Do you think it would be dangerous for me to meet him in a restaurant or a coffeehouse? In the middle of the day? Come on, Ian."

She smiled cajolingly at him—easier to smile than to argue. Easier to talk softly than to shout. Easier to hide her anger than to express it.

"I worry about you, Jen," he said, and he passed his fingers gently through her hair, sliding them through the newly dried ringlets of dark curls. "You're my little one, my very own elf, and I worry about you."

She smiled. It was nice to have someone who worried about her. A change for her who worried about everyone else, who as a child had worried about her parents' stormy marriage, about Elizabeth, her bitter and lonely sister. Now she worried about her sister, lonely and bitter in marriage and motherhood and about Elizabeth's son, her nephew, poor beautiful Adam with his beautiful dead dark eyes. She feared for her mother, widowed and infirm, and for Cynthia and Eric and their twin daughters. She thought of the little red-headed girls, peering out of the bay window of the upscale East Side brownstone, perhaps waiting for Eric, as she herself had so often peered out of the window of her family's apartment, looking for her father, dreading his return yet fearful that he would not return. Suffused with sadness, mired in memory, she allowed Ian to lead her back to the futon, to comfort her with tenderness and with passion.

Later, after he had left to meet some painter friends at a neighboring pub, she returned to her desk and completed the first panel of her comic strip, drawing a cloud that lightly touched the sun, a precursor of a slowly encroaching darkness. She thought again of "The Lottery."

Somehow, she had arrived at a new understanding of the story. Setting the charcoal stick down, she called Eric at his office and arranged to meet him for lunch later that week.

She had dinner with Donna two nights later but did not mention her appointment with Eric. Nor did she discuss it with Cynthia as they worked together on the Nightingale's spring catalog. She noted, for the first time, that Cynthia no longer wore her wedding band and that she had styled her auburn hair into a shoulder-length cut that Jen thought too girlish. Twice during their conference the phone rang, and during each conversation Cynthia reached for her Palm Pilot. "Dinner then," she said. "Great. I can only meet for drinks." Her voice apologetic. "The kids, you know."

She turned back to Jen, to the page proofs spread before them.

"I guess I'm in a new life," she said, as though an explanation was owed.

"But have you really finished with the old one?" Jen asked gently.

Cynthia did not answer, but as she moved her marking pen across the proofs her fingers trembled. It was Jen who pointed out two price changes that the copy writer had missed, errors that Cynthia had always automatically picked up.

"Good catch," Cynthia murmured. "I must be getting careless."

"Well, you have a lot on your mind." Excuses came easily to Jen.

Cynthia toyed with the fringes of the light wool paisley scarf that blended subtly with the light blue of her classic turtleneck cashmere dress. "Do I?" she smiled sadly, her enigmatic question requiring neither response nor comment.

The restaurant Eric had selected was a trendy bistro off Union Square. Jen noted that it was a significant distance from Nightingale's. Their privacy would be assured. There was no possibility that Cynthia or anyone else that they knew would venture that far downtown. He was already seated at a corner table, on which a candle burned in a smoke-clouded hurricane lamp although the day was bright and the restaurant was well lit. An overly attentive maître d' pulled out her chair and smiled benignly at them both, reminding her that Eric might be caught in a maelstrom of personal chaos, but to the outside world he was still Eric Anders, a mover and shaker, a well-known, well-respected producer who threw parties at restaurants like this when his documentaries premiered at the Film Forum. They accepted large, leather-covered menus, which neither of them opened, and he withdrew discreetly.

"Thanks for coming all the way down here, Jen," Eric said. "I have a screening later not far from here so this seemed like a good place."

He wore a tan suit of a light soft wool, a crisp yellow shirt and a narrow tie of mustard-colored silk, the costume of a successful producer on his way to a screening. He could easily stand in for a clothing model in an upscale catalog. Cynthia would approve, Jen thought disloyally. Still, she noted that his jacket sagged, as though it had been tailored for a larger man, and his avian face was newly haggard.

"It's fine," she said. "It's far enough away from Nightingale's."

She would not dissemble. She knew why he had chosen that restaurant. He nodded, brushing back the fair hair that always fell so boyishly across his forehead, and took a sip of the martini in front of him. She noted the redness that rimmed his eyes and wondered if it was his first drink of the day and if he would order another.

The waiter returned and he did order another. She asked for a glass of white wine and they both ordered salads.

"How's the book group?" he asked.

"Status quo," she replied. "We've been reading good stuff and the meetings have been interesting, if a little hectic."

It would surprise him, she knew, to learn that there was a new dimension to the book group meetings, the lingering postmortems that took place after Cynthia's departure, during which the mystery of his marriage was discussed and analyzed. Of course he would be surprised, surprised and disgusted, she thought. A wave of shame washed over her. Elizabeth had been right. She could not move to a moral high ground and absolve herself. She shared the obsessive curiosity of her friends.

"And Cynthia comes to all the meetings?"

"There haven't been that many meetings, but yes, Cynthia has been at them. In fact I don't think Cynthia has ever missed a book club meeting."

She had not thought about it before but it was true. Of all of them, Cynthia had been the most faithful attendee. Trish had missed meetings because of a work emergency; Donna because of a freebie pharmaceutical jaunt to the Caribbean with Ray, an out-of-town jazz concert with Tim; Rina because Jeremy was ill or a sitter didn't show up; Elizabeth because of a crisis with Adam; Jen herself because a deadline had to be met or her mother was having yet another panic attack. But nothing had ever kept busy Cynthia from a meeting. Jen had heard her reschedule buying trips and marketing conferences so that they would not conflict with the book group.

"I'm not surprised. The book group is very important to Cynthia," he said. "Probably more important than it is to the rest of you."

"Why?" Jen asked.

He sipped his drink, set it down.

"In case you haven't noticed, Cynthia doesn't have many woman friends. Pretty strange for a woman who went to Bryn Mawr. It's probably because she's always been so career oriented, so busy climbing the ladder and always a little afraid that some colleague might grease one of the rungs and make her slip. It was important to her from the get-go to make it to the top, to be totally self-reliant. And Cynthia is not a trustful person. No one knows that better than me."

Bitterness curdled his words. Cynthia had, after all, not trusted him, her own husband, the father of her children. She had not, after all, trusted him to remain in the home they had shared for so many years.

"The women in your book group are no threat to her," he continued. "You're all in different fields, have different lifestyles. You're the only one with whom she has any professional contact and she knows that you have no designs on a full-time job at Nightingale's, that you're apolitical. But more important than that, everyone in the book group shares her addiction to reading, to losing yourselves in fiction. I used to think that instead of friends Cynthia had books. You know, she read as though she was hypnotized. We took bags of books on our honeymoon and there were always pyramids of books on her night table. And when you introduced her to the book group, for the first time she was involved with women who shared her obsession with reading and wanted nothing more from her than her opinion of *Anna Karenina*. She was able to discuss, to share. She understood all of you and you understood her. I can't tell you how grateful she was—is—for that, how much she values it. When we traveled she searched out gifts for all of you because that's how Cynthia thinks she can keep affection, how she can show that she loves and cares, by giving." He touched his tie, his fingers caressing the fine silk. "Do you know how many ties I have? How many shirts, cuff links? All of them from Cynthia. All of them saying 'I love you. I care about you.'"

It occurred to Jen that she had never received a gift from Ian, although she had given him small and clever presents. A leather case for his Metrocard, a tie-dyed cotton ascot in the colors of a huge abstract he had sold to a small museum in Massachusetts, a Starbucks gift certificate. And yes, all those gifts did say that she cared about him. She had trained herself not to think about love. But Cynthia's gifts to Eric had been love offerings.

"So she did care about you. She did love you. What happened to change that, Eric?" she asked cautiously.

He drained the last of his martini and stared at a neighboring table where a young man and woman sat, their fingers linked, their faces bright with love. He did not answer her but waved to the waiter, pointed to his empty glass.

"Did you give her gifts also?" Jen persisted.

Their salads arrived and they both poked with disinterest at the expensive greens. He forked an anchovy, she a clump of goat cheese.

"I gave her gifts. I loved her. I cared about her. I still love her. I still care about her." Sadness softened and flattened his voice.

"Eric, why did you want to see me?" she asked.

"I want to know how Cynthia is. How she's holding up. She won't talk to me. Mae won't talk to me. When I see the twins, that dimwit au pair is with them watching, listening."

His eyes were dangerously bright. His lips trembled. She feared that at any moment he might weep.

"Eric, she probably needs time before she talks to you. Whatever happened between you…it can't be that terrible."

"It is. To her. Terrible. Her word. Unforgivable. Also her word," he said bitterly. "But you could be right. Maybe time will work some magic. But meanwhile I have to know how she's feeling, what she's feeling."

"She's okay, Eric. Really okay." She thought of Cynthia speaking so softly into the phone. "Dinner? Great." "Drinks? Great." Cynthia making dates with other men, Cynthia carefully building a new life.

His face sagged. Had he wanted to hear that she was ill, that she was suffering?

She looked away from his pain, studied diners at other tables. Two women in their twenties, chatting happily, engagement rings sparkling on their well-manicured fingers. Three florid-faced men passing documents back and forth across the table. A well-dressed elderly couple, the woman's silver hair swept upward, a diamond clip affixed to a scarf of shimmering fabric, studied the menu. The hand-holding couple made their way to the door, smiling, kissing lightly as they parted. They were all people in control of their lives, affluent, self-satisfied. They had found their way to the end of the rainbow. She thought, with a perverse stab of pride, that such words did not describe herself or her book-group friends. Not even Cynthia. Not now. They were seekers, not finders, intense readers in search of endings, happy or otherwise, in their own lives, in the books they read.

"And you, Eric? How are you?" she asked.

He shrugged, ripped apart a roll and ate it so carelessly that crumbs clung to his mustard tie.

"Me? I'm lousy. Oh, I'm working, sifting through scripts, taking meetings, going through the motions. I manage to get photographed at the right parties, the right openings, and no one has noticed yet that my smiling, upbeat, successful organized wife is no longer at my side. I'm not important enough to hit the major gossip columns. But then I go home and home is a sublet in the East Sixties. An unfurnished sublet, so I'm living in graduate-student squalor and paying yuppie rent. I'm over forty and I'm sleeping on a cot, storing my hundred-dollar ties in milk crates and piling my Brooks Brothers shirts on the carton that my television set came in. And I'm popping frozen dinners into the microwave when I remember to eat and sometimes I drink Scotch straight out of the bottle. That's how I am, Jen." His eyes brimmed over. He fumbled for a handkerchief and wiped his face, passed his fingers through his fair hair. "Sorry," he said. "I didn't mean to embarrass you."

"I'm not embarrassed," she said, although, in fact, she had dropped her eyes, unwilling to see his tears.

Once, after a fierce argument between her parents (and all their arguments had been fierce), she had stolen into the kitchen and seen her father, that diminutive, balding man, wearing striped pajama bottoms and a dingy white undershirt, seated at the kitchen table, weeping. The tears had trickled between his fingers, droplets of crystalline sorrow. She had thought that they might burn her fingers if she touched them, if she moved to comfort him, because then, as now, always her impulse was to comfort.

Her mother had come up behind her and hissed, "See, see what he's like? A grown man crying. See?"

She had understood that her father's tears validated her mother's wrath, her terrible anger at being married to a weak and unmanly man, a man who cried like a child. She had allowed that same wrath to consume her. The urge to comfort vanished, replaced by an angry contempt. *He had no right. He had no right.*

She had rushed, that night, into Elizabeth's room, and her sister had looked up from her book and said with icy calm, "Just stay away from them after a fight. He cries and she yells."

She tried to remember how old she had been then— ten, perhaps eleven—very young because she had read *Heidi* that night, huddled in a corner of Elizabeth's room. Always, the books that she read at an emotional crossroad became the landmarks of her memory. She had been envious of Heidi, the Swiss orphan who enchanted her grumpy grandfather, even as her father's tears leaked from eyes grown weak with disappointment, but the repulsion she had felt then unnerved her still. She had turned away when Ian wept because a prominent reviewer had disparaged one of his paintings in a small gallery show just as she refrained now from looking at Eric. The strong were not supposed to weep.

She remembered suddenly how Cynthia had stared with cool disdain at a young assistant, in tears because of an error in an important order. She would have been equally impatient with Eric's tears. But relationships, Jen knew, were not shattered by a man's tears followed by a woman's revulsion—not her parents', not Cynthia and Eric's, not hers and Ian's. It startled her that she had placed the six of them in the same equation. What, in fact, would cause her and Ian to go their separate ways? Again, unbidden, the thought came to her and she thrust it aside and looked at Eric.

"But you can change things, Eric," she said at last. "You can get yourself some decent furniture, do some light cooking."

"But I don't want to," he said fiercely. "I don't want a sofa and pots and pans and dishes and cutlery for one. I don't want to do anything that says 'This is for real. This is how things are going to be.' I want my life back."

His face was drained of color and he downed the last of his drink.

"Your life with Cynthia?"

"My life. My house. My children. And yes. My wife. Cynthia. I want it all back."

"Can that happen?" she asked softly.

"Oh, God, I don't know. I don't know."

She feared that he might weep again, but instead he glanced at his watch, motioned the waiter for the check and pulled out his credit card.

"Can I do anything?" she asked.

"You can listen. To me. To her. I suppose that's all anyone can do. Now. But you're probably right." His voice lifted. He was suddenly hopeful. "We need time to sort this out. Both of us."

He was more in control now, his tone brisk, his color restored. He opened his attaché case, glanced at a file and snapped it shut. He was en route to the world of his work. Like Cynthia, he was skilled at compartmentalizing, at working efficiently against all emotional odds. He paid the bill, added the tip.

"But, Jen, we'll stay in touch. It's important to me." Again that muted plea in his voice that tugged at her heart.

"Yes," she agreed. "We'll stay in touch."

"I'm late." He kissed her on the cheek and hurried out, a handsome man, expensively clothed, on his way to an important appointment. Watching him, she was oddly reminded of the James Harris character in Shirley Jackson's stories, that enigmatic, fair-haired man who drifted in and out of the sad lives of Jackson's wraith-like heroines.

She sat for a few more minutes over coffee grown tepid and bitter. Then she reached for her cell phone and called Donna.

"I just had lunch with Eric," she said.

"What did he want?" The question was asked too laconically, as though to mute the eager need for answers.

"I don't know," Jen said. "I honestly don't know." Swiftly she changed the subject. "I'm going to make a veal stew for the book-group meeting. Can you e-mail me a good recipe?"

"Sure. I have a good one with peppers, tomatoes and wine."

"Sounds great."

They both sighed, relieved to be on safer ground. It was simpler to discuss food and books, to trade casual comments about movies they had seen, parties they had attended, than to rehash speculations grown stale with repetition. It was newly threatening to discuss Cynthia and Eric. Like travelers about to embark on a journey who strain to avoid news stories about accidents and crashes, they struggled against their oppressive curiosity about their friends' imploding marriage.

Jen clicked off and saw that Eric had left his handkerchief on the table. She scooped up the damp square of linen and dropped it into her bag, as though to conceal all evidence of his misery.

Although Jen had told Ian weeks earlier that the book group would hold its December meeting in their loft, he was annoyed when she reminded him, some days earlier, that he would have to move his easel to make room for a coatrack. His irritation was compounded by the fact that Elizabeth had arranged to come to the loft that evening, an odd request. The date and time, as always, convenient to Elizabeth and scheduled with an indifference to whatever plans Jen and Ian might have had.

"I hate to move the easel," he said angrily. "I can never get the light exactly right when I move it back. And I'm at a crucial point in this painting. You know that. Why does the meeting have to be here?" he protested.

"Because it's my turn," she explained patiently. "We each take a turn. You know that."

She did not remind him that he had raised the same objection the previous year and the year before that and always she had offered him the same explanation. They had lived together now for almost three years, but he still seemed at once bewildered and annoyed by any aspect of her life that inconvenienced him.

"And what am I supposed to do while you're trading insights about the author of the month, whoever that might be?"

"Shirley Jackson. She's the 'author of the month,' as you put it. Do whatever you please, Ian. Go to the movies. Go to a coffeehouse."

Uncharacteristically, irritation edged her voice. She was tempted to remind him that the loft was leased to her, that she paid almost all the bills while his work dominated much of the space—his canvases stacked against the wall, his easel and, on occasion, more than one easel, positioned near the huge windows, swept with light during the day, curtained by darkness at night. But she contained herself. That, after all, had been their agreement, lazily reached only weeks after they met, as they sat side by side on the futon, his large hand resting on her head as though he would crown her with his tenderness.

They had met in a life-drawing class, working side by side as the nude model, a shivering old man, silver hairs like threads of wire streaking his pink scalp, crouched in an uncomfortable pose. Jen had used charcoal, each attempt to capture the model's bone structure and facial expression a struggle, her completed work so smudged and awkward that she ripped it up before the strolling instructor could pause to comment on it. Ian, two easels away, had worked swiftly, his hawkish features frozen in concentrated effort, using watercolors because, as he explained to her later, oils were so damn expensive that he reserved them for his real work, not studio exercises. His finished picture was fluid, the pathos of the elderly model captured in a pale, mournful wash of color. Jen, conscious of him throughout the hour, inhaling with strange pleasure the scent of his sweaty intensity, amused by the clot of green paint in his carrot-colored hair, had admired his work, had recognized his gift. He had, she had decided, what Andrew West, her favorite painting instructor at Tyler, called "the real thing," what Ian himself called his "real work." It was Andrew West who had gravely studied her portfolio at graduation and told her that while she had talent she would be wise to direct her efforts to a career in graphic design. Andrew West would not have suggested that to Ian. She had, that first evening, moved closer to Ian's easel, studied his work and shyly nodded her admiration.

She was not surprised when he asked her to join him for coffee after the session, nor was she surprised when he invited the model to come with them. His kindness to the elderly man (who, in fact, had declined the invitation with great dignity) had pleased her and she was pleased, too, by the gentle kiss with which he brushed her cheek when they parted at her door. Three weeks later they were lovers. Two months later he had moved into her loft and placed his easel in front of the huge window that faced the river. It was an arrangement that worked for both of them, at least most of the time. It worked, she knew, because she accommodated him when she could. She was, after all, used to accommodating others, well schooled in appeasement. But she stood firm when it came to the book group. It was too important to her.

"I'm going out," he said angrily, shrugging into his jacket and rooting through a drawer for his scarf. "You're right. There's always a coffeehouse or a movie. In fact, tonight there's a gallery opening. Erica Manning's show. I may drop in there."

She recognized the name. A young artist newly arrived from London. Pretty. Talented. Was Ian issuing a threat? No. That was not like him.

"I don't want to be here, anyway, if your damn sister is coming over," he continued. "What does she want?"

"I don't know," Jen admitted. Ian's question was not unreasonable A mid-week visit from Elizabeth, who worked long hours, overseeing the guidance program at her own school and consulting for a small private academy, was unusual. It was more likely than not that her sister did want something.

She held out his gloves and the black wool beret she had bought him only days earlier. A peace gesture. She stood on her toes so that he might lean down and kiss her, their familiar farewell ritual, but he ignored her, annoyance still glinting in his blue eyes. He slammed the door in punishment as he left, and she shivered. As always, any show of anger, no matter how mild, frightened her.

Within minutes the bell jangled and she sighed and buzzed Elizabeth in.

"What's wrong with Ian?" Elizabeth asked. "He rushed by me at the door, barely said 'hello.'"

Jen took her sister's long dark coat, threaded the coral wool scarf through the sleeve and held it while Elizabeth, who took excellent care of everything she owned, put the matching beret and gloves in the pocket. She had given Elizabeth the set after she had finished a fanciful drawing in which the scarf served as a jump rope and the mittens and beret cavorted over it, for the Nightingale's winter-accessory catalog. Cynthia had loved the layout and featured it on the cover, and Elizabeth, in her taciturn way, had thanked Jen. She had needed a hat, she had needed a scarf. Of course, she had added, coral was not a color she herself would have chosen.

"Oh, Ian's under a lot of tension. He's trying to get together enough new work for a gallery show. He's been working nights—a new impasto technique to capture darkness…"

Why was she explaining all this to Elizabeth, who didn't know a damn thing about painting and wasn't interested? She stopped midsentence.

"Anyway," she continued, "it threw him off when I told him that the book group would be meeting here next week."

"It threw him off?" Elizabeth asked sourly, stooping to remove her boots. She had walked the long blocks from the subway to the loft and she would walk back unless Bert managed to pick her up, which Jen knew would not happen. "It hasn't occurred to him that this is *your* loft, that *you* pay the bills and that gives you some rights?" She blew on her fingers, reddened by the cold despite the gloves.

"Look, Elizabeth, my arrangement with Ian is entirely my own business," Jen said quietly. "I believe in his talent. We're good together. He gives me what I need."

"Which doesn't happen to include a check at the end of the month. Or marriage."

In the sarcasm of her sister's words, Jen heard their mother's voice shrilling down the hallways of their childhood home and recalled the answering lob of her father's invective.

"Other things are more important to me," she said quietly.

She would not quantify those things for Elizabeth. Her life with Ian was not an emotional ledger in which she balanced his playful affection, his softness of touch and tone against her willingness to share her space, to pay their bills, to deal with his occasional foolish fits of petulance. Their togetherness, his gentle affection, were important to her. She did stand up to him when she had to, as she had that very evening. And she had seen him struggle toward a new reliability, a new consistency in his work that could only make life better for both of them. She cared for him. He cared for her. That was all that counted. They would work things out. They *were* working things out. Screw Elizabeth's judgmental attitude, her insistence on equal balance. Was there equal balance in her marriage to Bert? But that was a question that she would not, of course, ask her sister. What would be the point?

She went into the kitchen area, heated the pot of coffee, put cheese and a baguette on the long counter that served them as a table and waited for Elizabeth to finish pulling her light brown hair into an austere bun. Finally they sat side by side on the high stools, Elizabeth, as always with her back absolutely straight, and Jen, barefoot and tousle-haired, with her legs curled beneath her. She waited for the inevitable beginning of their conversation when Elizabeth would discuss their mother. She smiled when her sister did not prove her wrong.

"Bert and I went up to the nursing home last weekend to see her," Elizabeth said. "She seems fine."

"I know. I was there yesterday. I can't say she was particularly pleasant or particularly alert, but what else is new?" Jen cut herself a piece of cheese and wondered why they always seemed to refer to their mother by pronoun. A way of distancing themselves, she supposed, to mask their ambivalence toward the old woman, their mother who, during their childhood, had been painfully ambivalent toward both of them.

"Why do you think they even had children?" Jen had once asked Elizabeth. *"Maybe because they couldn't*

stand to be alone with each other," Elizabeth had replied bitterly.

Jen recalled her sister's words, so searingly accurate, as she herself discussed her last visit to their mother, a painful and pointless ill-spent hour.

"She seems happiest when she's with that disgusting aide. Fanya. The fat Russian woman with bad breath. I'd be glad to raise her salary if she'd splurge on a bottle of Listerine. Or maybe we should give her one for Christmas."

She waited for Elizabeth to laugh in agreement. They had, from childhood on, understood and appreciated each other's caustic observations. Sometimes Jen thought that their shared wry malice and their mutual addiction to reading were the only things they had in common. She did not factor into that commonality the odd commingling of love and envy, of muted anger and cultivated resentment, the *Rashomon* mix of childhood memories, that haunted their feelings for each other.

But Elizabeth did not laugh. She stirred her coffee, to which she had added neither sugar nor milk.

"Actually, it was about the aides that I wanted to talk to you," she said. "We have Fanya five days a week and the Filipina, Elena, on the weekends. Bert and I were talking about it. It's running us a lot of money."

"We're sharing it, though," Jen said. "I pay half. And you know she needs them. We've been through this. The home keeps a skeletal staff. The aides have to be there to make sure she eats at mealtimes, that she's clean, that she gets to go out. Insurance doesn't cover that."

"We can't afford it," Elizabeth said flatly. "Bert and I just don't have the money. We want to start Adam on a new program. Something called patterning. A one-on-

one approach for autistic kids. We would have to hire the special trainers they call 'shadows' who would work with him every day for hours at a time. It started in California and it worked there. It's very expensive, but if we cut back on other things we can just about make it."

"And one of the things you'd cut back on is what you pay toward the aides?" Jen asked.

"We just couldn't do it. It's not even fair of you to ask us to. We have to think of Adam. You don't have that sort of responsibility." She sat even straighter, her face frozen into a mask of stubborn resistance, thin lips pursed, eyes set in a hard stare.

"Adam's nine. You've been thinking of him for nine years. Therapists. Trainers. The residential facility. And now this patterning. Do you really think it will work, Elizabeth?" She spoke quietly, as though her tone might mitigate the harshness of her words.

"We have to try. We have to give it a chance."

"And if it doesn't work, then you'll resume contributing to the aides' salaries?"

Jen was grasping for straws now. Her very question indicated acquiescence, but she could manage if Elizabeth's withdrawal was finite, which she assumed it would be. No other program had worked. Her nephew, beautiful dark-eyed Adam, with his long, delicate fingers so like her own, and his pale high forehead, fell into the range of the profoundly autistic, those for whom there was virtually no hope. A social worker at his facility had told her so, intimating that she should try to persuade Elizabeth to accept that sad truth. Jen had not tried. She knew herself to be powerless against Elizabeth's rigid determination.

"No. If it doesn't work we're going to have to think about his future—what happens when he ages out of a youth facility. And that will cost even more than what we're paying now. Bert says we have to start saving for that and I can't argue with him."

Jen nodded. She understood. Arguments with Bert ended in violet explosions of temper, vicious exchanges. It was ironic that Elizabeth had fled from the angry ambience of their childhood home into an even angrier marriage.

"I've got to get out of here," she had told Jen the night she announced her engagement, a night of slamming doors and raised voices, of tears and crashing crockery.

And then it was from that marriage that she had tried to escape. She had left Bert when she was pregnant with Adam, sought refuge from his bursts of fury in their parents' home, however unwelcoming. She had spoken to Jen then of making a life for herself and her unborn child. She had a profession, a tenured job. She would arrange for day care, an apartment of her own, after the child's birth. She would not be trapped again. It all seemed feasible until it became clear that Adam neither chortled nor babbled, that he did not even weep as other children wept, that he did not play with his toys or meet the eyes of the concerned adults who bent over the crib, where he lay inert for hours at a time, staring up at the ceiling. The diagnosis had been decisive and shortly afterward Elizabeth and Bert had reconciled. Neither of them could deal with Adam alone. He was their charge and they were his prisoners, confined by responsibility and resentment in equal measure. Jen had watched Elizabeth rationalize her situation, retreat into the bitter self-righteousness of the eternal victim. Elizabeth spoke in clipped sentences, sat very straight, frowned at the excesses of others. She had surrendered her own life and sat in judgment of the way others lived. Since her inclusion in the book group she had told Jen that she thought Rina too careless, Trish too pedantic, Donna too casual and Cynthia too extravagant.

Jen sighed and refilled her sister's coffee cup.

"Look, Elizabeth," she said. "I know how hard it is for you. But I can't afford to carry it all on my own. I simply don't have enough income."

"You would if Ian pulled his weight. If he contributed toward expenses."

"I've told you before. That's none of your business."

"It *is* my business. You see for yourself that it affects me. Besides, you're my sister. I don't like to see what's happening."

"And what is happening?" Jen struggled to speak in an even tone.

"You're not getting younger. Your biological clock is running. In five, or is it six years, you'll be forty. There's no talk of marriage, of children. If you were married, if there were children, your life would be more secure. He'd recognize his obligations."

"You take it as a given then that marriage and children mean a secure life. That didn't happen with Cynthia and Eric, did it?" Jen asked. She stopped herself from offering Elizabeth's own marriage as an example.

"Cynthia. Eric. They're not typical. They don't live lives that we understand. They're like characters in a fairy tale. They might just as well have existed on another planet. Their twin daughters were beautiful princesses. Their brownstone house was a beautiful castle. They flew in silver airplanes and sailed on the bluest of seas smiling, and smiling and smiling some more."

Elizabeth spoke in singsong and Jen recognized the rhythm of Adam's high-pitched monotone voice. Was

autism contagious? Did caregivers catch the idiosyn-
crasies of their charges? She thought of how Fanya aped
her mother's whining monosyllabic sentences and shut
her mind against her own malice of thought.

"But they didn't live happily ever after," she said,
silencing her sister. "Why didn't they live happily ever
after? Will we ever know?"

"More to the point," Elizabeth said, in that burst of
honest insight that caused all of them to admire her,
"why has it become so important for all of us to know?"

It was a question that Jen supposed had occurred to
each book group member in turn.

She did not answer. She slid off the stool and went to
her desk. Swiftly, she turned the pages of her checkbook.

"Look, Elizabeth," she said. "I can manage to pay it all
for a few months. I've been asked to do some freelance
work for an ad agency and I guess I could take that on.
And if Ian's show goes well it could mean sales or com-
missions for him—maybe both. So I'll say yes, for a few
months at least, and then we'll see."

"I appreciate it." The words of gratitude were spoken
too softly, as though Elizabeth had wrenched them from
a bedrock of resistance. Jen felt a small surge of victory.
She had submitted to Elizabeth's request but not in its
entirety.

"How are you liking the Shirley Jackson?" she asked.
She wanted to end any further discussion of their mother,
any further mention of Adam.

"It depends which Shirley Jackson you're talking
about," Elizabeth replied. "The dark moody fiction writer
or the light whimsical teller of family tales?"

"The dark is way too dark," Jen said.

"And the light is way too light."

Elizabeth smiled and they both broke into laughter, pleased to have agreed on something, to find themselves back in the safe port of literature, their constant refuge, their constant delight.

Elizabeth left then and Ian returned an hour later. He encircled Jen with his strong arms in mute apology, pressed his cold cheek against her face and blew into her ear with warm and tender breath.

"I didn't go to Erica's opening," he said softly.

The next morning, as the first milky light of dawn spilled in through the uncurtained window, while Ian still slept, Jen went to her desk and opened her sketch book. Working swiftly, she filled in the next panel, peopling it with early arrivals to the village green—a slight young man in an oversize suit, an overly thin, rigidly erect woman whose hair was twisted into a severe bun (not unlike Elizabeth's, she realized as she worked) and a diminutive curly-haired impish figure (not unlike herself, she admitted) hidden behind a large tree. Satisfied, she snapped the pad shut just as Ian wakened and before he could ask her what she was working on. She could finish the cartoons easily before the book group meeting.

Jen prepared the veal stew for that evening's meeting in the early afternoon, working quietly so that Ian, who had been painting since first light, his brush strokes swift and kinetic, would not be disturbed. Now and again she glanced out the window and saw that the sky was slowly darkening. Snow had been predicted and she worried vaguely that a storm might keep some of her friends away. Rina would come because she had called Jen to assure her that she had arranged to swap baby-sitting hours with a woman in her building. Typical of egocentric Rina, Jen had thought, surprised by her own annoyance, to be certain that her arrangements were of prime concern. Trish's presence, however, would depend on Jason returning home in time to be with Mandy at bedtime.

"We're really working to accommodate each other's schedules," Trish had said. "When we didn't talk about it a lot of stuff slipped by and he was mad because I had overcommitted and I was depressed because I thought he wasn't thinking of me when he arranged business trips or conferences. We're making sure that doesn't happen now because it can be dangerous."

It seemed to Jen that they were all exercising new caution because of Cynthia and Eric. They were not unlike drivers who slowed their vehicles after witnessing an accident. She and Ian had neither quarreled nor disagreed since the evening of Elizabeth's visit.

Ian finished working and stepped back to study his morning's efforts, as she added the wine to the slowly simmering stew.

"What do you think, Jen?" he asked.

She crossed the room and studied the canvas. Glittering stars spangled a night sky, the darkness graduating from broad strokes of raven black to the naphthol blue-black that he bought in tiny tubes from a dealer in Chinatown. A single, nacreous cloud, shaped like a fist, almost obscured the largest of the stars.

"It's wonderful," she said honestly.

"It's almost finished. I'll have it in time for the gallery show. I'm almost sure of it."

He dipped his brushes in turpentine, scraped his palette. Very carefully, he moved the easel behind the rice-paper screen that Jen had bought when he first moved in and which he seldom used. She was grateful to him for remembering it now. In turn, she stood on tiptoe to wipe a wand of silver paint from his chin.

"I'll be going now," he said.

"But they won't be here for hours."

"I want to stop at the Maestrato Gallery and talk to the owner. And then I thought I'd spend some time at the League. I told Patrick I'd cover his studio class tonight. We can use the money."

"Yes, we can," she said gratefully.

She was reassured. He was trying; slowly, slowly, he was changing.

She had told him about Elizabeth's request, and her acquiescence, anticipating his annoyance but instead he had been quietly agreeable, even volunteering to try to contribute to their expenses when he could. And he was doing just that. She and Ian were, she supposed, like Jason and Trish, consciously trying to be more accommodating to each other.

He leaned down and planted a kiss on her nose.

"I won't be home too late," he said. "And I won't be home too early."

"Either way," she assured him, "I'll be here."

"I'm counting on it." He tousled her hair and closed the heavy door firmly behind him, waiting in the hall until she slipped the dead bolt into place. She loved that brief moment of concern, that loving caution that made her feel cared for and protected.

She added spices to the stew, stirred it, changed into a comfortable jumpsuit and went to her drawing table. She worked for a desultory hour on the layout for the ad agency. The art director had specified a caricature for a new citrus drink account. Jen made a series of small sketches and ripped them up. Working with Cynthia had spoiled her, she realized, because Cynthia always knew exactly what she wanted in a graphic design. She sighed and drew a weeping orange, a laughing lemon, an angry grapefruit. She tossed them all away, looked at the copywriter's tip sheet and drew all three fruits holding hands in a circle dance. That worked. It would do. She selected type for the logo and then, feeling vaguely satisfied, she turned back to her comic strip of "The Lottery." By the time early darkness fell, she had completed all the panels and, with great care, she glued them to two storyboards, which she placed on one of Ian's empty easels.

She wondered if this was the first illustration of "The Lottery" and she worried briefly about the book group's reaction to it. Her drawings captured Jackson's tale of the small town where, once a year, a scapegoat was chosen by lottery—an average, innocent citizen who would be stoned to death by neighbors who were equally average and innocent citizens. In Jackson's story, Tessie Hutchinson, a gentle wife and mother, was the victim. Jen studied her work critically, shading the pile of stones in one panel and adding a checked pattern to Tessie Hutchinson's apron. Jackson had not described the apron, but Jen felt that she would have approved. She was, after all, a writer who relied on visualization in her economical but evocative sentences. A writer who described the dots on the new linoleum kitchen floor in "Raising Demons" would not mind having her doomed character wear a checked apron. She turned the easel around and began to prepare the salad.

The phone rang as she was mixing the dressing. It was Rina, struggling to be heard over ambient voices and laughter.

"I'm still at the college. I had to cover someone's composition class. My baby-sitting arrangement fell through so I have to take Jeremy over to Cynthia's. She said that would be all right. So I'll be a little late. Oh, this has just been a day when everything went wrong. Well, when doesn't it?" She laughed harshly, resigned to the consistency of her bad luck.

"You're taking Jeremy to Cynthia's?" Jen asked in surprise.

"Yeah. Why not? He knows the twins. They're in his after-school art program at the Y. I thought of asking Trish, but I didn't think Jason would love the idea and Cynthia has Mae and the au pair and she said they wouldn't mind. Not that she'd care if they did. Anyway, I'll be late."

Of course Cynthia wouldn't care, no more than she cared about allowing a meeting to extend well past lunch hour. She paid those who worked for her well and, in turn, expected a great deal from them. *Perhaps she had expected more from Eric than he could give her? Would she treat a husband as she treated her employees?* Oddly, the question did not seem absurd.

She hung up and saw that the snow had begun to fall. Tiny star-shaped flakes clung to the windowpane and a vagrant wind sent them dancing toward the river. The doorbell rang and she released the dead bolt. Donna, bare-headed, her face wind-reddened, thrust a covered cake plate into her hands.

"Apple pie," she said. "There should always be warm apple pie the night of the first snowfall."

"You sound like the sort of woman Shirley Jackson would hate," Jen said as she carried the pie into the kitchen area.

"She would probably hate all of us. Except maybe Rina."

"Rina? Why Rina?" Jen was surprised.

"Because Rina is so like the women in her stories. Disorganized, vulnerable, always short of money and talking about it, always reinventing herself. But she's a good mother and so was Jackson."

"If you believe *Life Among the Savages* and *Raising Demons*, which I have to tell you I don't," Jen said.

"This should be an interesting meeting. Oh, Trish might be late. She was on intake and there was an emergency admission."

"And Rina will definitely be late. She has to get Jeremy over to Cynthia's."

But Trish and Rina arrived together, almost on time, trailed a few minutes later by Elizabeth, who handed Jen a bottle of very good wine. A guilt offering, Jen thought as she set out wineglasses and plunged the pasta into the water boiling on a burner. It pleased her to think that at least her sister had some recognition of the burden she had placed on her. Too often, Elizabeth's tone was accusatory, as it had been throughout their childhood. *Did you visit her this week? Did you speak to the nursing home office about the last bill? You were supposed to call and let me know.*

The veal stew simmered fragrantly and she reduced the heat. Donna's recipe had called for baking, but there was no oven in the loft. They had planned to buy one when Ian sold his next painting, a plan that was now on hold.

The bell rang again and Rina opened the door to Cynthia, elegant in a hooded fur cape and high black boots.

"Sorry I'm late," she said breathlessly. "I had to meet someone for drinks."

They looked knowingly at one another. *Someone. A man. Of course, a man.*

Cynthia slipped out of her cape and they saw that she wore a full-skirted, jewel-necked black cashmere dress that closely hugged her body. *Definitely a man.*

"Thanks for letting Jeremy stay with the twins," Rina said.

"Did you see the girls when you dropped him off?"

"Yes. You sound worried. But they seemed fine."

"I do worry. This is a pretty stressful time for them," Cynthia said irritably.

"But things will get better, Cynthia," Jen said soothingly. "Maybe you'll be able to work things out, you and Eric."

Cynthia shrugged.

"That depends on what you mean by 'working things out.' In any case, I don't want to discuss it."

"Of course not," Jen said hastily, and busied herself with the food, setting it out on the counter.

They filled their plates and sat on the cushions Jen had arranged around the small colorful plastic tables. She poured wine into their glasses. Trish took a long sip and sighed.

"I never thought I'd get here on time," she said. "I had a really difficult intake. A young girl who was sexually molested by a relative. She was admitted in a state of shock. She tore my heart out. All I could think of was my Mandy and how vulnerable kids are."

"A close relative?" Cynthia asked. Red blotches fanned out across her neck and she set her fork down because her hands were trembling.

"I really can't talk about it," Trish replied. "I shouldn't have said anything at all."

"I'm surprised that you did." Elizabeth again, self-righteous now. "I make it a point never to talk about anything that comes up in the guidance office. You never know."

"Well, I'll discuss my menus anytime," Donna said, laughing. "Anyone want to know what I'm planning for the hospital Christmas dinner?"

They all laughed and Jen was relieved to see that when she set out the apple pie, warm from the oven, Cynthia helped herself to a large piece. Cynthia's question did not mean anything, her brief distress might have been just tension. It was a question any one of them might have asked. It was impossible to think of Eric, quiet, soft-spoken Eric, as a predator. Although, of course, the thought had occurred to all of them.

They cleared away the dishes and Jen perched on a bright yellow floor cushion, the books she had used to prepare her introduction piled on the floor beside her. The others sat in a circle, their books on their laps, facing the frost-streaked window through which they could see the slowly falling snow.

Speaking slowly, from the notes she had made as Ian slept heavily beside her, Jen described the author's early life, the psychic wounds inflicted on the lonely, introspective child by a cold, exacting mother who yearned for a pretty, conforming daughter, and an ambitious, materialistic father devoted to the corporate life.

"I read somewhere that there wasn't a single book in their California home," Rina said.

It was the sort of detail that Rina would remember, Jen thought, annoyed by the interruption.

"They were probably guilty of worse sins than that," she continued. "They were narrow-minded anti-Semites, inveterate snobs. But Shirley managed to escape them by creating stories, thinking them and writing them. She called writing—I have the quote right here—'a delicious private thing.' I guess I marked that quote because it's exactly the way I feel about reading, that it is a delicious private thing."

They all nodded in mutual recognition. They knew enough about one another to know that for each of them reading had always meant exactly that. They felt themselves at one with the small girl in California, who had loved books and stories as they did. They understood that delicious privacy that had been as essential to her life as it was to theirs.

Jen spoke of the Jackson family's move to Rochester, New York, of Shirley's loneliness in that cold northern city and, at last, of her discovery of a community of like-minded writers and readers at Syracuse University. It was there that Stanley Edgar Hyman, a radical Jewish intellectual from Brooklyn, courted and won the daughter of the prejudiced Protestant country-club denizens.

"As far as both sets of parents were concerned, it was a marriage made in hell. Stanley's father, Moe, even sat *shiva* for him, you know, the traditional seven days of mourning in the Jewish religion when people die. Apparently they do it when there's an intermarriage if they're really religious. Do people still do that, Rina?" Jen asked.

"Hey, being the only Jew here doesn't make me a Talmudic expert," Rina said. "But I guess there are some really orthodox Jews who would disown their kids for marrying out. I don't think my parents would have been too happy about Jeremy's father not being a member of the tribe. They wouldn't have sat *shiva* for me—I mean I didn't get married, I only got pregnant—but they would have made their displeasure known."

They all looked at her in surprise. It was the first time she had said anything at all about Jeremy's father. They waited for her to elaborate, but she said nothing more and Jen continued to speak of Jackson's life, now and again referring to her notes.

She spoke of the early days of their marriage as a young struggling couple on the fringes of Manhattan's bohemian life, grappling with low-paying jobs, and how Shirley managed to wrest short humorous fiction from even the most frustrating experiences.

"She turned a short-term job at Macy's into 'My Life with R.H. Macy,'" Jen said.

"I loved that story," Rina added. "I even imitated it once when I worked as a salesgirl during Christmas rush my sophomore year. I signed my letter of resignation with my employee number just the way she did. I think I felt like her emotional twin, sort of."

"And I think I remember your telling me that you even pocketed the cash customers gave you, which was just what she did," Donna added.

"Right. It came to about fourteen dollars. I didn't think of it as stealing. I thought of it as striking a blow against a merchandising conglomerate, which, I think, is exactly how Jackson felt when she kept the seventy-five cents a Macy's customer paid her."

She laughed and searched through her oversize black leather purse for a tissue. Donna wondered if any of the others had noticed that the bag had a tortoiseshell handle. Did they recognize, as she did, that it exactly fit the description of the handbag, stolen, according to Rina's story, by that expensively dressed woman at Saks? She knew, with a sudden flash of certainty, that there had never been such a woman. She was entirely created by Rina, who was, it appeared, still striking blows against a merchandising conglomerate.

Shirley Jackson would approve of Rina's action, Donna supposed. Emma Bovary would understand it and Edith Wharton would simply be interested. She smiled at her own long-standing acceptance of Rina's vagaries and turned her attention back to Jen, who was now speaking of the birth of Shirley's son, Laurie, the family's move to Vermont and the odd double life she led in that New England hamlet where three other children were born and the writer of "The Lottery" became a conventional mother and homemaker.

"Why a double life?" Elizabeth asked. "I would say multiple lives, like the ones all of us lead. Our professional lives, our private lives. Our different roles. Daughter. Wife. Mother. Friend. Sister." She glanced at Jen, who looked down at her notebook.

"It's true that we all have multiple roles," Trish said. "But all of these roles are played out by a single intact personality. I think Jen is rightly pointing out a split in Shirley Jackson's personality and it's that split that's reflected in her writing. On the one hand, you have her wonderfully funny stories about her kids, about the pleasant aspects of daily life in small-town New England—Little League, birthday parties, men playing poker, women having coffee together, planning menus. And then you have her violent and terrifying stories of that same community, her recognition of the darkness of small-town life, of lurking evil, of the cruelty that she perceived in sunny kitchens and landscaped gardens. Two different writers were at work. Two different women, maybe more, were trapped in Shirley Jackson's body. It's something I see at the hospital every day."

"I think you're being entirely too clinical," Cynthia objected. "I'll try for another explanation. Money. Stanley Edgar Hyman was an academic. He wrote for the *New*

Yorker and the *New Republic* to make ends meet, and even with all that he could never quite make it. He said himself that he only made enough to pay the bar bill, which was a lot because they were both big drinkers. So it was her income that sustained the household, even though he controlled the actual money and she had to ask him for every penny. She needed his permission to spend the money that she earned. She was always the good subservient wife, bringing him his drinks, cooking his meals and endowing him with absolute power. She sold her stories about her children to magazines like *Woman's Home Companion* and *Good Housekeeping* and she got paid good money for them and that was fine. It was money they could count on to support their kids, their big house, their parties. And then she reached deep down into her soul for the other stories, the novels that she wrote from what Trish calls her dark side. Every artist who comes to grips with reality and the practical world does that at different points in their creative lives. Like Eric—he made these great documentaries but he also shoots commercials. For the money. Just as Jackson must have written for the money. She didn't feel compromised just as Eric doesn't feel compromised or…" She faltered, and fell silent in midsentence. She looked at her friends in bewilderment, as though her own words had startled her. She had spoken of Eric as though they were still together, as though she were defending his professional choices, a subtle wifely pride in her tone. It sounded to her, it sounded to all of them, as though he still shared her home, her life, the twins.

It was Donna who breached the embarrassing silence.

"It's true that Jackson was concerned about money. In the stories about the children, she's always discussing how much things cost, how they couldn't afford this or that, how they punished the kids by fining them or with-holding their allowances, and money may have figured into what she decided to write. But I don't think that it was money that really motivated her. I think that she tried to write her own reality, to create a scenario that conformed to her idea of what she wanted her life to be like and what she wanted her world to be like. So she wrote herself into the role of the witty, amused mother, a little overwhelmed but always able to cope, and her children became these charming tykes, mischievous and wildly imaginative, and they all lived in this quiet town and went to Little League games and she was a PTA mom and her husband played poker and she met other women for coffee. She reinvented herself, she reinvented her neighbors, she reinvented her world. I don't agree with Trish that you have to be a split personality in order to want to do that. We all want to invent lives that are dif-ferent from those we actually live. When I was a kid I used to imagine that I had a father who went to work every day and a happy, relaxed mother with enough free time to garden and read. And even now I sort of create separate worlds for myself. One night I'm with Tim at the Blue Note and the next night I'm at the symphony with Ray. I spent too many years watching my mother trapped in her kitchen, escaping her life by listening to books on tape. I don't want to give up my own freedom. I want to keep on reinventing myself. In a way that's what Jackson was doing in her work." Donna's words came in a rush, and she leaned back when she had finished speaking as though exhausted by her own revelations.

"But only in her so-called lighthearted work. The lives that you reinvent for yourself, Donna, are all preferable alternatives to the life you saw your mother living. But Jackson's agenda was entirely different. Take "The Lottery" for instance," Elizabeth said. "That small peaceful village where the action took place was definitely North Bennington, Vermont, where Jackson lived. And the villagers who participated in the so-called lottery, who were all too ready to stone an innocent woman to death, were the same kindly neighbors she describes with such amused affection in the stories about her children. If we agree with Donna's theory about her creating an idealized world, what do we do with the other world she created, using the same landscape, the same subjects?"

"I think she understood that it doesn't take much to turn the helpful neighbor into a tormentor, and it's a simple matter for the tormentor of today to be the kindly neighbor of tomorrow," Jen said. "Look, I hope you don't mind, but I did something a little unorthodox, even for us. I drew a comic strip based on 'The Lottery.' Just for us."

She pulled the easel forward, flipped the oak-tag sheets over and waited while they studied her drawings. Rina came forward to take a closer look.

"You've certainly caught the mood of the story," Cynthia said in the careful voice she used when Jen presented her with a graphic-design project. "I can actually feel the slowly growing tension, each panel a little darker than the one before it."

"And the changing faces," Donna observed admiringly. "Just like the story. In the beginning they look as though they've all come together for a holiday celebration, smiling, happy. And then at the end their faces are twisted, angry."

"But that's what people are like," Rina said. "There's a duality. They're capable of goodness and they're capable of evil. Probably like everyone else in the world. There's always a predisposition to prejudice, maybe a kind of internal stereotyping. Like a man asking a Jewish woman why Jews were always so sad." She paused and briefly closed her eyes, remembering the careless question of the man who became Jeremy's father, who did not know that Jeremy existed.

"That was something Jackson recognized," she continued. "Something she had to write about. Jen's drawing of the crowd in that last panel, with all of the villagers, even the victim's own son, caught up in the descending crowd while she cowers in the middle—it reminded me of the Nazis, of how supposedly innocent Germans who loved their children, kept their homes in good repair, listened to Beethoven and went to church, became a mob of killers descending on victims who cowered in the middle of their violent assault. There was good in them until the hatred was turned on, until a lottery was declared. The Jews were Tessie Hutchinson, Shirley Jackson's own scapegoat."

"You're being oversensitive, Rina," Elizabeth objected. "Try not to see anti-Semites under every bed."

"What I said has nothing to do with my being Jewish," Rina retorted hotly. "I'm surprised none of you see the parallel."

"I do," Trish said quietly. "And you're not wrong in your interpretation. I read an essay online about Jackson who, when she was asked what the story was about, said that it was about the Jews. And that would fit. Her husband was Jewish, her kids were half Jewish, and they suffered real anti-Semitism in that Vermont town. It was sort of ironic since they weren't practicing Jews, but they didn't have to be in the eyes of those Vermonters. They were from New York, they were intellectuals, they were different. Of course they contributed to their differentness. I guess it didn't help that he walked around in a cape brandishing a sword cane and she weighed about two hundred pounds and wore these flowing red-and-purple muumuus, but it was the anti-Semitism that got to her. She heard the slurs, she felt the prejudice and recognized it. After all, her own parents had been bona fide anti-Semites. She knew that those good kind folk who lived in her peaceful village were capable of evil. She understood that everyone, including herself, had the capacity for violence. She was a volatile personality. One minute she was hugging her kids and the next she was screaming at them. But she struggled against her anger and she struggled to love and be loved. She recognized her duality and it frightened her. She may have tried to overcome it by writing a story like "The Lottery." I think that her own imagination, her own creative power, terrified her. The family stories were her grip on normalcy. But in the end it was all too much for her. Even a normal family didn't offer her a lifeline."

"But the family wasn't normal," Elizabeth protested. "Not that any family is really normal," she added. She did not look at Jen.

"It seemed normal to the outside world. A big house, caring parents, creative kids, dinner on the table at a set time. She cooked, she baked. Who knows what goes on behind the closed doors of anyone's house? You should hear the stories I listen to in family-therapy groups." Trish sighed and got up to refill her cup.

"You don't have to be a therapist to know that every family has its secrets, that enchanted lives are sometimes haunted," Cynthia said softly.

They were silent. Each of them, through the years, had wondered what it would be like to live Cynthia's enchanted life of professional privilege and power. They had, each of them silently acknowledged, envied her the excitement of Eric's career and her own, her marriage, her gracious home and her beautiful well-behaved children. They had been wrong; their envy morphed into pity and a reflexive vulnerability. Impulsively, Donna reached out and placed her hand on Cynthia's shoulder. Cynthia smiled and walked to the easel, studying each panel of Jen's cartoon.

"I think you ought to submit these to a publisher, Jen," she said. "You might want to add cartoons based on other book or stories. Not necessarily Jackson's work. It would be marketable."

"You really think so?" Jen's face glowed with pleasure.

"Actually, cartoons as literature is becoming its own new genre, you know, like Spiegelman's *Maus*," Rina said.

"It could very well be marketable," Cynthia said thoughtfully. "I'll put you in touch with an agent when you have something more to show." She remained at the easel for a moment and then sat down beside Donna.

"I'm interested in the whole concept of reinvention," Rina said, resuming the discussion. "I think it goes to the heart of the writing process and it was something Shirley Jackson recognized. Remember, in her story "Charles" she has Laurie going off to kindergarten and coming home with tales of the class menace, a boy named Charles. Charles was terrible, Charles was horrible and then Charles got better and finally became a good boy. When Jackson goes up to school for a teacher's conference, she discovers that there's no Charles in the class, but that it was Laurie himself who had been doing

all the things he attributed to Charles. He had sort of invented himself. It's the ultimate act of fiction."

"Like crediting an invented character with something
you yourself might have done," Donna murmured,
thinking again of Rina's description of the elegant
shoplifter.

"Exactly." Rina smiled and touched her leather purse,
sliding her hand across the smooth tortoiseshell handle.

"I think it may also be at the heart of the reading process," Elizabeth said. "I think people like us turn to
books so that we can slide into other lives, other worlds.
We're not passive, casual readers. There are times when
the stories I read seem more real to me than my own life."

They all nodded in agreement, in mutual recognition.
They sat for a few moments in companionable silence,
leaning back against the bright floor cushions, their
books piled beside them. Elizabeth picked up the biography of the author that Jen had used for her research,
studied the photograph of Shirley Jackson on the jacket
and noted that the photographer was Laurence Hyman,
Jackson's older son. Her eyes clouded and Jen, watching
her, knew that Elizabeth was thinking of her own son,
Adam, who would never, never be able to take a picture
of his mother. Gently, she took the book from her sister
and placed it on her desk.

The phone rang, its harsh summons dispelling the
sweet and unusual quiet of the room. Jen reached for it.

"Hi, Mae," she said. "Cynthia's right here."

"Damn." Frowning, Cynthia took the phone. She listened for a few minutes, the annoyance in her expression replaced with a new gravity.

"All right, Mae. We'll leave now and grab a cab. We'll
be there as soon as we can."

She turned to Rina.

"Jeremy has a headache. A very bad headache, Mae says. He began complaining about two hours ago and she thought it would pass, but it seems to have gotten worse. And Mae thinks he's running a temperature."

"Jeremy? He's never had a headache." Rina's voice was anxious. "A headache? A temperature?" she repeated as she and Cynthia shrugged into their coats.

"He'll be fine, Rina," Jen said. "I'm sure he'll be fine. Give us a call and let us know."

"Yes. I will. We will. Thanks."

She was already at the door, Cynthia following close behind her, her hand slightly raised in a small wave, her delicate features set in a mask of worry.

The others moved to the huge window. The snow fell now in soft wind-tossed flurries. They watched as Cynthia and Rina left the building and waited briefly on the curb until a cruising yellow cab stopped and the two women entered it. They noticed that Cynthia leaned forward to give the driver her address while Rina sat rigidly in the darkness.

"Jeremy will be all right," Trish said as she called her own home and spoke softly to Jason. "Amanda's asleep?" she asked. "I'll be home soon, very soon."

They listened without surprise. Fear was contagious, reassurance was imperative.

Together then, they cleared away the dishes, piled the floor cushions neatly into a corner and, over one last cup of coffee, agreed that their next meeting would be held at Trish's apartment at the end of January and, with rare unanimity, they selected a relatively new book, *Reading Lolita in Tehran* by Azar Nafisi. The reviews had interested all of them. They had each mentally adopted the book group of Iranian women, claiming those distant readers as their own intellectual siblings.

"And let's try to read Nabokov's *Lolita* as well," Trish said.

"And then we can write a sequel—*Reading Lolita in Manhattan*," Elizabeth added caustically, and they all laughed.

The decision restored normalcy. They collected their coats, tossing hats and scarves to one another, giggling when Elizabeth's coral wool scarf settled on an empty easel. Gaeity had been restored to them; their anxiety had been appeased. They agreed that they would not call either Cynthia or Rina that night.

"A headache. Only a headache," Elizabeth said. "He'll be fine."

"Of course. Of course."

The snow had stopped falling by the time they left Jen's building, but a frigid wind whistled its way down the quiet street.

Chapter Five

But Jeremy was not fine. Rina's exhausted voice wakened Donna early the next morning.

"I'm home," she said. "I took Jeremy home in a cab last night. We thought that whatever was causing the headache would pass, but it hasn't. He hardly slept and he's worse this morning. He has a fever—not high, but a fever. I called my pediatrician, who told me to take him to the emergency room, but I don't want to take him out in this weather."

Donna carried the phone to her frost-patterned window and glanced out. The municipal snowplows had been at work and mountains of whiteness, already soot-spattered, lined the curbs. Icicles dangled from the narrow balcony and tanklike spreaders lumbered down the street, covering the sleek frozen surface with a thick layer of sand. A lone woman, bundled into a red down jacket, struggled to reach the corner, thrusting herself forward against the wind.

"I don't blame you," she said. "It looks fierce out there. Your doctor won't come to the apartment?"

Rina laughed harshly.

"What century are you living in? The age of house visits and cherry lollipops is over. I didn't even ask him and he sure as hell didn't suggest it. Donna, I'm so worried."

Her voice broke. Fear and fatigue had overwhelmed her.

"Rina, what can I do?" Donna asked gently. "Do you want me to come over?"

"No. But I thought that maybe you could tell Raymond, that maybe he was with you, and he could check Jeremy out."

"Ray isn't here. But I can reach him. I think he'll do it. I'm sure he'll do it." She spoke with the certainty of a woman who knows that her lover will accede to any request. Within reason. And this, of course, was a request well within reason. "I'll call you back as soon as I speak to him."

She splashed cold water on her face and brushed her long blond hair as she called Ray's apartment. There was no answer. He had probably left for the hospital. She called his cell phone and sighed with relief when he answered on the third ring.

"Dr. Goldman."

Concern replaced the professional curtness in his tone when he heard her voice. She had never, in the three years of their intimacy, called him in the morning.

"Are you all right, Donna?" he asked worriedly. She imagined his gray eyes darkening, his fingers passing through his thick silver hair in that familiar gesture of nervousness she had noticed when his service called about a patient's problem or when he was troubled about a diagnosis.

He was a kind, soft-spoken man, gifted with a gentleness that draped him like a cloak. It was that kindness, that gentleness, that had drawn Donna to him when they met. She had, from the first, felt protected when she was with him. It pleased her to sit beside him at concerts and the theater, to sit across from him in restaurants, conscious always of his solidity, his competent authority, his concern. Was her seat comfortable, her view unobstructed, was her cold better? He was caring and careful, always available and always undemanding. She had told him once that he would make a wonderful father and he had nodded pleasantly and said that yes, he would want to have children one day. The time was not now. But yes, of course. Children were important to him. His marriage had disappointed him, his wife's infidelity had baffled him, but he was not embittered.

He and Donna were at ease with each other, involved yet independent. He knew that he was not the only man in her life and she had never asked him about other women. It was sufficient, for now, that they were comfortable with each other and that, in that shared comfort zone, they found islands of safe haven.

"Yes. I'm fine," she assured him. "It's Rina's son, Jeremy. He has a horrific headache and fever. Rina's afraid to take him out in this weather, and, of course, she can't get a doctor to come to her apartment. She wondered if you could manage to stop by."

"But I'm a neurologist, not a pediatrician," he said.

"I know. And I'm sure he's all right. But if you could just examine him and reassure her. You know how she gets."

"Actually, I don't. Although I do have an idea."

He had met Rina only a few times and always he had been newly startled by her intensity, the fierceness of her

opinions and her sudden, incandescent bursts of wit.
The closeness of her friendship with Donna, who was always so calm and organized, surprised him, but he understood that there was a great deal that he did not know
about Donna, that there were questions he would not
ask. He listened while she and Rina chatted on the
phone, charmed by their intimacy but irritated now again
by Donna's placid acceptance even when Rina called
when they were in the middle of a meal or about to leave
for an appointment. Such calls were usually for venting
or in request for reassurance, which Donna proffered
without difficulty.

"You did the right things, Rina."

"Don't worry, it will all work out."

Always, when she spoke to her friend, Donna's voice
was calm and soothing. It was that serenity that he prized
and he would not risk disturbing it.

He thought that olive-skinned Rina, with her almond-
shaped eyes and angular face, was very beautiful, but he
had not mentioned that to Donna, although he did tell
her that the way Rina wore her hair, that single lustrous
black braid that fell almost to her waist, reminded him
of the grandmother who had raised him. He remembered himself, as a small boy, standing in the doorway of
her bedroom each evening and watching her plait her
long silver hair. He had thought the movements of her
hands magical, her nightly ritual rhythmic and soothing.

"She gets pretty overwrought about Jeremy," Donna
continued, almost apologetically. "It's not easy to be a single mother and it's especially hard for Rina. She has no
family at all, no support group. It's just her and Jeremy.
And myself and a couple of other friends for backup. So
she gets a little frantic when he gets sick. If you could

manage to get over there, that would be terrific. Although I'm sure it's nothing."

"I have office hours later today so it will have to be in the morning," he said. "Just give me her address and let her know I'll be there in about an hour."

"Great."

He heard the relief in her voice as she gave him Rina's address and phone number and the gratitude when she invited him for dinner that night.

"I'll have to let you know about dinner. I'm on overload today," he said. "You're a very good friend, Donna. A generous friend."

He smiled into the phone, grateful for her goodness, her generosity. His wife, the petulant, angry girl he had married during his last year in medical school and divorced with some relief when she told him, with chilling indifference, that she was having an affair and that it was not her first, had been neither good nor generous.

Donna stopped at Barnes & Noble on her way to work and bought two copies of *Reading Lolita in Tehran* and two copies of Nabokov's *Lolita*. She had told Rina that she would bring them over later that afternoon when she called to tell her that Ray had agreed to examine Jeremy.

"Please, Donna, I'm not hungry and I can't even think about reading," Rina had objected peevishly.

But Rina would need the books, Donna knew. They would be her barricade against anxiety, her escape route from the dark fears that would surely crowd about her in the overheated room where Jeremy lay, inert and pale. As always, reading would be her refuge, narratives and ideas a vital distraction. She would not be alone as she turned the pages of the books the group had selected for its next meeting. Across the city, her friends would also be reading Nabokov, sharing the memories and insights of brave Azar Nafisi who had read *Lolita* in Tehran. Like all of them, she belonged to a community of readers and dreamers, bonded by words, each of them hypnotized by a story that would touch each of them differently. Donna herself had read the first few pages at her desk, even before calling Rina, and had felt herself drawn into the chronicle of the seven young Iranian women who had held clandestine meetings in the home of their courageous literature professor, Azar Nafisi. They met to drink tea, eat pastries and to discuss works of fiction, a dangerous activity in the repressive, totalitarian society ruthlessly ruled by the Ayatollah Khomeni.

"You'll be feeling better by the time I get there," Donna had said. "And so will Jeremy, I'm sure. Ray will probably prescribe some antibiotic. He said that there are a lot of viruses floating around this time of year. Don't worry. Please don't worry."

He had said nothing like that, but as always she scavenged for words that would soothe and reassure her friend, the pattern of their college years redux. *Of course you passed, Rina. Of course he'll call you again. Don't worry. Please don't worry.*

Rina's neediness, never defined or solidified, adhered to her like a shadow.

At lunchtime she ran into Trish in the hospital cafeteria, and over sandwiches and coffee, Donna told her about Rina's phone call.

"I'm sure it's nothing. Kids get sick in the wintertime. Rina tends to overreact."

"I'm not sure," Trish said. "Bad headaches in kids aren't the norm. Did Rina say anything about his neck hurting?"

"No. And I didn't ask. You're thinking meningitis?"

"It occurred to me," Trish admitted. "But it's highly unlikely. Forget it."

"It's forgotten," Donna said.

She sipped her coffee but Trish called her apartment and spoke to her baby-sitter, clutching her phone too tightly.

"Amanda ate her lunch?" Trish asked. "She seems okay? I mean, she was a little tired when I dropped her at nursery school and I thought she might be coming down with something." She paused, clicked a spoon against her plate as she listened. "I don't think it would be a good idea for her to go outside today. Too cold. Just take her to the playroom, maybe pop in a video. Thanks."

She hung up and flashed Donna an embarrassed smile.

"All right. So I'm an obsessive guilt-ridden working mother. Maybe woman doctors shouldn't have children. We know too much."

"So maybe men doctors shouldn't have children, either. They know too much," Donna retorted.

"Your Ray didn't have any children with his ex-wife?" Trish asked.

"He's not *my Ray* and no, they didn't have any children. Which is too bad because he'd be a terrific father. He says she was too worried about her figure, too selfish, afraid to give. Who knows? That's his story and because he's Ray I believe him. But I'm sure she has her own tale of woe."

They smiled at each other conspiratorially. They were clever women who understood the men in their lives, insights gained by their struggle to understand the men who peopled the pages of the books that absorbed them. Just as they had pondered the vagaries of Vronsky, the weaknesses of Charles Bovary, so they might agree on the limits of Ray's explanations and Jason's occasional inconsistencies. Reading in depth honed their skepticism and offered them a defense against disappointment.

Trish glanced at her watch. She did not want to be late for a consultation. They cleared their trays and hurried back to their offices.

"Call me if you hear anything from Rina or Ray," Trish called as she turned the corner onto her own corridor.

"I will," Donna said, pausing at the copier to pick up the day's menus she had ordered. She was experimenting with a new low-carb diet, which, still in its early stages, had won the enthusiasm of the endocrinologists. Ray had told her that she could probably get an NIH grant to develop it and she had played with the idea. But that might mean relocating to Washington and she had no desire to leave New York. She liked her apartment, her job, the gentle evenings with Ray, the more exciting late nights with Tim. And the book group. Always the book group.

She listened to the messages on her voice mail. Tim telling her he had a gig in the Village that night. Did she want to have dinner downtown? She jotted down the number he had left. Then she listened to Ray speaking with a gravity she instantly recognized.

"I'm a little concerned about Jeremy," he said. "If the symptoms haven't abated in the next twenty-four hours he'll have to be admitted to the hospital for tests. I prescribed something for the fever, something for the headache and I wanted to prescribe a sedative for Rina, but she categorically refused. She's a very gutsy dame, your friend. Anyway, we'll talk. You can reach me on my cell."

She heard the admiration in his voice when he spoke of Rina and felt a pang of jealousy. He was right, of course. Rina was a very gutsy dame, a little bit nuts, but definitely gutsy. It was stupid and selfish of her to begrudge her friend Ray's casual, and probably indifferent, approval. In penance, she called Rina.

"I'll be over after work," she said. "I have the books for you. Do you need any food? I can raid the hospital kitchen for a care package or stop at Whole Foods."

"I'm not sure it's a good idea for you to come." Rina sounded exhausted. "Jeremy might be contagious. Ray said he'd be back later. Maybe you'd better talk to him."

"I will. But don't worry. I can always wear a protective mask. I work in a hospital, remember? So what can I bring?"

"Juices, I suppose." Rina's acquiescence to her visit was a surrender. "Jeremy's supposed to drink a lot, although he doesn't seem interested in eating or drinking. He doesn't seem interested in anything. He just lies there. Oh, Donna, I'm so scared."

"Listen to me, Rina. He'll be all right. Kids get sick. Ray is a great doctor. Everything always turns out okay." Her voice was firm as she uttered the requisite platitudes, although her hands trembled. Everything did not always turn out okay. Neither she nor Rina believed that. Their own lives and the books they loved had taught them otherwise. Happy endings were not the norm.

"Tell that to Anna Karenina. Tell that to Edith Wharton," Rina retorted caustically, and they both laughed, their anxiety abated by their shared bitter humor.

She called Ray and left a message with his secretary. An hour later he returned her call.

"I think I'll have to take a rain check on dinner tonight," he said. "I'm jammed up here and then I want to go back to Rina's and check on Jeremy. I'm a little worried."

"I'm going there myself. I want to bring her some food, juices, the books for our next meeting."

"Donna, I don't think it's a good idea for you to go over there. We don't have a diagnosis. There may be contagion," he cautioned.

"I'll wear a mask," she assured him. "Trish thought meningitis, maybe. Is that where you are?"

"It's too early to tell. We have to see how he reacts to the medication. I don't think so, but I'm not ruling it out. I just don't want to order invasive tests if they're not necessary." He was, as always, conservative, considerate, a patient doctor, a patient friend, a very patient lover.

"Ray, Jeremy stayed at Cynthia's last night. He was with her children. The twins."

"Then Cynthia and her husband should be advised of the situation just in case one of the twins presents with the same symptoms."

"But you know that Cynthia and Eric are separated. He's not in the house."

"That's irrelevant. He's the father. He has to be informed." He spoke with professional certainty and Donna wondered how Cynthia would react. But that, too, was irrelevant. All that should concern them now was the health of the children.

"Listen, Donna. Maybe you should go to Rina's apartment. She's been alone all day. It's important to keep her calm. Wear a mask, gloves. I might see you there."

"Okay."

Again she felt a pang of jealousy. He had placed his concern for Rina above his concern for her. And again, she chastised herself for irrational resentment. He had cautioned her and it was only natural that he should be concerned for Rina. Flushed with shame and annoyance,

she called Cynthia and bullied her way through two protective secretaries so that she could tell her friend about
Jeremy's illness, about the unlikely but possible threat to
the twins, about the need to inform Eric.

"Why Eric?" Cynthia asked edgily, keeping her voice
very low.

"He's the children's father. Apparently the protocol is
that both parents have to be informed of possible danger, of suggested precautions. At least that's what Ray implied," Donna said.

Cynthia sighed.

"I suppose this won't be the first situation we'll have
to deal with if…" Her voice drifted off.

There were voices in the background; a telephone
rang. Donna imagined Cynthia's huge cluttered desk,
the flowers bought that morning (because there were always fresh flowers on Cynthia's desk) drooping in a crystal vase, secretaries and assistants scurrying in and out
of the thickly carpeted office while Cynthia herself sat
in grim, indecisive silence.

"If what?" Donna pressed.

"If we don't resolve our current situation. If. If. If. I really can't talk now." Irritation coated her words. "Okay,
Donna. I'll take care of it. Thanks. Oh, I hope Jeremy feels
better," she added as yet another phone rang, and she
called to an assistant to answer it, for God's sake.

Donna went into the hospital kitchen, commandeered
two casseroles for Rina and, wrapped in her heavy green
woolen cape, she went into the frigid night and hailed a
cab. Huddled in the back seat as the driver navigated his
way down the ice bound streets, she pondered Cynthia's
words. *If,* her friend had said, *if.* Uncertainty was implied.
Things had clearly changed. Cynthia was newly hesitant.

Donna felt a surge of hope. Like all committed readers, she yearned for the ever-elusive happy ending.

She did not stay long at Rina's. Jeremy was asleep, and as Rina put the food she had brought from the hospital and the juices she had purchased at the corner bodega into the fridge, she peered into the bedroom. The small boy lay motionless on the high bed, his sweat-dampened dark hair spread across the yellow pillow slip on which a benevolent Babar ruled his jungle kingdom. *Babar,* Donna remembered, was his favorite book. His face was pale but his cheeks burned with a febrile brightness.

"I'm glad he's sleeping," Rina said softly. "Sleeping and not crying."

Her own face was ashen with fatigue, her dark eyes red rimmed, but her hair was neatly braided and, oddly enough, she wore a long red velvet shift, plucked months before from the outdoor bin of a vintage clothing shop.

"Jeremy's favorite," she said, touching the high collar.

She had dressed to please her son, who would not open his eyes to admire the color, who would not pass his small fingers across the soft fabric weathered by age.

Donna admired her for the hope of that small act. She had, in fact, always admired Rina for her daring, her intensity, her ability to act on impulse. She herself had always chosen to remain strictly on course, the motivated student, the organized professional, her lovers carefully chosen, her involvements carefully restrained. Her mother's advice had not been forgotten.

She put her arm on Rina's shoulder.

"I want a red velvet robe," she said. "The next time you see one, buy it for me."

"I will. But you won't wear it," Rina replied and, laughing, they went together into the living room.

Donna noticed, at once, that the room, normally cluttered with magazines, books and toys, the sofa bed rarely folded, was unusually orderly. The papers on Rina's desk were arranged in neat piles, her marking pens neatly lined up. Colorful throw pillows covered the shabby sofa. A single lamp burned on Rina's computer table, but the pale gray screen was blank.

"I couldn't concentrate on work so I cleaned up," Rina said.

"Good idea."

"I think your Ray was a little shocked by the chaos."

"He's not my Ray," Donna said for the second time that day.

The phone rang then and Rina picked up.

"I took his temperature about an hour ago. It was lower. Only 103. But he said that his head still ached."

Ray, Donna realized, calling for an update, hopeful perhaps that he would not have to make a return visit.

"Yes. Donna's here," Rina continued. "All right. I'll tell her."

She hung up.

"Tell me what?" Donna asked.

"He has an emergency at the hospital so he had to rush. He won't be here until later, much later. He said he'd call you tomorrow."

"Okay. That's fine. Rina, do you want me to stay? Do you need anything?"

"No. Actually I'm going to try to get some sleep myself. And then maybe eat something and start one of the books. A pretty strange time to launch myself on *Lolita*, isn't it?"

"Maybe any time would be strange for that book." Donna smiled, kissed Rina on the cheek and left, closing the door softly behind her.

Waiting for the elevator, she fumbled for her cell phone and realized that she had never bothered to put on either the protective mask or the gloves. It did not matter. Standing outside Rina's building, shivering against the cold, she called Tim to tell him that yes, she was up for dinner and she wouldn't mind listening to some guitar. She wanted his sad and wistful music to wash over her as she sat in a candlelit cellar club.

The news of Jeremy's illness ignited sparks of worry in each member of the book group. They called one another to exchange information, to trade suggestions, to relieve the anxiety that iced their hearts and caused their hands to tremble. Donna's cell phone rang again and again as she sat opposite Tim in a village bistro, picking at a salad she had no desire to eat. Trish called to ask if she had heard from Ray. Elizabeth, who was seldom forthcoming, wanted to know if Rina needed anything, but then Elizabeth understood what it was like to care for a sick child. Finally Jen called to discuss her conversation with Cynthia.

"Cynthia said you told her that Jeremy might be seriously ill, that it might affect the twins," Jen said. She did not use the word *contagion*. She did not speak of danger.

"It might." Donna flashed Tim an apologetic glance. He nodded indifferently and poured ketchup on his hamburger and, as always, slouched in his seat.

He was a tall man who seemed embarrassed by his height. He wore a cap tonight, as he always did before a gig. It perched uneasily on his unruly chestnut-colored curls and she reached across the table, as she listened to Jen, and straightened it. He frowned.

Unlike Ray, Tim was impatient with her book club friendships. He was a man whose music absorbed him totally. His friendships were with other musicians; they spent afternoons and evenings jamming together or listening to one another play. Sweet mournful clarinet notes and intricate string arrangements stirred their hearts and caused their feet to tap, their heads to nod as they sipped their beers and took long pulls on their hand-rolled joints.

"You and your friends talk too much," he had told Donna accusingly. "Too many words between you."

"And you play too many notes," she had retorted playfully. He did not laugh, although laughter came easily to him.

She had recognized from the beginning, from their first meeting at a party where they had danced in smiling silence, that it was his reluctance to talk that relaxed her, offering her as it did a respite from the intensity of her exchanges with her friends and her own thoughts. He provided her with balance, with the odd luxury of silence. She even liked it when he ejected a recording of a novel from her CD player and replaced it with a lively new rendition of Cumberland Gap music. Those were the times that he flashed her a boyish smile, put his large hands about her waist and whirled her around her small kitchen in an energetic jig that left her excited and breathless. But he did not smile as she continued to speak to Jen.

"Ray thinks that Cynthia should tell Eric about it," she murmured into the phone.

"Cynthia wants me to be there if she does meet with Eric," Jen said. "I don't want to say yes and I can't say no."

Donna sighed.

"It's tricky. Look, Jeremy may be fine by tomorrow and it won't even be a decision you'll have to make. I'll call you if I hear anything."

She clicked off and, in apology, pressed the mute button on her phone.

"Cynthia wants Jen to be there when she tells Eric that the twins might have been exposed to whatever it is that's causing Jeremy's fever, that they might have to undergo some invasive tests," she said. "It's an uncomfortable situation for Jen."

"Why? You and your friends have done nothing but discuss Cynthia and Eric for months. It's almost like a refrain in one of those old folk songs." He transformed his voice into a mock croon. "What did he do to make her say what she said?"

"That's not fair," Donna protested, smiling in spite of herself.

"Not fair but accurate. So now Jen gets to sit down with them and then she reports back to all of you. A bonus for all of you. What he said. What she said. How they looked at each other. Hey, I've got another three choruses here all backed up by a bass guitar."

She glared at him, in mock anger, and he smiled and changed the subject.

"Listen," he said, reaching for her hand. "There's a bluegrass festival in one of the Florida Keys over Christmas and I'm going to do a workshop. It's terrific. A Florida spa in the dead of winter. I get to play, to teach, I get to bring a friend along and I collect a big fat check. How about it, Donna? Want to be that friend? Can you get time off?"

He himself was unconstrained by a work schedule. He picked up gigs haphazardly, accepting this one, turning that one down. He had big pay days at uptown clubs, then played gratis at smoke-filled Village joints because he wanted to sit in with a particular group. He recorded CDs, some of which sold and some of which didn't. His laid-back, unworried approach to life was a pleasant mystery to Donna, whose life had been so carefully programmed.

"I don't know. I'll think about it. I haven't figured out winter vacation yet. But it sounds good."

It sounded better than good. It sounded wonderful. She imagined herself sitting on the beach, sunlight dappling the pages of the open book on her lap. She wondered if Ray had any vacation plans, recalling that he had gone with her the previous year to the lavish party Cynthia and Eric threw each Christmas Eve. The book group had always been invited. Sipping eggnog, munching on strawberries dipped in chocolate, they had joined the excited groups who wandered through the brightly lit rooms, decorated for the holiday with red-ribboned boughs of pine and sprigs of mistletoe, tall candles burning in every window. They had stood around the giant spruce, its branches hung with delicate ornaments purchased by Cynthia in small Tuscan villages and seabound Irish towns, and watched as Liza and Julie, flushed with excitement and laughter, vagrant strands of silver tinsel spangling their auburn hair, were hoisted by a beaming Eric to set the last star and the last angel in place. But Eric would not be there this year, and in all probability, Cynthia would not host a Christmas party without him. Not that Ray would miss it. Christmas, after all, was not his holiday, he had told her quietly.

"I'm Jewish, not seriously Jewish but Jewish enough not to do Christmas," he had said, unknowingly echoing sentiments Rina had expressed more than once.

Still, he remembered to buy her a gemstone brooch that year. Tim, of course, had never given her a gift.

"Okay. Think about it. Let's get out of here. And please turn your damn phone off. I don't want any of your friends calling during a clarinet solo."

"I will."

She kept her promise, and so it was not until she returned to her apartment, after ducking out on Tim's last set, that she heard Ray's message. She listened to his grave voice as she shrugged into her warmest nightgown and crept into bed.

"Jeremy's fever hasn't broken and the headache seems to have intensified. I don't think we can wait much longer. If there's no change by the morning I'm going to schedule a spinal tap. Don't call Rina. I gave her something to help her sleep." His own voice was brittle with exhaustion. "Take care, Donna," he added, almost in an afterthought. The words were new for him. Almost always he ended a nightly phone message saying, "I'll be thinking about you."

Vaguely troubled, she opened *Reading Lolita in Tehran,* which she had begun that morning. Once again she entered that house in the Iranian capital where a woman who lived surrounded by books and flowers listened to a young friend laughingly describe a poem. The writer's children played in an adjacent hallway, and as she and her friend spoke, the scent of fresh-brewed coffee drifted toward them. The graceful idyllic scene, which the author had so skillfully painted, was shattered by the ominous ringing of a doorbell.

Donna stopped reading. She did not want to know who had rung the doorbell. She wanted the women to continue talking, the children to continue playing. But

that, she knew, was not what would happen. She closed
the book and glanced at her bedside clock. It was late,
too late to call Ray, too late to call anyone. She sighed and
switched off her reading light.

Rina wakened in the half light of dawn. She remained
motionless on the sofa bed, listening, in brief bewilderment, to Ray's rhythmic breathing. He lay sprawled
across a makeshift bed of blankets on her living room
floor. She had forgotten that he had elected to stay the
night, a choice that had both frightened and relieved
her. He slept heavily now, although she had heard him,
during the night, pad into the bedroom. His presence had
allowed her to sink again into the deep and magical sleep
that had overtaken her minutes after swallowing the
oversize pink pill Ray had held out to her. If Ray had allowed himself to sleep, then surely the fever had broken
and Jeremy was all right. Hope spurred her into wakefulness and she tiptoed past Ray into the bedroom.

Rhomboids of morning light danced across Jeremy's
thin face, and Rina rushed to the window and pulled the
shade down against the morning's wintry brightness. She
bent over the bed, brushed away the cowlick of dark hair
and passed her lips across her son's high, pale forehead.
It was feverish still, but it seemed cooler to her than it
had been the previous evening. And Jeremy's breathing
was less labored. His hands, which had seemed to twitch
spasmodically, rested quietly on the coverlet. He was
better, definitely better. She should not have been so
pessimistic. She should have had the courage of those
young women in Tehran who had faced arbitrary and irrational danger, the loss of freedom and family, and
would have coped with the illness of a child with the

same steadfastness with which they coped with the illness of their society. She had begun to read about the Tehran book club as Jeremy slept, inevitably comparing herself and her book club to that small sorority of readers who argued about Lolita as sirens shrieked through the streets of their city. *I need their bravery,* she told herself, and thought that perhaps she might assign that book to her class in the coming semester. But for now, she had to dress and reclaim her life.

Rina tiptoed hurriedly about the room collecting fresh underwear, clean jeans and a sweatshirt. She took a long, hot shower and dressed quickly, leaving the bathroom door ajar so that she could hear Jeremy if he called out to her. As she plaited her long black hair, she looked up and saw that Ray stood in the doorway watching her. She blushed, as though he had interrupted her in an act of intimacy and, strangely, his color, too, rose and he averted his eyes.

"Sorry," he said softly. "I didn't mean to startle you."

"It's all right. Thanks so much for staying the night. And for the pill. I feel like a new woman. But that's probably because Jeremy seems so much better."

She smiled but his expression was grave.

"He does seem better. But there's still a fever. And that worries me."

"But it's much diminished. I could tell."

"I'm sure it's not as high. But with all the antibiotics he's had, if it was a simple bacterial infection it would be gone by now. Entirely. But this is a persistent fever. I don't want to take a chance."

"A chance on what?" She finished braiding her hair, but she did not look at herself in the mirror.

"I want to be sure that it's not meningitis." The word fell heavily from his lips.

"Meningitis." She struggled to remember what she knew about the disease. Something to do with the brain, she knew. An infection or an inflammation. It was dangerous. Newscasters spoke of it in tones of gravity.

"That's serious, isn't it?" she asked at last.

"Very."

"Is it life threatening?"

She trembled. Jeremy could not die, could not be taken from her. He was her baby, her little boy, her child, hers alone. She hugged herself and rocked from side to side, remembering how she had rocked him and kept him safe through all the days, all the short years of his life. He was hers, all she had, all she might ever have. She did not weep. Her tears had been sucked away in a vacuum of fear.

"It can be, but not if it's caught early enough. And it's just a supposition on my part. That's why I waited. He's not presenting with any of the classic symptoms. He doesn't seem to experience pain when he bends his head forward. There's no acute sensitivity to light. No vomiting. No convulsions. But there is the fever and the headache. I'd rather err on the side of caution. That's why I would suggest a lumbar puncture, a spinal tap. Then we would know for certain." Ray spoke with a gentle patience.

"Is a spinal tap dangerous?" she asked.

"Not dangerous. But painful. Which is another reason for my hesitation. We don't want to cause a small child to suffer."

"And if he does have meningitis…what do we do then?"

"If it's bacterial we have powerful antibiotics. If it's viral, then it will clear up by itself."

"And what happens if it's not treated immediately?" she asked.

He understood that she was pleading for time, time for the fever to dissipate, for the headache to disappear, time for all the symptoms to vanish so that Jeremy, mischievous, playful Jeremy, would be restored to her. But time was a luxury he could not guarantee her.

"There could be mental retardation, cerebral palsy. And Rina, I must tell you that when there have been long delays in treatment, patients have died."

"If you recommend the spinal tap then, of course, it will have to be done," she said. She leaned against the doorjamb, her body slack, her mouth dry. She would submit, as she had to, to his authority, his concern.

"One more question." He spoke hesitantly.

"Yes?"

"Jeremy's father. Should he be informed?"

"Jeremy's father doesn't know that Jeremy exists," she replied. And then, although she had no reason to, she told him about that one night she had spent with the ascetic academic whose bright blue eyes Jeremy had inherited.

"I've never told anyone about it before," she said. "Not even Donna. I didn't want to be judged."

"I would only judge you as courageous," he said gravely, and briefly rested his hand on her shoulder, the first time he had touched her. The warmth of his tenderness melted the icy terror that gripped her heart.

He went to the phone then and called the hospital. She listened as he spoke of scheduling, as he specified a particular nurse, a technician. He would do the procedure himself, he told them, and again she felt a rush of gratitude. Clearly, he had departed from his routine to personally work with Jeremy.

He hung up and smiled at her.

"It will be all right," he said. "Everything is on our side. I have a top nurse, a top technician. My troops are ready."

They were engaged in battle then, doctor and mother, Donna's lover and Donna's friend.

They stood in the doorway of the bedroom and looked at the child, at small Jeremy, who still slept, oblivious to the danger that threatened him. Ray put his arm about Rina then and led her to the sofa. They sat together in the half light of morning, her head on his shoulder, her long silken braid caught between his fingers. Her book, discarded amid the bedclothes the night before, fell softly to the floor and she looked down at the photograph of two young Iranian women, clad in black, scarves obscuring hair that was surely as dark as her own. The sorrow etched across their lovely faces frightened her and she willed herself to separate herself from their despair, so distant and different from her own. She would remain strong, she had to remain strong, for Jeremy and for herself.

It was at Jen's loft that Cynthia and Eric would meet, a decision that angered Ian. Angrily he scrubbed his canvas clean, wiping away the morning's work. Deliberately, his lips pursed, he scraped at the remaining traces of paint, the stubborn celadon green that he hated to waste because it was so expensive and so difficult to come by.

"Why here?" he asked. "Why not at their East Side Mc-Mansion where their fat housekeeper can serve them tea and pick up their Kleenexes should either Mr. or Mrs. Dysfunctional Marriage have a crying jag?"

"Precisely because they don't want Mae to hear any of the discussion. They don't want her or the au pair to get into a panic about the disease being contagious," Jen said patiently. She would not allow Ian to escalate the argument, to ignite her fury with his own. She was, after all, skilled at banking emotional blazes.

"Then why don't they meet at her office—okay, I can see how that wouldn't work. But why not at a café, a restaurant?"

"Because they don't want a gossip columnist to spot them and drop poisonous paragraphs into the evening news. You know, 'prize winning director Eric Anders and his beautiful wife, the marketing manager at Nightingale's, who have not been seen together recently, were spotted at Orsini's in intimate conversation….' They don't need to have their names appear in gossip columns. They're not up for a sound bite on the *Today* show," she replied, keeping her voice level. "They'll be here for less than an hour and after all—"

"Do what you want. It is your loft," he said bitterly.

He completed her sentence with words she had not thought to use, but once said, she claimed them.

"Yes. Actually, it *is* my loft," she replied, repressing an anger that was slowly accruing.

She had paid the monthly bills the previous day, and although he had promised to contribute to that month's rent, had even undertaken an extra class to do just that, no money had been credited to their account. He had needed to buy new paints, a specially treated canvas, a set of sable brushes, he said sullenly when she asked him why there had been no deposit. She had not answered, hugging her resentment in silence. But now that silence had been breached. She recognized, with sudden clarity, that if she made no demands on Ian, there would be no change. And, she acknowledged, Elizabeth was right about that much. He had to change if they were to go forward, whatever that might mean. She sighed. Of course she knew what that meant. Going forward equaled commitment, perhaps marriage, children. It meant that Ian's responsibility would have to match her own.

She watched as he shrugged into his loden coat. A toggle had broken loose and she had meant to sew it on. She would try to do it that evening. An act of atonement, although she did not need Elizabeth to assure her that she had nothing at all to atone for. She did not regret her words.

He slammed the heavy door as he left. She picked up the turpentine-soaked cleaning rag he had tossed to the floor. It had left a mark on the hardwood floor, which angered her. Grimly, she wiped it away. No, she told herself firmly. I will not sew on his damn toggle. She wondered, a ghost of a smile playing at her lips, if that new determination echoed the determination Cynthia had felt when she asked Eric to leave their home. What might she say to Ian? *I will not tolerate you in this loft a moment longer because you do not pay your share, because you slam doors and mar floors and because you want to rule over space that is mine.* She would not, of course, issue such an ultimatum. She forgave him much because of his talent and because she needed the tenderness of his touch, the seductive softness of his voice when things were good between them. And they were good more often than not, she reminded herself. And he was trying. That much she knew.

Cynthia arrived within minutes of Ian's departure. She was dressed for a journey, her auburn hair tucked into a mink cloche, the mink collar of the long black coat that reached the tops of her soft black leather boots, turned up. She carried a heavy matching tote bag and pulled a wheeled, compact suitcase into the loft. When she reached the airport, Jen knew, she would immediately be taken to the first-class lounge. Men would smile at her and then avert their eyes. Exhausted flight attendants would stare at her with ill-concealed envy.

But Jen saw that beneath the smooth veneer of Cynthia's expensive and expertly applied makeup, her face was tight with tension, her green eyes narrowed by sleeplessness. She did not remove her coat but peeled off her gloves. Crimson lacquer glittered on her manicured fingernails. Jen thought suddenly of Sanaz, a participant in the Tehran book group, who had painted her fingernails in defiance of the religious edict against nail polish. Sanaz wore black gloves to conceal her disobedience but, nevertheless, the coloring of her nails was a small and courageous act of defiance. And Cynthia—busy, organized and frequently overwhelmed Cynthia—painted her own nails to combat the unease and sadness, the myriad of responsibilities and the compounded indecisiveness that robbed her of sleep. Another small and courageous act. Jen smiled at her, in sympathy and in admiration.

"You're traveling today?" she asked.

"L.A. Just for two days. Nightingale's is opening a new store on Rodeo Drive and I'm meeting with the execs there to set up the boutique marketing plan. Didn't you do the promo for it?"

Jen nodded.

"Months ago. Before the summer."

The word hung between them. Before Cynthia's marriage had so mysteriously erupted, an unexpected minor volcano that sent aftershocks through the lives of her friends. *Before* winter, with all its discontents, its threatening illnesses, had surrounded them. *Before* their book group became obsessed with curiosity about that seemingly fissured marriage. *Before* Eric had sat opposite her with tears in his eyes.

"But Cynthia, what if the twins have to have these tests? Donna said that they might have to have the same spinal tap as Jeremy if it is meningitis, because they were so exposed to him. Will you still go to California?"

She wanted Cynthia to say no, to deliver a small speech about how the twins were her priority, how she could not think of leaving New York if they had to undergo a painful, invasive procedure. But Cynthia sat down on the futon and studied her hands. She did not wear her wedding band, Jen noted. She had replaced it with a gold snake ring that coiled its way about her finger.

"I don't know," she said. "I guess that's one of the things Eric and I will be talking about. You'll have to play referee if we need one, Jen."

"You won't need one," Jen replied. It occurred to her that she had never heard either of them speak in anger, not to each other, not to their children. Grace and civility were the hallmarks of their marriage. She corrected herself. *Had been* the hallmarks of their marriage.

"And we'll have to decide quickly," Cynthia continued. "I have a car coming to take me to the airport in just an hour." She glanced at her watch. "Eric is late," she said, but even as she spoke, the doorbell rang.

"No," Jen called in relief as she hurried to the door. "He's right on time."

Eric kissed Jen on the cheek and hurried across the room to Cynthia.

She eased herself up and took off her cloche so that her hair circled her slender face in a fiery frame. A dramatic gesture, reserved for his moment of entry, Jen thought unkindly, watching as Eric touched Cynthia's head lightly and then pressed his palm gently against her chin.

"Cynthia."

"Eric."

Softly they uttered each other's names, searchingly they looked at each other. They had not, after all, been together since summer's end, when their skin had still been brushed by the gold of the Mediterranean sun, and whatever words they had spoken then had surely burned with anger and regret. Now it was winter and they stood before a frost-laced window, their faces pale, their eyes dulled with worry.

Jen busied herself making tea, filling the mugs, foraging in the pantry for biscotti, which she arranged on a ceramic plate. She heard their voices as she worked, the steady, susurrant flow of words that seemed to come with surprising ease. She would have suspected awkward ebbs after the long months of silence. They had not seen each other, she knew, but of course they had talked. There were the twins' visits with Eric to be arranged, household and financial matters to be discussed, perhaps lawyers' appointments to be scheduled—although, oddly, she realized suddenly, neither Eric nor Cynthia had mentioned seeing a lawyer.

The thought teased her as she set the laden tray in front of them. Cynthia, so used to being served, so sure that Jen knew exactly how they liked their tea, took her mug and sipped the hot drink. She motioned Jen to a chair, but Jen shook her head and went to her worktable. She selected fonts for a new layout as their words drifted toward her.

"I've asked around," Eric said. "The general agreement is that meningitis is dangerous enough to warrant extreme vigilance if there's been any exposure at all. The people I spoke to, that doctor in the U.K. with whom I worked on the documentary about contagious diseases in the Third World, and a specialist at the Cleveland Clinic, all said as much. If Jeremy is diagnosed with meningitis and if the twins played with him the night he got sick, they're at risk and will have to undergo the lumbar punctures. I don't think we have any choice." He was the well trained, expert researcher, the caring and careful father. He had done his homework and made his decision.

"You're right." Cynthia's voice was subdued. There was no battle to be fought. They were in agreement.

"You said on the phone that you had to go to California?"

"I don't have to go. No one will die if I don't go to the meeting."

"But there's no reason why you shouldn't go. I'm available. My new film doesn't go into production for another week."

"But I should be with them."

"Cynthia, you kept watch often enough when I had to be away. I can do as much for you now."

She was silent. Jen waited for her to protest, to express concern, establish conditions. Would she allow him to stay in the house during her absence? Would she trust him? She tried to remember Cynthia's exact words—*I discovered something that makes it impossible for me to live with him. I can't allow him to sleep in this house for another night*—that was what she said or at least something very similar. Had that mysterious and terrible discovery been somehow mitigated or perhaps clarified over the months? Had that distrust been diluted so that now she was no longer uneasy about Eric being with the children?

Jen set her drawing pen down. The silence stretched. Cynthia's car would arrive shortly. She would have to decide whether to stay or to go. Jen wondered if they were waiting for her to speak and she struggled to think of what she might say. Elizabeth would have known intuitively. Elizabeth, after all, was a mother.

The phone rang, its harsh summons piercing the thick canopy of tense quiet that had settled over them. She reached for it. Cynthia and Eric sprang to their feet. It was Donna, speaking too quickly, her voice breathless with relief.

"It's all right. Truly all right. Jeremy wakened from this long sleep. The headache was gone, his temperature was almost normal. Ray says there's no danger of meningitis. It must have been some sort of infection. He's canceled the spinal tap. Oh, Jen, Rina was crying and me—I'm so relieved. I can breathe again."

"I know how you feel," Jen said. "Cynthia and Eric are here. I'll tell them. We'll talk later."

She danced toward them.

"It's okay. Jeremy's okay. Fully recovered. No danger. Not to him, so definitely not to the twins."

They gripped her hands, their faces newly bright.

"Oh, Jen, that's marvelous," they said. "Thank God."

"Oh, Eric. They're all right."

"Our Julie."

"Our Liza."

Their voices melted into a chorus of caring and then a horn blared up from the street below. Cynthia's car had arrived. She grabbed her hat, her bag, Eric took up her

overnight case. Each gripped Jen in a swift hug of gratitude and they were gone.

She watched from the window as Eric handed Cynthia's bag to the driver, as he held the door of the town
car for her. He leaned toward her and, for the briefest moment, Jen thought that they might melt into each other's
arms, that they might kiss, but instead Cynthia held her
gloved hand out to him and disappeared into the car,
sinking from sight behind the car's tinted windows. Eric
stood motionless as the driver pulled away and then,
turning up the collar of his long camel-hair coat, he
knotted his soft yellow wool scarf and walked swiftly
down the street, bracing himself against the whirling
wind.

They gathered at Rina's apartment that evening, an
unusual impromptu meeting of the book group. But they
had not met to discuss books, although copies of *Reading Lolita in Tehran* and the Nabokov novel weighted
their briefcases and tote bags. They would read as they
sat on buses and subways, as they waited in line at the
checkout counter, paragraphs and pages greedily consumed in scavenged minutes. The books would be finished when they met at Trish's home and they would
discuss them then. But tonight they had come together
to reassure themselves that Jeremy was indeed recovered
and to offer Rina respite and support.

And Jeremy was recovered. He sat up in bed, smiling
mischievously, his dark hair as thick as Rina's, damp
from the bath. He wore new blue pajamas of the softest
flannel that exactly matched the piercing blue of his eyes.

"Messengered over from Nightingale's this afternoon,"
Rina said, straightening the collar of the pajama top and

jerking her hand away to avoid his playful slap of protest. "Cynthia works fast."

"She probably called in the order on her way to the airport," Jen guessed.

She imagined Cynthia leaning back against the leather seat of the town car, cradling her phone as she told her assistant Jeremy's size, specified the color, spelled out the name and address. Capable, organized Cynthia, present even in her absence. They looked at her gift approvingly. Soon, they all knew, they would talk about her, about her and Eric. They would press Jen for details about their meeting and struggle to fit the jagged piece of information into the puzzle they could not complete.

They, too, had brought offerings. Elizabeth presented Jeremy with a model airplane kit and she watched as he assembled the pieces on his bed tray. Deftly, he arranged the wings, puzzled over the tail. Elizabeth put a piece of the flimsy balsa wood into place and smiled wistfully. Adam would never be able to assemble a model plane. All that the new expensive therapy program promised, and even that promise was carefully tentative, was a "semblance of normalcy." The construction of a model plane was probably far beyond the expectations of that "semblance."

Donna had brought a meatball casserole, which they ate from paper plates. Rina poured the red wine that was Jen's gift into plastic cups, and they toasted themselves and Jeremy.

"And a toast to Ray," Rina said. "He was great."

"To Ray," they said in unison, and Jeremy called from the next room, "Who's Ray? I don't know Ray. Can I have some wine?"

They all laughed.

"Ray is Donna's friend, the nice doctor who took care of you," Rina called back. "And you know very well you can't have any wine. Drink your juice."

She refilled her glass and turned back to her friends. "I guess he's almost fully recovered. This is really good wine, Jen."

"Actually, it's from Ian. A peace offering. We had words because I had agreed to let Cynthia and Eric meet at our loft, and I guess he felt badly about giving me a hard time. He was painting a snowscape and he lost the light when he left."

Jen swirled her own wine, thinking of Ian's rueful smile when he returned to the loft carrying the gaily wrapped bottle.

"I was wrong," he had said, holding her close, and she had lifted her hand to his face gesturing forgiveness.

"It won't happen again," he had added, but she had not replied.

She had grown up in a home where such promises were made on a daily basis by both her father and her mother but never kept. Still, Ian's tone had been determined, his eyes soft with regret. He understood what was at stake. Jen, weak with relief, faint with gratitude, had hugged him.

"Poor Ian," Elizabeth muttered sarcastically.

Jen shot her sister an angry glance but said nothing.

"How did Cynthia and Eric seem?" Trish asked, distributing the pastries she had brought.

"They were okay," Jen said. "At least they seemed okay. It was a little weird. Weird for me. They acted almost as though nothing had happened between them. It was all very civilized. They were concerned about the twins and they were concerned about each other."

"The prince and princess of grace and civility," Elizabeth said, and, too swiftly, apologized for the harshness of her words. "I'm sorry. I was just thinking of how it would be if Bert and I ever had to have such a discussion in such a situation. But it doesn't really bear thinking about."

They were silent. They knew the strains in Elizabeth's marriage; they pitied her because she was Bert's wife and Adam's mother. They understood that she armed herself with arrows of anger, that her stringent sarcasm was a shield against their sympathy and her own melancholy. They excused her, they valued her opinions, admired the sharpness of her insights, but they did not like her. Jen, looking at her sister, wished with a sudden intensity that it had been Elizabeth and not Cynthia who had announced the dissolution of her marriage. They would not have had to guess at the reasons.

"So you think that things are better between them, that they might get back together?" Donna asked.

"I don't know," Jen answered impatiently. "If we don't know why they split, how can we have any idea of whether they'll reconcile? I only know that I think about it too damn much. We all do."

"I've wondered about that myself," Trish said. "I guess if I were doing a clinical evaluation, I'd say that we were all engaged in transference of a kind."

"Transference?" Elizabeth asked sharply.

"Yes. I mean, we've probably transferred a lot of our own anxieties onto Cynthia's situation. Maybe, in a kind of projection even imagined ourselves as Cynthia. A game of trading places. I'll be very honest. That's what I found myself doing."

"You mean Cynthia and Eric became Trish and Jason?" Jen's question was hesitant, but she had recognized the truth in Trish's words. In a way she, too, had traded places. She had, often enough over the past months, weighed Ian's actions on the mysterious scales of Cynthia's judgment. That was why she had, at last, let Ian feel her resentment, her anger. But how could those scales be balanced if she did not know what Eric had done? She took up an empty paper plate, plucked one of Jeremy's crayons from the floor and idly drew a series of stick figures, men and women holding hands in a circle, the female figures facing one way, the males the other. She thought about her cartoon drawings of "The Lottery." She wondered why it was that she had never shown them to Ian. Probably because she feared his criticism. She would study them when she got home, perhaps work on them again. And she just might show them to him.

"I think you're wrong, Trish," Donna said quietly. "I think our fascination is rooted in something entirely different. Having Cynthia in our book group was sort of like having the homecoming queen in your college sorority. You wanted to be close to the girl everyone wanted to claim as a friend because she had everything. She was beautiful, that was a given, but somehow the homecoming queen was also a terrific student, dean's list and Phi Bet—at least that's the way it was at our university. Remember, Rina?"

Rina nodded.

"And she was rich to boot. Our queens always seemed to have very thin, aristocratic-looking parents who drove long, sleek, late-model cars. The queen wore real pearls and had a drawer full of cashmere sweater sets." She smiled, went to the bedroom door to check on Jeremy. He had fallen asleep and she gently moved the model airplane pieces onto his bedside table, switched off the light and closed the door.

"Were the sweaters all pastel colored?" Trish asked.

"They were. And of course, she was pinned. Usually to the president of the student union, who was also handsome and brilliant. No wonder everyone wanted to sit next to her in the cafeteria or walk home with her from the library or be in her study group. Some of the charm in her life might rub off," Donna continued.

"And Cynthia is our book group's homecoming queen," Elizabeth agreed, her voice flat. "She has the life that all of us would want."

"Had. Had the life," Donna corrected her. "But yes. She was the homecoming queen of our adult life. Beautiful, smart as a whip, great marriage, great job, great kids, great house. See the society pages for additional information."

"Great money," Rina contributed, and they all laughed.

"Yeah. Great money. And to top it off she's a great friend. A great friend to all of us."

"With great taste in boy's pajamas," Rina said, and again they laughed.

"She sort of brought us into her glamorous life. At least halfway in. We got invitations to Eric's openings, to events at Nightingale's, presents from her trips to the Adriatic and the Caribbean. There was her Christmas Eve party. It was even a perk to spot her picture in the Styles section on Sunday mornings and say, 'Hey, she's my friend.' We sort of lived vicariously through her. I'll be as honest as Trish. I did just that. In fantasy, I turned my life into hers. It was *me* jetting off to the Riviera. It was *me* living in that great house, arranging yellow roses in copper bowls before going to my gorgeous office. It was *me* having it all. Maybe that's what Trish calls transference," Donna continued.

"No," Trish protested. "It's not."

"But go on, Donna. I like your thesis better than Trish's," Rina said lightly.

"So then Cynthia tells us that she's asked Eric to leave and, in a way, the whole house of cards comes tumbling down. We're disappointed. Maybe we even feel betrayed. Like finding out that the homecoming queen wore falsies and cheated on her exams. In a way we sort of have vested interest in wanting to know why it happened. And we're a little frightened, too. If it happened to Cynthia, it could happen to us. Any relationship could shatter. Tim, who's tired of hearing about it, even turned it into a kind of ballad." She laughed and imitated Tim's soft croon. "'What did he do to make her say what she said?' So yes," she went on, "we are a little obsessed with it. But I don't think we have to be ashamed. It's not a malicious obsession." She leaned back, as though exhausted.

Her own words had surprised her. It was unusual for her to speak at such length, with such intensity. From childhood on, she had cultivated an internal quiet, a self-imposed calm, that enabled her to be gentle to her constantly agitated father and work beside her mother in companionable silence. Together, in that very clean kitchen with its latched door, they had diced and chopped and stirred, listening all the while to the mellifluous voices reading from the novels that sustained them. Their thoughts had seldom overflowed into speech, perhaps because they feared to give them voice.

Speaking to her friends with such honesty was different. She took courage from the intellectual intimacy they had shared, from the honesty of their exchanges over the years. She thought suddenly of the book group in Tehran. As she read Nafisi's book, she had realized that it was not the danger and cruelty of their lives that moved her, but the emotional support they offered one another. Different as they were from her friends, different as their lives were, they shared a commonality. They, too, had speculated about one another's secrets and puzzled over the personal revelations that filtered through their discussions of Henry James and Jane Austen. They, too, understood and forgave one another's weaknesses and welcomed an honesty that did not seek to wound.

"I think you're right, Donna," Jen said. "But you left something out. I think everyone must have been jealous of the prom queen. You didn't say anything about our envying Cynthia."

"But we did. Donna didn't have to say it. We all know that it's true," Elizabeth interjected. "How could we have helped envying her? She had everything. She still has more than some of us do." Bitterness encased her words. Cynthia had healthy children. And if her children were ill she could easily afford treatment. Of course she had envied Cynthia.

"But no one, no one in this room, is taking delight in what's going on now between her and Eric." Trish looked at each of them in turn and each of them nodded. "There's no schadenfreude here. I guess we can congratulate ourselves on that."

"Even if our curiosity can't be contained," Jen said, turning the paper plate over and tossing the crayon aside. "I guess I agree with Trish and Donna both. We—or at least me—I'm caught up in a combo of transference and prom-queen syndrome. Even though my art school never had a prom queen."

"You don't have to know a prom queen to envy her," Rina said, and they all laughed.

It was Trish who declared a moratorium on all further discussion of Cynthia and Eric.

Their conversation drifted then into plans for the winter holidays. Elizabeth and Bert had been invited to visit friends in Vermont but Elizabeth was wary about being so far away from Adam.

"Vermont isn't the South Pole," Jen said. "Go for it, Elizabeth. Action is a great antidote for envy."

They looked at her curiously. She seldom challenged her sister. It surprised them that Elizabeth did not respond with a verbal attack but sat very still, her back held straight as always.

"Actually we're waiting for a call from Adam's new therapist right now. He's on this new program and they think it might help him to adjust if Bert and I didn't visit for a while so, depending on what they recommend, we might actually go to Vermont," she said. "Of course, that means my mother would be alone over Christmas."

"*Our* mother," Jen corrected. "And if you and Bert go away I'll schedule whatever I decide to do so that I'll be at the home on Christmas Eve. Not that Mommy dearest was ever big on Christmas merriment."

Jen herself was thinking about a couple of days in Mexico if she could swing it, she told them. "I'd take the sketches for 'The Lottery' down there and work on them and I've got a brochure to design for some foundation that I could do. I have this fantasy about working in the sun just for a couple of days."

She did not mention Ian and no one asked about him. Slowly, deliberately, she tore the paper plate on which she had been doodling in half.

Trish and Jason had found a child-friendly cruise to the Caribbean.

"We're kind of programming ourselves to get away, to have fun. To stockpile good times. And it's working. We're easing ourselves out of the rut we were in," she said.

They nodded. They did not have to ask when Trish had recognized that she and Jason were in a rut and what had motivated her to work her way free. They had all experienced the same wake-up call.

Donna thought that she might go to a bluegrass festival in Florida with Tim.

"It's at some spa in the Keys and I've never been to the Keys. Or to a spa, for that matter."

"Would you mind then if I invited Ray over for Hanukkah? I'm thinking of having a small party, a couple of Jeremy's classmates and their parents," Rina said. "It would be a way of thanking him. He was so great with Jeremy."

"No, of course I wouldn't mind," Donna said quietly. That would be okay. That would be terrific. Neither Ray nor Rina celebrated Christmas, and Hanukkah was probably important to each of them despite the fact that they had each told her in turn that they were not "seriously Jewish." "Sure. Have a terrific party. I even have some latke recipes I could give you."

Trish stared at her. She thought Donna's calm deceptive. She worked closely with Donna at the hospital and she recognized the almost imperceptible change in her tone, the slight edge in her voice that signified mild annoyance. But annoyance never morphed into irritation or anger. It occurred to her that, even in the most frenetic of situations, she had never seen Donna lose her temper. Her serenity, in fact, had been noticed by the floor nurses who affectionately referred to her as "Madonna." She watched as Donna carried her casserole dish to the sink and concentrated on washing it. Swiftly then, she changed the topic.

"Listen, wherever we are—Mexico, Vermont, the Caribbean—finish the books for the next meeting," she said. "Although *Lolita* isn't exactly holiday reading."

"Since when are we into seasonal correctness?" Rina asked.

She yawned and they looked at their watches, startled by the lateness of the hour.

They shrugged into their coats, rummaged in their purses for their Metrocards. Trish's cell phone rang and she assured Jason that she was on her way home. Donna put her empty casserole dish into a plastic shopping bag. It was not large enough, and Rina handed her a bedraggled Saks Fifth Avenue bag, shaking loose a scrap of paper that fell to the floor. Donna picked it up. It was a receipt for a black leather handbag. She shook her head wearily. They had known each other so long that Rina neither surprised nor disappointed her but she did remain a puzzlement. It occurred to her that she should tell Ray that Rina occasionally imposed fantasy on reality, but she dismissed the thought. They were all adults. They were not her responsibility. And why would Ray care, why would she even think that he would care? She crumbled the receipt, self-exonerated but aware of a new and elusive sadness that slowed her movements as she shrugged into her heavy winter coat and tucked her long fair hair into her beret.

Elizabeth called Bert, and although she spoke very softly into the phone they heard her mention Adam's name once and then again.

"Did the therapist say anything else about Adam, Bert? How is Adam reacting?" The son who could not meet their eyes was always on their minds.

She hung up and Jen handed her her coat, held out the coral scarf that Elizabeth wrapped too tightly about her neck.

"Good night, Rina."

Their farewells were a chorus of affection, her response lilting and grateful.

"Thanks so much for coming. And thanks for all the goodies."

"Take care."

"Love to Jeremy. Tell him no more headaches."

Rina stood in the doorway and waved as they laughingly crowded their way into the waiting elevator. The phone rang and she hurried inside to answer it.

"Oh, he's better. So much better. Thanks for calling, Ray."

She smiled as she hung up and went into the bedroom where Jeremy slept, his brow cool, his breathing steady. She touched his head and gently entwined a circlet of his dark silken hair about her fingers. For the first time in years, she felt a flutter of happiness.

Chapter Six

Trish hated January. It was the month when abandoned Christmas trees, their branches stripped and dry, were dumped atop the graying snowdrifts that lined the sidewalks. Tall garbage pails overflowed with the soggy cartons that had contained oversize plastic toys. Flattened gift boxes, spattered with coffee grounds and tomato stains, formed awkward curbside pyramids. The brief elation of the holiday season had been punctured and pedestrians trudged through murky puddles with their heads bent low against the wind. In January, darkness came too early and the workday ended too slowly. In the office windows of tall buildings, fluorescent bulbs emitted artificially bright promises of warmth and welcome, but those who stared impassively at computer screens and answered ringing telephones were not fooled.

Pale women drew the drapes of their windows closed, as though to protect their homes from the threat of cold and darkness. Children sat too close to television sets and quarreled. They were tired. They were bored. The days were long and the weeks even longer. It was a month unpunctuated by expectations. There would be no holidays; nothing would break the monotony of winter's chill. January's cruelty was unnerving, freezing memory, dulling desire.

Trish's calendar was crowded. January was the month when disappointment simmered to a boil, when misery congealed in overheated rooms. Depressed patients called for emergency appointments. Bits of Kleenex, shredded by weeping women, littered her desk after each therapy session. They were not understood. They would never be understood. Men smashed their fists against the arms of her leather armchairs, slammed the door as they left her office, furious that their misery had not been diluted, that renegade rages had not been magically harnessed. She had no silver bullets to offer them, but she wrote prescriptions for Paxil and Zoloft and Prozac in the neat script she had been taught in her rural school, whose graduates had been expected to apply for jobs with letters written in their own hand.

She talked quietly to the adolescent girls who could not remain seated during therapy sessions, but roamed the room nervously, picking up books and magazines and setting them down. They stared out the window and turned abruptly to again sit opposite her, their faces blanched, their hands trembling. She did not ask them about the thoughts that crowded their minds as they looked down at the windswept street. She thought it likely that they had been wondering if they would sail with feathery lightness through the gray air, into the beckoning abyss of the nothingness they struggled to describe to her. Many of them were thin, almost skeletal. Fragile wrist bones shone through thin layers of pink flesh, more often than not braceleted with the welts of slowly healing scars.

Bitterness tinged voices that often did not rise above a whisper. Their holidays had sucked. Their lives sucked. They would starve themselves into death. She struggled to find the words to corral them back into life, and in the end, she surrendered and offered them pills that more often than not, they did not take.

"I hate January," a girl on leave of absence from Barnard screamed. Her voice shrilled with anger and discontent. Trish thought of Nabokov's description of Lolita's voice, the nymphet's preadolescent wail.

"I hate January, too," Trish said, a professional breach that resulted in a professional breakthrough. The girl wept. Words poured forth. Trish extended the therapeutic hour and was late for her lunch date with Donna.

"I hate January," she repeated as she slipped into the seat opposite her friend in the hospital cafeteria. "The suicide rate probably doubles. Admissions skyrocket. My phone doesn't stop ringing."

"Seasonal affective disorder," Donna replied calmly. "Has anyone ever done a study comparing the rate of depression in cold climates as opposed to warmer ones?"

"I'm sure they have. And if they haven't, there's a grant proposal for such a study on the desk of some foundation executive even as we speak." Trish bit into her chicken salad sandwich. "Anyway, I'm glad the book group's meeting at our place this month. It gives me something to focus on, something to take my mind off my patient load. Although actually, reading about Lolita is a kind of clinical experience."

"It should be an interesting meeting," Donna said. "Talking about *Lolita* in Manhattan is going to be a lot different from talking about *Lolita* in Tehran."

"You finished both books?" Trish asked.

Donna nodded. She had read both paperback volumes lying on the pearl-white beach of Sunset Key, her fingers shadowing the pages ablaze with sunlight. It was a luxury to read and think and read again, occasionally dozing off into a sweet, brief sleep. She had allowed Tim to lead her into the ocean, had danced through the waves with him, but plucked up her book again, not even bothering to towel herself dry, indifferent to the imprint left on the thin paper by her dripping fingers. Both books had engrossed her, carried her deep inside of herself. She had particularly liked *Reading Lolita in Tehran,* the author's account of a clandestine book group, young women who had studied literature with her at the university and then convened in her living room, a daring salon of intellectual protest.

Once during that vacation she had called Ray but he had not been at home and she had not left a message. The next day she had dialed Rina's number but hung up before the phone even rang.

"I think probably everyone did the reading," she said. "Jen said she finished both books before New Year's and then went back and read them again. She told me that Elizabeth wasn't crazy about the Nabokov. I don't know about Cynthia, but probably she's finished them, in between decorating the house, wrapping gifts, cooking a gourmet dinner and probably negotiating with Eric about who got to spend the holidays with the kids. And, of course, remaining in touch with her office every hour. You know Cynthia. She gets everything done."

"Prom queens always do. Maybe because they have so many ladies in waiting," Trish teased. "Not that fat Mae or that au pair with the pierced belly button would qualify as ladies in waiting."

Donna laughed.

"I'm going to be haunted by that analogy forever, I suppose."

"That's because it was pretty accurate. It's the accurate insights that endure. First lesson of analytic training. No. Not first. Maybe second or third. Have you spoken to Rina?"

"Briefly. Very briefly. Jeremy's good. Fully recovered. One of those fluke infections, Ray thinks." Donna answered with her usual calm, but Trish sensed a remoteness.

"And Ray, how is he?" she asked cautiously.

"He's fine. Of course he's fine." A defensive note edged her voice, and she hesitated as though she would say more but instead busied herself piling their dishes on a tray. "I have to get going. I'm meeting with the dialysis nurses. New nutrition guidelines. Trish, I'm writing a grant proposal myself. Would you have time to look at it?"

"No problem."

Trish watched as Donna walked through the cafeteria, her gait unhurried, her soft hips swaying. Her white lab coat was immaculate and she had sculpted her thick blond hair into a loose chignon that rested easily on the nape of her neck. As always she had been calm and unflustered but strangely reticent. She reflected that Donna had said very little about Tim and almost nothing at all about Ray. But then, neither had she herself spoken of Jason and Amanda. Words did not come easy in January. Bitterly she blamed the month. They were all turned inward on themselves.

She took out a pad and thought about a menu for the book club dinner. Something different, something complicated and colorful enough to offset the bleakness of the season. Bouillabaisse. The very word intrigued her, diverted her thoughts from weeping girls and snow-bound streets.

The meeting was scheduled for a Monday evening. Trish, Jason and Mandy spent Saturday happily shopping. It was the sort of excursion Trish had made a conscious effort to arrange over the past several months.

"We have to learn to have fun together," she had told Jason.

"Can fun be programmed, written into a prospectus?" he had asked warily. "You could write a therapist's guide—*The Family that Plays Together Stays Together* and I could market it. Come on, Trish. I don't think we have to schedule any artificial togetherness."

"We have to try something different," she had insisted stubbornly, and in the end, he had agreed. They did not speak of Cynthia and Eric's separation, but it hung between them like a shadowy scrim, an ominous reminder of hidden dangers. Like homeowners who install burglar alarms after a neighbor has been robbed, they put new protective programs into place, newly aware of their own vulnerability.

They concentrated. They each worked less and made plans that included Amanda. The search for a new apartment, a new country house, carefully planned, morphed into engaging adventures. They cooked together as they had during the early days of their marriage, admitting Amanda into their fun, encouraging her to shape dumplings, to stir sweet and sticky mixtures. Trish arranged for more household help. Irene, a competent Finnish woman was pleased to relieve the babysitter in the late afternoon and do light housework and cooking. Jason cut his travel schedule. And, to their shared surprise, it was working. Slowly a new ease had evolved between them and Amanda, too, seemed happier. She no longer awakened fitfully in the middle of the night, her small voice squeaky with terror, her tiny body tense. The Caribbean cruise over the Christmas holiday had both relaxed and excited them. The memories of the golden days at sea, of the long hours spent reading on deck, cushioned Trish against the harshness of winter's chill, helped her to race against the depression that threatened to overtake her in the dark and sober month of the year's beginning.

A skilled diagnostician of her own symptoms, always remembering the alienation she had felt as a child and the sadness and uncertainty of her student years, she struggled to counteract her incipient depression. She organized the weekend to combat her encroaching sadness and focused her attention on the book group. She was impatient to see her friends again, to exchange stories of their winter getaways, to wryly chronicle the annoyances and amusements of the weeks gone by.

It occurred to her, as she analyzed her melancholy and her corresponding eagerness to sit in a circle of friends in her lamp-lit living room, book groups were not unlike the consciousness-raising groups of the early days of feminism. Those hours during which ideas and insights were traded with passion and honesty represented a refuge of a kind, a safe haven where anything and everything could be discussed. Holding their books and notebooks, fortified by food and friendship, they could say anything without fear of rejection or ridicule. The lives of writers and their fictional characters expanded their own horizons, added new dimensions to their self-awareness. Trish found herself anticipating the meeting with an almost childish excitement, happily scheduling her preparations, drawing up marketing lists, checking her spice rack late at night for ingredients that suddenly occurred to her.

"We'll shop on Saturday," she told Jason and Amanda, "and cook on Sunday."

"And I'll help," Amanda agreed enthusiastically. "I'll shop. I'll cook."

"We'll all shop. We'll all cook," Jason said.

Trish's enthusiasm was contagious.

That Saturday they traveled down to Fulton Street and wandered through the fish market, laughing as Amanda held her nose against the odors, smiling when she admired the heaps of shining mackerel, their gills flashing silver against the hillocks of ice chips on which they were displayed.

"Look, Mommy, their skin is like *jools,*" she cried.

Her mispronunciation delighted them. Trish hugged her and allowed her to slide smooth white slices of lemon sole onto layers of newspaper as she herself selected firm-fleshed, gelatinous halibut steaks and a long sheet of winter flounder. Jason added a small pollock and the fishmonger tossed in two large lemons. Amanda sniffed her fingers and grimaced, and they laughed as they each wiped one small hand with tissues plucked from their pockets.

Trish was amused to note that they had, without intent, dressed alike that morning in worn jeans, heavy sweaters and padded jackets. She had jammed a red

woolen cap over the thick, slowly silvering dark hair a
Madison Avenue stylist (Cynthia's own hairdresser) had
so laboriously fashioned into a layered cut. Her own indifference to fashion pleased her.

"Lobster?" Jason asked. "I remember that Cynthia
made it with lobster."

"No lobster," she decided. "I'm not Cynthia."

Cynthia of course had opted for the shellfish that
added color and glamour to the simple dish, exotic in
New York but a staple of the fisherman's diet, but then
Cynthia had merely selected the recipe. It would have
been Mae who had done the cooking for the Anders's dinner party at which they had eaten the bouillabaisse. And,
of course Cynthia would not have shopped for the fish,
although she might have phoned the order into Citarella.

Trish tried to imagine Cynthia and Eric, with the twins
trailing behind them, moving through the teeming Fulton fish market, jostled by crowds of shoppers. Cynthia
would be casually elegant in a loose coat and a long
woolen scarf, walking slightly ahead of Eric. She imagined
him in his soft leather jacket and Italian boots and the
twins in matching slickers and bright red duck shoes. She
shook her head. The image would not hold. The Anders
family was too elegant to slosh through sawdust rank
with the blood and guts of eviscerated fish. The twins,
pampered little girls who played their Suzuki violins in
flower-filled rooms, would whine. Cynthia would pull her
scarf over her hair to protect it from the shower of shimmering fish scales that skittered through the fetid air.

Eric might study the scene with the shrewd observation of a professional filmmaker, interested but unsmiling.

She wondered suddenly why she was balancing her
pleasure on the unreadable scale of Cynthia's vanished

life. The thought troubled her, and as though to banish it, she pulled her own hat off and thrust it into Jason's pocket. He took her hand in his in gratitude for the small intimacy.

They went out that evening. A client of Jason's had invested in an off-Broadway show and offered him tickets, which Jason knew was not an invitation but a command.

"I'll go alone if you're tired," he offered.

"No. It might be fun," she said.

Silently, they congratulated themselves on their new determination to accommodate each other.

They took a cab down to the East Village. The play, as both Trish and Jason had anticipated, was wordy and pretentious and Jason's client and his wife stole away before the first act ended.

"No goodbye. No thanks for coming," Trish whispered.

"When you're that rich, you don't have to be polite," Jason said.

"Then I don't ever want to be that rich."

"I'll keep that in mind."

They both laughed. He ran his fingers through the layered thickness of her hair, then rested his hand on the nape of her neck, the tender gesture of their brief courtship reclaimed.

At intermission, they, too, left the theater. There was a small bistro on the same street and they went in and took a booth in the rear of the smoke-filled room. They sipped their lattes and idly observed the other patrons. A young couple sat pale and silent, their meals untouched, and then abruptly, wordlessly, the husband tossed a bill onto the table and left. His wife stared after him, her eyes filled with tears. She opened her mouth, perhaps to call to him, but no words came. Instead, she turned her attention to her omelette, finished it and pulled his plate over, eating his as well. She wiped her mouth carefully, dabbed at her eyes with the same napkin, put on her coat and glided out of the restaurant.

"January," Trish said bitterly.

She blamed the quarrel on the perversity of winter, on the wind's harsh and chilly breath of sadness.

"Husbands and wives have spats in spring and summer," Jason protested.

"And in the fall," she said, and thought of the amber-colored zinnias she had brought Cynthia as a gift on that autumn evening when their book group first convened and Cynthia dropped her bombshell. *"I am divorcing Eric," she had said.* But there had been no mention of arguments or disagreements and *spat* was not a word she would use in connection with Cynthia and Eric. It was, in fact, a rather archaic word she would not use at all, but it was amusing, even endearing, that Jason had chosen it. She smiled at him, afloat on a wave of affection, grateful that they had rediscovered each other. She supposed that for that rediscovery she owed a debt of a kind to Cynthia and Eric.

Two men at a neighboring table rose and somewhat shyly walked over to a banquette where two young women sat. Trish watched as they hovered uneasily over the small table until the women motioned them to join them. The shorter of the men blushed. Absorbed in their interaction, wondering if the four strangers might in fact become two couples, she did not notice that the table abandoned by the pale young woman was newly occupied by two men whose backs were toward her.

Jason gripped her hand.

"Trish, Eric just came in," he said. "Eric and some guy. A very young guy."

She saw that it was indeed Eric who was studying the oversize menu, his hair grown a bit longer and flecked with silver, a single irrepressible lock falling, as always, onto his high forehead. His vulpine face was leaner than she remembered. He was elegantly dressed, tan corduroy slacks, a V-necked green cashmere sweater over a soft-collared yellow shirt. His companion wore the uniform of a graduate student, faded jeans, a gray sweater, battered hiking boots. His hair, like Eric's, was pale gold in color and, like Eric's, his gray eyes were oddly long and thickly lashed. Their similarity startled Trish and she thought suddenly of a patient she had treated years ago, a young attorney who, amid his other, less interesting revelations, had told her that he could only successfully make love to a woman who closely resembled him, a woman who shared both his coloring and his facial characteristics.

"The epitome of narcissism," Trish's training analyst told her when she went to him for a consult. "A man who wants to make love to himself."

But she had never noticed any narcissistic tendencies in Eric and, she told herself firmly, it was ridiculous to conclude that the younger man was Eric's lover. Two men having dinner together did not a homosexual relationship make. That would be a new height of homophobia. But even as the thought and counter-thought fluttered through her mind, Eric closed the menu and rested his hand on his companion's shoulder.

"What do we do?" Jason asked anxiously.

He considered Eric a friend. He and Trish had occasionally had dinner with Eric and Cynthia, had, for one season, shared a concert subscription. The two men, thrust together by their wives' friendship, had liked each other, and Jason had on occasion given Eric investment advice. But he had not seen Eric since his separation from Cynthia, although he had, once or twice, thought of calling him. That he had not done so shamed him. It would be cruel to ignore him now.

"I don't know. Say hello, I suppose," Trish said, but even as she spoke the waiter brought their bill and, as Jason paid it, Eric left his table and headed toward the men's room.

Without speaking, Trish and Jason, walking too rapidly, left the bistro. At the door, Trish turned and looked back at the youth who sat alone at the table, folding and refolding his paper napkin.

"Do you think…?" she asked Jason as they walked to the subway, fearful of finishing her question, knowing that he would surmise the words she left unsaid.

"I don't know what to think," he said harshly.

"It would explain everything," she murmured.

"Or nothing," he retorted with an impatience that bordered on anger. "My God, why can't you and your friends leave the whole damn situation alone. Whatever happened is Cynthia's business, Eric's business. It has nothing to do with you."

But it has everything to do with us. She thought the thought but did not say the words. She rested her hand on his arm as they made their way home locked in silence.

They made love that night swiftly and tenderly, and held each other close in a protective embrace as they drifted off to sleep.

She cooked on Sunday. Amanda perched on a stool beside her as she chopped garlic and sliced the leeks. When boredom overtook her she went to the park with Jason, who was happily compliant because a merger he had been working on for weeks had just been settled. He brandished the newly received fax as though it were a flag of triumph. Neither of them spoke of Eric.

Trish thought of calling Jen, gentle, quiescent Jen, who had the confidence of both Cynthia and Eric. She lifted the receiver and set it down again. What would be the point? What could Jen say? Was it Rina who had suggested that Eric was gay or had that simply been another conjecture that they had tossed into the melting pot of their suppositions? She could not remember.

She brought the broth to a boil, submerged the fish and added the herbs and spices, smiling as the aromatic scent of the stew filled the kitchen. Suffused with contentment, she allowed it to simmer and marveled that this new happiness of hers had been so easily attained. *Not so easily.* She corrected herself with professional objectivity. They had been frightened, she and Jason, into restructuring their lives and that fear persisted. They would not so easily abandon caution.

That night, with an exhausted Amanda safely asleep, she reread her notes on *Lolita*. The story, of course, centered on middle-aged Humbert Humbert's obsessive sexual fixation on the preadolescent Lolita and their trans-American odyssey. Still, Trish found herself strangely sympathetic to Charlotte Haze, the nymphet Lolita's mother. Poor, repressed, striving Charlotte. The Tehran readers, so repressed and striving themselves, should have understood her, but Charlotte seemed not to have interested them at all. Trish wondered if Charlotte, killed off so conveniently by Nabokov, would engage the imaginations of her own group. She made a checklist in anticipation of their reactions. Donna. Jen. Elizabeth. Rina. *Cynthia.*

She underlined Cynthia's name once and then again. She wondered, not for the first time, if it had been insensitive of them to have selected *Lolita,* given their conjectures about Eric. She acknowledged that it was entirely possible that a subconscious perversity had led them to that selection. She thought of Eric, his hand resting on the shoulder of the sullen young man as they sat together in the dimly lit bistro and she scowled at her own thought. Stupid to equate Eric with Humbert. The comparison was ludicrous.

"Well, at least we didn't choose *Maurice,*" she said aloud, remembering her shock as an undergraduate, when she first read the Forster novel with its graphic and erotic descriptions of male homosexuality. Smiling at the naive girl she had been, she closed the books and placed them, with her notes, in readiness on the end table.

"What did you say?" Jason called from the bathroom.

"Nothing."

She shrugged, switched off her lamp and went into the bedroom where Jason, his face wind-ruddied, his newly gray hair still damp from the shower, waited for her.

It was the aroma of the bouillabaisse that wafted toward her when Trish arrived home the next day. The fragrance immediately canceled out the tensions of the afternoon, her rush to dictate patient evaluations, her too swift and perhaps too peremptory conversation with the mother of the Barnard girl, her irritation with a resident who misunderstood a directive. She had been determined to escape the hospital early that day and she had succeeded. She would remedy everything tomorrow, but tonight there would be a terrific meal, gossipy catch-ups and a literary escape into the unfamiliar worlds created by Nabokov and Nafisi.

She would draw the drapes against the wintry darkness, and seated in the brightly lit living room, she and her friends would follow their sister readers on a distant continent through the threatening streets of Tehran. Like those Iranian women, they would insinuate themselves into the dark fantasies and darker actions of Humbert Humbert. She felt an anticipatory thrill of intellectual excitement and a guilty pleasure in the knowledge that Amanda was spending the night at a playmate's home and Jason had a late meeting. The evening was entirely her own.

"Thanks for heating the stew, Irene," she called to the pleasant, florid-faced housekeeper who was running the vacuum in the living room. She congratulated herself on hiring Irene. She should have followed Cynthia's lead and done it long ago.

She set her purchases down on the kitchen counter, breathing in the mingled odors of the long-stemmed yellow roses and the freshly baked baguettes. As Irene set the table, Trish made a large green salad, sliced the long French bread and separated the flowers into two vases, which she placed in the living room. It had intrigued her that despite all the uncertainty and unpleasantness of life in a city controlled by Islamic fundamentalists, Azar Nafisi always welcomed her reading group into a home redolent with the fragrance of freshly cut flowers. It was touching, too, that her students, no matter how fearful or anxious they were, never failed to bring sweet pastries to their meetings.

It was Cynthia who would bring the pastries that night. She had called Trish earlier in the day to volunteer.

"I will be like a Tehran maiden, arriving with my box of éclairs," she had said, and they had both laughed briefly.

"Poor girls," Cynthia said.

"Poor girls," Trish agreed.

Trish had wondered if Cynthia compared the sadness in her own life with the sadness that had adhered to the young women who had been forced to veil their faces, to conceal their hair beneath dark scarves and hide their bodies in the folds of heavy robes. But misery, of course, was not relative. A mourner was not consoled by losses others had sustained. Cynthia's sadness was her own, as overwhelming to her as the sadness and suffering of a woman in Tehran whose husband beat her or her friend who had been abandoned by her lover.

"Do you want me to stay and help you to serve and wash up?" Irene asked.

"No. But thank you, anyway," Trish said. "I'll see you at the end of the week."

It would have been nice to have Irene's help, but she wanted to be alone with her friends, to claim sole dominion, for that one evening, over her home.

"It's what I love about my life," Donna had said that day at lunch. "When I close the door to my apartment I'm alone and free." Trish had felt a twinge of envy. Solitude eluded women with husbands and children. Their homes were seldom their own. There was no space that was exempt from invasion.

"Have a nice party," Irene said wistfully, and closed the front door softly behind her.

Trish knew that Irene's husband worked the night shift, that her children were grown and her evenings were long and lonely. And, of course, she could use the extra money. Trish felt sorry for her as she had felt sorry for Tahereh Khanoom, the servant who had padded through Nafisi's Tehran apartment in slippered feet, and for Louise, the maid who cleaned Charlotte Haze's home three times a week, picking up after Lolita, scraping plates left too long unwashed. There had been no mention of Tahereh Khanoom's fate after Nafisi's departure for America. Louise had vanished from Nabokov's narrative after Charlotte's death.

Trish thought of efficient, sullen Mae, who moved through Cynthia's East Side town house in the sneakers that matched her track suits, preparing meals, straightening bedclothes. Mae, of course, knew Cynthia's secrets, exercised dominion over her home, but Mae, too, was expendable. In life, as in literature, servants who moved soundlessly, wearing slippers or sneakers, became domestic ghosts; they disappeared without protest, carrying with them the grim secrets of households in disarray and hugging close their observations and resentments.

The doorbell rang and she hurried to answer it. Laughing and chattering, excited at being together again after the long holiday hiatus, her friends converged upon her, shedding their heavy dark winter coats, thrusting their gifts into her hands or setting them on the low table amid the requisite cheese and crackers and the small tinted wineglasses. There were pastries from Cynthia in a large white box, which Trish carried into the kitchen. Forced narcissi from Jen and Elizabeth, a paperback copy of Nabokov's *Pnin* from Rina, who boasted of discovering it in the Strand bookstore. A nacreous conch shell from Donna, who had carried it home from the Keys.

"Hold it to your ear and it sings but it doesn't sigh," Donna said teasingly. Trish had complained to her often enough about the sighs and silences of her patients.

They settled themselves in the living room. Their brightly colored sweaters, their shimmering silk scarves, formed a brave rainbow of color against Trish's beige couch and matching chairs. Their cheeks glowed pinkly as they sipped their wine, as they laughed and chattered. Donna loosened her hair. Jen kicked off her shoes. Their talk grew more and more animated; their voices were lilting and musical. January's grayness would not defeat them.

They traded vacation stories, swapped anecdotes from work, discussed holiday gatherings. Jen did a cruel parody of the Christmas Eve celebration at her mother's old age home.

"Two old ladies on walkers, two old men in wheelchairs and our mother, front-runner in the misery sweepstakes, all gathered around a skinny tree decorated by obese Girl Scouts who couldn't get the lights to work and who didn't know the words to a single carol. And of course it was our dear and gentle mother who finally said to them, 'Go home, girls. We're deaf, anyway. And take your cookies with you. We're all diabetic.'"

They all laughed, even Elizabeth, who shook her head ruefully.

"Come on, Jen, be nice," she coaxed, the elder sister setting standards.

"I don't have to be nice. I was there. That earned me the right to be nasty," Jen retorted, but she grinned as she refilled her wineglass. "It also earned me the right to go to Mexico with a clear conscience."

"And Ian survived," Elizabeth observed dryly.

"I never doubted that he would. He even got a lot of work done. His show may become a reality. Hey, how did your Hanukkah do go, Rina? Let's be a little ecumenical here." Jen turned to Rina.

"It was fun. Jeremy liked it. It was a first for me. I even had to borrow a menorah," Rina replied. "But it was good to reconnect with a past that really was mine." She fingered her long braid, toyed with the wooden buttons of her buttercup-yellow cardigan.

Donna looked at her sharply. She had never before heard Rina acknowledge her propensity for reinventing herself, for disconnecting and reconnecting. "Ray said he had a very good time," she said, keeping her tone light, busying herself with rearranging the crackers.

He had, in fact, said more than that. He had taken Donna to dinner at the very good small French restaurant they had often frequented and told her that he had seen Rina several times during the vacation, that he had enjoyed being with her, that he found her interesting.

"And Jeremy's a wonderful kid," he had added.

Donna knew and had always known that Ray lusted for the fatherhood his ex-wife, concerned about her figure and worried about pain, had denied him.

"Rina's a very interesting gal," Donna had agreed.

"And a terrific mother."

"Yes. A terrific mother."

They looked sadly at each other, acknowledging words unsaid.

When he took her home he had not come in nor had he kissed her good-night. He had, instead, pressed his hand gently against her cheek, a gesture of affection and, she knew, of farewell. She was saddened but not surprised. She wondered how it was that she could so deeply feel the loss of that which she had never really wanted. She and Ray had recognized from the outset that they provided comfort and companionship for each other and very little else. *And yet. And yet.* She could not articulate her sadness.

"Yes, he seemed to." Rina blushed and averted her eyes. She and Donna would have to talk soon, very soon.

The others swirled their wine. The muted exchange between Rina and Donna unsettled them. They were newly initiated into the fragility of friendship, the impermanence of love; Cynthia and Eric's vulnerability had rendered them all vulnerable. They foraged for scraps of conversation. *Would winter ever end? The upcoming election was crazy.* They each complained about the stress of their jobs, trading war stories about superiors and subordinates. The spontaneity of their first meeting and greeting had vanished.

Trish hurried into the kitchen, checked the bouillabaisse and summoned them to the table. The brief tension dissipated as they passed their plates to her, busily buttered the chunks of baguette and ate the fragrant fish stew.

"Delicious."

"Fantastic."

"What a terrific idea, Trish."

Their enthusiasm was genuine. They were women who loved good food, who read cookbooks with pleasure and were at home at famous fictional tables—sideboard breakfasts at Henry James's English country houses, the sparse spinster dinners prepared by Barbara Pym's heroines, Philip Roth's lavish Jewish smorgasbords, Tom Jones's orgy of eating.

Flushed with pride and pleasure, Trish passed the green salad, told them how much Amanda had loved going down to the Fulton fish market, asked worriedly if she had used too much garlic.

"Just right," Cynthia assured her, soaking up the soup with the heel of the bread. "Eric always talked about taking the twins down to the market but somehow we never did."

"But maybe you will," Jen said, remembering the softness in their eyes when they met in her loft—Eric's generosity, Cynthia's gratitude.

They waited for her answer but she simply nodded and said nothing.

Disappointed, they assembled in the living room, coffee mugs in hand, their books on their laps. Trish set the pastries on a large platter and placed it on the table, cleared now of the cheese and wine.

"It's interesting, isn't it, that the women in the Tehran book group never seemed to share a meal. It was always pastry or cookies," Donna observed.

"Living such bitter lives, they probably hungered for sweetness," Elizabeth suggested, and she bit into an éclair, licking the cream that trickled out of the flaky crust. Her life, too, was bitter. She too hungered for sweetness.

Trish briefly discussed the authors of both books, emphasizing the similarities in their backgrounds.

"Both Nafisi and Nabokov were refugees. Not perhaps in the conventional sense, you know, they didn't belong to those huddled masses yearning to be free that Emma Lazarus wrote about," she said.

"And they certainly were not the wretched refuse of teeming shores," Rina added. "I tried to teach that poem and my students took it personally. They're mostly immigrants or the children of immigrants, but no way do they consider themselves part of the huddled masses or the wretched refuse."

"Poor Emma Lazarus, politically incorrect by today's standards. Anyway, what I meant was that both writers were refugees in the literal sense, even though they were kind of aristocratic," Trish continued. "Nabokov's family were Russian gentry. Nafisi's father had been the mayor of Tehran, her mother a member of the parliament. They each took refuge in this country from repressive regimes in the lands of their birth. Nabokov fled the Bolsheviks, she fled the Ayatollah. They both became academics and both of them were fascinated by the United States and American culture. Lolita is a kind of travelogue, cross-country journeys from Pennsylvania to the West, a literary window on American high school culture, the provinciality of small-town life, weird motels and weirder families, all of it one hundred percent American. Nafisi chooses Lolita for her reading group because it's a book that's going to catapult them into honesty, into a recognition that even by daring to meet in secret they were not unlike Lolita who, in a typically American way, broke all the rules and then some."

"What about the other books they discussed?" Elizabeth asked. "*The Great Gatsby, Daisy Miller* and Jane Austen, the one non-American writer she chose. I take it you're thinking of Nabokov as an American?"

"I think that *Lolita* is a quintessentially American novel," Trish agreed, and they all nodded.

"But in a way it's not even a novel. It's more like a fairy tale," Jen said. "Nabokov himself said that every great novel is a fairy tale, good fighting evil, the innocent in need of protection, evil witches and beneficent godmothers. Nafisi even quotes him."

"Then in the same way every life is a fairy tale," Cynthia interjected, her voice so soft that they leaned close to catch her words. "We're all caught between good and evil. We all want to protect the innocent. And sometimes it's hard to know just how to do that. Could Lolita have been protected? Could the girl in the Tehran book group who goes off on vacation with her friends and is detained and forced to submit to sexual examinations have been protected? Can we even protect our own children? All we can do is try and sometimes the effort that we make is wrong."

Anguish threaded her voice. Each word was wrenched loose from the stubborn sorrow, the terrible uncertainty, that rested on her heart. She bent her head and her hair fell in a fiery curtain across her face. They could not read her eyes.

"It was probably stupid of us to choose these books, Cynthia," Jen said apologetically. "Considering."

"Considering what?" Cynthia asked blankly.

They did not answer, shamed by Cynthia's bewilderment, her ignorance of their obsessive conjectures.

It was Elizabeth who broke the silence.

"Cynthia's right. We do have to try," she said. "The tragedy lies in not trying. Humbert didn't try to overcome his impulses. He didn't even think of protecting Lolita. He thought only of assaulting her. So he is as villainous as any fairy tale ogre. And so, in a way, is Charlotte, her mother, who would have sent her away, banished her from the kingdom of her home."

"But what if a decision is made and it's the wrong decision?" Rina asked hesitantly.

Cynthia, who had been turning the pages of her book looked up sharply and immediately cast her eyes down.

"Decisions can be reversed," Donna said curtly. "It happens every day. Separations and reconciliations. Codicils to established contracts. Broken leases. Lawsuits instituted and then withdrawn. Enmities reversed. Writers know that. They begin a new chapter, change an ending. If they're as lucky as Nabokov and Nafisi, they move to another city, another country, and write another book."

"Not all endings can be changed," Rina retorted. "In real life things are not always in our control." Jeremy's illness, his vulnerability and thus her own, still haunted her. Weeks after his recovery, she wakened in the night to touch his forehead, to listen to his rhythmic breathing, to bend close so that she might inhale the soapy sweetness of his skin and his hair.

"You might not understand that, Donna. Not having children. Not being married," Elizabeth said.

They forgave the aspersion. They resented her but they pitied her. They knew that her own life had careened out of control, her careful plan ambushed by Adam's autism. Donna calmly poured herself another cup of coffee.

Jen recognized the patronizing tone in her sister's voice, familiar to her from the days of their shared childhood. Elizabeth used it when she spoke to the aides and nurses at the home and, Jen assumed, when she conferred with the parents of a difficult student. Which was perhaps why the nurses and aides disliked her, preferring to talk to Jen. She waited for Donna to respond irritably, defensively.

But Donna merely smiled.

"You're right, Elizabeth," she said serenely. "Of course there are endings that can't be changed. But I'm talking about situations that can be altered. Take the girls in Nafisi's reading group. Some of them, like Nafisi herself, made choices that changed their lives. Nassrin, the youngest of them, escaped to England. Mitra went to Canada. Yassi—I love her name—is in Texas and that glamorous Azin is in California. Remember, Azin had a daughter whom she abandoned in Tehran so that she could live her own life. I think that what gave them the courage to make those choices was the books they read, their power to imagine worlds beyond their own, to use the fictional characters whom they came to know as examples of how their own lives might be changed."

"And what of the nonfictional characters, the real young women in the Tehran book group? Do they also serve as examples? Azin abandons a daughter in Tehran in order to live with her new husband in California? Can we countenance a mother's abandoning a child and call it courage?" Elizabeth asked harshly.

She was thinking, they knew, of Adam, whose needs imprisoned her in her marriage, chained her to her job. Could she abandon him and lay claim to her own life?

"There is such a thing as responsible abandonment. Azin left her daughter with her ex-husband. The child will be well cared for, and if she had stayed, he would never have allowed Azin to impart her values to her daughter. So she saved her own life. In a way she had no choice. Even Charlotte Haze, Lolita's horrible mother, intent as she was on getting Lolita out of her life, made arrangements for a boarding school education. Not an ideal arrangement but, in its own way, a responsible abandonment," Trish said. "I was wondering, last night, how some of you felt about Charlotte."

"I couldn't stand her," Cynthia said. "She was a vulgar, pretentious bitch."

"I felt sorry for her," Donna admitted. "A widow with romantic fantasies trapped in a provincial town."

"She was definitely not a fictional character who could serve as an example to those struggling young women in Tehran," Rina said. "Whereas Lolita herself could."

"Lolita? How could Lolita serve as an example? She was a victim, Humbert's victim, just as the Tehran women were the victims of the Ayatollah's henchmen," Jen protested.

"But she wasn't an acquiescent victim," Trish pointed out. "She fought back. She talked back. She was moody and foulmouthed and gave as good as she got—sometimes better. I would have liked to have had her as a patient. No passive-aggressive anorexic, our Lolita. Somewhere Nafisi discusses that. She talks about their small rebellions, allowing some hair to show, having a manicure. Small acts, but assertive."

"And what about the characters in the other books they read—Fitzgerald's *Gatsby,* James's *Daisy Miller,* Jane Austen's girls in search of suitable husbands? Would you call them courageous?" Cynthia asked softly.

They seized upon her question. Answers poured forth in an avalanche. Words atop words. They interrupted one another, apologized, interrupted again. They spun about in a whirlwind of ideas, their eyes bright, their faces flushed. As always, they reveled in the swift exchanges, exhilarated by agreements and disagreements alike. They turned pages feverishly, finding a sentence, a paragraph, to prove an argument.

"Yes, Gatsby had been courageous. A man who totally reinvented himself." Donna glanced at Rina. Rina smiled slyly and looked away.

They all had words for Gatsby.

"Tenacious in his love for Daisy," Jen said, and Trish nodded.

"A risk-taker, unafraid of consorting with criminals, unafraid of being a criminal." An odd observation from Elizabeth.

"And Daisy Miller, poor Daisy, she was really daring. An American girl bucking the snobbery of European aristocracy, courageous enough to wander into the Roman forum in the dangerous chill of evening. It might have been that she was actually courting death, which takes a certain amount of courage." Rina sighed wistfully. She had always loved Henry James's willful heroines.

"Do you think it takes courage to court death?" Donna asked softly, her color high, and Rina flinched. She cursed herself for her insensitivity and reached for her friend's hand, but Rina rose abruptly and went to stand by the window, her finger tracing its way across the damp and glistening pane.

"And then there are the Bennet sisters, so proud and prejudiced. Austen really caught them," Cynthia said. "Give me Jane Austen over Vladimir Nabokov anytime, although I have to admit he was a great observer."

They laughed, pleased with one another and with themselves. They traded favorite scenes from each of the books, the small literary gems they kept in the safe boxes of memory. Cynthia read from Nabokov's own afterward in her edition of the novel, in which he described his own favorite images, the still lifes of his imagination, the sounds that echoed in memory, his skillful evocation of elusive landscapes.

Trish brewed another pot of coffee and refilled their cups.

Their mood mellowed. Languidly, they discussed the minor characters in the books, speculated about possible alternative endings. What would have happened to Lolita if Humbert Humbert had not stumbled into her life? Rina thought she might have become a checkout girl in a supermarket. Donna, more charitably, sent her off to a junior college, where she met and married a pharmacy student.

"A nurse's aide in an old-age home," Jen said.

"Who seduces an elderly amputee," Elizabeth added in a rare burst of whimsical malice.

They all laughed.

"I'm not going to play," Cynthia said. "You know I don't like entering the kingdom of 'what ifs.'"

She uncoiled herself from the low chair, adjusted the cowl collar of her crimson sweater and peered out the window. They marveled at her daring in choosing to wear such a color given her coloring, but she had not erred. It looked terrific. The marketing director of Nightingale's would, of course, have no margin for error when it came to fashion.

"My car's downstairs. I have an early-morning conference scheduled for tomorrow. Anyone need a lift?"

They shook their heads, watched as she shrugged into her coat and hoisted her attaché case.

"Great pastries, Cynthia," Trish said.

"Loved them myself." She smiled, gracious, generous Cynthia, whose expertly applied makeup had worn off so that they could see the dark circles beneath her eyes and note the new thinness of her face. "Where will we meet next?"

"My place," said Elizabeth. "I'm pretty sure it's my turn next."

"Elizabeth's place," Trish agreed. "And we'll figure out a date. Sometime in March, I think."

She walked Cynthia to the door, kissed her on the cheek and returned to her living room, which was suddenly eerily quiet. The women sat wordlessly until they heard the elevator door open and close. Jen went to the window, saw Cynthia duck into the waiting black car and returned to the couch. Her coffee had grown cold, but she drank it, anyway, oddly pleased by its punishing bitterness. It was Trish who shattered the odd silence.

"We saw Eric last night," she said softly. "Jason and I."

"Where?" Jen asked warily.

As always Jen felt protective of Eric. She had meant to call him after her return from Mexico but somehow there had been no time. She had taken on additional work for an advertising agency and she spent long hours on the comic panels of her "Lottery" drawings. And then, too, her absence seemed to have energized Ian. He had completed another large canvas and had finally begun work on a series of watercolors based on his Rhode Island sketchbook. Plans were in place for a major exhibit and Jen fielded phone calls from the gallery owner, designed a program and answered his urgent calls to critique a work in progress.

"I feel that I'm getting to where I want to be, which means that I'm getting to where I want us to be," Ian had told her, holding her close, a new resolve mingling with his tenderness.

All that meant that there had been little enough time to visit her mother and no time at all to arrange a meeting with Eric, who had, in fact, left several messages on her answering machine. She would call him soon, she promised herself. Very soon.

"In a bistro in the West Village," Trish replied. "He was with someone. A man. A very young man."

She looked down at her hands. She had not been sure that she would share what Jason had sarcastically called her "Eric sighting" with the group, but the impulse to do so had been too strong. It would have been a betrayal of sorts if she had not told them. They were all secret sharers, all of them equally and guiltily complicit in ferreting out Cynthia's secret, a secret that was at once tantalizing and threatening.

"Men have friends of the same sex. It doesn't mean that they're gay," Jen said.

"He and Cynthia have been married for a long time. They have children. That says something about his sexuality." Rina twisted her handkerchief. She wished that Trish had remained silent. She wished that Trish had not seen Eric. Her own life was newly simplified. She did not want those of her friends to become complicated.

"And how many times do we hear about married men, some with long and supposedly happy marriages, who suddenly reveal that they're gay, that they've been living double lives?" Elizabeth asked. "Bert has a colleague, a boring man with a boring wife and three boring children who suddenly turned out not to be so boring after all. He came out of the closet, revealed that he'd been living a double life for twenty-five years, and now that his pension had vested, he was moving down to Key West with his partner. The boring wife and the boring children get the pension because the partner seems to be independently wealthy and everyone lives happily ever after. Or unhappily ever after as the case may be." She laughed harshly. She was familiar with unhappy endings.

"And there are married women who suddenly come out of the closet," Donna added. "Trish and I know a nurse at the hospital who did just that. And in today's climate no one cared."

"But probably her husband cared," Trish said. "And Cynthia would care."

"If it's true," Jen said crisply. "And it may not be. Eric could have been with a nephew, a colleague, a student from the film class he teaches. There could be any number of explanations. Look, we've all know him for years. Did any of you ever think he was gay?"

They shook their heads. They had thought him gentle. They had thought him caring and accommodating. They had thought him attractive. They had admired his career, the glamour of his life so generously shared. And they had thought him a good husband and a good father, a suitably successful consort for the prom queen.

"But then how well does anyone really know anyone else?" Donna asked. Again her gaze flitted toward Rina, her college roommate, the friend of her heart. It was Rina who had stood beside her at her mother's funeral and it was only Rina who knew how her mother had died. She remembered sitting in the hospital waiting room through the long night of Jeremy's birth, consumed with worry about Rina, whose courage she admired, whose impulsive decisions she feared, whose child she had taken to her heart.

She had baked Jeremy's birthday cakes year after year, bought his shoes, taken him to the Children's Museum. She was Aunt Donna, his mother's best friend. Yet how well did she know Rina, a friend who constantly reinvented herself, who hugged her secrets, and who now sat opposite Ray in restaurants and beside him at concerts? It was strange, she knew, how easily she had accepted the fact that her best friend and the gentle, sweet man who had been her lover were newly joined in a profound and impenetrable intimacy. How well, then, did she know herself?

In fact, did she really know the others—Cynthia and Trish, Elizabeth and Jen? Had the women in the Tehran reading group really known one another? Did the very books they read serve as shields, warding off a deeper emotional involvement? The question saddened her. She looked at her friends, who sat in reflective silence.

Slowly, one by one, they closed their books. Elizabeth, who took notes at every discussion, carefully capped her pen and put it in her bag. Trish cleared away the pastries.

"The next book?" Elizabeth asked.

"You get to choose. We're meeting at your apartment," Rina said.

"Would you mind if we read *The Bell Jar* and the *Ariel* poems?" Elizabeth asked Rina. "I know it's your turf, but I thought Sylvia Plath would make interesting winter reading."

Jen recognized the provocative slyness in her sister's question.

"I don't mind," Rina replied. "It would probably be helpful to me, if none of you object to having your insights steal into my dissertation."

"We'd be flattered," Trish said, and they all laughed.

Their mood lifted. They smiled at one another, Cynthia and Eric banished from their thoughts, and gathered up their coats and bags.

"A great meal," Donna told Trish, hugging her at the door.

"Great," they agreed in unison.

"And a terrific discussion," Jen added, and they nodded vigorously.

Jason's key turned in the lock as they stood in the doorway and they greeted him with affection and laughter. His presence was the final punctuation mark on their shared evening. He put his arm on Trish's shoulder as though to reclaim her, and husband and wife stood together in the doorway and waved as the chattering group of friends entered the elevator.

Chapter Seven

"Hi, Jen, can we watch you work?"

Jen, seated at a drawing table in the studio of Nightingale's art department, looked up and was surprised to see Cynthia's twin daughters standing in the doorway.

"Hey Liza, hey Julie, what are you doing here? No school? Or are you two playing hookey?"

The girls giggled and shook their heads vigorously, their glossy auburn ponytails bobbing up and down, Liza's held in place with a blue ribbon to match her pale blue T-shirt and Julie's gathered in a pink scrunchy the same color as her pink shirt. Jen did not have to look down to know that Liza's socks were blue and Julie's pink. Cynthia was obsessive about such details. She might not be on hand to dress her daughters in the morning, but their school outfits would always be perfectly co-ordinated. It was Cynthia's way.

"The boiler at our school broke. Mae was out shopping and Ingrid wasn't home. She's off when we're at school. So they called Mom at work and she sent a car for us and said that we could hang out here until she took us home. She told us where to find you," Liza said, beaming with the accuracy of her report. "She said you could teach us something about what you do. Because I want to be an artist."

"I don't want to be an artist but I'll watch." Julie edged closer to the drawing board and stared down at Jen's drawing.

"Great," Jen said, masking her annoyance. What was Cynthia thinking? She had called Jen, last minute (very last minute) to clean up the layout of an ad that a staff artist had messed up, and now she expected her to baby-sit. That was a first. It wasn't like Cynthia to take advantage of her—or maybe it was. After all, when Cynthia needed a project completed she needed it at once and the hell with anyone else's schedule. Maybe she had taken advantage of Eric one time too often and he, in turn, had done something vengeful and maybe, just maybe, unforgivable by Cynthia's lights. Almost at once, she acknowledged the disloyalty of the thought. Cynthia was her friend, her very good friend, and to compensate she drew the girls toward her and kissed each of them on the cheek.

"So here's what I do," she said. "I have this photograph of a couple of things your mother wants to put on sale— there's a paperweight, bookends, a candleholder. And what I have to do is arrange them and then draw a picture of my arrangement so that people reading their newspapers will see my drawing and say, 'Hey, that looks terrific. I think I'll buy that paperweight' and rush over

to Nightingale's to grab it up." As she spoke, she shuffled the photographs and then deftly sketched in three
books between the bookends, added the candleholder
with a burning taper and drew in the paperweight resting on an open book.

"Why couldn't the newspaper just show the photographs?" Liza asked.

"Why don't you do it on a computer?" Julie leaned forward. She was the more serious twin. "Why don't you
draw in a shadow? Candles glow best when there's a
shadow." She was her father's daughter. She had Eric's eye
for composition and nuance.

Jen glanced at the phone. Eric had left her two messages, his voice vaguely apologetic. She would call him
soon, before the end of the week, she promised herself.
She smiled at his daughters, noticing for the first time
that their lashes, like his, were long and curling, fiery ten-
drils that brushed their cheeks.

"You're right," Jen agreed, and added a shadow. "Your
mom wants to use a drawing instead of a photograph because she thinks a drawing will get more attention. I can
do this sort of work better by hand than I could with a
computer. And do you girls ever stop asking 'why?'"

"But there are lots of things we want to know," Julie said.
"You answered us but not everyone does. We keep asking
why about stuff, important stuff, but no one tells us."

"Like what do you keep asking?" Jen sprayed the
drawing with fixative, then pasted on the text that would
head the ad. *Let Your Desk Say Romance.* Her own desk
did not say "romance," she reflected wryly. The piles of
unfinished sketches and unpaid bills said "overload."

"Like why doesn't our dad live with us anymore. Why
did he go away?"

Both girls stared hard at Jen, their green eyes aglitter with a dangerous brightness, their color high.

"I'm sorry. That's a question you'll have to ask your mother," Jen said, and turned away.

If they wept, her own tears might fall. She thought of how different their question was from the "why" that had haunted her own childhood. *Why do they stay together? Why don't they separate?* she had asked herself when her parents' quarrels reached a frightening crescendo. She had wished them apart. She had longed for the sound of a slamming door, yearned for an irrevocable departure.

"Ask me what?" Cynthia stood in the doorway of the studio, casually elegant in her black pantsuit. She hugged her clipboard and muted the ringing cell phone that dangled from her narrow silver belt.

She glided over to the drawing board, studied Jen's drawing and smiled.

"That's what I wanted. Exactly," she said. "I hope these imps of mine didn't bother you too much."

"No. They were fine," Jen replied.

"Great. Liza, Julie, I got a hold of Mae and she'll be by to pick you up. Now, what did Jen tell you to ask me?"

"We wanted to know if we could go for ice cream," Julie said, and glanced slyly at Jen.

"Sure. I'll tell Mae that's fine. But just a single scoop each. Thank Jen."

"Thanks, Jen," they chortled in unison, and dashed out.

"And I thank you, too," Cynthia said. "Are you done for the day?"

"No. I have another meeting and then I want to get over to the bookstore to see if I can find a copy of *The Bell Jar.* I haven't even started the reading for our next meeting."

"Good luck. My secretary couldn't find it in the stores. She finally went to Amazon. I don't know why I was in such a hurry to read it. It's depressing the life out of me." Cynthia turned to go but paused suddenly.

"You thought the girls were all right, didn't you?" she asked. "They're handling the situation okay, don't you think?"

Jen hesitated.

"They seem to be coping," she said at last. "But I do think it's pretty hard on them." She would not lie and she did not know the truth.

Cynthia raised her eyebrows. It was not the answer she had anticipated. It was not the answer she wanted.

"I see," she said coldly. "Well, don't work too hard, Jen."

"I'll try not to."

But she did work hard, dashing from Nightingale's to a meeting with an art director at an ad agency who needed instant and extensive reworking of a mock-up. It was late when she finally made her way through the cobalt-tinged darkness of the late winter evening to the Strand Bookstore on Tenth Street. Happy amid the shelves of books, she wandered through the crowded store, revisiting titles read and loved, leafing through one book and then another until she finally found a battered copy of *The Bell Jar.* A copy of Plath's own journal, the pages still uncut, the poet smiling too brightly in an odd photo that showed the hand of an unseen admirer offering her a white rose, was placed next to it, and Jen hesitated before deciding to buy both books. Ten dollars was a lot for her to spend considering that money was tight again. Her Mexican trip, though closely budgeted, had been an extravagance, and the bills for her mother's care were mounting. Still, she wanted the journal. Ian's show would almost certainly be mounted in the late spring and she had no doubt that the larger paintings would be swiftly sold. In any event, with his work for the show completed he could resume his teaching schedule at the League and they would be able to count on some steady income. He had promised her as much and these days he kept his promises.

"Damn it, I can afford ten dollars for a book," she muttered aloud, and took her place in line at the register. The ponytailed girl with wind-reddened cheeks who stood beside her, clutching a copy of *Mastering the Art of French Cooking,* glanced at Jen's selections and averted her eyes.

"Our book club is doing Sylvia Plath," Jen said, and wondered why she felt she had to explain. Reading Sylvia Plath did not make her a depressive. But then she was always intent on offering explanations, avoiding misunderstandings, even in the briefest of encounters.

"Oh. Great," the girl said. She gestured to her own selection. "I'm buying this because I'm just learning how to cook. My boyfriend was in Paris for his junior year and he loves French food."

"Well, that's a good book to begin with," Jen said approvingly. She tried to remember the last time she had prepared a dish to please Ian. Then she tried to remember the last time they had shared a meal. Weeks ago, she realized. The extra work she had taken on to cover their expenses meant that she was out late and, of course, too exhausted to cook. Occasionally, when she returned to the loft in the evening Ian was gone, leaving a scrawled note of explanation on her desk. He had to meet with the gallery owner or perhaps catch the early showing of an art film. Now and again he visited exhibits by other artists.

Too often, she crumbled the notes irritably, then straightened them out and shoved them beneath the storyboards of her cartoons, in penance for her annoyance. She could not blame him for wanting to leave the loft after a day spent painting and, she acknowledged, she welcomed the few hours of solitude that came with his absence. It afforded her time to get on with her own work, to read quietly while she ate her pickup dinner.

Watching the cashier thrust the Plath volumes into a shopping bag, she realized that she half hoped that Ian would be gone when she arrived home. She wanted to cut the pages of the journal very carefully, to inhale the scent of crisp quality paper untouched by previous readers. Always a book that shimmered with newness filled her with anticipatory excitement. She imagined the mellow amber light of her bed lamp casting its glow across the sharply printed text as she slowly turned the pages and slipped into the life of the young poet that had ended so tragically. She tried to remember how old Sylvia Plath had been when she committed suicide on a frigid London night. Somewhere around the age of the members of the book group, she supposed.

She shivered and thought that she would begin the reading of the journal that night. Hopefully she could finish it in record time and pass it on to Elizabeth before the book club meeting. That, at least, would justify the expense.

"Happy cooking," she called to the girl as they exited the store together.

Ian was gone when she reached the loft, another of his notes attached by a magnet to the refrigerator. *I'm at a lecture on impressionism at Cooper Union. Waited for you because I thought you might want to go. I.* Just an intial. No affectionate regret. No *I love you* or *It would have been more fun with you.*

She felt a surge of righteous anger, unfamiliar but empowering. She was late because she had worked on a job that would pay their next month's rent. And she had told him about the appointment that morning. He had no right to guilt her. That sudden vehemence frightened her. She reread the note and calmed herself. She had overreacted. He had implied no blame. The phone rang and she picked up the receiver with trembling fingers, annoyed with herself, hopeful that the caller was Ian.

"Jen." Elizabeth, as always, curt and to the point. A simple "Hi, how are you?" constituted a waste of time.

"Hi, Elizabeth." She kept her tone calm. Her sister could always discern any anxiety or irritation in her voice and was always swift to exploit even the most transitory vulnerability. Siblings, Trish had told her, had an instinct for the jugular, a too-intimate knowledge of the wounds and weaknesses of childhood, inevitably carried into adulthood. She would not tell Elizabeth about Ian's note. It would only add fuel to the dully burning flame of her sister's disapproval of Ian, of her contempt for their relationship.

"I was just thinking about you," she said too swiftly. "I bought Sylvia Plath's journal and I thought you might want it when I've finished. It might flesh out your intro for the book group."

"I already took it out of the library. I'm almost halfway through it and it's not making me love the lady poet. But that's not what I called about."

No, it wouldn't be, Jen thought. Elizabeth's calls were never casual. She said nothing and slowly ripped Ian's note into small pieces.

"Has the nursing home called you?" Elizabeth asked.

"No. Is something wrong?"

"It's not clear. They think there may have been a series of ministrokes. She's slightly incoherent and Fanya, that's the Russian aide…"

"I know who Fanya is," Jen interrupted. "I write checks out to her."

Elizabeth was briefly silent, as surprised by Jen's irritated retort as Jen herself was.

"What about Fanya?" Jen asked more gently.

"Fanya says she's noticed some weakness on the right side. She's having difficulty with eating utensils—that sort of thing."

It occurred to Jen that they had not mentioned their mother by name. On this, at least, they were united. They were dutiful toward the woman who had birthed them but they did not pretend to love her. She, after all, had never acknowledged any love for them. They had spent their childhoods defending themselves against her irrational rages. Elizabeth, armed with sullen resentment, slammed her bedroom door against the moods of morning, the quarrels of evening, while Jen retreated into subdued acquiescence. Both of them took refuge in a book, reading their way out of reality. Anything to avoid a scene, anything to prevent an argument.

Their mother had startled them with the fierceness, the near hysteria, of her grief when their father, that weak, ineffectual man whom they had pitied but never respected, died suddenly of a heart attack. It was only later that they realized that she grieved for herself because she had lost the target of her anger. Bereft of fury, hugging her bitterness, she indulged in illnesses that compounded through the passing years—hypertension, fatigue, anemia—the inevitable, chronic complaints of the aged and the lonely. Her face shriveled into a mask of sunken features, her body diminished, she spat out invective and accusation, blamed them for her ailments as she had blamed their father for her unhappiness. It was their cruel indifference that caused her blood pressure to peak, her glucose count to rocket. Her irrational shouts echoed down the corridors of the nursing home, caused aides and nurses to stare at them and turn away in embarrassment.

Numbed by the years of abuse, Elizabeth and Jen no longer speculated about the source of her bitterness. There had been another man, they knew, before their father. He had abandoned her, and somewhere in the dark mythology of her family, there lurked a tale of her own father's, their grandfather's, betrayal. Their mother's life, they supposed, had been one of serial disappointments. But that, they had each decided separately, did not excuse the misery she had caused them.

Dutifully, they made arrangements for her care, dealt with her affairs, ran interference for her at the nursing home and made the requisite visits. She never thanked them. And they in turn were grateful for that lack of gratitude. It absolved them of the responsibility of loving her.

"What are we supposed to do?" Jen asked.

"I suppose one of us ought to go and see her. But I really can't. Work is crazy and we had a call from Adam's therapist. He wants to confer with us. It's an important part of this new program. So you'll have to do it."

"I can't," Jen said firmly. "I'm juggling three jobs now plus my regular assignments. Cynthia's set a deadline for the graphics for her summer catalog. Look, Elizabeth, there's not much we can do. She's getting decent care. What difference would it make if we showed up at the home?"

"I suppose you're right." Elizabeth's agreement was tinged with both relief and reluctance.

"I'll call the home and explain," Jen said. "Anyway, how are you liking the Plath stuff, the poems, the journal?" She was eager to change the subject, to escape the shadow of their shared past. As always, books were their safe havens, discussions of writers and their works neutral territory.

"Mixed," Elizabeth said carefully. "I find a lot of her work pretty disturbing. Not just *The Bell Jar* but the *Ariel* poems and the way she disses her mother in her journal."

"Mothers get a bad rap," Jen said lightly, inviting her sister's complicity. "Except our mother. She earned it."

"According to Bert, mothers are the source of all evil." Weariness weighted Elizabeth's words. "At least that's what he used to think. Now that we know more about autism he's changed his tune. In fact, I think he's changing in other ways."

Jen sighed. She knew that Bert had blamed Elizabeth for Adam's autism. He had pelted her with Bettelheim's essays on maternal rejection, downloaded Internet entries that alluded to the acidic impacts on small children by reluctant and unloving women. Ian had told her that Bert had cautioned him against having children with Jen.

"Their mother screwed them up. Elizabeth screwed Adam up. You don't want a replay."

Ian had quoted him word for word.

"And what did you say?" Jen had asked.

"I told him to mind his own damn business."

Jen had felt a surge of pride. Where she avoided confrontation, Ian was fearlessly direct. His strength compensated for her weakness. They provided balance for each other. In gratitude then, she had stood on tiptoe and kissed his chin, delighting in the smoothness of his flesh against her lips.

"Am I your business, then?" she had asked.

"Damn right, you are," he had assured her, entangling his paint-stained fingers in her dark curls.

"Oh, Bert," Jen said now. "He can be such an asshole." She crumbled the shreds of Ian's note, balled them up and tossed them away.

"Yes, he can, can't he?" Elizabeth agreed, "But actually he's a lot better than he used to be."

"Oh?" Jen was surprised. Elizabeth had seldom discussed Bert with her, and when she did she was more often than not defensive, excusing his behavior as she probably excused her own. Adam's condition, the burden of his care, validated the bitter anger that cloaked their lives, the resentment that edged every conversation.

"I'm thinking of doing a cheese fondue for the book club dinner," Elizabeth said, switching tracks. Cooking was an even safer topic than literature. "What do you think?"

"Use English cheddar. Appropriate for a discussion of Sylvia Plath, given her whole obsession with the U.K. And then, too, Ted Hughes, her husband, was the poet laureate of England, so you'll be right on target," Jen said. "Maybe that's what we ought to do next year. Coordinate our menus with the books we discuss. Like for dinner with *Anna Karenina* we could have had blinis or beef Stroganoff." The thought amused her and she smiled into the phone.

"Is that what they use for fondue?" Elizabeth asked. "English cheddar?"

"I don't know. Fondue was not exactly a staple of our childhood." The sisters laughed, newly relaxed and at ease with each other.

"I'll check it out," Elizabeth said. "Good night."

"Good night. And don't worry about her."

"No. No, I won't."

Jen hung up and thought of her mother lying helpless in bed, trying to lift her right arm, to flex the fingers of her right hand. She struggled to summon sympathy, a semblance of compassion (*"She is old, she is ill, she is your mother," she told herself sternly*) but all she felt was a heavy, undefined sadness. She sighed and plucked a bowl of spaghetti from the refrigerator, which she ate cold. She did not cut the pages of the journal that night, but lying in bed, after a hot shower, she opened *The Bell Jar.*

"Sylvia Plath," the introductory essay informed her, "wrote this novel using the pseudonym Victoria Lucas, in order to protect her mother."

Jen studied the sentence again and lifted her pencil. *"To protect her mother from what?"* she scrawled in the margin. She would pose the question at the book club meeting. She closed her eyes and thought of the twins, saw again the glint in those four green eyes, heard their voices sweetly raised in the lie about wanting ice cream that would protect their mother from their own desperate need to understand what was happening in their home.

Why doesn't Daddy live here anymore? Why? Cynthia's children, like Cynthia's friends, suing for the knowledge that was denied them. *Why and again why?* She heard their question as the refrain of a duet sung oh-so-sadly by the twins, their bright hair now brushed loose and hanging to their shoulders. With that image dancing through her mind she drifted into a light sleep and wakened only when Ian's lips brushed her eyelids and his hand rested gently on her head.

"I'm sorry I left without you," he said. "You're not angry, are you?"

"No, I'm not angry." She drew him down beside her, allowed the book to fall to the floor.

"The nursing home called," he said. "I forgot to leave a message. A problem with your mother."

"I know."

"Everything will be all right."

"I know." The lie was effortless.

He switched the bed light off and they lay side by side, his hand still resting on her head, safely cocooned in the comforting darkness.

Elizabeth did not go to work the day the book club was to meet at her house. She called her school, instructed the clerk to mark her absence against her personal leave, leaned back against the pillows and watched Bert pack for his overnight trip to Washington. In this, as in all things, he was careful and methodical. He counted out two pair of socks, two pair of shorts, two undershirts, two shirts, although he would only be gone one night. But always he anticipated small disasters, a delayed flight, a spilled drink, a food stain, a sudden burst of perspiration soaking his skin, creating embarrassing circlets of dampness beneath his arms. His pessimism (declared phobic by Trish, knowingly and maliciously—she did not like Bert, none of the book club members did) was temporized by these precautions. Elizabeth watched him select two hand-kerchiefs and then add two more. His tension level must be especially high today, she decided but said nothing. She had learned, over the years, when to keep silent.

"Why are you taking the day off?" he asked. "Don't you usually save your personal leave? We might need it."

"I'm giving myself a day off," she replied lightly. "I've accrued more leave than I'll ever be able to use. I need the day to shop and cook. You know that the book club is meeting here tonight."

"Ah, the book club. The holy book club." He snapped his overnight case shut. "At least I'll miss that. I suppose it's some compensation for having to go to Washington. I hate these trips. I hate all the nitpicking over the reports and eating alone in the damn hotel."

"Maybe I could go with you next time," she said ten-tatively.

"Would you want to?" His reply was as uncertain as her question.

Embarrassed by his own surprise, he turned to the mirror and concentrated on knotting his tie, an expen-sive nubby teal wool that Elizabeth had bought because she thought it matched his eyes. It did, she realized with an odd pleasure. His deep-set eyes retained their color, although his sand-colored hair had thinned and disap-pointment had honed his features into a new sharpness.

She remembered still how he had charmed her at their first meeting, a blind date arranged by a Hunter College classmate. His voice so deep, his large hands so comfort-able and competent on the steering wheel. He had argued clearly and decisively with the waiter, who had over-charged a single item on their restaurant bill, and she, the daughter of a weak and weeping father, had admired his persistence. He had plans, he had told her that very first night. He was good with numbers, great with computers. He thought to open his own firm specializing in the analysis of corporate statistics. His ambition thrilled her. His assertiveness had bewitched her. She had thought him attractive, had loved the touch of his large hands on her body. Within three months they were engaged. Within six months they were married. She had escaped the home she hated, the parents who had incurred her contempt. All she took from her childhood home was her clothing and a carton of books. She left her bed lamp for Jen. Marriage had freed her to read whenever or wherever she pleased.

In less than a year she knew that she had made a mistake. Bert's strength was laced with impatience, the persistence that she had so admired was both aggressive and obsessive. He sought to control her, monitoring her movements, laying claim to her paycheck, pumping her salary into the business that stubbornly refused to take off. The arguments in her marriage seemed a vivid replay of the angry exchanges of her childhood.

Although she was already pregnant with Adam, she fled. She would not live as her parents had. This she told Jen when she left Bert, her tone taciturn and decisive as always. She had not taken into account that the child born to her might be impaired, that Adam's profound autism would necessitate the care of two parents, that two steady incomes would be needed to pay his small army of doctors and sitters. Duty—and both she and Bert were dutiful—that much they shared—overwhelmed all other options.

Bert abandoned the business that hovered near success and took a civil service job. She abandoned her dream of an independent life and returned to the marriage. Adam, his beautiful eyes so deep and empty, his long graceful fingers restlessly roaming, dominated their days, haunted their nights, poisoned their dreams and their reality. They entered the arena of blame, hurling accusations and counteraccusations at each other and then, briefly uniting when a glimmer of optimism—a new program, a new medication, a new intervention—briefly flickered. As it had now. Love for their son, hope for his future, however fragile that hope was, brought them together.

"You'll call Dr. Theobald and schedule another appointment?" Bert asked as he checked his briefcase. "You won't be too busy with your book club preparations to do that?"

She ignored the sarcasm of his tone. He disliked the women in the book group, resented the worlds they opened to Elizabeth. "Pseudointellectuals," he called them dismissively.

He did not speculate as to why Cynthia had made Eric leave their home. He claimed absolute knowledge.

"It's because she's a selfish, manipulative bitch," he had said. "It would be clear to anyone except your over-analytical, self-pitying friends."

Elizabeth had not contradicted him. There would have been no point.

Swiftly, perhaps too swiftly, he amended his words.

"I don't place you in that category," he had said, and paused as though he would say more, but she had turned away.

"I'll talk to Theobald," she said. "Although it's probably too soon after our conference for him to have anything else to say to us."

They had, over the weekend, journeyed out to southern New Jersey to visit Adam and to meet with Dr. Theobald, who was in charge of the new program. Although they both thought they could discern a change in Adam, the doctor had not been encouraging.

"It's my feeling and the feeling of the team that the patterning intervention came too late in his development," he had told them, his eyes cast down, his voice so low they had to strain to hear him.

He was a small man whose heavy tweed suit seemed too large for him, as though his body had been diminished by the sorrows of others. Strands of silver threaded their way through his dark, bushy beard and his thick, unkempt hair although he was very young, forty according to the profile Bert had found on the Internet. Elizabeth thought it probable that his early grayness was the result of having not one but two autistic children of his own, a son and a daughter. That information had appeared in an article written about him based on an interview. It angered her to see such intimate knowledge displayed on the computer screen. Still, it had been somewhat reassuring to learn that it was the dilemma of his own children that had caused Dr. Theobald to develop the patterning program. He was personally vested in it. She wondered if his own children had, in fact, been helped, but perhaps they, too, had been too old.

"We thought that there was a difference in Adam," she had protested at their meeting. "His hands were still. And he seemed to look directly at us."

"You want there to be a difference," Dr. Theobald had replied patiently. His own hands were not still. He flexed his fingers, clasped them, straightened them. He did not look directly at either Elizabeth or Bert.

"We know what we saw," Bert said in the same clear, decisive tone he had used with the waiter on their very first date. And again she felt a flutter of admiration, a glimpse of the man she had married.

"I know that participation in this program represents a significant financial sacrifice for you," the doctor said. "I don't want it to be in vain."

"That's our business, not yours." Bert hardened his voice.

"You understand that there is some risk. We're going to take the kids who are participating out of the sheltered atmosphere of the school. We want to expand their horizons. We plan to take them to parks, perhaps even to the mall. In stages, of course, and always with their shadows."

Elizabeth cringed. She knew that the team of attendants who worked with each child, following them every hour of the day, were defined as "shadows," but she thought the word offensive. It was as though Adam and the other children were like Peter Schlemiel, the legendary hero of a German folk tale who had no shadow of his own. That would be yet another deficit in a life defined by deficits.

Unbidden, a line from a Sylvia Plath poem she had read the previous evening sprang to mind: "I see myself, flat, ridiculous, a cut-paper shadow…" The poem had been called "Tulips," she remembered suddenly and irrelevantly. Perhaps Plath herself feared the loss of her shadow, as she had feared so many other things. And it was that fear that had at last overwhelmed her and driven her to suicide. Although the doctor's consulting room had been very warm, Elizabeth had shivered.

"So what's the risk?" Bert had asked.

"Adam can be unpredictable, sometimes deaf to the simplest instruction."

"But sometimes aware?" Elizabeth spoke for the first time, saw Bert nod with approval.

"Sometimes."

"You're not absolutely certain that there has been no progress, are you?" Bert was on the offensive now.

"There are no absolutes in this field."

"Then in spite of what you said, we want to continue to have Adam receive the patterning therapy. Don't worry. You warned us. You covered your ass." Bert stood.

"Bert," Elizabeth protested. The violence of his tone, the rudeness of his words shamed her, and yet she admired him for his courage, for his concern for Adam. Their son. They were locked, she and Bert, into a complicity of paternal love.

The doctor placed his hand soothingly on her own.

"I understand your husband's frustration, Mrs. Crawford. Indeed I share it. All right, then. We'll continue for the time being. But call me next week. It's important that we stay in touch."

She would call him, she told herself, after she returned from shopping for the food. She would speak to him as she cooked. The scent of the food, the knowledge that a pleasant evening of shared ideas lay ahead of her, would give her the comfort she needed for that conversation. She watched as Bert checked his airline tickets.

"Okay then. I'll see you tomorrow night."

"Fine. And Bert…"

"What?"

"Have a good trip, a good meeting."

He looked at her, a new softness in his eyes.

"Thanks. And I hope your book group meeting goes well."

And then he surprised them both by leaning over to touch her cheek, his fingers warm against her skin. He left then, suitcase in one hand, briefcase in the other. The front door closed softly behind him and she was alone.

She got out of bed and stood for a brief moment in the sliver of sunlight that danced its way across the bedroom floor. She watched as its brightness washed over the books she had piled on the floor late last night—*The Bell Jar,* Plath's unabridged journals, the *Ariel* poems. The closely written notebook on which she had carefully recorded the points she wanted to make during that evening's discussion lay open on her bedside table. She closed it. She would review it after she had finished the shopping, the cooking, the cleaning of the small apartment, which was, in fact, already clean. Disorder did not descend where lives were stingily lived. Still, after she had washed her own breakfast dishes and the mug that Bert had left in the sink, she managed a few peremptory swipes with the dust cloth. Only then did she pull out her pristine copy of *The Joy of Cooking,* barely opened because cooking for Bert had never afforded her even a modicum of joy. She flipped to the recipe for cheese fondue, which she had never made before, but she had been inspired by Plath's vivid discussions of food, the poet's excitement at shopping for ingredients, the pleasure of the chopping and dicing. "How I love to cook," Sylvia Plath had written from the cottage she and Ted Hughes shared in Spain during the brief idyll of their honeymoon before reality had poisoned their marriage.

Elizabeth had imagined Plath, the young bride, stirring the bubbling cheese and wine and had remembered the fondue set, a wedding gift from the teachers at her school, never used, stored in a kitchen cabinet. She and Bert would not be a couple who sat with friends over dinner, extending long forks into a fragrant golden mixture. She had never even opened the carton, but neither had she given it away.

"Why not?" Elizabeth had asked herself. "Why shouldn't I try making it?"

She looked forward to preparing it and anticipated the pleasure of the book group at her daring, and their praise. The fondue, of course, would be delicious. Of that much she was certain. Whatever Elizabeth did, she did well. Her supervisor's reports had recorded excellent evaluations year after year, and even Bert, at his most recalcitrant moments, admitted as much. She herself added a bitter amendment to that judgment: *Whatever I can control I do well.* Birthing a normal child had been beyond her control.

The rush of that thought impelled her to call Dr. Theobald. She was relieved to learn that he was not available, that he was, in fact, accompanying students on an off-campus excursion. Gratefully then, she left the apartment, excited by her clandestine freedom and the adventure of shopping for the new and different foods.

She ignored the large supermarket where she usually shopped and headed for the smaller esoteric shops scattered through their Inwood neighborhood. They lived so far to the north because it was cheaper than lower Manhattan, but there were compensations. Although she would never admit it to Bert, Elizabeth loved the river scent, the profusion of wild-leafed trees that lined the heights above the Hudson and the varied ethnic populations, each with their own restaurants and food markets.

The streets throbbed with energy. Women, carrying laden shopping bags, greeted one another in Spanish, in Russian, in Portuguese. A graceful Indian girl, wearing a bright pink sari that swirled about her narrow ankles, walked down the street carrying a large pizza box. Workmen called to one another in languages she did not recognize.

Elizabeth averted her eyes from mothers who wheeled baby carriages and held the hands of small children. She crossed the street to avoid the neighborhood playground, where laughing toddlers slid down slides that glinted silver in the sunlight, their laughter and their quarrels rising in sweet symphony. Adam had balked at even entering the playground, had clung so tightly to the fence surrounding it that she had had to pry his fingers loose.

She stopped at a cheese store for slabs of Gruyère (she had read with regret that fondue was not generally made with cheddar), tasted the samples of different cheeses arrayed on the marble counter and, impulsively, added a jar of nicoise olives and caper berries to her order. At the Italian bakery, she bought crusty loaves of bread, still warm from the oven, and at the small shop that sold only wine she opted for a dry Chablis, defiantly choosing two bottles of the higher-priced selections. She bought her produce from the wizened old Italian woman whose gnarled hands sorted through the fruits and vegetables, angrily discarding shriveled leaves and bruised skin. Elizabeth filled her string bag with the romaine and arugula she would use for the salad and added an out-of-season melon, remembering Plath's description of the dessert at her birthday lunch: "…new green honeydew melon… wild cold honey-flavored, melon-flesh…" She had memorized the vivid descriptions and she thought she might surprise the book group by repeating them when she served the melon that night.

The meal itself would surprise them, she knew, but then they had all surprised one another since that autumn evening when Cynthia had dropped her bombshell. Her announcement, so laced with mystery, so startling and unexpected, had impacted on each of them, igniting latent fears, sparking new resolutions. The fragility of Cynthia and Eric's marriage had rendered all their own relationships fragile, had carried each of them to an unfamiliar crossroad. She thought of how she and Bert had parted that morning, the new and inexplicable softness between them. It might signify reconciliation; it might signify separation. *Where do I want to go?* she wondered. *What road must I take?* She thought of Bert seated on the Washington plane, worriedly reviewing his presentation, his high, pale brow already beaded with sweat, and a wave of compassion for him swept over her.

She shrugged the image away and added a wreath of garlic to her purchases. She would hang it from a hook in her kitchen, as Plath had done in the early days of her marriage, before she knew that her love, like the thinly layered bulbs she thought so beautiful, would decay. Elizabeth could lay no claim to such innocence. Her parents had been excellent teachers.

She hurried home, hugging her purchases, her face flushed with the cold, her short, pale hair ruffled by the wind. There were two messages on her answering machine and her heart raced faster as she waited for the recording. Every phone call filled her with apprehension. *Adam. Let Adam be all right.* The mental mantra, so often repeated, came automatically to mind. With relief, she heard Jen tell her that she had spoken to the charge nurse at the home and their mother seemed all right. With even greater relief she heard Dr. Theobald's gentle voice assure them that in fact Adam seemed to be responding to the patterning. Perhaps he had only needed more time. The doctor's voice was apologetic. He was sorry to have been so negative at their meeting. Adam was now adhering to instructions. He was in a group that would be making a trip out of the facility that afternoon. They would be walking to a playground several blocks away. The doctor was no longer worried about the risk. Elizabeth breathed easier. She played the message again. His reassuring voice soothed her.

The fondue, as the cookbook had promised, was simple to prepare. She worked slowly, stirring in the wine, the kirsch, adding more garlic than the recipe called for. "When I am quiet at my cooking," Plath had written in the poem called "A Birthday Present."

"I am quiet at my cooking." Elizabeth repeated the line aloud as she sliced the bread, made the salad and set the table.

When she was done she called Jen and left a message on her machine, thanking her for her call. Then she called Bert and left a message at his hotel, telling him about Dr. Theobald's new assessment. Both her messages would surprise, she knew. Her sister, with good reason, did not anticipate her gratitude. Her husband did not anticipate good news.

Then she lay down on her bed, turned the pages of her notebook, now picking up Plath's journal, then idly riffling the pages of the *Ariel* poems but never opening *The Bell Jar*. The edition of the novel on her bedside table was her own worn copy, first read in her parents' home as her mother shouted and her father whined, and reread over the years at moments of misery. It was a fictional account of the author's adolescent odyssey into madness, culminating in her failed suicide attempt.

It was, for Elizabeth, a literary admonition, a warning of imminent danger, of what might happen if she did not seize emotional control, if she did not rein in the despair that so often threatened to overcome her.

She studied her notes, added one idea and deleted another. She had to be very careful. Rina had been studying Plath for years and surely knew a great deal more about her than Elizabeth did. But then Rina's concentration was a bit diluted these days. Elizabeth thought about Rina and Ray. Was she the only one in the group who found that new relationship puzzling? Ray had been Donna's lover, and Rina was Donna's closest friend. But then, she supposed, Ray had been a lover of convenience who suited Donna's passionless serenity. Did Donna even regret the loss? Would she herself regret losing Bert, if it came to that? Once she would have been able to answer that question with certainty, but not now, not today. And what about Cynthia? Was she riddled with regret? Did she think about Eric in sympathy and sorrow? The questions teased but did not wound.

The phone rang—Jen, telling her that she would be sharing a cab uptown with Cynthia. Cynthia had bought cannolis. Did Elizabeth need anything else?

"No. I'm all set," Elizabeth said. "I guess Donna and Trish will come up from the hospital together."

"I guess so. I don't know about Rina."

"Maybe Ray will drive her."

"Maybe."

Jen, too, had difficulty thinking of Rina and Ray as a couple. Donna's acceptance of their relationship had surprised her, but then a great deal about Donna surprised and mystified.

"See you soon," Jen said. "You got my message. About the nursing home report."

"Yes. I called to thank you."

"Did you?" Jen did not mask the surprise in her voice.

"It's a relief that she's all right."

"Yes. She seems to be."

Yet again they did not refer to their mother by name.

Elizabeth showered and dressed quickly. Black slacks and a black turtleneck, Plath's favored costume and, she supposed, her own. She set out the dips, the olives, the wineglasses, and was just arranging the napkins when the doorbell rang. Rina, after all, was the first to arrive. A swift hello and then she hurried to the window and waved down to the street. Elizabeth followed her and saw Ray parked in front of her apartment building in the smart little yellow sports car in which he had so often driven Donna to book club meetings. He waved and drove off, and Rina smiled and blushed, her eyes bright. She had released her long dark hair from the single braid and it tumbled about her shoulders. She shrugged out of her coat.

"He worries," she said. "I have to tell him where I'm going, when I'm coming home, show him that I got safely up to your apartment." She laughed. His concern pleased her, validated his love.

"Do you think he worried like that about Donna?" Elizabeth asked, with a sudden coldness.

"No. Things were different between him and Donna."

"And you know that because…"

"Because he has said so." Rina hung her coat up.

"And Donna? Has Donna said so?"

"Donna and I will be talking about it. But you know, Elizabeth, it's really none of your business." She spoke calmly, fighting the anger that had flared at Elizabeth's question.

"You're right," Elizabeth agreed. "I'm sorry."

Her apology startled Rina, who smiled sadly.

"I guess we've become awfully ensnared in one another's lives this year," Rina said. "All of us. We're in a tangle. I guess it's because of Cynthia and Eric."

"Yes. Just a few hours ago I was thinking of how it's affected us," Elizabeth agreed, and glanced at her watch. Bert would have already presented his paper. He would be sitting alone in the hotel coffee shop. Her heart turned as she thought of him listlessly studying the menu, solitude souring his mouth. It was with relief that she hurried to answer the ringing doorbell.

Donna and Trish entered together, still laughing over a comment their cab driver had made.

"He called us sweet girls," Trish enthused. "Us. Sweet girls. The nicest thing anyone said to me all day. One patient called me a white-coated bitch. Another one said I was a bitter old lady. My own daughter called me a mean mommy because I wasn't coming home for dinner tonight. Ah, but he saw the real me, a sweet girl."

"I think he really just wanted a big tip," Donna said mildly. "Elizabeth, is that fondue I smell? Rina, you look terrific. I haven't seen your hair loose for years."

Rina curtsied, tossed her hair over one shoulder and then the other. Smiling, she kissed Donna on the cheek. Donna smiled, touched her friend's hair, and then allowed it to fall through her fingers in long dark sheaths.

Cynthia and Jen burst in without even ringing the bell. They, too, were laughing. There had been difficulty persuading their cabdriver to come so far uptown, even more difficulty in directing him back to the highway.

"He kept saying, 'No, no, you ladies not want to go there.'" Jen grimaced as she imitated his accent.

"He was surer about where we should go than I am about most things in my life," Cynthia said, and gave Elizabeth the bakery box, granules of sugar clinging like small diamonds to the stiff white cardboard.

"For dessert, for discussion. We're going to need something sweet and creamy to counteract our Sylvia's bitterness. Why, oh why, Elizabeth, did you choose her?" Cynthia asked plaintively.

"Come on. You're talking about the writer on whom my entire academic career depends," Rina interposed. "Although I'm taking a break from her—a long break."

They sipped their wine and nibbled the olives as Elizabeth set out the salad, the bread and finally the bubbling fondue.

"Marvelous."

"Delicious."

"An inspired choice," Rina said. "Very Plathian, as the women in my seminar would say. You know she's become the heroine of a new generation of feminists, the exploited woman, the victim, the exhausted artist mother. Her husband, Ted Hughes, published like mad while she changed diapers."

"Let's agree to pity her after dinner," Donna said. "I'm famished."

"I don't pity her," Elizabeth said firmly as they assembled around the table.

They speared the bread with their long forks, dipped it into the cheese mixture, took swift swallows of chilled wine and ate slowly, their faces bright with pleasure.

"That was one of the few uplifting things about Plath," Donna said. "She loved food, loved to cook, although even there she was pretty obsessive about preparing everything perfectly."

"Well, you have that in common," Trish observed. "Not the obsessive bit, but the love of food and cooking."

"We have a great deal more in common than that, Sylvia and I," Donna said softly. She looked at Rina and did not move away when Rina covered her hand with her own. The others marked the gesture but did not comment.

"But even in her cooking she was competitive. Competitive and mother-hating. When she peeled potatoes she couldn't help remembering how her mother had always corrected the way she held her knife, the thickness of the peels. I suppose it's really hard to forgive parents for their faults," Cynthia said. "I understand that." She licked her fork, turned her attention to the salad.

Her comment surprised them. Cynthia rarely mentioned her parents. They had always assumed that her childhood had been as enchanted as the life into which she had graduated, a prom princess effortlessly morphed into a prom queen. *Until.* That word, unsaid, hovered in their thoughts.

"It's not hard to understand if you've had a rejecting, angry mother," Elizabeth observed quietly, and she and Jen exchanged a sharp look.

She collected the empty plates, replaced them with dessert dishes and carried out the melon decorated with lemon wedges.

"I bought it because of how Plath described the melon she bought at the Spanish market," Elizabeth said. She opened the journal and read aloud the sentence she had recalled earlier that day.

"A bit over the top like so much of her work," Cynthia said. "I know I'm being sacrilegious but I have to say it reminds me a bit of advertising copy—I might use a phrase like that in an ad for a line of face creams."

"And she might have sold it to you. She was that money-obsessed, that determined to see anything she wrote in print, anywhere, any way," Rina said.

"Rina, she's your thesis subject," Donna reminded her reprovingly.

"Which doesn't mean I have to like her," Rina retorted, and ran her fingers through her hair. She loved it loose about her shoulders, sweeping down across her back, and she loved the way Ray smiled as he watched her braid it, plait over plait, her fingers deft in the dance that preceded desire.

"Okay, let's get down to business." Trish glanced at her watch as she went into the living room, carrying her coffee mug. The discussion would be long, she knew, and she did not want to be too late getting home. Jason would be waiting up for her, eager to discuss a new apartment they were contemplating buying, eager for her advice, her opinion. And she wanted to tell him about a particularly interesting patient she had admitted that day. She and Jason had bridged the emotional gap that had for so long yawned between them. She acknowledged that this had taken a conscious effort, but that effort had been successful. Whereas once she had relished time away from him, she now treasured their time together.

As always, with the meal over, the friends sat in a circle. Cynthia and Trish pulled the unmatched armchairs closer to each other. Jen perched on an ottoman with Rina and Donna seated side by side on the rigid hard-cushioned beige sofa. Their books were in easy reach, on their laps, at their feet. All of them, except Elizabeth, wore light wool slacks and sweaters in the soft pastel shades of the early flowers of spring, as though they would hurry the slowly approaching season.

"We're in a floral mode," Cynthia said approvingly as she tossed her gentian-colored cardigan over her chair and adjusted its matching turtleneck shell.

The gentle colors they wore relieved the colorless austerity of the room, where the bulbs in the shaded lamps burned too dimly and the windows were so narrow that even during the day they admitted little light. Jen had long thought that it was like Elizabeth and Bert to live amid gloom, as though to emulate the mysterious darkness of their son's emotional life.

Elizabeth herself sat on a wooden chair, her notebook open on her lap, her Plath books on the coffee table where Cynthia had placed the pastries that oozed sweetened ricotta cheese and a pile of paper plates and plastic forks from Nightingale's party-accessories department.

"Cynthia always thinks of everything," Rina said as she reached for a plate. She recalled the disposable soup bowls she had brought for the wonton soup. Poor Eric. It couldn't be easy to be married to a woman who thought of everything. She smiled fleetingly, remembering Ray's exasperated amusement at her own absentmindedness. *Ray.* She looked at Donna and looked away.

Elizabeth glanced at her notebook and began with a brief discussion of Plath's life.

"Before she even entered Smith College, she'd published poems in *Seventeen* and the *Christian Science Monitor,*" Elizabeth reported.

"She was a gal in a hurry," Trish said. "Probably even then she knew that she wouldn't live a long life, that she didn't want to live a long life. I feel that in a lot of my suicidal patients. I worry more about the ones who are obsessed about getting a lot done than I do about the passive ones."

"And at Smith, she plunged into everything—classes, clubs, the *Smith Review,* weekends at Yale or wherever Smith girls went on weekends," Elizabeth continued. "One of her friends said that it was as though she couldn't wait for life to come to her…she rushed out to make things happen." Elizabeth read the quote in a monotone. She understood Plath's hurry, her sense of urgency. Her marriage to Bert had been based on her own rush to make things happen, to break free of her parents' home, of their angers. She, too, had been unable to wait for life to come to her.

"She even rushed into her relationship with Ted Hughes. Life had to move very fast for her," she added.

"But all the time she was flirting with death," Trish insisted quietly. "Her fictional heroine in *The Bell Jar,* Esther Greenwood, and the real Sylvia—both of them playing a role. Did any of you pick up on the fact that Sylvia wrote in her journal that one of the writers she most wanted to meet when she went to New York for *Mademoiselle* was Shirley Jackson. Shirley Jackson! That's pretty telling. The girl who sees herself as the eternal victim wants to meet the author of 'The Lottery,' the classic tale of victimization."

Trish warmed to her subject, her words coming quickly as idea followed idea. They listened closely, exhilarated by her interpretation, her rarefied professional insights. As always the book group discussion expanded their own horizons, invigorated them with an excitement of thought and feeling.

"She wrote a guest editor column for *Mademoiselle*," Trish went on, "using words like 'stargazers' and 'evening blue.' Cynthia was exactly right—she had a gift for writing advertising copy. Anyway, within weeks, she's forgotten all about being a stargazer, whatever the hell that is, she's in a massive depression, inviting her mother to die with her. If I had to diagnose her, then I would have said that she could no longer bear the burden of her double life. Suicide was her way out, a selfish exit." Trish sat back and speared a cannoli. She ate it slowly, licking the silken cream that settled on her lips.

"You would count all suicides as selfish?" Donna asked quietly.

"Perhaps not all. But most," Trish said. "At least that's been my clinical experience. Suicide is a narcissistic act. Most suicides think only of ending their own pain. They don't think of the pain they will cause their survivors."

"It hasn't been my personal experience," Donna spoke very softly, her eyes cast down. "Only Rina knows this, but my mother committed suicide. She swallowed too many pills while a tape of Dickinson poems played. I think she did it out of exhaustion. And I think for her it was an unselfish act. She did it for me. She wanted me to be free. To live my life unburdened, without being trapped by emotional slavery. She didn't want me to live as she had, listening to tales of other people's poems and stories on tape while she prepared meals for strangers. It frightened her that her loneliness, her sadness would hold me back. She wrote me a note telling me to live the life that she'd been denied because of my father's illness. She wanted me to live, to be unencumbered by commitments. It's just possible that Plath might have killed herself to spare her children the burden of her own terrible sadness. She understood that she was ill, that psychiatric care hadn't helped her. That would make her suicide a selfless act Like my mother's." Donna's clear blue eyes were lucent with the tears that glided down her cheeks, tears that she did not wipe away.

They sat for a brief moment in shocked silence. Always they had considered Donna, so self-contained, so serene, so competent and contented, to be the strongest of their group. She was, they had thought admiringly, unconflicted about the men with whom she spent her time, at ease with Ray, at ease with Tim, at ease even with the new relationship between Rina and Ray. She did as she pleased, always accepting, always calm, her life neatly compartmentalized. They had never suspected that her mother's death had cast a long shadow across her life and that what they saw as an untroubled serenity was, in fact, a numbness, an odd obedience to that melancholy deathbed mandate. She would not be trapped. She had been warned by a mother who had herself been trapped.

"Oh, Donna!" Sadness softened their voices, their hands trembled. Rina leaned toward her and gently pressed a handkerchief to her cheeks, wiping away Donna's tears, tender toward the friend on whose tenderness she had relied for so many years.

They clustered about her, knelt before her, forming a circle of sympathy. Trish placed her hand on Donna's shoulder.

"Sweetie, I'm so sorry. I should have realized. I should have known."

Her voice was faint with regret, wretched with shame. Of course she should have known, they all should have known. There had been enough hints.

Donna shook her head.

"It's all right. I'm all right. Let's go on." She smiled at Rina, reached for her book.

Elizabeth looked at her notes and then bravely she began again, focusing now on *The Bell Jar*.

"Plath clearly based the novel on her own life, but her heroine, Esther Greenwood, didn't have what I think was one of the key ingredients in Sylvia's emotional makeup."

"And what might that be?" Rina asked sarcastically. "I've been studying Plath and her work for years now and I've yet to pinpoint what you call that key ingredient."

Jen shot her an angry look. She felt suddenly protective of her sister. But Elizabeth was not cowed.

"Envy," she said. "That's what propelled Sylvia Plath, although that's not how she drew Esther Greenwood."

"Envy." They uttered the word in unison, as though its truth was suddenly and simultaneously evident to each of them.

"She said it herself in her journal," Elizabeth said. "She admitted being jealous of anyone who thought more deeply, wrote better, lived better than she did. She was envious of anyone who was prettier than she was, envious, I think, of Ted Hughes, her own husband. Her words were pretty explicit."

"Actually, I marked those words in my copy." Cynthia showed them the page in her book, the entry highlighted in the violet ink she favored. "But then I read on—I do a lot of middle-of-the-night reading just now—and almost nine years later she talks about defeating envy by taking joy in herself. So she recognized the dangers of that envy and she was fighting it."

"But she wasn't winning the fight. If she had won it she'd be alive today and the feminist movement would have lost its literary icon," Rina said. "Elizabeth's right. Envy is at the root of her life, of her work. I see it now. It poisoned her, crippled her. I'm glad you picked that up, Elizabeth."

Elizabeth smiled thinly. Rina's intellectual generosity was unexpected—Ray's influence, she supposed.

"I don't think she's really an icon for today's feminists." Donna had regained her composure and she spoke in the confident tone that they had always found reassuring. "But I do think that envy is pretty hard to overcome, and while it doesn't poison everyone's life the way it clearly poisoned hers, I don't think that there's anyone who's un-affected by it. We could go around the room right now, and if we're honest, we'd each reveal a kernel of envy that's pretty hard to decimate."

"Let's try it," Cynthia said. "And since you introduced the game, Donna, you go first. What or whom do you envy?"

"Aren't we too old to be playing 'truth or dare'?" Elizabeth asked irritably. She glanced down at her notes. There was so much more that she had prepared but hadn't yet talked about. But her friends were already poised for the game, leaning toward Donna.

"Cynthia's right. This should be interesting," Rina said.

Donna hesitated, stirred her coffee.

"All right," she said finally. "We're going for absolute honesty here."

She turned to Rina, who went suddenly pale. Even as Donna looked hard at her she lowered her eyes.

"Don't be frightened, Rina," Donna said softly. "I don't envy you Ray. I envy you your feelings for him, your ability to get emotionally involved with him. I could only care up to a point, for him, for Tim, for the other

men I've been with. I was always too careful, too frightened of allowing myself to feel deeply, of finding myself
caged in a life I didn't really want. I took my mother's
life as a message, accepted her instructions—'Live, be
free, hug your independence.' Because she never lived,
never had freedom, never had independence. So I was
careful, too careful. I held back. I envied you when you
had the courage to have Jeremy on your own without
worrying about your independence, and now I envy
you because you're free enough to accept Ray's love and
offer him your own. You taught me something. In fact,
this entire year, everything that's happened, our talks,
our books, has made me realize that I have to grab hold
of my own life, I can't wait for something to jolt me into
a decision."

Her gaze shifted from Rina to Cynthia, who had, ex-
plicably, been jolted into a decision.

Slowly she shredded her paper napkin, allowed the
long, thin white strips to cling to the soft yellow wool of
her sweater. Donna did not tell them how she planned
to change her life, nor did they ask her. Her honesty
stunned and challenged them. Their expressions were
grave. They knew that their own revelations would have
to match Donna's painful candor.

"Elizabeth." Cynthia clapped her hands, ever the executive skilled at assigning presentations, taking control
of the game that was no longer a game.

Elizabeth spoke slowly, each word uttered with care
and pain. "I envy every mother of normal children. I
envy the mothers who come to consult with me about
where their kids should go to college or whether or not
they should be tutored in math or what can be done
about their lateness, their low self-esteem, their possible

marijuana problem. I envy the mothers in the play-ground, even the ones who can't stop yelling at their kids. Why the hell are they yelling? Don't they know how happy they should be that their kids aren't like my Adam?"

She was very pale, and Jen, for the first time, noted her sister's fragility. She looked around Elizabeth's living room, devoid of family photographs, not even her wed-ding portrait or a picture of Adam. The furniture and dra-peries were of muted browns and beiges; black-and-white framed photographs of autumnal woodlands and empty windswept beaches hung on the pale walls. She saw Eliz-abeth's life and Elizabeth herself from a new perspective. Her sister had neutralized her home just as she had, from girlhood on, neutralized her emotions, confining them to a harsh protective carapace of brusque colorless remoteness. Always Jen had seen her sister's taciturn cynicism as rejection. But while Jen had taken refuge in compliant acquiescence, Elizabeth had simply with-drawn, first from their parents' bitterness and then from the unhappiness of her marriage, the tragedy of her son. Emotional distance protected her from emotional dam-age. But tonight, and even over the past several months, there were signs of change, of easy laughter, a new soft-ness, and now, this sudden openness.

"I'm sorry," Trish said. "It's hard for you, really hard, Elizabeth."

They all nodded; her pain, acknowledged and shared, became their own. They had, since she had joined the book group, tolerated Elizabeth, first because she was Jen's sister and then because her knowledge and eclectic insights enriched their discussions. But tonight that stingy toleration had turned into sympathetic affection.

It was Cynthia who reached out and touched Elizabeth's head lightly.

"Oh, I envy other things as well," Elizabeth said, struggling for lightness of tone. "I envy people who aren't as clumsy as I am. I'm always falling or bumping into something or burning or cutting myself. Sometimes I get into bed and notice a bruise and I can't remember how I got it. So I guess you could say I envy grace."

Jen remembered suddenly how their mother had mocked Elizabeth's clumsiness, her stumbling attempts to master social dancing, each criticism compounding Elizabeth's uncertainty until at last she abandoned all efforts.

Donna and Trish looked at each other, remembering all the times they had noticed her bruises and silently blamed Bert for a black-and-blue mark on Elizabeth's arm, a welt on her leg. They had spoken of it in worried tones over lunch in the hospital cafeteria, had contemplated discussing it with her or at least with Jen. They sighed, relieved to have been wrong, relieved that they had remained silent.

Rina reached for a cannoli but set it down as Cynthia murmured her name, her turn. She would hold it in reserve, a reward placed in escrow, a reward for own painful revelations.

"I have to tell you all that I think I identify with Plath's profusion of jealousies. Now I realize that may even be why I chose her for a thesis topic. Somewhere she says, 'I wanted to live many lives.'"

"She says it everywhere," Trish interposed dryly.

"Well, I did, too. I wanted to know what it felt like to be poor so I played at having no money. I was an only child so I invented a fantasy family of brothers and sisters. Actually I invented and reinvented myself, dropped clues about the mysterious person I really wasn't, invented stories—a shoplifting woman, a vanished lover. One month I was fiercely Jewish, the next month I was totally indifferent to anything that smacked of religion. I imagined parents more interesting than my mother and father. And then when they were killed in that accident, I envied anyone who had parents at all, interesting or uninteresting. I couldn't bear the thought of being alone in the world, the only child of parents who had both been only children, no biological connection anywhere. I envied people with families, and so Jeremy became my family and then the real envy began. Envy of women who had husbands, who had money, who didn't have to scrounge for love and leftovers, envy of academics who managed to complete their doctorates because someone else was taking care of them, taking care of their children, and probably just ambient envy. I'm not proud of it but that's what I was like."

"*Was?*" Trish asked, in her probing clinical voice.

"Was," Rina said firmly. "And now no more. Because with Ray I feel protected. Loved, protected and connected. And more than that. I love, I protect. I connect. I have Ray, I have Jeremy, I have Donna and I have all of you. I feel flush with my own luck. Probably I don't deserve it."

"You deserve it." Donna looked at her friend, smiled. "You were very brave, Rina. In fact, when I said that I envied you your feelings for Ray, I should have told you I remember sitting in the hospital the night Jeremy was born and thinking of how courageous it was of you to have this baby, to be prepared to raise him alone. And now I'm glad that you won't have to, that Ray will be with you. I mean that. I'm glad for both of you and I'm glad for myself, and for all of us. It's wonderful that we can be so honest with one another."

"Your turn, Jen. Who do you envy? What do you envy?" Cynthia asked softly. They were all gentle with Jen, their diminutive pixieish friend who now ran her fingers through the ringlets of dark hair that helmeted her head and toyed with the collar of her pale green sweater.

"That's easy. I envy Ian his talent," she said quietly.

"But you're talented yourself," Cynthia protested. "You're the most talented artist I work with at Nightingale's."

"Oh, I have a sort of minor gift. I'm skilled, competent and really good at what I do. But Ian is an *artist*. The real thing. I wish I could use my brush as he does but I can't and I know that. I could never compete with him. Not the way Plath competed with Ted Hughes. She thought that she was as good a poet as he was, and maybe she was or maybe she could have been. I'm realistic. I see Ian's work and I see my own and I know that creatively we're in two different worlds. Most of the time I'm glad that I can help him get to where he's going, help him to mount his show, help him reach for greatness. Not all the time, of course. I'm no saint. Sometimes I'm mad as hell that I'm supporting him almost totally, that he doesn't even bother to pick up his dirty underwear, that he's taken over most of the work space in the loft. And I've begun to fight it, to complain and make demands. I'm telling Ian how I feel and he's actually listening to me. He's changing. Things are better between us. I'm not Sylvia Plath. She pretended to sainthood, the sacrificing wife, the sacrificing mother. Hughes goes off to live with a lover and she stays in a freezing flat with two small children complaining to everyone but him. What she couldn't forgive was his dishonesty. Those were her exact words. She didn't seem to care as much about his fucking someone else as she cared about the fact that he lied about it."

"But dishonesty in a marriage is very hard to forgive, maybe impossible," Cynthia said quietly, flipping through the pages of the journal. "Plath herself says that there is no love without trust. I understand what she meant. When trust dies in a marriage, the marriage dies as well. It would take a lot to revive it." Her voice grew faint. She closed her book, opened it again and stared blindly down at the blank frontispiece.

They looked at one another and willed her to continue—perhaps to speak of Eric's dishonesty, the secret or secrets he had for so long hidden from her. What had he done to betray her trust, to turn her love and his own into a lie? Their speculations, compounded month after month, rushed to mind. They thought of how Trish had seen him at a café with that young man, of how Jen had smelled alcohol on his breath. Now perhaps Cynthia might tell them why she lived alone in their beautiful home and read the anguished journals of a poet deep into the night. But Cynthia closed her eyes and remained silent.

Jen waited for a moment, sighed and steered the conversation back to Sylvia Plath.

"Plath wasn't too unlike Shirley Jackson, if you think about it," she said. "Jackson wrote to pay the bills, cooked, baked, took care of the kids while her husband charmed Bennington coeds. Plath was Jackson redux, another lottery victim. And speaking of that, I have some news." She smiled shyly. "I sold my comic strip of 'The

Lottery.' Here's the letter of acceptance. It seems what they're calling graphic lit is very hot just now." She beamed, her elfin face alight with pleasure.

"Jen, that's marvelous."

"Great."

"Way to go, girl!"

Their love, their enthusiasm, the generosity of their friendship, radiated toward her. They hugged her, kissed her cheeks, encircled her in a dance of friendship.

"Why did you wait so long to tell us?" Elizabeth asked.

"I wanted to get my envy confession out of the way," Jen said. "Or maybe I wanted all of you to talk so no one could say they were envious of me."

They laughed.

"Who's left?" Rina asked. "Everyone has to step up to the plate."

"Me. And Cynthia." Trish looked up from her pad. A trained facilitator, she had ticked off their names. "And I'll go first."

She flushed and spoke very slowly, her gaze fixed on Cynthia.

"Here's a discarded envy. I envied you, Cynthia. I envied you your life, how you were able to arrange for enough help, how you never stinted on surrounding yourself with beauty, how your job was exciting. I kept envying you even though I knew that I could probably afford to do everything that you did—or almost everything—even though I knew that my own work was important and that I was good at it." She did not look at Cynthia as she spoke.

"And my marriage? Did you envy me my marriage?" Cynthia asked dryly.

"I think we all did." It was Jen who answered, her voice hesitant. "You had it all. The perfect life."

"That's what I thought. In retrospect, I envy it myself." Cynthia laughed bitterly. "It was great, better than great. I would wake up smiling. I could hardly wait for each day to begin. Now I can hardly wait for each day to end. And that's my own answer to the question of who or what I envy. I envy the life that was mine."

"Then why…?" The question froze on Jen's lips. It would not be answered. Cynthia had shut down, her face a mask, at once sorrowful and angry.

"I'm out of the game," she said. "Truth or dare. And I dared. I told the truth. I'm done."

Jen recognized the cold finality of her tone. That was how Cynthia ended meetings when she had lost patience with a presentation, when she wanted to be done with a project.

"All right. Cynthia's done. We're all done."

Rina, newly happy Rina, her own jealousies jettisoned, wanted the game to be over. It had reached its nadir. Trish had pierced the envy that had been common to all of them, their envy of Cynthia, which was now terminated. They all knew why. It was simply that Cynthia's life had ceased to be enviable. She was bereft and alone and their envy had morphed into pity. They did not understand what had happened to her, to Eric. That question obsessed them still but it had mutated through the long months and weeks of speculation; it had dislodged their own hidden longings, altered the plans and patterns of their own lives.

Elizabeth stood and went to the window. She stared down at the street, where a woman walked alone through the darkness, looking up at the lights in other people's windows. In the house across the way she saw a mother sit beside her son in the circlet of light cast by a bedside lamp. She had watched them before. The boy, a redhead, was Adam's age, perhaps a year younger or older. *Adam.* The thought of her son was like an arrow in her heart. Surely he was safely back from the outing to the playground. She wondered how many streets he had crossed and whether the expensive aide they called his shadow had been at his side all the way, guiding him safely from one curbstone to another. She closed her eyes and listened to Trish, who, in a lighter vein, was recounting other whimsical envies.

"I envy Miranda Richardson because she gets to sleep with Liam Neeson. And I envy women with smaller waistlines, more manageable hair, women who are more patient mothers. I envy anyone with an extended family and anyone who can bake a birthday cake," Trish concluded, her face flushed with relief and embarrassment.

"You have us for an extended family," Donna said. "Invite us for Thanksgiving, for Mother's Day, for Christmas."

"It's a deal," Trish said, laughing. "It's an open invite."

They all nodded and smiled, glad that the exercise was over, that their revelations and their pain had been shared, and thus diluted. They were, at once, proud and bewildered by their honesty. Something had been achieved, an emotional wall had been scaled, but they were not yet ready to examine the new terrain.

"What do we read next?" Trish asked.

"You mean who do we read next?" Rina retorted. "I think we're getting more involved with the writers than with their books. But that's all right," she added benignly.

"Whose turn?"

"Cynthia's. First session at Cynthia's. Last session at Cynthia's." Trish was the record-keeper, the arbiter.

"Then Cynthia gets to choose."

"No more suicidal authors. No more victims. We need a happy ending. We've had our dinner with Anna Karenina. We need a return to innocence." Cynthia hesitated. "What would you say to revisiting our reading past? What would you say to Little Women?"

They clapped their hands in enthusiastic pleasure.

"Louisa May. Our wonderful Louisa May."

"Perfect."

"Wonderful."

"I can't wait."

Their excitement bubbled over. The idea delighted them. They each recalled their girlhoods when they had read themselves into the lives of the March girls, the heroines of the Alcott saga. The names of the sisters were joyously recalled. "Jo!" "Meg!" "Poor Beth!" "Amy!"

"Oh, Amy. I always wanted to be Amy," Cynthia said wistfully.

They laughed. Her choice did not surprise them. Amy had loved clothing and small luxuries, flowers and furnishings. And it was Amy, like Cynthia, who had married into a prosperous and exciting life. But then Amy's happily ever after, unlike Cynthia's, had never been interrupted.

Calendars and PDAs were whipped out. A date was selected. Elizabeth volunteered to discuss *Transcendental Wild Oats* and *Excerpts from the Fruitlands Diary,* in which Louisa chronicled the efforts of her father, Bronson Alcott, to establish a utopian transcendental community by that name. Elizabeth, whose reading was strangely eclectic, had found a copy of the diary at a book sale.

"We could learn a lot from it," she told them as though determined to restore a modicum of gravity to their purpose. But their newfound gaiety would not be diminished.

Laughing, they refilled their coffee cups, plucked up the cannolis. They tasted the pastries with darting tongues, punctured them with swift, small bites so that the filling oozed free as they discussed the sweet dessert with the contented complacency peculiar to women who pride themselves on their knowledge of food.

"Better than the ones I buy in Little Italy," Trish said.

"Too much cinnamon," Rina observed.

"Not *enough* cinnamon," Donna contradicted her.

Jen reached for the one remaining pastry and suddenly all their hands were extended as they playfully grappled for the cake, giggling as they crushed it and their fingers were covered with the sweet cream. Greedily, they licked it away, their laughter as mischievous as that of small girls misbehaving at a party.

The phone rang as Elizabeth distributed paper napkins. She reached for it reluctantly.

"Bert, probably," she said. "Wanting to know about Adam. He knows that I spoke to his therapist today."

"What about Adam?" Jen asked quickly. She felt a special closeness to her nephew. She had held him close when he was an infant and, even then, had felt the unnatural rigidity of his small body, his resistance to tenderness. She pitied him then and pitied him still. She moved closer to her sister, who held the receiver so tightly that her knuckles whitened, her lips moving silently.

"Is it Adam?" Jen asked fearfully. "Has something happened to Adam?"

But Elizabeth did not answer her. She swayed as though she might fall beneath the weight of her own sadness. Jen's heart tightened. Something was wrong, something was terribly wrong.

"When?" Elizabeth asked, speaking so softly into the phone that Jen could barely hear her. "You're sure, absolutely sure? The doctor has been there?"

"Elizabeth, what is it? What's happened?"

Jen knelt beside her. She reached for her hand and Elizabeth gripped her fingers tightly as she continued to speak in that robotic voice drained of all expression.

"My husband is out of town. I'll try to reach him. But my sister is here. We'll decide what to do. Arrangements will have to be made. I'll call you back. Yes. Thank you."

Gently, too gently, she replaced the receiver and sat motionless.

"Elizabeth, tell me." Jen's cry was wrenching. Tears already filled her eyes, grief convulsed her gamin face. "Is it Adam?"

Elizabeth shook her head. "No. Thank God it's not Adam. It's her, our mother. It was the nursing home, the supervisor, who called. She died. She's gone. The charge nurse said it happened so suddenly. They couldn't do anything. She, Mother, just pitched herself out of her chair, thrust herself forward and fell to the floor. She was dead when they reached her. They're sorry. That's what the woman who called said. 'We're sorry.' Oh, Jen, it sounds as though she willed herself to die."

Shaking her head in disbelief, she opened her arms and Jen slipped into them. The two sisters wept, overwhelmed with grief for the woman they had not loved, for all the small and terrible losses of their lives, from the days of their frightened childhood until this wintry night when their mother had chosen a death as bitter and punitive as her life.

Their friends gathered about them, murmuring their sympathy, pledging their help. It was Trish who called Ian, and Cynthia who found a bottle of brandy and made them each sip the golden liquid that seared their throats and soothed their sorrow. When the phone rang, Trish answered it and spoke to Bert in a calm and measured tone, telling him what had happened, relaying his reply to Elizabeth. He would take the first flight out in the morning. He would call the nursing home. He would arrange everything. His reaction surprised them, but then, they would reflect later, everything about that evening had surprised them.

They had known that Plath country was treacherous territory, but they had not thought it would trigger intimacies that haunted and overwhelmed. First there had been Donna's revelation, then their odd confessional game, and finally the death of the old woman, Elizabeth and Jen's mother, unloving and unloved. Mysteriously, her daughters were bereft. Or perhaps not so mysteriously. She had not been a good mother, but she had been *their* mother. Her death, her *willed* death, denying any reconciliation, left them stranded on an isle of loss and grief.

It had startled them that Bert, a man they had never liked, a man whom they had even feared, had suddenly assumed a new role. Alone in a hotel room, in a distant city, he was making arrangements, assuming responsibility, relieving Elizabeth and Jen of the grim task of dealing with the logistics of death's aftermath. Or perhaps, they admitted reluctantly, it was not so new. They saw for the first time the man Elizabeth had married—a man who was decisive and assertive. He was, they acknowledged grudgingly, a man who had not abandoned his son or the wife who had, in fact, abandoned him, a man who knew and would always know where his duty lay. Elizabeth, sad, bitter Elizabeth, had always recognized that much. They would think of him differently after this night.

Silently they cleared away the remaining food and washed the dishes, gliding through the room in stockinged feet. One by one they gathered their books, murmured their condolences, hugged Jen, touched Elizabeth's hand and left. Only Trish remained.

"Jen, do you want to stay here with Elizabeth tonight?" she asked gently. "If not, I'll take you home. Jason is sending a car."

Jen looked at her sister.

"I'll be fine, Jen," Elizabeth said. "And you'll want to be with Ian. He'll take care of you."

Jen nodded. She was unsurprised that her sister recognized that. Elizabeth, of course, with piercing sororial insight, understood her, perhaps even better than she understood herself. Gratefully, she hugged her, gathered up her books and followed Trish into the night.

Chapter Eight

Jen was jarred into wakefulness the next morning.

"Jen, I'm sorry, so sorry. Is there anything I can do?"

Still sleep-fogged, she recognized Eric's voice. She recalled the urgent ringing of the telephone but she could not remember answering it. It was, she supposed, the effect of the small pink pill Trish had given to Ian and that he, in turn, had pressed upon her tongue, then lifted a glass of very cold water to her lips to wash it down. Trish was a doctor. She routinely carried antidotes to grief.

"No. I don't think so, but thank you," she told Eric, and glanced at her watch, her hand trembling. She had thought she would not sleep at all and now it was mid-morning. She wondered absently why her answer to Eric's question sounded so childlike. Perhaps it was because she was so newly orphaned, she thought suddenly. *Orphan.* The word intrigued her. As a child she had dreamed of being orphaned, of being adopted by a be-

nign Daddy Long Legs, an indulgent Daddy Warbucks.
Such caring surrogate fathers would pluck her from her
unhappy home; they would coddle and spoil her, those
powerful fictional parents. She sat up in bed, smiled at
the memory, and wondered if it had been Ian who had
slipped the long white nightshirt over her head, or if
Trish, who had taken her home, had selected it. It did not
matter.

"I know that there will be a lot to do, arrangements to
be made." Eric was gently persistent.

Cynthia had, in the golden days of her marriage, spoken with admiration of Eric's persistence. "That's how he
gets the funding for his documentaries, the cooperation
of his subjects. No one likes to say no to Eric," she had
reported proudly.

"I want to help, Jen." He would not be put off.

She wondered, unkindly, if he wanted more than that.
Closeness to Jen would mean closeness to Cynthia. Immediately, she regretted the thought. Eric had always
been generous, always ready to offer support. She knew
that he had a special feeling for her as she had a special
feeling for him. Theirs had been a spontaneous and in-
stinctive friendship, independent of Cynthia, independent of Ian. There had been laughter between them and
sudden exchanges of thoughts and feelings, islands of intimacy amid the waves of gaiety at large holiday parties.
It was Jen to whom Eric had turned when the need to
talk about Cynthia had overwhelmed him. Of course he
had no ulterior motive.

"That's sweet of you, Eric," she said softly. "But Bert and
Ian are seeing to everything. At least that's what I think."

She vaguely recalled Ian saying something about meeting Bert to make funeral arrangements, to see what had

to be done. She had been half asleep as he moved through the loft in the milky light of early morning. She remembered now that Elizabeth had called and Ian had spoken to her, his hand resting on Jen's head. Even in half sleep, that conversation had surprised her. Ian and Elizabeth rarely talked, but clearly today was different. Death had brushed their lives, redrawn their perspective. They had a common cause, Elizabeth and Bert, Jen and Ian.

Now, in the daylight brightness, it seemed only reasonable that Ian had chosen to be involved, that Elizabeth had turned to him and that he, in turn, had chosen to help Bert. There was a funeral to be organized, papers to be signed, calls to be made. This was a family affair and Ian was her family just as Bert was Elizabeth's family. It had taken their mother's death for her sister to recognize that.

What could Eric, so newly bereft of his own family, do to help?

She stared helplessly at the receiver, thinking of words to forestall him, and saw that a note in Ian's broad hand lay on the bedside table.

"Just a minute, Eric."

She scanned it quickly. Ian was meeting Bert at the nursing home. The director had wanted to meet with the family, to assure them, he presumed, that the home had in no way been negligent. He would call her when he knew more. *Get some rest, babe. I love you.*

In place of a signature he had drawn a long-stalked sunflower with curling petals, their secret symbol of love.

She read it again and tucked it into the pocket of her nightshirt.

"Bert and Ian are at the nursing home, Eric. I'm going to wait for him to call. And then maybe we can meet."

"I'll call you later, then. You're all right?"

"Yes, yes, I'm all right. But, Eric, how did you know about my mother?"

"Cynthia called to tell me."

"Cynthia?" She could not mute the surprise in her voice.

"Yes. She knows how much I care about you. She understands that you and I are friends, good friends. She wanted me to know. She thought that maybe I could be helpful, do something for you. Juggle. Stand on my head, make you laugh. Take you out for an expensive brunch."

"That was good of her."

"Cynthia's a very good person," he said. "I know that. I've always known that. I should have trusted her goodness."

She heard the regret in his voice, feared that he might weep yet again and that his tears would trigger her own.

"You two should really talk, you and Cynthia," she said carefully. "Couldn't you still work things out?"

It was not a question, she knew, that she had any right to ask. It did not surprise her that he did not answer it.

"I'll call you soon, Jen," he said gently. "You should have something to eat. Brunch. Let's meet for brunch."

"Maybe. We'll see." But she knew, even as she hung up, that she would meet him. It was only right that she accept his kindness.

She dialed Elizabeth's number. No answer. Her sister, she knew with certainty, had gone to her office. It would be like her. Easier for Elizabeth to deal with private grief in a public venue, shielded behind piles of papers, the silence of sorrow banished by urgently ringing phones, inter-office memos, meetings and the admiration of her colleagues. *So wonderful to come to work in the face of such a loss. Such dedication.*

Jen would not go to work. The Nightingale's summer catalog could wait a day, two days, a week, forever.

She took a shower, shrugged into a robe, made coffee. There was no bread for toast. The butter was rancid. Ian had promised to shop but he had forgotten. She wandered over to his easel, studied the painting he had probably completed late in the evening. A late winter urban skyscape, gray clouds colliding, pierced by spires, buffeting the cylindrical cisterns on the rooftops of high-rises. It was wonderful. It beckoned her skyward. She forgave him for neglecting the shopping. No, he had not forgotten. He had gotten lost in his work. He could not have paused in his work to buy bread and butter. She touched the canvas. The paint was dry.

The phone rang. Ian, his voice tender, laced with worry.

"Are you all right? You were really zonked out when I left."

"That would be Trish's little pink pill. I'm fine. What's happening?"

"They want to do an autopsy. They say it's called for. Do you object?"

"No. Does Elizabeth object?"

"Bert doesn't think she will. She's at work. He's calling her at the school. She's a cold one, your sister, going to work today."

"No. She's not cold. She deals with things in her own way." She would share her new perception of Elizabeth with him, but not now, not today, not on the phone.

"All right. Whatever you say. I'll be home in two or three hours. We're supposed to pack up your mother's stuff, go over to the hospital, sign papers."

"Ian, thank you. And I loved your painting."

"Ah, my painting. Yeah. It's okay. Actually, I think it's more than okay."

She heard the pleasure in his voice and knew that he had to be smiling, running his fingers through his bright hair. A difficult work completed, another hurdle won. There would be a show. He was almost there.

"Anyway, I'm going to brunch with Eric."

"With Eric?"

"There's nothing to eat in the house. He called. He wants to help, to do something. And I'm hungry."

"Have a good brunch, then." Amusement rather than anger tinged his voice.

"And I loved your sunflower."

"And I love you."

He hung up then, and when Eric called she thanked him and asked when and where they could meet.

"The Bryant Park Grill," he said. "Twelve-thirty. I have to meet someone there just before noon, but I'll be done by then. So is twelve-thirty good?"

"That's fine," she agreed.

Cynthia called just as she was leaving the loft. She was messengering over a black suit in Jen's size that had been used in a catalog shoot.

"You'll need it," Cynthia said. "You know."

"Yes. For the funeral," Jen agreed.

The word did not frighten her. Her mother had died and would be buried. There would be a funeral, arranged by Bert with Ian's help.

Nor did Cynthia's gesture surprise her. It was like Cynthia to be concerned about appropriate clothing, to be attentive to details. She would outfit Jen for the funeral as she outfitted her daughters each day in matching socks and T-shirts, as she had for so many years, filled Eric's drawers with pastel shirts and paisley ties. She would dress all of them in the uniforms of her love. It was what she did best and she loved doing it. That Jen knew and for that she was grateful.

"Thanks for taking care of that, Cynthia," she said, surprised that her voice broke. Her friends' kindness, Cynthia's and Eric's both, undermined her calm.

"Should I look for something for Elizabeth?" Cynthia asked. "I thought a plain black linen dress."

"No. I don't think so."

Elizabeth would not welcome a gift from Cynthia, would perhaps see it as an intrusion, an unwelcome exercise of control.

"You know Elizabeth," she added by way of apology. "But thanks for thinking of her, Cynthia. Thanks for thinking of both of us."

It occurred to Jen, as she walked out into the pale sunlight of waning winter, that she had not told Cynthia she would be meeting Eric. An innocent omission, but one that nagged at her as she slowly made her way through the crowded streets to Bryant Park.

Although the day was chilly the park was crowded. Chess players bent over boards set up on small tables and moved their pieces with gloved hands. Urban readers, their canvas bags overflowing with books, sat on benches and turned pages. Young mothers, colored scarves loosely dangling, pushed canvas strollers and called to the toddlers in bulky jackets who scurried ahead of them. They lifted their faces to the teasing platinum orb of the sun, struggling to free itself from the encroaching mist of gossamer clouds.

Jen saw an artist, with whom she had taken a life drawing class, perched on a stool, an open sketch pad on his lap. She wanted to see what he was drawing, but she hurried on before he could recognize her. She did not want him to ask her how she was. What would she say? *I'm feeling sad today because my mother died last night and I don't know how to mourn her.* She imagined his bewilderment, his uneasy laughter.

She walked swiftly to the Grill where, despite the weather, tables had been set up on the terrace for a few intrepid patrons. Three women bundled into fur coats studied a swatch book spread open before them as they sipped their coffee, turning the pages with their gloved hands. She glanced at an elderly man and woman, seated side by side. The sun gilded their white hair and they smiled at each other as they stirred their hot chocolate. *Had her mother and father ever smiled at each other, had they ever reveled in an hour of leisure on a wintry morning?* The thought saddened her and she turned toward the northern corner of the terrace where two men sat, their table placed in a patch of sunlight, their backs toward her.

"Waiter, our check, please."

One of the men was Eric. She recognized his voice even before he turned and she saw his face in profile. Unseen, she watched from the entryway as he waved to the waiter and reached for his briefcase. His companion stood. He was a very young man, a boy, really, as fair-haired and fine-featured as Eric himself. He wore the requisite uniform of the graduate student—faded jeans, a heavy gray sweater, leather patches on the elbows, shabby and expensive. The waiter gave Eric the bill as the boy struggled with his backpack. Stooped by his burden, he bent and kissed Eric on the cheek. Eric fumbled for his credit card and removed several bills from his wallet, which he pressed into the boy's hand, closing his resistant fingers over them. They embraced then, an awkward male entanglement of shoulders and arms.

Jen moved indoors, her heart pounding, her face flushed. She tried to remember Trish's description of the youth she and Jason had seen with Eric in the East Village. Fair-haired, she had said, and slender, oddly resembling Eric himself. The descriptions matched.

"May I help you, madam?"

The young woman at the reservations desk leaned toward her, but it was Eric who suddenly appeared at her side who answered.

"We have a reservation. Eric Anders."

He took Jen's hand, pressed it in friendship and compassion.

"Yes. Of course, Mr. Anders."

Dutifully, they followed her to a table that overlooked the terrace table he had just vacated. Jen stared out at the coffee cup he had left behind, at the napkin that fluttered in the wind. A yellow pencil remained on the table, forgotten by the young man who had kissed Eric goodbye.

She opened the menu. She had not realized how hungry she was. Too quickly she ordered an omelet, croissants.

"I'll have the same," he said.

She filled her own coffee cup and reached for Eric's.

"Not yet," he said. "I just had a cup of coffee."

"Oh, yes. I saw you and your—friend. He was leaving just as I arrived. Who was he—someone you're working with? Are you researching a new film?" she asked, hating herself for the guile that coated her question. Eric deserved better from her.

He looked at her through narrowed eyes.

"It wasn't a business meeting, Jen," he said shortly, and she was relieved and shamed that he had not lied.

He reached across the table and took her hand in
his own.

"This must be a very hard day for you." His voice was
softer, his brief irritation forgotten. He had, after all, volunteered to comfort her on this, her first day of mourning.

She nodded. "It's hard because it was so sudden. She was
old and she wasn't well, but we never thought that she was
that ill. Yes, it was a shock. She was a difficult woman, my
mother, and things were never really good between us, but
I am sad, very sad. I'm sad because her life was so filled
with bitterness. Because she didn't know how to love. I
guess it's not her death that grieves me—it's her life."

Her eyes filled with tears. Eric held her hand tightly.
He would comfort her as she had comforted him. His
compassion soothed her, eased her words. Always there
had been this special rapport between them.

"Do you know," she said, "I never heard her laugh. Not
her and not my father. Isn't that terrible—to have lived
in a house with a mother and father who never laughed?"

"Terrible and sad," he agreed, and fell silent as their
food arrived and the waiter, with great care, arranged the
dishes before them.

"Terrible and sad for the parents. Terrible and sad for
the kids," he repeated as the waiter brought a bread basket and glided away.

"They say that divorce causes horrific harm to kids,"
she said. "But I think it's far worse for children to grow
up in a house where there is so much anger between their
parents that they live in fear. Elizabeth and I used to shut
our bedroom doors against their arguments. We buried
ourselves in books. We wanted the words on the page to
block out the words our parents shouted at each other,

his insults, her accusations. I used to pray that they would separate, that they would never again live in the same house and that I would live far away from both of them. Divorce, separation, they can't be as bad as a childhood lived on a battleground."

He set down his fork, his face blanched.

"No. I suppose not." He spoke so softly that she had to strain to hear him.

"Oh, Eric, I'm sorry." Her voice trembled with regret. "Stupid of me to talk to you like that. I forgot what you're going through, you and Cynthia." Her words tumbled awkwardly over one another. She had not meant to cause him pain.

"No. It's all right, Jen. What you said doesn't apply to Cynthia and myself." He spoke softly but calmly. "There was never any anger between us. Julie and Liza were never frightened that an explosion would erupt. No shouting. No loud arguments. Considering all that's happened, it's a strange thing to say but we were a very happy family. That's the irony of it. And that's why I suppose our separation is so shocking, so unbelievable to everyone who knew us. You know, I still can't believe it myself. I wake up in my lousy little apartment and I have to remind myself that I'm alone, that everything in my life has changed, that in another part of the city my little girls are brushing their hair, that my wife, my beautiful wife, is getting dressed. I loved watching them brush their hair. I loved watching Cynthia choose her clothes."

He crushed a roll and lifted the crumbs one by one from the white cloth to his mouth. It was as though each kernel of grain was a memory to be discreetly savored.

"We all thought of you as happy. The ideal marriage. The ideal life. At our book group meeting last night we talked about envy and the consensus was that each of us envied Cynthia. Envied her the happiness of her family, of her life. I could never compare my parents' situation to whatever is happening between you and Cynthia. I didn't mean to. But I should have been more sensitive when I talked about kids and divorce. It upset you and I'm sorry."

Jen flushed. She had said too much yet not enough.

Eric nodded. His words of reply came slowly and he spoke with his eyes downcast as though he feared to meet her gaze.

"What you said upset me because your parents' marriage sounded so much like another relationship I was in when I was very young. Before I met Cynthia. It was a bad time in my life. I was foolish and careless and I caused a great deal of damage. Actually, we both caused a great deal of damage, the woman I was with and myself. The worst of it is that I never told Cynthia about it. And one thing that Cynthia cannot bear is deception. I don't know if Cynthia ever told you that her father had deceived her mother. He had pretended that they were the all-American happy family while secretly he had another life, another family in Philly. She had had to cope with that in her childhood. She had lived a lie and she had promised herself that her own marriage would be different, that it would be absolutely honest. She didn't want Liza and Julie to have to deal with the kind of pain she had suffered. She didn't want them to have a father who lied and concealed. And I agreed with her. I reassured her. And all the while I had a secret. A secret that I could not bring myself to share with her." His voice was flat, his eyes soft with sorrow.

"She discovered your secret?" Jen asked.

She remembered Cynthia's reaction when they discussed Sylvia Plath's anguished journal entry when she learned that her husband, Ted Hughes, had lied to her. "What I cannot forgive is dishonesty," the poet had written. Cynthia had quoted her words, had agreed with them unequivocally. Dishonesty was the unforgivable sin.

"No. She didn't discover it. The time came when I had to tell her. Jen, I would be betraying her if I told you anything more. We agreed, Cynthia and myself, to get through this without involving anyone else. You understand that?" he asked pleadingly.

"I understand that." She hesitated. "Eric, who were you with this morning? Who was the young man I saw you with?"

"Paul," he said, a smile playing at his lips. "His name is Paul. But, Jen, it's not what you think."

"It doesn't matter. It doesn't matter what I think." She reached for his mound of crumbs, scattered them across the white cloth. "You are my friend. My good and kind friend. And Cynthia is my friend. And I am lucky to have both of you. Especially today."

Her tears fell freely then and he waited patiently until her grief subsided, his hand covering hers. He offered her a silk handkerchief that surely had been a gift from Cynthia.

"You'll be at the funeral?" she asked as they left the restaurant.

"I'll be there," he promised, and bent to kiss her on the cheek, his lips soft and warm against her skin.

The funeral, a graveside service, was held at a small cemetery in New Jersey not far from the roaring waters of the Hudson, filled to overflowing that week by

the northeastern rains that marked the onset of spring.
Jen, her gamin face pale, her black curls subdued by
the beret that Cynthia had included with the elegant
but simple black dress and cape, stood beside Ian. He
wore a newly purchased blazer and khaki slacks, his
carrot-colored hair tucked into a tweed cap. He was,
Jen thought, making a statement of a kind, an ac-
knowledgment that he was graduating into a new time
of life, an era of responsibility. He and Bert had seen to
funeral arrangements. He had called relatives of Jen's
whom he had never met, speaking in hushed tones to
strangers even while Guy Maestrato, the gallery owner
who had long been interested in his work, crouched on
the floor of the loft and studied the new canvases approvingly. He spoke of a contract, of potential collectors, of percentages.

Ian would have a one-man show. He would meet with
critics and collectors, deposit money in the bank and
write checks. He had inched slowly toward this new beginning. It was Jen who had prodded him, her gathering self-awareness spurring him to a realization of all
that he could do, of all that he had to do, for himself,
for their life together. But in the end, the accomplish-
ment was his. He felt a new pride, a new confidence.

"Let me take care of you," he had told Jen when Maestrato left. "Will you let me take care of you?"

Wordlessly she had nodded her assent. Of course she
would let him. And she in turn would care for him, as
she had through all their time together. But now there
would be mutuality, reciprocity. They were moving forward, their lives entwined, each dependent on the other,
free of secrets, unafraid of betrayal. They would not re-

peat the mistakes of others. They would not part from each other amid whispers and wonderings.

A cold breeze blew through the cemetery and Jen shivered. Ian took her hand in his own, first one and then the other, warming her fingers.

Elizabeth and Bert stood opposite her, Bert's hand resting on his wife's shoulder. They both wore charcoal-gray suits and white shirts; Elizabeth held Adam's hand. The handsome dark-haired boy, his face expressionless, his dark eyes wide with bewilderment, shifted rhythmically from one foot to another as though the controlled pattern of his movement might contain the gathering chaos that haunted him.

There had been much discussion as to whether or not he should attend the funeral. It was, after all, his grandmother who had died, although he had seldom seen her and she had rarely asked about him. And yet, when they cleared out the old woman's bedside table they had found a framed photograph of Adam in the drawer, the glass smudged with fingerprints. She had, they realized, often studied the photo of the grandson whose existence she had ignored. It had been Bert who thought that Adam should be with them at the funeral and it was he who had consulted with Dr. Theobald, who, surprisingly, had agreed.

"It may penetrate," the weary doctor had said. "It may mean something to him. And, as you say, she was his grandmother."

Penetrate. A new code word, Elizabeth had thought bitterly, but when she pressed Adam's hand as he stood beside her, he returned the pressure, and when Jen stood on tiptoe to kiss him, he lowered his head.

"You're short," he told his aunt.

"Very short," she agreed.

He did not flinch when Ian put his large hand on his head.

"I'm your Uncle Ian," he told the boy, who repeated the word, now placing his weight on his left foot and then on his right.

"Uncle," he said without expression, and stared vacantly ahead as another funeral cortege moved down the narrow pathway, opposite the open gravesite where their own small group had assembled.

The relatives, a scattering of distant cousins, their pale faces masks of resentment and irritation, stood together. They had done their duty by coming, and now they stole surreptitious glances at their watches, murmuring softly to one another. One elderly man consulted a train schedule. A woman whose rusted black hat perched precariously on her silver hair, slid a pill under her tongue. Two old women leaned on their canes and stared into the grave. They were residents of the nursing home and, they told Jen and Elizabeth, had often played canasta with their mother. The sisters looked at each other. They had not known their mother played canasta. That lack of knowledge intensified their sadness. She had hidden the smallest pleasures of her life from them.

A group of teachers from Elizabeth's school clustered near her in a show of professional solidarity. Former neighbors approached and kissed the sisters, then shuffled back to stand at a distance from the mound of dirt that would be shoveled over the coffin soon enough. Jen wondered how many of them remembered the angry shouts that had emanated from their home, but then her mother had always been careful to slam the windows shut, to draw the curtains. Appearances had been important to her. The hatreds of the household had been contained.

All the members of the book club were there. Cynthia and Eric had arrived in separate cars but now stood side by side. He studied the scene with his cinematographer's eye, brushing that recalcitrant shock of fair hair from his forehead. Cynthia had pulled her bright hair back and clipped it into place with a black velvet bow that matched the trim of her well-cut black suit.

Rina and Ray, Jeremy walking between them, approached slowly, a newly formed family. Jeremy carried two white roses, which he held with great care. His presence did not surprise them. It was like Rina to offer her son the experience of death.

Trish looked at Jason and shook her head. They would not have brought Amanda to a cemetery, but then all their lives, all their choices were so different. She would not stand in judgment of her friends. Nor would she answer her cell phone, although its insistent ring shattered the ominous silence. The demands of her office no longer controlled her. She switched it off and turned to nod to Donna and Tim.

It seemed natural for Donna and Tim to move toward Rina and Ray, for Donna to bend to kiss Jeremy and straighten the boy's tie, for Ray to kiss her on the cheek as Tim removed his clarinet from its case.

A very young minister spoke briefly. He had not known the deceased, but he knew that her life had not been a happy one. Still, her daughters, Jen and Elizabeth (he stumbled over their names, newly learned that morning) had been dutiful and caring and her death had been mercifully swift and painless. For that he invited the gratitude of those who had come to pay their last respects. He did not speak of love nor did he lift his eyes from his notes.

The coffin was lowered into the grave, ribs of sunlight dancing across the pale wood. The minister offered a short prayer and stepped back as the mourners softly intoned the requisite "amen."

Tim lifted his clarinet to his lips. The tremolos of a mournful Dvorák sonata filled the air. Jen and Elizabeth lifted clumps of earth and dropped them onto the coffin. They turned to each other and walked hand in hand toward Adam, who had not ceased his restless movement. Left foot. Right foot. Left foot. Right foot. Bert and Ian each shoveled earth into the grave and then stood aside to allow others to take their turns. The last to approach the grave was Jeremy, who walked beside Rina, clutching his white roses. Abruptly, he turned to Adam and held out a flower.

"Here," he said. "For your grandmother."

Adam stared at him, hesitated, and took the flower. Together, the two boys dropped the full-blown blossoms onto the pale wooden coffin. The soft white petals scattered like oversize teardrops across the thin layer of rich, dark earth that blanketed it. Adam stepped back. A single tear glistened on his cheek. Elizabeth gently wiped her son's face, grateful for the gift of his sorrow.

The notes of the clarinet shivered against the sweep of the wind as slowly, slowly, their small group turned to leave. Trish noted that Cynthia walked beside Eric and she listened as Cynthia spoke, her words not addressed to him but softly murmured, a grief offering of a kind, like the strains of music that lingered in the quiet air.

"Two children, two roses," she said.

The words, Trish remembered, were reminiscent of Sylvia Plath's poem "Kindness." "Two children. Two roses," Eric repeated. "We have two children, Cynthia." His words were a plea.

Trish turned away so that she would not hear Cynthia's whispered reply, so that she would not see the pain that surely swept across Eric's narrow face. She did notice that Eric waved away the town car that had chauffeured him to the cemetery and took a seat beside Cynthia in the limo in which she had arrived.

She turned and linked her arm through Jason's, pleased that he placed his hand over hers as though to rescue her from the loneliness inevitable in any brush with death. They would not return to their offices after this funeral. They would go home and hold each other close, their bodies throbbing with warmth and love and life, their eyes closed against the memory of these serried acres of death marked by the chiseled gravestones of remembrance.

The wind ceased and the new and unfamiliar warmth of spring caused the mourners to remove their dark outer clothing and lift their faces to the sun's brightness. Then swiftly, too swiftly, they all hurried to their waiting cars.

Chapter Nine

Sunlight flooded the huge windows of Cynthia's office and spangled the broad surface of her desk with dancing beams. Cynthia frowned and drew the shades.

"It's not that I don't love the rays," she said apologetically to Jen, who sat opposite her. "It's just that seeing them makes me want to rush toward summer. I begin to think about beaches and boat trips and vacations when I should be getting ideas for the fall catalog and scheduling meetings with the buyers to discuss Christmas ideas."

"Forget winter holidays. I saw my first daffodil today," Jen protested. "It's spring. Why shouldn't you be thinking about the summer?"

"I guess because it will be hard to make plans this year. Eric and I have to talk about it. But then Eric and I have to talk about so many things." Sadness tinged her voice.

"Then why don't you?" Jen asked daringly.

"This isn't the time or place to talk about that," Cynthia said, her tone abruptly changing. She moved her desk chair back as though to place a distance between them. "And I do have to think about the November catalog. You know Nightingale's marketing strategy—think ahead, plan ahead or else get left behind in the great merchandising rat race."

She shrugged and plucked an embossed invitation from the small pile of correspondence on her desk.

"This is what I wanted to talk to you about. Have you ever done runway sketches at any of the fashion shows?"

She held the invitation out and Jen studied it. A group of young designers had banded together and scheduled a show at the New York Botanical Garden. A gutsy and expensive enterprise, Jen thought, although some of the names were familiar. They were young, newcomers to the glitzy fashion scene who were just beginning to get some name recognition but were still far from the top. Cynthia was famous in the fashion world for her ability to spot emerging talent and sign her new discoveries to exclusive Nightingale's contracts.

"No. I've never done runway sketches. I've done layouts from photographs, and to be honest, I think photography works best for fashion promotions," Jen said. "If I were you I would go with a standard photo shoot."

"That's getting boring and the models get more attention than the clothing. What I have in mind are whimsical, fluid sketches. Pen and ink, really. Maybe some swift soft brushwork. I think you'd be great at it and it would be a new approach for Nightingale's."

Jen hesitated. She did not want to reject an assignment from Cynthia, who had so often gone out of her way to find work for her, but she had determined to cut back.

She had been asked to add panels to her "Lottery" sketches and Ian wanted her to design the invitation to his show and do the graphics for the brochure. The need for additional income was no longer as pressing as it had been. Her mother's death had changed that. Not only was she free of paying for her mother's care, but she and Elizabeth had been astonished to learn that their mother had left them a small estate.

"Her parting blow," Elizabeth had said. "Asking for our help when she didn't need it. Even though she knew it was hard for us to come up with the money."

"I think she wanted to maintain some sort of contact with us and that was her way of doing it. She made sure we had to visit the damn nursing home to settle bills and make arrangements," Jen had conjectured. "It was a dirty trick but then she wasn't exactly Marmee."

"And we're not exactly little women," Elizabeth had agreed, and they had laughed at the ludicrousness of the comparison.

But then they, like the others, had been catapulted into the domestic idyll Alcott had created. Now that the book club was newly immersed in *Little Women,* the March family formed a new frame of reference for all the members of the group. The tale of the four sisters, whose father was gallantly attached to the Union army and whose mother was the selfless and beatific Marmee, had captured them. The all-but-forgotten secret language of the glory reading days of their girlhoods, the elegant archaic Alcott style that had once enchanted them, was now wondrously retrieved.

"Fiddlesticks," Rina said to Donna during one of their late-night phone conversations.

"Stop jabbering," Cynthia said to her mystified daughters.

"Oh, dear me!" Trish murmured to an amused Jason when he talked about a deal that had fallen through.

They burst into giggles at each usage and smiled because the secret coda of their younger selves had been restored to them.

"I'd love to try it, Cynthia," Jen said at last. "But I'm sort of overloaded. And I'm not sure how good I'd be at it."

"Why don't you let me be the judge of that?" Cynthia said. "Look, it's just the one afternoon. We could go up to the Botanical Garden together and then have dinner. It's been so long since you and I had time just to talk."

There was a new urgency in her voice, almost a plea. The assignment was a pretext, Jen realized. Cynthia might want the drawings, but what she really wanted was time alone with Jen, an exchange of confidences, an hour of intimacy, but being Cynthia, she wanted it on her terms. She would pick the time and place for such a meeting. She would choose the topic and set the parameters of discussion. What did she want to talk about— Eric, her children, a new professional opportunity? Jen could not know, but she did know that she had to agree. She sighed.

"All right," she said. "I'll do it."

Dutifully she copied the time and date into her diary.

"I'll get a car," Cynthia said. "It's a nice ride up there. And the garden is beautiful now. Eric took the twins there last Sunday."

Carelessly she tossed his name into the conversation, and carefully Jen avoided responding.

"See you then."

She picked up her oversize leather portfolio. She was meeting Donna for dinner, but there was still time to go to the printer and look at the stock for Ian's invitations, still time to stop at Barnes & Noble to pick up the biography of Louisa May Alcott that she had ordered.

Donna was already at Gino's when Jen, breathless from racing across town, hurried to their usual corner table.

"Sorry I'm late," she apologized, placing her portfolio on the floor beside her. "But I had this meeting with Cynthia and it went on for longer than I thought it would."

"I thought you were going to cut back on the Nightingale's work," Donna said.

"I was. But she had this one assignment that she wanted me to accept. And she wants to have dinner afterward. It's been a really long time since she and I met alone outside of Nightingale's. She wants to talk."

"So she suckered you in." Donna grinned. "Great confidences in the offing. The mystery revealed. All our wondering put to rest. I don't blame you for agreeing."

Jen laughed.

"Yup. She suckered me in. Although you may have noticed that I've gotten a lot better at saying no this year. I said yes because it seemed so important to her and because I half wanted to do it. And yeah, I am curious. Aren't we all?"

"Not curious. Obsessed. But it's all right. You don't owe me any explanation." Donna turned her attention to the menu, as Jen bent yet again to straighten out her portfolio and find a place for her book bag.

Settled at last, she looked across the table at her friend. There was something different about Donna. It took her a few seconds to realize what it was.

"Donna, your hair. You've cut your hair," she said in surprise.

Donna, they had all noted, had always styled her hair to define her role. At the hospital she wore it coiled into a bun, as much a part of her uniform as her long white coat. She loosened it after work, allowing it to fall to her shoulders in lucent waves, a sensual invitation, an announcement of careless freedom, a silken gift to her lovers.

"Do you like it?" Donna ran her fingers through the shimmering layers of thick golden hair that helmeted her head.

"I'm thinking."

Jen studied her friend's face carefully, saw how the new cut more sharply defined Donna's soft features. She noticed, for the first time, the thick golden arcs of Donna's eyebrows, the curling, amber-colored lashes that swept the rise of her rose-gold cheeks.

"I like it," she said at last. "It suits you."

The waiter approached, hovered over them. A shy young Italian, barely out of his teens, his English halting, his gaze fixed on Donna's hair. Swiftly, they ordered. Linguini, salad, a carafe of Chianti. His smile, as he withdrew, was for Donna.

"Well, our waiter clearly approves of your hair," Jen said. "What does Tim think?"

She broke off a piece of garlic bread and thought that only months ago she would have asked about Ray's reaction as well. Always she had marveled at the way Donna managed to split her life between Tim and Ray but, of course, all that had changed. It was Rina and Ray now, a seemingly effortless shift in relationships.

"Oh, Tim." Donna laughed carelessly. "He said he likes it. But it wouldn't be important if he didn't like it. It's not as though Tim and I are at the center of each other's lives. We're not like you and Ian."

Jen recognized the truth of her words. She and Ian were, at last, at the center of each other's lives, sharers and partners. She no longer felt put upon, ever the conciliatory victim. Things were good between them and slowly, slowly getting better. She smiled at Donna, grateful to her friend for recognizing the change.

"What *is* it like, between you and Tim?" she asked. It was not a question she had ever asked before.

"It's as it always was between us," Donna replied calmly. "Comfortable. Pleasant. We fit ourselves into each other's lives. No strings attached. No questions asked. No answers necessary. My being with Ray didn't bother him. I don't care if he sees another woman. We're free. It's much like the rest of my life. Comfortable. Easy. All part of the scenario. *Donna Saunders and Her Fabulous Life.* A sitcom featuring one character. The great apartment. The good job at the hospital that guarantees me security. Time off whenever I want to take a trip to Europe, a couple of weeks in the Caribbean. So there, too, I'm free. My mother's legacy fulfilled. I'm not trapped as she was. I have the good life she always wanted. I can read for pleasure, not for escape. I'm my own person, in a way that she never was. My only responsibility is to myself."

Her voice thickened and she leaned forward conspiratorially.

"But now somehow, that's not enough. I need more. A challenge, a connection. Professionally. Personally. I want to start over—something my mother was never able to do. I think maybe I took courage from Nafisi and the women of the Tehran book group, from Edith Wharton and I guess even from Cynthia. If they changed their lives, I could change mine. So I've made some plans."

"What sort of plans?"

"I applied for a grant at the National Institute for Health in Washington. I have an idea for a new approach to a low-carb diet linked to psychotherapy geared to patients with eating disorders—something that hasn't been tried before. It's experimental and may not work. And the grant is for a year without a guarantee of renewal, so I'd be taking a chance, but I guess, for all of us, this has been a year of taking chances. Or at least making changes."

"Or accepting changes," Jen added.

The odd reconfiguring of their lives, all the gains and losses of the seasons past, dizzied her. Cynthia without Eric, Rina with Ray, she and Ian at a new and happier place, her mother's death and now Donna's move: change upon change in an endlessly winding pathway. Cynthia's decision had plunged them into a maze of discovery, had provided each of them with an odd compass that had guided them to new emotional clearings.

"Then you'll be moving to D.C.?" she asked.

"If I get the grant. Which I think I will. Trish wrote a terrific letter of recommendation and so did some of the other doctors."

"Then Trish doesn't mind your leaving?"

"I suppose she does. We're good friends and we worked so well together. But her life is pretty centered around Jason and Amanda these days. She found a vacation house in the Berkshires and she's excited about that. A shift for her. For a while there, I thought she was drowning in boredom à la Emma Bovary and Anna Karenina pre-Vronsky. But not now. Anyway she's supportive of my decision."

The waiter set their plates before them, filled their wineglasses and left the carafe of Chianti on the table.

Jen lifted a glass.

"To you and your new life," she said.

Donna touched Jen's glass with her own.

"To you and Ian. To Ian's show. To our friendship. Washington's not the end of the world. Shuttle flights. The Metroliner. I'll come in."

"We'll schedule book group meetings around your trips to New York," Jen promised recklessly. "Maybe we'll all come to Washington. A weekend book group marathon. We'll do two books, three books, watch a movie. We'll have another dinner with Anna Karenina. As Jo said at Meg's wedding, 'Long life to your resolution.' Let's drink to that."

"Whatever that means," Donna said as she took a sip of wine. "I have to tell you, Jen, I'm finding our little women a bit over the top—all that damn sanctimony and self-sacrifice."

"Oh no, don't say that, Donna. That's sacrilege!" Jen giggled and refilled their wineglasses. "But you're right. And I'll bet Cynthia leads off the discussion by asking us which of the March girls we would want to be."

"A lot less challenging than our envy revelations," Donna said. "You can ask her that over dinner. Although that's probably not what she wants to talk to you about."

"I don't think she has an agenda," Jen replied vaguely. She did not want to talk about Cynthia. She did not want to think about Cynthia and Eric. At night, lying in bed beside Ian, his hand resting on her head, she thought of the sadness in Eric's eyes, the edge in Cynthia's voice. Their misery tarnished the glow of her new happiness.

She filled her glass yet again and asked Donna what she thought of the Smith illustrations in the Centennial Edition of *Little Women*, which both of them were reading. She could see them as the kind of drawings Cynthia envisioned for the holiday catalog.

"Not such a great idea," Donna replied. "Louisa May Alcott is a bit too retro for today's young mods. I don't think anyone except nostalgic readers like our group would relate to her heroines, and actually I'm getting a bit tired of them myself."

"Have you gotten up to Beth's death yet?" Jen asked.

"Not yet."

"You'll cry. No matter how irritated you may be with the March girls, you'll cry. All the sophisticated dames like us cried their eyes out at the Broadway show a while back."

"Probably," Donna agreed. "I intend to have a box of Kleenex ready."

They smiled at each other and, having drained their wineglasses, ordered anisette, which the handsome waiter brought. The after-dinner drink was complimentary, he told them. Jen noticed that his hand brushed Donna's hair as he set the tray down.

Banks of daffodils, their golden heads nodding in the soft spring breeze, bordered the green velvet carpet of the improvised runway that had been set up in the heart of the garden. As each model made her way down, she bent and plucked a flower. The lithe blonde whose loose mint-colored chiffon dress resembled a cloud of sea foam, lifted the flower to her nose and inhaled its aroma. The very tall African American whose gray-black hair hugged her head, tucked her blossom into the pleated frontage of her magenta silk gown. The Asian model in the yellow pantsuit threaded it through the shining folds of her black hair. Jen, her charcoal stick moving rapidly across the broad sheets of her sketch pad, included the flower in each drawing. It was a clever idea, she thought. It gave cohesiveness to the vastly different styles of the diverse collections.

Cynthia, seated beside her, studied each drawing after making notes in her own elegant small cloth-covered journal. Shielded by her rimless sunglasses, her gaze was impervious but she nodded her approval.

The young designers clustered together in the rear, stared nervously at her and at the other buyers and merchandising directors they had invited. They hugged press kits, decorated with daffodils, which they handed to the fashion reporters who approached them. This was a make-or-break show for them, Jen knew and, in sympathy, she added a flowing grace to the skirt of an informal gown that she did not really like.

It was late afternoon when the last model made her way down the runway. The auburn-haired beauty in a copper-colored maternity dress pirouetted when she reached the podium, gathered the ample folds of her skirt and curtsied elegantly. The applause at this valedictory gesture was both relieved and admiring. The day had turned unseasonably warm and there was no shade in that area of the garden. Programs became fans and bottles of water were discreetly drained.

The show was a success. Orders were placed, queries made, but the audience was pleased that it was over. Cynthia, always correct, always gracious, accepted a glass of champagne, which she did not drink. She glided over to congratulate the designers. Jen lingered, her own sketch pad thrust into her huge woven shoulder bag.

"Look, there's Cynthia Anders," said one young woman who was gathering up abandoned press kits to another who was carrying order forms. Administrative assistants, Jen knew, chafing at the menial tasks of their first jobs, ready to climb the first rungs of the ladder that would eventually elevate them to a wide windowed office like Cynthia's own.

"I interviewed with her when I got out of college. She's got the dream job," her companion said.

"The dream life."

The pile of press kits slid to the ground. The girl cursed briefly and bent to pick them up, still thinking about Cynthia.

"God, I envy her."

Don't, Jen wanted to say. *Cynthia Anders's life is not enviable. She lies awake, alone in her bed, with only her books for company. And she weeps as she reads.*

But she remained silent and watched as Cynthia chatted with a buyer from Bergdorf's and then moved on to shake the hand of the reed-thin young man in faded jeans whose shock of jet-black hair seemed to stand straight up. He had designed the copper-colored gown and Jen knew that Cynthia had marked his entry with a large star. In the coming weeks she would have lunch with him, look through his portfolio and sign him to an exclusive but not overly indulgent contract. It was her way, the secret of her professional success.

At last Cynthia was ready to leave and they slid into the Nightingale's limo.

"City Island," Cynthia told the driver, and she leaned back. "I feel as though I'm playing hookey," she told Jen. "City Island in the middle of the week when my desk is piled high and Mae is waiting at home to complain about all sorts of domestic crap. But what the hell!" She smiled mischievously.

"And the twins? You don't feel badly about not having dinner with them?" Jen asked. She knew that Cynthia tried to be with the girls as much as possible.

"Eric picked them up after school today. They're having dinner with him."

Her smile faded at the mention of his name, and she did not speak as the car made its way over the causeway and onto the island.

It was only after they entered the restaurant and were seated at a window table that overlooked the gentle waters of the Sound, that she seemed to relax again.

"A good runway show, I thought," she said. "And I liked your drawings. My instinct about sketches instead of photos was right."

"Your instincts usually are," Jen said.

"Except when they're horribly off." She laughed nervously, pulled out her phone, checked for messages and thrust it back into her bag.

The waiter approached. Jen ordered a glass of Chablis and waited for Cynthia to ask for her usual red wine.

"Just sparkling water," Cynthia said, and Jen, who was buttering her roll, lifted her eyebrows in surprise.

"No wine?" she asked. "Come on. Drinking alone is never any fun."

"But pregnant women shouldn't drink."

Jen's knife clattered to the table as she stared at her friend in disbelief.

"Cynthia, I don't understand," she said at last, stumbling over her words.

"I'm not sure I do, either, but there you are," Cynthia replied evenly. "I'm having a baby. The rabbit doesn't lie. Nor do the three pregnancy test kits I used. I am very definitely with child, as our friend Louisa May would say."

"But who…?" Jen's cheeks burned.

Cynthia stared at her.

"You want to know who the father is? I'm still married, you know. Who could it be but Eric?" she asked calmly, a trace of amusement in her voice.

Startled, Jen dropped her eyes. She marveled at the steadiness of Cynthia's hands as she lifted the menu, her attentiveness as she listened to the specials recited by the waiter who had returned with their drinks.

They ordered. Scrod for Cynthia. Jen wondered if pregnant women were supposed to avoid shellfish. Spitefully she opted for the lobster, and then, in a whir of confusion, changed her mind and asked for sea bass. It did not matter. The food would be ashen in her mouth.

"Eric." She repeated his name and took a long sip of her wine.

"You're surprised?" Cynthia asked teasingly.

"I'm surprised," Jen admitted. "I'm more than surprised."

She thought of Eric embracing the young man he called Paul, surely the same youth Trish and Jason had seen him with in the Village coffee bar that distant Saturday night. She remembered his sadness, the softness of regret in his eyes. She hesitated before replying, but there were things she had to say to Cynthia. Her silence would be a betrayal, a dishonesty of a kind, and Cynthia, like Sylvia Plath, could not tolerate dishonesty. She took a long sip of her wine and, impulsively, reached across the table to touch Cynthia's hand before speaking. She would comfort her friend against the impact of words as yet unsaid.

"Eric and I had brunch the day after my mother's death. At the Bryant Grill. He was very kind. He wanted to cheer me up, be supportive," she murmured.

"I know," Cynthia said. "He told me. I was glad that he did that. It's hard enough to lose a parent, but it's even harder when it's a parent with whom you never made peace. I knew how terrible it was for you because I was angry with my father when he died. In fact, I'm still angry with him. Which makes it difficult to mourn him, even after all these years. So I was glad that Eric could ease things for you."

"He did. He was—he always is, so gentle, so understanding." Jen hesitated. "But what I wanted to tell you was that I got to the Grill early. Eric was on the terrace."

She paused, twisted her napkin, gripped anew by uncertainty. And then, gathering strength, she continued. "He wasn't alone."

"Oh?"

"He was with someone. A very young man."

Cynthia nodded. "Paul." She said his name softly. It was not unfamiliar to her.

"They seemed very close. Eric and Paul."

Jen closed her eyes against the memory of her own panic at seeing them together, at watching them embrace, at her unease as she watched Eric give Paul money, at her own reluctance to ask him about it.

"I was sorry I saw them," she told Cynthia miserably. "I would have liked not to know, not to think about what I saw."

"Jen, did you think that Paul and Eric were lovers? Did you think that Eric was gay?"

Incredulity rimmed Cynthia's voice. Her cheeks were flushed. She set her glass down and smiled absently at the waiter, who was busily placing their dishes on the table, spattering their salad with pepper that neither of them wanted. "That's wild. You thought that, after know-ing Eric, knowing both of us, all these years?"

"Yes, that's what I thought," Jen admitted.

"Of course Eric isn't gay. Paul is his son, the child I never knew he had fathered." There was no amusement in her voice now, only the flatness of a sorrow too closely held through too many seasons.

"I don't understand."

"I didn't, either. Not at first. Not even now, after all these months. Although, actually it's not all that com-plex. When Eric was very young, when he was still a stu-dent, he had a relationship with a classmate. A love affair, actually. Her name was Judy. She was a film student in his program. They were in love and then they were out of love. 'We were kids,' he told me, as though that ex-plained everything." She laughed bitterly. "They broke up, but months later she called him. She was pregnant and she was going to have the child. That child was Paul. Eric supported her, supported the child although Judy didn't want him in her life or in Paul's life. She didn't mind if he saw him occasionally. It was, apparently, all very amicable. Judy moved to the coast with Paul and Eric saw them when he went to California. I, of course, never knew that they existed. Eventually Judy married and her husband adopted Paul. He and Judy had no other children and Eric was all right with the adoption although he remained in close touch—or as close as he could be, all things considered. Paul knew Eric was his biological father and he was okay with that. At least that's what Eric claims now. He was a California kid and I guess a lot of kids he knew had even stranger stories. Judy's husband knew about Eric but I never knew about Judy or about Paul. A minor omission." She took a sip of water and looked through the huge picture window at the harbor, where a sloop with brightly colored sails was drifting into the dock, and then continued, her voice growing softer and softer. "Eric neglected to tell me, he says, because he thought I wouldn't be able to handle it, because he thought that Paul's existence would never impact on our life. He was being sensitive to my feelings. He had all sorts of excuses for keeping silent. He didn't want me to think about him with another woman and he truly thought that I would never have to find out. And he might have been right. But last fall, just before our first book club meeting, Judy and her husband were both killed in an automobile accident and Paul came East. He's twenty years old, a kid really, and all of a sudden he was alone in the world. The only parent, the only relative, he had was Eric. He needed a father, up close and personal. He transferred from UCLA to NYU and Eric set him up in a student apartment. But Paul needed a family. He was going to be a real part of Eric's life. Which meant that Eric had to tell me about him."

"Then that's why…" Again Jen's shocked voice trailed off.

"That's why I asked Eric to leave," Cynthia continued in that same flat tone. "I felt betrayed. It was as though our entire marriage had been a lie. It wasn't so much that I minded about Paul. I didn't know him, but just knowing how alone he was made me feel sorry for him. What I minded, what made me miserable, was that Eric had never told me about him. All the years of our marriage, he had had a secret life, just like my father. Eric was doing to me what my father had done to my mother. He had deceived us. Liza and Julie have a half brother they never knew about, whom they had never met. I couldn't forgive him for deceiving me, for deceiving our daughters. Eric had taken our orderly life, our beautiful life, and thrown it into chaos without any warning. I was furious. Furious and disappointed and hurt. I couldn't bear to live with him. After all our years together he didn't know me and I didn't know him. I couldn't share my bed with a stranger. I didn't want that stranger to be with our daughters, to share their home, their lives."

Her green eyes glittered with unshed tears. "Oh, Jen. I don't know what to do. What should I do?"

Her voice, always so vested with authority, was plaintive now and Jen's heart turned as she struggled to understand all that Cynthia had told her.

"But you're pregnant," she said at last. "When? Why? After all that you said, all that you felt? If you can't forgive him, if you felt so betrayed?"

Her questions quivered with confusion. Cynthia's revelation overwhelmed her, filled her with pity and bewilderment.

"When? It was after your mother's funeral. We left together, Eric and I. We both felt so lost, so alone. Death, the finality of death, does that. I can't explain it, but any brush with death—a funeral, the obituary of someone I knew—makes me hungry for life. Eric and I talked about it once, talked about how whenever we went to a funeral together, we would come home and make love. We were affirming our own lives, our own vitality. Sex and death. The one canceling out the other. We looked at each other when Tim began to play the clarinet at the funeral and it was as though a single thought linked us. We didn't talk when we left the cemetery. We were simply together, for the first time in all those months. Together in a kind of sweet, sad silence. We held hands in the car as we drove back to the city. I didn't think about that life he had hidden from me. I didn't feel Paul's shadow between us. I was just glad that I was with Eric. We went to his apartment, his terrible little bachelor apartment, and we made love. I thought that I could smell his loneliness. Oh, I was so sorry for him, so sorry for myself, so sorry for our girls, sorry even for Paul. But I guess I felt a kind of joy as well. Eric and I were with each other. We had been brushed by death but we were alive. I loved him that morning. I think I loved him more than I had ever loved him before." She fell silent.

Jen nodded. "I think I understand," she said.

She imagined them walking hand in hand into that apartment, shedding the dark clothing of mourners, their naked bodies shimmering with life. Sex—no, not sex alone, but love—love triumphing over death.

"That was it. Those few hours. And then…"

"You found out that you were going to have a child."

"Yes. That's the one thing I'm certain about. I am going to have this child." Cynthia lifted her chin and smiled defiantly. "It's about the only thing I've been certain about over the past months."

"Does Eric know about the baby?" Jen asked.

"No. Not yet. I need time. I don't know if I can forgive him. I don't know if I'll ever be able to trust him again. It's as though I'm trapped on an emotional seesaw. I go up and think that everything will be okay, that we'll be able to work things out, that Eric and I will live happily ever after, and then suddenly I'm down again and I think that I can't live with a man who deceived me the way he did. I don't want my mother's life. I want what I thought I had for all those years we were together."

"But it's not your mother's life," Jen protested. "It wasn't an ongoing deception."

"Paul is twenty years old. Eric and I have been married for fourteen years. So for all those years it was an ongoing deception. Can I live with that? Could you?"

"I think I could," Jen replied hesitantly. "Everything is relative. I've been creating a kind of ledger over these past months, the credits and debits of my relationship with Ian. A stupid balance sheet. What had to be changed, what I could cope with. Ian's faults. My faults. How I could change, how he could change. His guilt. My guilt. Red and black."

"Not such a bad thing to do," Cynthia said wistfully.

"Okay, then. Let's see if it can work for you, if we can factor what Eric did into my crazy emotional bookkeeping. I think it would fall somewhere in the gray zone. Eric was responsible for his son. He supported him and remained in contact with him. And he loved you and wanted to spare you any pain. He didn't want you to suffer for something that had happened years before you even met. So he didn't tell you at first. He didn't want to chance putting you off. Later, after you were married, he realized how you felt about dishonesty, about deception, so he was afraid to tell you. And the longer he waited, the more difficult it probably became for him. I'm sure that all the while he thought he was protecting you. He didn't want to put your marriage at risk. There was no way he could have predicted that Paul would come East, that he would have to become part of your family, part of your life. He didn't realize how deeply you would be hurt. Oh, Cynthia, can't you accept that and forgive him?"

"I don't know. I think about it all the time. Sometimes I think yes and sometimes I think no. That seesaw goes

up and down. Up and down. Jen, please don't tell anyone about this." Cynthia's voice broke.

"Of course I won't tell anyone. Not Eric. Not Ian. Not
anyone in the group. Cynthia, things will work out."

"You're sure?" Cynthia asked. Her voice was plaintive, almost childlike.

"I'm sure." Jen's reply was firm, although her hands
trembled and her heart beat too rapidly.

They sat very still then and watched the red-gold sun
sink slowly into the cobalt waters, its waning light trim-
ming the foaming wavelets with dancing fringes of radiance.

Chapter Ten

The Korean florist on Cynthia's corner had arranged his tulips in the large ceramic containers that bordered his shop. In bud and full bloom, in shades of red and yellow, pink and pale orange, the graceful tall-stalked blossoms nodded in the mild evening breeze. Trish paused and studied them. She wavered between buying pink blossoms for Cynthia or perhaps a mingled bunch of the pink and yellow separated by baby's breath.

"She'll have flowers, you know. Cynthia always has flowers. You remember you brought those beautiful zinnias to the fall meeting and of course she already had a vase of asters on the table."

Trish veered about and smiled at Jen, who had sidled up to her and was now holding a pot of forced narcissi in each hand. "I couldn't resist them," Jen explained. "They're for the twins," she said. "For their bedroom."

It was an apology of a kind, she knew. She could not offer Liza and Julie an answer to the troubling question they had asked her; it was not up to her to explain why their father no longer lived in their home, but she could offer them the gold-hearted flowers whose fragrance might filter comfortingly into their dreams.

"I know that Cynthia will have flowers. But I'm buying these tulips for her just the same. You can't have too many flowers. That's what Louisa May would say," Trish said defensively. "You know how she explained why old Mr. Laurence, the March's next door neighbor, kept sending them flowers. 'Their house is so full and we are so fond of them.'" Wryly, she affected a falsetto. "Frankly, by the end of the book I was getting sort of sick of the March sisters and their flowers. All those dainty bouquets they were always making for one another—ugh."

Trish grimaced and began to select the tulips, choosing only those already in full bloom.

"Nothing dainty about your bouquet," Jen said. "Rather sensuous, I think."

"They *are* pretty sexy. Spring does that to you. I had a patient today who offered me a very long sex dream. In place of her vagina she had a huge rose and the petals parted to admit a fat phallus-shaped branch all covered with moss. I was glad the hour was up before she could continue." She laughed and Jen smiled.

"Pretty Freudian. It would have shocked our little women, but then Freud wasn't even on the horizon in Alcott's day," Jen said as the shopkeeper's wife took the flowers Trish had selected and wrapped them in crisp white paper. "Which is really too bad. Her family could have used therapy big-time. Did you read her biography, Trish?"

"I did. Now, that's what you call dysfunctional—everyone could have used intensive treatment. Her father, her mother, her sisters and probably Louisa herself, who thought that she could make everything better. Pathology galore! I'm glad I didn't know about Alcott's life when I was a girl. I envied the March girls, how they all seemed to be friends as well as sisters. I used to pretend that their home was my home. In my own family I was the alien, this weird girl who read books and got great grades and had the crazy idea that she could be a doctor. It was as though E.T. had been dropped into their midst. We didn't connect and we still don't. which is too bad because it means that Amanda doesn't really have an extended family. But things could be worse. A great deal worse." Trish smiled ruefully and bent her head to the flowers, inhaling their earthy fragrance.

Jen noted that, at other times, Trish had spoken of her distant family, her lonely childhood, with a bitterness that bordered on anger. But that bitterness had vanished, replaced with regret and a residual sadness. She no longer lingered in the past. It was the future that concerned her now, the future and the present. And there was a new vibrancy in her marriage, an almost determined closeness between Trish and Jason that morphed mysteriously into spontaneity. Their laughter came with ease and they spoke excitedly about their new house in the Berkshires, where they would hang the large nightscape they had purchased from the Maestrato Gallery even before Ian's show opened. Had Trish, like herself, been spurred by Cynthia's revelation, into a new accounting of her life with Jason? Jen wondered, but decided not to ask. She turned the conversation back to the Alcotts, withdrawing, as always, into the safe harbor of books and writers.

"Actually," she said as they mounted the steps of Cynthia's brownstone, "I would have found it comforting to know about the tensions in the Alcott family. It would have been a relief to know that my family didn't have a monopoly on misery, that other families had their own issues, that not everyone gathered happily around the dining room table like the March girls and said grace, holding hands. I would have loved a series of books about unhappy families. I would have been able to relate to them."

"Unhappy families. Tolstoy's literary flagship. Remember that first crushing line of Anna Karenina—'Happy families are all alike, every unhappy family is unhappy in its own way,'" Trish quoted as she lifted the heavy brass knocker. "We argued about that, remember? That first night."

"Can it really be almost a year since we read Anna Karenina?" Jen asked.

"Almost a year. Autumn, winter and spring. It seems almost longer than that given all our dinners together, everything that we've read, everything that's happened," Trish replied as the door swung open and a sullen Mae admitted them without a greeting.

"Great sweatsuit, Mae. And great sneakers," Jen said brightly.

Mae nodded and adjusted the collar of her magenta jacket. Jen noted that she even wore magenta socks. It must have been a feat even for Cynthia, merchandising genius that she was, to have located sneakers and socks in that color.

"Are the others here yet?" she asked.

"They're in the living room," Mae said shortly. "I'll take the flowers."

"Actually, we'd prefer to give them to Cynthia and to the girls," Trish said.

"Suit yourself." Mae shrugged.

Elizabeth and Donna, each sipping a glass of white wine, sat side by side on the sofa opposite Cynthia, who was, once again, seated in a deep leather chair. Liza and Julie perched on the armrests, their bright hair tied back with ribbons that matched their pajamas, apple green for Julie and yellow for Liza. Cynthia herself wore a flowing silk robe in shimmering shades of green and yellow. It had been modeled in the runway show, Jen recalled, the work of a promising young Asian designer. She had done a pen-and-ink sketch of it and then brushed in the colors. Had Cynthia bought it, Jen wondered with a touch of malice, to create this color-coded tableau with her daughters? She quickly discarded the thought. Cynthia had chosen it, she realized, because it fell in loose and graceful folds, ideal for the early months of a pregnancy not yet revealed. She wondered if Cynthia had also bought the shimmering copper-colored maternity gown.

"Cynthia, you look positively radiant," Trish said. She held out the tulips and noted, without surprise, that all the vases in the room overflowed with great sprays of forsythia, and tall branches of pussy willow filled the copper urns beside the fireplace. But no tulips, she thought with satisfaction.

Cynthia smiled. There was a subtle glow to her skin, a glinting brightness to her eyes, and she moved forward with balletic grace to accept the flowers.

"Oh, Trish, they're beautiful."

She inhaled their fragrance and then handed them to Mae, who had crept up soundlessly behind them, a vase already filled with water in her hand.

Jen held the narcissi out to the twins, who blushed shyly as they accepted them.

"I love flowers," Liza said. "Mommy said we're going to have a big garden in the house we're going to this summer, and I'm going to plant loads of bulbs and watch them come up."

"Silly," Julia said. "You have to plant bulbs in the fall and we won't be going to the country until the summer."

"You can plant some bulbs later," Jen assured Liza. "In July. Even in August."

She did not ask where the country house would be or who would be going to it. Elizabeth and Donna also remained silent. They would not trespass into territory that Cynthia's silence declared off-limits.

"Rina's not here yet?" Trish asked.

"She called and said she might be a little late. She can't leave until Ray gets home and he's had some sort of emergency at the hospital," Cynthia said. She rearranged the ribbon in Liza's hair, gently massaged Julie's back.

"Home?" Elizabeth raised her eyebrows. "I didn't know they were living together."

"Yes. Rina's home is now Ray's home."

It was Donna who answered, her voice very calm, almost amused.

"Although I imagine they'll be looking for a larger apartment in a few months. After their wedding," she added. "They're planning to marry very soon."

"And you don't mind, Donna?" Elizabeth asked, curiosity triumphing over her feigned indifference.

Jen averted her eyes in embarrassment. It was like her sister to pose the question directly although clearly all of them had wondered about it.

"I don't mind," Donna replied quietly. "Not anymore. It was difficult at first but now I'm glad of it, glad that they have each other. I've been taking care of Rina in a way since we were college roommates. It's great for me that she has Ray to rely on now. He's a wonderful man. He's terrific with Jeremy. He'll be a great husband, a great father. He loves her stories, her fantasies. He loves Rina. I mean, I won't say that I wasn't a little put off when they first got serious. I'm not a saint and Ray and I had been together for a pretty long time, even though it was understood that neither of us was monogamous. We never talked about a long-term commitment. We knew that it wasn't in the cards for us. But it was only a blow to my ego and I recovered. Now I'm fine with it. It means that I could get on with my own life without feeling guilty." Donna refilled her wineglass. "To a guilt-free life." She smiled as she offered the toast.

"To a guilt-free life," they echoed in unison as the knocker sounded again and Mae shuffled off to answer it.

It was Rina, her cheeks flushed and her dark hair wind-tousled, her arms laden with books and shopping bags. Shrugging out of her bright orange stole, she apologized breathlessly. Ray had been late, she couldn't get a cab and had run all the way from the bus stop. She burrowed through her large canvas bag for two brightly wrapped packages, which she held out to the twins.

"From Jeremy," she said. "Bookends. He made them in his woodworking class. And here's a set for Adam."

She held a third package out to Elizabeth, who accepted it in bewilderment. It was unusual for Adam to receive a gift. Her fingers traced the pattern of the plaid wrapping paper as though in wonderment at her son's inclusion.

"Thank you. Thank you very much. And thank Jeremy," she said.

The twins ripped off the wrapping and displayed the triangles carved out of blond wood and unevenly lacquered.

"Cool," Liza said.

"I love them," Julie crowed.

"Go upstairs and put them in your rooms. And take the great narcissi that Jen brought you. And then brush your teeth and go to bed. But kisses first. Kisses all around." Cynthia was, as always, at once firm and gentle.

The girls pouted and then, obediently, circled the room. They kissed their mother's friends and, hugging their gifts, they dashed up the stairs. The assembled women watched their scrambling ascent, marveling at Cynthia's maternal power. They smiled at her, each of them noting how relaxed she was, how gracefully she rose from her chair.

"Hungry?" she asked, and led the way into the dining room.

She had ordered a spring menu for this, their last dinner of the year. Bright yellow bowls of cold curried pea soup were set on each flowered place mat. There was poached salmon and a green salad, saffron rice and roasted fennel on the table. As always, they ate with enthusiasm, their laughter and talk rising above the clatter of the cutlery and clink of crystal as they passed serving dishes to one another. Mae, in her usual efficient and unpleasant manner, collected the soup plates and filled their water and wineglasses. As always, they refrained from discussing book and author during the meal. Dinner was catch-up time. Summer was approaching. There were vacation plans to share. Rina and Ray planned a trip to the Pacific Northwest. She did not speak of a honeymoon and they did not introduce the word.

Elizabeth and Bert were going to France, their first trip abroad, their first real vacation ever. Dr Theobald thought that it would be safe, perhaps even beneficial for them to leave Adam, and their financial situation was improved.

"It's sort of a trial run for us," she said with the blunt honesty that did not surprise them. "We want to see if we can work things out, if we have a chance to work things out, to maybe get to know each other. Again." She studied the plate of food she had barely tasted.

They nodded and avoided one another's eyes. It was improbable but not impossible, they supposed. Bert had, after all, taken charge with such swiftness when her mother died. He had stood so quietly beside Adam at the funeral. It could go either way and it seemed that Elizabeth was trying and that he was trying. Things changed. Relationships changed. That much they had learned. Cynthia looked at Elizabeth as though to ask a question, but she remained silent, clasping and unclasping her hands.

Jen and Ian had scheduled a trip to Mexico.

"If the gallery show goes well," she said. "Ian is in love with the idea of painting down there and I want to work on the new panels for my 'Lottery' book."

"But there's every sign that it will go well," Trish observed. "When we bought our painting Maestrato told us that a lot of the paintings in the show were already pre-sold."

Jen nodded.

"I know, but I guess we've lived too long on the edge to be really certain about anything. Although we're beginning to feel pretty certain about each other," she added. The words that she would not have spoken months earlier came easily to her.

Trish talked about the house she and Jason had found in the Berkshires.

"Two acres and a wraparound porch," she said happily. "You'll all have to come up. Together. We'll go to the Mount, pay our respects to the ghost of Edith Wharton. Let's pick out a date. Sometime in August."

Donna carefully placed a scoop of rice on her plate.

"August is out for me," she said. "I'll be living in Washington then. I got word today that my grant proposal was accepted and I'll be starting work at the NIH."

They stared at her in surprise.

"I didn't know you were planning a move to Washington, Donna," Cynthia exclaimed. "Is this a sudden decision?"

"No." She framed her answer carefully. "I've been thinking about it all year. In a way it had a lot to do with our reading, our discussions. Each book we read, each author we discussed made me realize that I had to change my life before life changed me. I realized that it was entirely possible that in five years' time, in ten years' time, I might suddenly ask myself why I hadn't made the changes I thought about, why I had remained inert when I could have moved forward. I knew that I had to make a choice. I couldn't let my mother choose for me. Like Nafisi said in the Tehran book, people have to make their own choices. I think that this year, from our very first dinner with Anna Karenina, for all sorts of reasons, has been a year of choice and change for each of us."

They were silent, remembering that first meeting, the crispness of the autumn air, their pleasure at coming together in this beautiful room after the long summer hiatus, and then their pleasure was shattered, their ease destroyed, by Cynthia's words, so unexpected and so devastating. Her perfect world, so beautifully and expensively constructed, so generously and carefully maintained, had mysteriously erupted, and in the aftershocks of that eruption the fragile structures of their own relationships, their own lives, had been rendered newly vulnerable.

In the rush of the changing seasons, in the books that informed their lives and haunted their dreams, they had assessed that vulnerability.

They had read, throughout the year, as though they were weavers, stretching discreet threads of narrative across the looms of their imaginations. They had traded color schemes and patterns, offered one another fragments of tapestries in varicolored skeins that they had no hope of finishing. They had argued over plot and character development, symbolism and motivation; their intense discussions and sudden insights had infused fiction with vitality. Reading late into the night, they had insinuated their own reality, their own yearnings, on imagined lives, but that, in the end, had not sufficed.

Still, on this spring evening, with sprigs of parsley on their plates and rose-gold tulips centered on the table, questions lingered. It was their truth that Donna had spoken. They had, through the long year—wondering always about Cynthia and Eric but wondering, too, about themselves—made their own choices, their own changes.

The window was open and a soft spring breeze drifted through the room. The tall flowers trembled and the women smiled.

Cynthia rose from her seat.

"It's time to talk about *Little Women*," she said, and led the way into the living room.

Relieved, the spell of memory broken, they gathered their books, followed her and arranged themselves in the usual circle. They waited for Mae to serve the coffee and set the platters of pastries and fresh fruit on the low round table. Only when she had shuffled from the room did they turn their attention to Cynthia, who opened her notebook, exquisitely bound in pale blue linen, its thick ivory-colored pages covered with notes in her distinctive violet ink.

"I have to confess," she said, "that when I chose *Little Women* it was a selfish choice. I wanted to be transported back to my girlhood when I read it over and over. I think I even knew parts of it by heart. I would lie awake and pretend to be a different sister each night. I was spoiled Amy, gentle Beth, bold Jo and motherly Meg. The March girls had the life I wanted. A brave father, an understanding, self-sacrificing mother, a loving home. Honest, idealistic New Englanders. Everyone in the family was exactly who they seemed. There was no deception, no masquerade."

"I felt exactly the same way," Donna interjected. "I imagined myself in the role of each sister. When Beth was dying I practiced dying myself. I would speak in a whispery voice and I put baby powder on my face so that I'd fit the description of the dying Beth, all wan and pale, too weak to even pick up a needle. My mother used to laugh at me and tell me that I wasn't too weak to beat a couple of eggs for the soufflé she had to deliver to someone's dinner party. But she told me that she cried herself when Beth died and I think I did get out of whipping those eggs."

They all nodded. They had all cried when Beth died. They were proud of that grief. It had marked them as readers, gifted each of them with the DNA of the book absorbed.

"Now that I think back," she continued, "I realize that I wasn't so much in love with Beth as I was intrigued with the idea of death. The romanticism of the preadolescent, I guess Trish would say."

She laughed ruefully, in mocking sympathy with her younger self.

"But there was actually nothing romantic about Louisa May Alcott," Cynthia said. She glanced down at her notebook. "She wrote to make money so she could support her family. That happy fictional family I envied was nothing like Louisa's real family. Bronson Alcott, her father, was a madman, so interested in transcending the real world that he didn't notice that his children were starving and his wife was heading for nervous-breakdown country. He was an operator who borrowed money wherever he could—from his wife's family, from Ralph Waldo Emerson, from Margaret Fuller. He moved his poor family to Fruitlands, a kind of collective farm near Concord, where he proceeded to practically starve them to death. Breakfast was a wafer, a slice of apple, a cup of cold water, and the other meals weren't much better. They had to follow the philosophy of Charles Lane, his crazy English mentor, who made the girls take ice-cold showers and wear canvas shoes because leather was forbidden. Apparently he thought that the lives of animals were more sacred than the health of children. And of course it got worse and worse."

She sighed and looked up from her notes.

"If he were around today he'd be investigated by children's services," Elizabeth said darkly.

She leaned forward to select a miniature éclair and added sugar to her coffee. Jen looked at her in surprise. Elizabeth never ate desserts, never sweetened her coffee. But of course, this had been a year of changes and choices. She smiled at her sister.

"It's interesting that the father in *Little Women* is hardly in the story," Rina mused. "Sylvia Plath's father, who died when she was eight, haunts her poems and journals."

"Comparing Plath and Alcott is like comparing apples and oranges. Different time periods, different genres," Elizabeth said daringly.

Always they were deferential to Rina's literary insights. She was, after all, an academic, immersed for all these years in her unfinished thesis on Plath, even launched on a novel of her own. But now they nodded in agreement with Elizabeth. Undeterred, Rina continued.

"Alcott was a writer who mined her own life, her own experiences. Her sisters are in her books, reinvented, of course, but clearly the Alcott girls. There are hints of Emerson's generosity and humanity in her descriptions of old Mr. Laurence. Marmee is an idealized portrait of her mother, Abba Alcott. But there's no reference to Charles Lane, although, cruel and eccentric as he was, he would have made a great character. I think it was denial. She refused to acknowledge that there was probably a homosexual dimension to her father's relationship with Charles Lane."

They stared hard at her, newly tense. She had overstepped an invisible line. Trish flushed angrily. It was insensitive of Rina to discuss homosexuality given their speculations about Eric. She thought of the young man who had sat beside him in the café all those months ago and remembered afresh the affection she had seen in

Eric's eyes when he looked at him. It surprised her that Jen did not seem perturbed by Rina's comment, that she continued to thumb through the pages of the Edna Cheney biography of Louisa, searching for a reference. Trish herself was suffused with embarrassment for themselves, with pity for Cynthia.

But Cynthia responded with an almost amused calm.

"I don't imagine that *homosexuality* was even a word in Alcott's lexicon. Remember the era she lived in. If it was recognized at all it wasn't spoken of, certainly not in front of women and children, no matter how sophisticated they might seem. And the Alcott family might have been intellectual, but they were hardly worldly. It's true that Louisa, her older sister, Anna and their mother were all concerned about Lane's influence on Bronson. The final straw for them was Lane's insistence that Bronson cut himself off from his family, abandon Fruitlands and join the Shaker community, where everyone would be celibate and live unhappily ever after."

"But that didn't happen," Jen said. She had found the passage she wanted in the Cheney biography and she summarized it.

"Apparently there was a family meeting. Abba and Bronson, Louisa and Anna. Together they gave Bronson an ultimatum. If he went to the Shaker community with Charles Lane, Abba would divorce him."

"In effect, what we would call in today's family-therapy language, an intervention," Trish said dryly. "Traumatic for the kids. And, of course, ultimatums are pretty tricky even if they work. Should a marriage be held together at gunpoint?"

"There are marriages that shouldn't be held together at all," Donna said. "And there are marriages that exist in name only. Did my mother really have a marriage? Oh, she was loyal and self-sacrificing, everyone admired her courage, her hard work, but in fact she was a caregiver, not a wife. And so was Abba Alcott."

She stared down at the photograph of Bronson Alcott in her book and sighed. The only picture she had of her father was the one taken on his wedding day, before her birth, before Korea and his illness.

"I understand why my mother lived as she did, but I think it would have been more courageous of her to have made a different choice. She should have divorced my father. He was sick, incurably sick, and Louisa's father was just as hopeless. He was selfish, indifferent and, like my father, he'd never overcome that selfishness, that indifference. Finally he was even unfaithful, which sort of punctures Rina's homosexual theory. In any case, I think that, family meeting or not, Louisa's mother should have left him and taken her precious little women with her."

Donna snapped her book shut and reached for a strawberry, allowing its juice to redden her lips.

"We're talking about the nineteenth century. Divorce wasn't an easy option then," Rina pointed out.

"And it's not an easy option now," Elizabeth agreed. "There are economic consequences. Divorce is expensive."

They looked down at their books. They knew about Elizabeth's separation from Bert during her pregnancy and they understood why they had reconciled when Adam was diagnosed. An economic necessity. There was no money for two households if they were to give their son proper care, to offer him every opportunity no matter how hopeless his condition might seem. On that they had always been in agreement.

"And it can happen, that given enough time, a marriage, even a really bad marriage, can be made to work."

Elizabeth flushed, then rushed on, speaking too quickly.

"And there's always the impact on the children."

Her words slowed. She was on safer ground now, speaking from professional experience.

"The kids I see in the guidance office, if they come from broken homes, they're angry, guilt-ridden, low self-esteem, low achievers. They come to me when the college application crunch is on and their grades are a problem. They're sometimes split between two households, there's confusion about texts and homework assignments, different rules about studying, which means they don't follow any rules at all. Divorce is tough on kids."

"And so are lousy marriages," Jen said angrily. "You and I should know that."

"Every situation is different." Cynthia's voice trembled. "Just as every marriage is different. You know, happy families and unhappy families, et cetera. And perhaps every divorce."

She fell silent then and looked around the room, at the lovely, welcoming haven she had created for her family and friends, the soft carpets and colorful cushions, the muted lamplight, the fresh flowers in the graceful vases collected over many years in many lands. Her eyes rested on a silver-framed portrait of Eric and herself taken aboard a sailing ship. They held Liza and Julie close and the sun was bright upon their faces as they laughed into the wind. Her friends watched her as she clutched her notebook, closed it, opened it.

They waited. Mae entered with a fresh carafe of coffee. She murmured something to Cynthia, who nodded impatiently.

"Just leave everything on the counter," she said. "I'll deal with it."

She smiled apologetically at her friends, her composure restored.

"Okay. Back to the Alcotts. In defense of Louisa's dad, of Bronson Alcott, we have to admit that no matter what his faults were, and I don't deny that he had plenty, he never dissimulated. He was honest. He told his wife about Lane's insistence that they join the Shakers. He told her when he lost money. He told her when he fell in love with another woman. He wasn't an admirable man but there was a kind of integrity in his honesty, and honesty was a value that Louisa incorporated into her work, something that she prized. You remember when Amy gets into trouble at school over those pickled limes…"

"Oh, those pickled limes!" they cried out, almost in unison, and then they laughed that all of them should remember that episode so well. They loved it when they were in synch, when memory and reaction were shared. It validated the bond of their friendship, their rare mutuality, their sisterhood in life and in literature.

"What do you think they tasted like?" Cynthia asked, and grimaced. "Anyway, you remember that when Amy's teacher confronts her and asks if she has given him all the limes she says, in that proud March manner, 'I never lie.' Jo tells Laurie the truth, hurtful as it was, when he asks her to marry him. And, of course, saintly Beth never told a lie. She was truthful even on her deathbed. Truth was a priority for Alcott. Maybe that was why she could forgive her father—because he didn't dissemble, because he revealed everything. Maybe in that she was like Sylvia Plath, who could forgive her husband's infidelity but not his deception."

"But deceit is grist for the novelist's mill," Donna said. "Emma Bovary deceives and lies. So does Anna Karenina. Do you think that Tolstoy and Flaubert were making a case for absolute honesty in marriage?"

"But there are levels of honesty and sometimes there are compelling reasons for not telling the truth or concealing a secret," Jen protested. "Choosing not to reveal something doesn't necessarily mean being complicit in a lie. Especially if the person who makes that choice does it to avoid causing pain."

Cynthia looked hard at her and went to the window. She stared into the night and leaned forward, then turned back to them.

"Anyway," Jen continued, more faintly now, "I have to tell you that although it was fun to reread Little Women, it was a bit much. Too didactic. Too much sweetness and light, goodness and self-sacrifice. And so dated. It was like spending time with a friend you've outgrown. I found the Alcott biographies a lot more interesting. I guess I prefer the writer to her work, at least at this point in my life. What did you guys think?"

They shook their heads, agreeing, disagreeing. Their answers converged, words tumbled over one another. They were in agreement that her prose was naive, her character development simplistic. And yet they had each read on and rejoiced when, at last, Jo married her German professor. They agreed that they were glad that they had known so little about the author's life. It would have marred the innocence of their enchanted immersion into her world.

Their voices soared as they discussed favorite scenes. Cynthia had loved the description of Meg's wedding. Trish spoke wistfully about Amy and Laurie's encounter in Europe.

"Not too contrived, was it?" Elizabeth asked caustically.

"Who cares?" Trish asked, and laughter overtook them.

They were wafted back to their girlhood days, when reading was magical and loneliness was banished as they compulsively turned the pages, and plunged deeper and deeper into the story. Not for the first time, they traded tales of how they had read late into the night, ignoring parental threats, shifting the books so that they could read by the rib of light that stole in through a partially opened bedroom door or the diffused radiance of a street lamp reflected in a window. Jen had read by the light of a flashlight concealed within the tent she created with her blankets. Trish had hidden her books beneath her bed to avoid the teasing of her siblings. Rina had created her own happy endings, scrawling them into the notebooks she hid in her underwear drawer.

They reveled now in the autonomy of their womanhood. They could read when they pleased, whether late into the night or at daybreak, inhibited only by the needs of family or the demands of their jobs. *Little Women* had been a nostalgic read and, they confessed, had spurred them to revisit other girlhood favorites.

They had sought to reclaim the safe havens, the refuges of fantasy that had kept them safe from family bitterness, that had sheltered them from rejection and the inexplicable mists of youthful sadness. If those refuges no longer satisfied, it did not matter because they had, after all, each in turn, reached safe harbor of a kind.

There had been disappointments. Old favorites had bored them. Elizabeth had hated *Little Men* when she was much younger and hated it even more the second time around.

"I'm not sure Alcott really understood boys," Rina observed. "But who am I to talk? I'm never sure that I understand Jeremy. But Ray does."

She hesitated and then told them what they already knew. She and Ray would be married soon. In a month's time. Perhaps two months. They were meeting with a rabbi. Rina wanted her marriage to be rooted in tradition. They understood that for her the operative word was *rooted*.

"Rina, that's marvelous."

"Great."

"Terrific."

Their joy was effusive. Their laughter and talk bubbled over, waking the twins, who stood in the doorway, sleepily rubbing their eyes

Cynthia offered to help Rina shop for a dress.

"Or maybe we can rescue something from a bridal shoot," she said.

They laughed, imagining bohemian Rina, the thrift-shop queen, in a Nightingale's gown.

"You can have the wedding at our Berkshire house," Trish said. "We can probably manage fifty people without a problem."

"Do I know fifty people?" Rina asked.

"Who needs fifty people?" Jen replied. They did not need fifty friends. They needed only one another.

"I'll make the cake," Donna volunteered. "I've baked wedding cakes before. Remember, I'm a caterer's daughter."

Jen glanced at her watch. It was getting late and she did not want Ian to be worried. She smiled at the thought so new to her, so new to both of them. They were linked by a new intensity, a need to hear each other's voices, to verify the times of their arrivals and departures.

Taking her cell phone, she went into the vestibule but ceased punching in the number when she heard the metallic sound of a key turning in the lock. The front door swung open and Eric and Paul walked in, slamming it shut behind them. Eric shook out his umbrella and placed it in the ceramic stand with the casual ease of a man who has arrived home, who has come in out of the rain. Paul shrugged out of his jacket and passed his fingers through the damp shock of fair hair that, like Eric's, fell onto his high forehead.

Speechless with surprise, Jen watched as Cynthia walked toward them. Cynthia had had no need for her homily on honesty, Jen realized. Her friend's decision had been made days, perhaps even weeks, earlier. She felt a twinge of annoyance and then a wave of joy. Her friends, Cynthia and her Eric, had been restored to each other and that was all that mattered.

Eric bent to kiss his wife's cheek, his fingers resting briefly on her neck. And then Liza and Julie hurtled toward them.

"Daddy! Paul!" they screamed excitedly, and pulled the two men into the living room. "Daddy's here. Paul's here."

The women half rose from their seats, smiling in bewilderment. Their books slipped from their laps and fell soundlessly onto the thick carpet.

"I want you all to meet Paul," Cynthia said. "Eric's son."

They nodded as Paul hoisted the twins up, each one straddling a shoulder. He smiled shyly at them as Eric circled the room, his hand extended in greeting. He was, once again, their friend, their host, Cynthia's husband.

"Mae left food on the counter for you," Cynthia told him.

She waved them, father and son, into the kitchen and, obediently, they smiled at the book group and disappeared, the twins giggling wildly, their faces bright with happiness. Their father was home, they had a brother, newly and mysteriously arrived, strong and playful, who would help them plant bulbs in the garden of their summerhouse—and no one was rushing them back to bed.

Cynthia reclaimed her seat in the circle of friends and waited for the question she knew would come. It was Donna who broke the silence.

"I didn't know Eric had a son!" she said.

"Neither did I," Cynthia replied quietly. "Not until last autumn. And now he may have yet another."

She rested her hands on the gentle rise of her abdomen, barely perceptible beneath the folds of her green-and-gold gown, her secret, so carefully kept, now joyously revealed.

They looked at her, first in wonderment, and then with a new and gentle understanding.

"Oh, Cynthia." They spoke her name in a lilting chorus of affection.

Their hands touched, fingers linked, soft palm upon soft palm. They sat quietly, all questions stilled. They were bonded in friendship, their hearts and minds linked. They had shared so much and they would share more. Smiling, they listened to the patter of the sudden soft spring rain upon the new and tender grass, and then they bent to gather up their books, which they held close to their hearts as the chatter and laughter of the men and the two small girls drifted into the room.